Cursed with a poor [...]
propensity to read, A[...]
her childhood lost in [...]
Literature followed by [...] [com]puting
didn't lead directly to [the] perfect job—writing
romance for Mills & Boon—but she has no
regrets in taking the scenic route. She lives in
London: a city where getting lost can be a joy.

Louisa Heaton lives on Hayling Island,
Hampshire, with her husband, four children and
a small zoo. She has worked in various roles in
the health industry—most recently four years
as a Community First Responder, answering
999 calls. When not writing Louisa enjoys other
creative pursuits, including reading, quilting and
patchwork—usually instead of the things she
ought to be doing!

Also by Annie Claydon

Snowbound with Her Off-Limits GP
Cinderella in the Surgeon's Castle
Children's Doc to Heal Her Heart
One Summer in Sydney

Also by Louisa Heaton

Miracle Twins for the Midwife

Greenbeck Village GPs miniseries

The Brooding Doc and the Single Mum
Second Chance for the Village Nurse

Discover more at millsandboon.co.uk.

HEALED BY HER RIVAL DOC

ANNIE CLAYDON

SNOWED IN WITH THE CHILDREN'S DOCTOR

LOUISA HEATON

MILLS & BOON

First published in Great Britain 2023
by Mills & Boon, an imprint of HarperCollins*Publishers* Ltd,
1 London Bridge Street, London, SE1 9GF

www.harpercollins.co.uk

HarperCollins*Publishers* Macken House, 39/40 Mayor Street Upper, Dublin 1, D01 C9W8, Ireland

Healed by Her Rival Doc © 2023 Annie Claydon

Snowed In with the Children's Doctor © 2023 Louisa Heaton

ISBN: 978-0-263-30619-4

09/23

MIX
Paper | Supporting
responsible forestry
FSC™ C007454

This book is produced from independently certified FSC™ paper to ensure responsible forest management.
For more information visit: www.harpercollins.co.uk/green.

Printed and Bound in the UK using 100% Renewable Electricity at CPI Group (UK) Ltd, Croydon, CR0 4YY

HEALED BY
HER RIVAL DOC

ANNIE CLAYDON

MILLS & BOON

For Richard

CHAPTER ONE

'MY APOLOGIES… After you.'

On a wet Monday morning, in a crowded coffee shop, those cheerful tones could only belong to one person. Everyone else here was focused on getting to work, and didn't have time for pleasantries.

'I'm so sorry, did I spill coffee on you? I really should have looked where I was going,' a woman's voice replied.

Dr Will Bradley was probably giving a 'no matter' shrug right now, which indicated that even if she had he wasn't going to take it personally.

'It's nothing. Have a great day.'

Lark Foster heard the woman laugh. 'You too.'

She turned, to see Will joining the end of the queue behind her. She motioned to the man between them to take her place, and Will gave her the smile that he specialised in. The one that made everyone in receipt of it feel as if they were the only person in the room, and always seemed to bring out the best in people.

'Good weekend?'

'Yes, thanks.' Lark grinned back at him, because even after four years of working with Will it was impossible not to react to his effortless invitation to see the nicer side of life.

When the handsome, charming neurologist had joined the staff of Migraine Community Action, working alongside Lark at the charity for two days a week, she'd had three reservations. Handsome—gorgeous, actually—was hard to ignore, but determination could work wonders, and Lark had no time for that kind of distraction. Will's charm was a difficulty, because it was always difficult to tell what he was really thinking. And a consultant neurologist? Lark had been assured that their jobs for the remaining three days a week were irrelevant to their equal status at the charity, but wouldn't he take it for granted that his opinion would carry more weight than that of a paramedic?

Will had put that concern to rest straight away. On his first day he'd mentioned the paper she'd written on childhood migraine, and asked several questions that betrayed a genuine interest in her work. He didn't expect her to defer to him, and he never deferred to her either, assuming that as equals she'd make her case as well as he could.

She reached forward, brushing a drop of coffee from the sleeve of his raincoat. 'I see you had a good weekend too.' No one, not even Will, apologised when someone spilled coffee on them, unless they were in a good mood.

'Right in one, Sherlock.' The smile slipped from Will's face. Clearly the good part of his weekend hadn't been as effortless as he liked to make out. 'I popped in to the hospital to see Howard yesterday.'

This was what Lark shared with Will. As their friendship had grown, Will had started to smile a little less when he was with her, coming out from behind his barrage of charm to tell her what was really on his mind. That was what made *her* feel special, because it was something that Will didn't bestow on just anyone.

'I heard from Alyssa, that you did a little more than just

pop in.' Lark had spent some time on the phone with Howard's wife on Sunday evening, to see how she was coping.

Will shrugged off his own good deeds, as if they meant no more than a drop of coffee. 'He's still very frustrated over not being able to tell us everything that he thinks we need to know, so we can keep things running smoothly.'

Lark nodded. Howard's stroke had struck like a bolt out of the blue, a healthy, vigorous man in his early sixties, suddenly partially paralysed on the right side of his body and affected by expressive aphasia, which meant he could read and understand the spoken word, but speaking and writing were major challenges for him right now. One source of his frustration was that the charity he'd founded twenty-five years ago, where Lark and Will worked as joint seconds-in-command, could no longer rely on his guiding hand.

'I don't know how I'd manage. Knowing exactly what I want to say and not being able to say it.'

'Yeah. Particularly for someone like Howard, who knows how everything works, and keeps a lot of it filed away in his head. I told him you'd been through everything on his desk...'

Lark turned the corners of her mouth down. 'I don't expect he liked that very much.'

Will's smile, again. This time it wasn't just the random good humour that he shared with everyone but had a point to it. 'Howard understands that we have to go through everything and pick up what needs to be done while he's away. You have to leave him the option of not liking it very much, even if he knows you're doing a great job.'

It was good to hear someone say that. Everyone else at the charity had made jokes about venturing into the lion's den, but Will had stayed late with her after work, quietly keeping her supplied with mugs of tea and some very nice home-made biscuits that he'd obtained from somewhere, while Lark sorted through correspondence and to-do lists, trying to make sense of it all, and hoping she hadn't missed anything.

'I don't suppose he mentioned the Board of Trustees?' They'd been suspiciously quiet over the last week, and not one of them had set foot in the charity's offices.

'He did, actually. They're there to guide and help us but it's up to us to keep things running. We make decisions together, as we always have, and the only difference is that we have to do it without Howard to help us.'

'He didn't *say* all that, did he?' Lark smirked at Will.

'No, I started off with a set of Yes/No options and we worked from there. I read it all back to him and asked if it was correct, and he gave me an emphatic thumbs-up. He may not be able to put things into words at the moment, but he still knows what he wants.'

Lark nodded. 'Alyssa said that he's starting to speak a little now.'

'A few words, yes and no mainly, and some names. He's getting to grips with different sounds, and names that begin with *M* are easiest at the moment, so we'll both have to wait our turn. It's a lot of hard work for him and I'd be tearing my hair out in his shoes.'

They'd reached the head of the queue, and he turned to the young woman behind the counter, who grinned back at him as she suddenly found herself the only person in the room.

'A cappuccino and a black coffee, both large, please.' Will shot her a twinkle from his baby-blue eyes. He might be tall, dark-haired and handsome, but it was the softness of his eyes that caught people's attention, every time.

'And a chocolate croissant…' Lark nudged Will and he nodded.

'Make that two croissants, please.' Before Lark could get

out her purse, Will had produced a note from his wallet, telling her that it must be his turn to pay.

Lark had known Howard ever since she'd first come to London, when he was a tutor for her university course in Paramedic Science, running the charity from home in his spare time. When he'd taken the step of renting a dark and not particularly welcoming space on the top floor of a solid building in central London, she'd been one of the students who'd turned up to help with the painting, and her interest in childhood migraine meant that she'd become a regular volunteer with Migraine Community Action.

Now the space was unrecognisable, a light, cream-painted space divided up by glazed walls, which conveyed accessibility and calm. With offices on one side and a large clinic on the other, the charity's staff had one central hub for their activities. As the operation had expanded, Howard had offered Lark a job, and a year later he'd recruited Will.

Will had brought his own stamp to the area that greeted them when the lift doors opened. He'd consulted his never-ending contacts list and managed to persuade a range of artists to work for free in support of a good cause. The artwork on the walls lent an air of sophistication, tempered by a touch of quirky humour, and a few practical suggestions from Lark had brought it all together beautifully. Visitors often commented on the stylish and welcoming feel of the space, and the people who worked here had been pleased and proud when a leading interiors magazine had run a feature on the low-cost, high-impact transformation.

'Your place or mine?' Will couldn't help a slight quirk of his lips as he asked the question, and Lark ignored the idea that he probably had plenty of practice with it. That was his business, and here it was an easy-going, unchallenging query about where they would drink their coffee and discuss the upcoming week, before anyone else arrived.

'Yours. Take the coffee and I'll go and see if the helpline staff had a chance to sort the post over the weekend.'

The call logs were in her pigeonhole, and she scanned them, noting that nothing was marked for her or Will's attention. The helpline had clearly been busy and the post was unsorted, so she picked up the bundles of envelopes, taking them through to Will's office.

Will was sitting on one of the two large sofas in his office, already in his shirtsleeves, the coffee and croissants laid out on the bulky coffee table that separated the sofas. His desk was pushed into an alcove in one corner, and was scrupulously tidy, largely because he very seldom sat at it. As far as Will was concerned, ergonomic seating and a large computer screen took second place to sprawling on the sofa with his laptop.

He sprang to his feet, taking her raincoat and hanging it up next to his. 'Did you have any thoughts about staffing while Howard's away, over the weekend?'

'Yes, I did. If Carole's willing to work three days instead of two, then it would be really helpful if she could take over the accounting. And you said that Dev's happy to cover for Howard in the office and with any medical questions from Tuesday to Thursday?'

Will nodded. 'Yes, he said that's no problem. In fact, three days in the office, plus being available during the evenings to liaise with us, suits him a great deal better than the five days a week doing home visits that he does at the moment. He'll be home a lot more and I think his wife could do with some extra help with the new baby.'

'Let's do that, then.' Lark sat down, dumping the post onto the table.

'You don't think that we should change our days? I could adjust my schedule and cover a couple of days when you're not here.' Will took a gulp of his coffee and started to sort through the post.

'No, the whole office structure's designed to be flexible and it runs itself most of the time. Dev will be here mid-week to give everyone the confidence of having someone to go to if they need it and our clinics are already fixed for Mondays and Fridays. I think we'll be better off working together on the policy and decision-making we'll have to do while Howard's away.' These were the roles they'd settled into. Lark was a facilitator while Will dealt with ideas, and the reason they were so effective as a team was that they each saw the importance of the other's way of working.

Will gave her his you're-the-only-person-in-the-room smile. It had somehow become much more effective since they'd had to deal with the worry of Howard's stroke.

'You don't think we ought to take a break from each other, then?'

It felt good to laugh with him over it. 'I'll let you know if things get to that, Will.'

Wordlessly, they fell into the usual Monday morning ritual of glancing through their post while they drank coffee. Lark's pile of opened letters grew steadily, while Will seemed to have got stuck on the first of his, reading through the pages and then taking a gulp of his coffee before he went back to the beginning to read it all again.

'What's that?' Whatever the letter contained, Will didn't look too pleased about it.

'It's…' He shook his head, reaching across to sort through

her letters and picking one out of the pile. 'You have one as well. This is outrageous...'

'Okay.' Lark could take outrageous or amazing, or any other extreme that Will came up with, and turn his flair and creativity into a practical proposition.

'No, I mean... It actually *is* outrageous. Read it.'

The letter was typed on the charity's headed notepaper and signed by the Chair of the Board of Trustees. Lark read it through carefully, with a growing sense of horror. For once, outrageous was an understatement.

'They want us to...*what*...?'

Will nodded. 'Yep. Sir Terence isn't satisfied with the two of us working together as we usually do to run the charity while Howard's away. He thinks we should explore the possibility of one of us stepping into his shoes on a temporary basis...'

'Which isn't going to work, because we both have other jobs.' That had always been important to Howard, he wanted the charity's employees and policy-makers to retain an ongoing involvement in treating patients with the NHS. It worked well, and Lark couldn't imagine why Sir Terence was now trying to fix something that wasn't broken.

'Exactly. I'm not in a position to give up my job, even if I wanted to, and I doubt you feel any differently. And this...' He jabbed his finger at the first paragraph on the second page, which had made Lark swallow hard when she'd read it.

'Since we have very different roles here, he wants each of us to consider how well we'd be able to take on overall responsibility...' Lark turned the corners of her mouth down, numbness beginning to take over from shock. 'That opens a whole can of worms.'

'Too right it does. They have two people who already work together well... We *do* work together well, don't we?'

'Yes. I couldn't do what you do…'

'And I wouldn't know where to begin with what you do.' Warmth flashed in Will's eyes. 'And they've chosen now—when we're having to manage without Howard—to ask us to experiment with reversing those roles. Instead of asking us what we need, and trying to help, which would be much more to the point.'

Lark nodded in agreement. 'It's not helpful at all. This last paragraph…' She flipped the paper with her finger.

Sir Terence had worked his way around to what he really wanted to say in the last paragraph, and everything that was implicit in the rest of the letter was horrifyingly explicit here. This was a time of change and they should embrace it. She and Will were in competition, not just to show how well they could do each other's jobs, or even for the post of temporary Chief Executive, but to gain Sir Terence's backing to succeed Howard when he retired.

'He's assuming Howard *will* retire. I think he's got a lot more left to do.'

'So do I. No one's going to write him off without a fight from me.' Will threw the letter down onto the coffee table. 'Do you suppose Alyssa knows about this?' Howard's wife was a GP and had been involved with the charity from the very start, and she brought a great deal of expertise and common sense to her role as a trustee.

'She would have said something when I spoke to her yesterday. And we mustn't involve her, Will, she's got enough on her plate at the moment.'

Will nodded in agreement. 'Well, I'm going to call Sir Terence and tell him that this isn't on. He can't move us around like pieces on a chessboard, to see what happens.'

He jumped to his feet, making for the phone on his desk. Things were getting very serious.

'Wait… Will, wait. It's eight in the morning and you know that Sir Terence is usually at his desk between nine and twelve. That's the best time to call him.'

'Interrupting his breakfast or, better still, hauling him out of bed, will no doubt convince him that this is a very poor idea. And that he needs to row back on it immediately.'

This was why Lark generally called Sir Terence, when Howard wasn't available to speak to him. The Board of Trustees might love Will's ideas, but they loved them best when she outlined them, after having added a few practical adjustments.

'Stop, Will. I've got another idea.'

He smiled suddenly, returning to his seat. 'Okay. Hit me with it…'

'We do what we've always done, with every challenge. We work together. The only way that we get to be in competition with each other is if we allow that to happen.'

Will thought for a moment. 'You mean play Sir Terence at his own game?'

'Not entirely. I mean go along with it and make it ours. Show him that we're a strong enough team to address anything that's thrown at us. I reckon that's far more effective than objecting to a situation that he's trying to put us in.'

'And this management consultant who's supposed to be coming in to see us?'

'Same thing. We put up a united front and make it work for us. Who knows, we might actually learn something from switching roles?'

'I already know I couldn't do what you do.'

Lark felt the warmth of a blush begin to rise to her cheeks. She'd always thought it a little odd that Will's you're-the-only-other-person-in-the-room brand of charm still worked when she actually *was* the only other person in the room.

'And who knows where exploring that would lead?'

Asking Will to plunge into something and find out where it led was always like a red rag to a bull. He seemed to relax suddenly, savouring the idea.

'And one big advantage of that is that we don't rock the boat. If Howard gets wind of this and thinks we're unhappy with it, then he'll just start to worry even more than he is already. If we can just take it all in our stride, then it's not an issue.'

Lark nodded. 'That's what I'm thinking. So we do as we're intending with everything else, and make this work. When Howard gets out of hospital he'll be in rehab for about six weeks, so for that time at least we need to fight our own battles, and do it together and in our own way.'

Will leaned back against the sofa cushions, regarding her thoughtfully. A little tingle ran down Lark's spine. Already they were negotiating new challenges together, and even stepping that far out of their roles was surprisingly confronting. Deliciously so, actually, as if she was seeing Will anew.

'Yes, we can do that. We'll make this okay.'

Lark wasn't entirely sure that they could. But in Will's mind *okay* was the polar opposite of *outrageous,* and it was her preferred option as well.

'Agreed then?'

'Yes, agreed. You always *were* the voice of reason, Lark. We'll let Sir Terence have his breakfast in peace, shall we?'

Nightingales were overrated. Will had had his share of dates that had ended on the pavement that ran around Berkeley Square, and he'd swept his partner into a few dance steps, crooning the words of the old song into her ear. They'd ended with laughter and a kiss and sometimes a little more…

But the lark, whose song Romeo and Juliet had so dreaded in the warmth of the night… The lark was something different. A songbird of the morning, whose brown plumage became shot with gold in the sunshine, in much the same way that Lark's hair and eyes did. If he'd dared to mention nightingales to her at midnight, somewhere in the vicinity of Berkeley Square, she would have laughed and waved down a taxi, leaving him with a more authentic warmth to take home with him.

She was practical, all-seeing, and she was the only woman that Will had ever met who teased him so deliciously. Their friendship had been cemented when she'd reproved him for gaining everyone's agreement to a project that they'd jointly proposed, with the help of a couple of well-chosen quotes from Shakespeare and a smile.

'Charm takes you a very long way, Will. But what happens if the figures don't stack up?' Lark had waved a copy of her carefully thought-out spreadsheet at him.

'If we're going to be strictly practical, then none of it stacks up. All that we do is based on the premise of commitment and passion.'

Lark had considered the matter for a moment. *'I suppose so. Maybe I'll just have to get used to the idea that no one likes facts and figures quite as much as sweeping ideas.'*

Will had begged to differ on that, and they'd ended up laughing about it. Lark was charming in a way that he could never be, and he never tired of watching her mind work, sorting and clarifying until an idea so thin that it was practically translucent became something solid and workable. The slight furrow of her brow, the twist of her lips as she called him out on the flaws in his logic.

Their strength was in their differences. Together they were a force to be reckoned with, but it was with a trace of regret that Will admitted to himself that there was one thing they'd never be able to do. They'd never welcome the call of the nightingale, in the velvet darkness of an embrace.

Lark had suggested that they start as they meant to go on and write a joint letter of reply to the Board of Trustees. Will had agreed to draft one up, and he'd emailed his first thoughts through to her so they could review them over sandwiches at lunchtime.

She read the letter through carefully, voicing her approval of a couple of the points he'd made and suggesting a few improvements elsewhere.

'I left my favourite quote out…'

'Good choice. It's a great quote and very appropriate, but in this instance it's our own words that are important.'

This wasn't like the fleeting pleasure of a kiss. Lark made him feel good in an entirely different way, one that took up residence somewhere in his consciousness.

He called up the document on his laptop and made the changes that Lark had suggested, before hitting the print button. They both added their signatures, side by side at the bottom of the letter, in a gesture that felt a lot like a plunge into unknown waters.

'So we'll see what this Management Consultant has to say for himself on Friday.' Will fetched an envelope from his desk, folding the letter into it and sealing it.

'I suppose so.' Lark took one moment to frown and then turned her mind to the present. 'In the meantime, it's business as usual. You're free for the two new referrals this afternoon?'

Will nodded. They'd started to see new referrals to the charity's clinic together, before discussing which of them would take on the lead role in each patient's care. Lark had suggested that it might save a lot of time further down the line, in terms of liaison and briefing each other, and she'd been right.

'Yep. You fancy dinner this evening?' That was one nice thing about their relationship being firmly rooted in friendship. Will could ask Lark to dinner, knowing that she took it solely as an invitation to eat.

'That would be really nice. Some time out of the office to sit back and review things.'

Will chuckled. 'Right. Don't bring your laptop, it'll spoil the mood.'

CHAPTER TWO

WILL SEEMED TO be taking all of this in his stride. There were times when Lark envied his commitment to ideas, and his blithe certainty that awkward details would shrivel in the heat of what was indisputably right. All they knew about the Management Consultant who would be visiting on Friday afternoon was his name—Pete Mason—and not knowing what their upcoming meeting would entail made it difficult for Lark to plan for it. That made her very nervous.

The meeting took longer than the expected hour, which was an annoyance, since Will and Lark had had to reschedule a couple of other appointments to make time for it. By the time they'd finished the office was empty and Will unlocked the glazed doors which led out into the lift lobby and shook Pete's hand.

'Thanks. Plenty of food for thought...'

Pete nodded. 'I'll see you next Friday?'

'Looking forward to it.' Will glanced at Lark and she nodded. They watched Pete into the lift, and as the doors closed they turned to face each other.

'He's thorough. I'll give him that...' Will puffed out a breath, the smile disappearing from his face.

'This isn't what we signed up for, Will.' Pete had employed all of the techniques of a counsellor, which Lark recognised because she'd used a few of them herself with her own patients. Listening, asking questions.

'No, it's not. Although, in truth, management is a lot about personalities.'

'That's not the point. How we operate at work is fair game, but this is clearly an exercise in delving into our personal lives.' Lark turned the corners of her mouth down.

Will understood immediately what was nagging at her. 'You mean all of the questions about Robyn.'

Lark's younger sister. An accident when Robyn was five years old had left her legs partially paralysed, and when she'd landed a place at art school in London their parents had vetoed the idea of Robyn studying so far from home. Robyn's adventurous spirit had clashed head-on with their parents' protective instincts and everyone had appealed to Lark, who had just qualified as a paramedic, to speak to everyone else and talk some sense into them.

It had felt a lot like being a peace negotiator in a war-torn province. They'd all had to give a little, love a lot. But Lark had liaised with the college that had offered Robyn a place, and found a ground floor flat that was suitable for wheelchair use and gave easy access to the campus. When their parents had driven away, leaving the sisters together in their new home, she and Robyn had hugged each other, both talking excitedly about the adventures ahead of them.

They'd both worked hard and supported each other. Lark had been able to save enough to afford a deposit and bought a bungalow in the London suburbs, which gave her and Robyn more room than they'd had in the flat. Of course, it hadn't all been plain sailing. Helping Robyn to gain her independence and land a good job had provided a few challenges. In the six years that she and Robyn had lived together, they'd both changed. Both learned a bit, because that was what you were supposed to do when faced with a new phase in life.

'My home situation *does* have some bearing on the way I work, I suppose...'

Will's brow darkened. 'Maybe. Everything we do influences us in some way. But I wasn't happy with the question about whether you feel you're trying to recreate a caring situation at work because that's the one you had at home.'

Will had said as much during the session, coming to her defence with an unusual burst of anger. Lark had appreciated that, even if it wasn't strictly necessary, and she'd been forced to wonder whether Pete had a point.

'I do miss having Robyn around, now that she's married...' Lark could admit to that now that she wasn't under Pete's calculating gaze.

'Not the same thing. You miss Robyn as your sister, or as a wheelchair user?'

Will's questions were just as pointed as Pete's had been but they came from a different place. One of knowing her and Robyn.

'Right now, we could do with her as a volunteer.' Lark looked over at the empty reception area, which Robyn had presided over for a couple of evenings every week, dispensing the same kindness and understanding to their patients as she had when they were children and the migraine headaches had brought Lark to a standstill.

'Yeah, me too.' Will grinned. 'I dare say she would have made some comment to Pete about us being too busy for his session to have overrun. I'm rather regretting that she and Matt live so far away...'

He always made her laugh, even through the most difficult and confusing times. 'That would have been nice.'

'Look, you cared for your sister because she's your sister, and Robyn cared for you in return.' Will turned the corners of his mouth down. 'It's very easy to take one look at people and assign roles, particularly with families. The truth's a bit more complicated and takes work.'

His face had darkened, and this was clearly something that Will felt strongly about. Lark raised her eyebrows in a silent question, and Will shook his head in a wordless answer. Sometimes—just sometimes—Lark got the impression that there were things that Will never talked about, even to her. Suddenly he smiled, and the moment of asking was lost.

'I'm perfectly aware of who's boss around here.'

'That would be Howard.'

He let out a derisive laugh. 'Yeah, right. How many times has he said that he defers to your good sense?'

'And how many times has he said that we depend on your ideas?'

'So he's a great boss. An idea isn't much good unless you can put it into practice, Lark. You're the glue that holds this place together, and that's true leadership.'

It was nice to hear Will say that, because the meeting with Pete had given Lark the feeling that, in the nicest possible way, she was being attacked and undermined. A tear rolled down her cheek, and she shrugged it away.

But Will always knew how to make people feel better about things, and it appeared that Lark wasn't entirely immune to his talents. When he stepped forward, curling his arm around her shoulder and hugging her, he made her feel much, much better.

She knew all about his touch already. They'd spent the last four years bumping into each other in corridors, Will had caught her a couple of times when she'd tripped, and Lark had lost count of the number of times she'd grabbed his arm to prevent Will from acting on an impulse that they hadn't thought through yet. Will had even brushed his lips against her cheek at the Christmas party. But none of that was like this. A sudden feeling of warmth that held nothing of the everyday, but was an exquisite, one-time token of friendly affection.

And she'd just learned that Will was a really great hugger. He didn't hold her too tight, but somehow he took her breath away. Not clinging or intrusive but there for her, letting her sink into the heat that was suddenly surrounding her.

'What are we going to do, then?' She took the risk of laying her head against his shoulder, and realised that his heart was beating fast. Even that made her feel better, as if his every instinct was readying him to come to her defence.

'We'll do what we said we would, even if I noticed you weren't entirely convinced...'

'Neither were you.'

Will's chuckle was even more enticing when she could feel as well as hear it. She should probably step away from him now, but this was far too nice to do anything of the sort. Even if it probably meant a great deal more to her than it did to him.

'I must be slipping. I was doing my best to put my doubts aside and not give too much away. Look, he's outlined the different roles that he supposes we fit into, and asked us to swap...'

'He's not entirely wrong, we are very different.'

'He *is* entirely wrong, because he reckons that our roles confine us instead of empowering us. And now it's just you and me, we'll do things our way, as you suggested.'

Lark nodded. Will sounded so certain that they weren't confined by their roles and she'd take his word for it until she'd worked the idea through in her head. 'And *our way* is?'

'We have a way of working here that benefits the charity

and our patients, and I don't think we should meddle with that right now. But we could have some fun with it, and get to know each other's weekends a little better, couldn't we? If that informs our work roles then so be it.'

Lark thought for a moment. Spending a weekend with Will sounded… Delicious. That probably wasn't what Pete had been thinking, and she shouldn't think that way either.

'So… I'll spend a weekend going out and sweet-talking everyone I meet…?' Possibly taking someone home for a night of sweet romance, even. There was a problem with that, because the last few years hadn't given her much time for the complex negotiations that starting a relationship required. Although Will didn't seem to need that, his relationships might only have a shelf life of about a month, but there were enough of them.

He knew what she was thinking, and his face took on a look of gentle reproach. 'See how little you really know me?'

She couldn't resist that temptation. 'Okay. Surprise me, then. And I'll surprise you, maybe.'

Lark couldn't help squeezing him a little tighter and she felt Will catch his breath. Too much. It was too sweet, too comforting, and she was suddenly far too aware of his body. This was a world away from being able to tease him about keeping in shape, and a mere whisper away from testing out every movement and reaction. She patted his shoulder and stepped back.

Even that was delicious. The look in Will's eyes made her feel that she was the only person in the universe. There was understanding, warmth, and the slightest trace of regret that the moment was over. And it *was* over, because Lark wasn't sure she could risk doing that again.

'Okay, so this weekend I have to be at my parents' cocktail evening in aid of a hospice that's local to them. *Next* weekend's the evening they're holding in support of Migraine Community Action, that Howard and I were going to go to. I can't do that alone.'

Lark reckoned he probably could. She'd seen Will work a room, and decided on the spot that she was better off sticking with what she was good at. 'I don't have anything quite so glittering planned.'

He grinned. 'That's all in the eye of the beholder. Parties can lose their shine if you go to enough of them...'

The coffee shop was always busy at seven on a Monday morning. People deciding to make an early start and vanquish the coming week before it could throw anything in their way. As Lark held the glass door open for someone who was exiting with their coffee, the sight of Will's broad shoulders at the end of the queue made her feel a lot more confident about the vanquishing part of the week.

'Hey...' She tapped him on his right shoulder, ducking around to his left side and waiting until Will looked back at her. Worked every time.

'There you are...' He always made their first greeting of the day sound as if it were something special that he'd been waiting for. This morning that produced an unusual quiver that ran deliciously down her spine.

'You look a little weary.' Will was showing definite signs of a couple of very late nights, and Lark swallowed down the impulse to demand to know what he'd been up to. *That* was new, too.

'Yeah. It was my mother's birthday yesterday and we made a thing of it.'

The Bradley family made a thing of everything. William Bradley senior did a lot of entertaining in connection with his mechanical engineering company, and Priscilla Bradley worked hard for a carefully selected list of charities. Lark and Robyn had been to a New Year's celebration held at his parents' large house in Hertfordshire, and Lark had been astonished that one couple could know so many people.

'She had a nice day?'

'She had a great day.' Will narrowed his eyes. 'I suppose you could always mention Dad's parties to Pete. If he thinks you're trapped in a role that's dictated by your family, he'd have a field day with mine.'

Will's family *were* fertile ground, if you had a mind to look at it that way. People often commented on how different the three brothers were, Will handsome and charming, Edward quiet and businesslike and Joel the academic. Of course that didn't take account of Will's ferocious intellect and his years of study to become a doctor, or the fact that he could advise his patients calmly and precisely when he wanted to.

'I'm not going to get Pete off my back by focusing his attention on you.'

'That's very noble of you.' Will grinned at her.

'So how was the party?'

'Great. Some really interesting people there. I got distracted, though, and ended up in the kitchen, talking until two in the morning.'

'Was she nice?' Lark felt her heart sink, as if it had suddenly taken on more weight than it could handle.

'Gorgeous. Amazing, actually, and very interesting. Emma...' He grinned as Lark's eyebrows shot up.

'I thought a gentleman never tells.' She heard a cool edge creep into her tone, and pressed her lips closed. Will's conquests had never particularly bothered her before now.

'It depends what there is to tell. Miss Emma Salisbury.'

'You mean...*the* Emma Salisbury?' One half of the Salisbury sisters who had taken a small local newspaper and trans-formed it into a popular and well-regarded national publication. Emma was the eldest, and must be in her eighties.

'Yep. Fascinating woman. She was telling me about how, by coincidence, she'd been in America when JFK was assassinated. She drove all the way to Texas in a beat-up old Chevy, and her pictures and interviews formed the basis of the book that she and her sister produced some years later.'

'I hear it's a wonderful book.' *Witnesses* concentrated on the reactions of ordinary people who had been caught up in world-changing events, and had won a string of literary and journalistic prizes.

'Yes, it is. When I saw the guest list I looked out my copy and put it into the car, in case I had a chance to ask her to sign it for me. She was very gracious.' Will tapped his briefcase, in an indication that he'd brought the now precious book to show her. 'I took up far too much of her time, but she said that these days she prefers sandwiches and cocoa in the kitchen to kicking up her heels.'

That was Lark's go-to position, as well. 'I don't blame her.'

'Me neither.' He grinned at Lark's raised eyebrows. 'Sometimes my father's expectations do get a little heavy to carry. So what did *you* get up to at the weekend?'

Lark shrugged. 'Not a great deal. I spent Saturday after-noon with Howard, and he's in good form. He was showing off some of the words he's been working on with his speech therapist. Alyssa says he'll be moving into rehab soon.'

'That's great. Good for him.'

'And I chose some paint for my sitting room...' Lark dredged up the only other thing she'd done that was even vaguely remarkable.

'Yeah? What colour...?'

* * *

Will had somehow contrived to make Lark's weekend sound more interesting than his own, and by the time they reached the office he'd started to interrogate her about the lighter shades she had in mind for the ceiling. He broke off as the phone rang, and Lark leaned over the reception desk to answer the call.

'Hello, Migraine Community Action. How can we help you?'

'My name's Stan Copeland. It's my wife, Sandra…' The voice on the other end of the line sounded ragged and stressed. 'She came to see you at one of your clinics…'

Lark thought for a moment. 'I remember—I saw Sandra a few weeks ago, didn't I. How is she now?'

'She's been following the advice you gave and she's been much better. But over the weekend—she's had the most dreadful headache that she just can't shake. I called the doctor this morning and he said that it might be stress—Sandra had her phone stolen in the street last week.'

'Was she hurt?'

'It was a lad on a bike, he rode past her on the pavement and snatched it from her hand. Sandra tried to hang on to the phone and he shoved her… I said she should have just let him have it, but she said that she hadn't had time to think, it was just instinct.'

'I'm sorry to hear that. Did Sandra fall over?'

'No, but he elbowed her away, and she was a bit dazed afterwards. The police said that we should go to A&E, but she said she felt fine, and she just wanted to go home. I wanted to take her home, to be honest. Did I do the wrong thing?'

The man's voice hitched with emotion.

'I would have wanted to do the same. Take her home, where she's safe.' Lark would have preferred it if her husband had taken Sandra to be checked over, but she could understand why he hadn't. 'Let's concentrate on how she is now. She's been feeling unwell for three days?'

'It started on Friday evening. She took her painkillers and we went to bed, usually that stops the migraine, but she woke up early on Saturday with a thumping headache.'

'And she's been taking her medication since then? How often has she needed it?'

'She's been in so much pain and the pills don't seem to make any difference. I was afraid she'd take too many, and I took them away and only let her have them according to the instructions on the packet.'

'That's good. Really sensible. Stan, I understand how worried you are, but I need you to hold on for a moment, so I can look up my record of having seen Sandra…'

Will had been sorting through the bundles of post, but now he reached for the secure cabinet under the reception desk, unlocking it. He handed Lark her tablet and she called up the notes she'd made when Sandra had come to the clinic.

'You're only ten minutes away from here…'

'Yes. We don't like to make a fuss, but if someone could see Sandra… This doesn't seem right.'

That was often the most telling thing. A member of a patient's family who knew that something wasn't right shouldn't be ignored.

'I've got a better idea, Stan. You and Sandra sit tight and I'll come to you…'

Will waited for her to end the call, and Lark handed the tablet over to him as she put the phone down.

'It's a patient I saw last week. I gave her some lifestyle advice on how to manage her migraine, and her husband says she's been better, but now she's been incapacitated all weekend.'

'Could be the result of her relaxing after stress.' Will looked up at her. 'You don't think so?'

'It's a possibility. But she had her phone snatched in the street last week. Apparently, she tried to hang onto it and was shoved. And now the headache doesn't seem to be responding to her usual medication...'

'She was seen by someone?'

Lark shook her head. 'She said she felt okay, and that she just wanted to go home. There's a small chance that this isn't a migraine.'

Will nodded. 'Would you like me to come with you?'

That would be good. Will assessed people for possible head and neck injuries every day, and as a doctor he was able to write a prescription if one was needed.

'Maybe I should stay here. Pete said that he'd be emailing a list of suggestions through to us this weekend...' Even as Lark said the words, she realised that she had her priorities upside down.

'So...what? You're going to wait for an email when you could be coming with me to see a patient? I know you're worried—'

'Yes, I am. But you're right, hanging around waiting for emails isn't the way to deal with it,' Lark interrupted him, reaching for her jacket. Hopefully, whoever had last used the charity's electric car, garaged in the basement car park, had remembered to leave it charged up.

CHAPTER THREE

WILL WAS GLAD that he'd decided to come along. When he parked outside the small house on one of the central London housing estates he saw a man open the door. Lark introduced them, and they were shown into a neat sitting room where a woman was lying on the sofa. Stan was hovering, clearly worried about Sandra, and Lark drew him to one side so that Will could examine her.

'I'm so sorry to bring you out...' Sandra was trying to sit up, her head obviously hurting her badly. Will helped her, then knelt down beside her.

'It's no trouble. May I just check your head for any bumps?' It was often difficult to distinguish between the symptoms of a migraine and a concussion or mild traumatic brain injury, and looking for any signs of the head injury itself was a good place to start.

Sandra was bleary-eyed and clearly in a lot of pain. Will couldn't quite assess what the look on her face meant, but when she touched the side of her head, Lark noticed the action too. She murmured to Stan that maybe they should leave Sandra and Will alone, and Stan offered to make a cup of tea.

Then he realised. Sandra *had* been hurt and she'd been keeping it from Stan. He reached out, gently exploring the side of her head, and found the bump. 'Do you know when this happened? Was it when you had your phone snatched?'

'Yes. Stan was so upset and angry… He'd walked on ahead.'

'Yeah. Blamed himself?' Will could identify with that. If it had happened to Lark, he would have felt just the same.

'Yes. It's stupid, but…' Sandra shrugged miserably.

'No, it's not. We've all been there, Sandra, someone we love is hurt and we're unable to help.' The old agony began to stir in Will's heart. Echoes of when someone *he'd* loved had been hurt. Now wasn't the time to think about that, he had a job to do here. Will repeated the old mantra to himself. He was okay and he could function. He could carry on, the way he'd done for more than ten years, now.

'You didn't tell him?'

'It's probably nothing. I've bumped my head before now.' Sandra straightened a little, but the effort seemed too much for her and she leaned back onto the sofa cushions.

'Yes, you're right. The overwhelming possibility is that it *is* nothing, and that what you're experiencing is a bad migraine. But I think we need to check, just to be sure. Just knowing may well help you to feel a bit better.'

'Yes. All right.'

'There are a few more tests I'd like to do first. One of them is going to involve shining a light in your eyes, just for a moment. I know that's not what you want right now…'

'It's all right, Doctor. I'll manage.'

Sandra had managed, even though she'd begun to retch when Will had checked the reactions of her pupils to light. Lark came hurrying into the room, holding a roll of kitchen towel, and deftly caught up a disposable vomit bowl from the medical kit they'd brought with them. When he took it from her, she grinned at him and Will reckoned he'd be in for one of Lark's dry comments about doctors not being supposed to take vomit bowls from paramedics, later. Lark had always been more aware of that difference than he was, even if her reaction had turned from looks of quiet suspicion to teasing a long time ago.

'What do you think?' Sandra was leaning against her, her eyes closed, and Lark held her gently. Her ability to calm and reassure people was something she never measured against his qualifications, and Will always felt that was an omission on her part, which wasn't like Lark because her sharp mind usually took in everything.

'She has a bump on her head and a very slight dilation of the pupil, both on the right side, which is the side of the headache. It may be nothing but we need to make sure.'

Lark nodded. 'You want me to call an ambulance?'

He was quite capable of doing that himself. Now wasn't the time to remind her of that. And they were only five minutes from the hospital where Will worked.

'It'll be much quicker and better all round if we take her ourselves. I can phone ahead and speak to someone in Neurology.'

'Yes. Good. I'll go and let Stan know, and explain that we're just being ultra-careful. He didn't mention to me that Sandra had banged her head.'

'It was when her phone was snatched. Sandra didn't think it was anything, and didn't mention it to Stan.'

'Ah, okay.' She nodded. No need to say any more, he could rely on Lark to break the news gently.

They carried a folding wheelchair in the boot of the car, for just this eventuality, and Lark went to fetch it while Stan came to sit with Sandra. He shook his head in gentle reproach and Sandra managed a smile as Will took out his phone, dialling the number of the neurology department at the hospital.

* * *

Lark didn't come to this hospital much, but since the neurology department was a centre of excellence she'd transported a few patients here. From the moment they walked into the building it became apparent that Will was well regarded. He didn't push, but his quiet conversation with the A&E receptionist brought a nurse out to show them through to a cubicle almost immediately, and a young woman doctor appeared as soon as Sandra was settled on the couch.

'Such a fuss…' Sandra whispered to her, blinking in the bright overhead lighting. Lark held her hand up to shade Sandra's face from the glare.

'It's okay, just close your eyes if the light's hurting you. Let them make a fuss if they want to, we want to make sure you're all right.' Lark was becoming more and more convinced that there was cause for concern, and that this wasn't a simple migraine.

She handed her tablet to Will, containing the observations from when she'd first seen Sandra, along with today's notes. He fiddled with it for a moment and then walked over to the nurses' station, plucking a sheet of paper from the printer and handing it over to the doctor. There was a quiet conversation, in which Will appeared to do most of the talking, and then the young woman walked over to Sandra.

'Hi, Sandra, my name's Dr Shireen Madani-Porter and I'm from the neurology department here in the hospital. Dr Bradley's already examined you and I'm afraid I have a few more tests I need to do, now that you're here. I know your head's hurting, so I'll be as quick as I can.'

'Thank you, Doctor,' Stan replied for Sandra, watching as Shireen carefully checked Sandra's responses, noting everything down. Lark motioned him to a seat, sitting down next to him.

When she'd finished, Shireen walked over to Will, who was standing in the corner of the cubicle, watching silently. She proffered her notes, and Will ignored them.

'I'd like to do a CT scan, and keep Sandra in until we can be sure exactly what's going on,' Shireen murmured and Will gave her one of his brightest smiles.

'Great. Thank you.' He nodded towards Stan, in an indication that Shireen should now tell him what would be happening next, and she hurried over to him, sitting down in the seat that Lark had just vacated for her, and began to talk to him.

It was time to go. Lark squeezed Sandra's hand, smiling at her and reminding her to do as she was told, and then nudged Will out of the cubicle.

'We can't hang around here all day...'

'No.' Will frowned. Something was clearly bugging him. 'What?'

'Nothing. Just...how do you do this? Bringing people into the hospital and just leaving them here. Don't you wonder about what comes next for them?'

'Yes, of course I do. But there's always the next person waiting for me. It's a matter of trust, and knowing I'm handing my patients on to people who will care for them well.'

'Mm. Suppose so. Shireen's very thorough and she's a good doctor. A little new, and she's still finding her feet...' Will looked round as the cubicle door opened behind them, and Shireen appeared. 'Everything okay?'

'Yes, thanks. I'm just going to order the CT scan, and I'll make sure that Sandra's taken up to the ward as soon as possible.'

'Give me a call...'

Shireen's face fell and Lark resisted the temptation to kick Will. 'It would be great to know how Sandra's doing. If you have the time, that is.' She smiled at Shireen.

'Oh. Yes, of course.' Shireen got the message that Will wasn't checking up on her and grinned, hurrying away.

'Really? *Give me a call?*' Lark waited until they were outside, walking back to the car.

'It's a perfectly reasonable request.'

'You're happy that she can manage Sandra's case?'

'Of course. I have absolutely no doubt of that.'

'Then let her do it. Ask tomorrow. Or ask today if you must, but make it clear that you're not questioning her ability, you'd just like to know. Or you could call Stan, he's given me his number and I said I'd give him a call this afternoon.'

'Oh. Now you tell me.' Will feigned outrage. 'So much for your ability to walk away and not look back, then.'

'You're not the only one who's human,' Lark flashed back at him, getting into the car.

When they returned to the charity's office, riding up in the lift with the receptionist, they found their morning coffees still standing on the front desk. Grace tutted at them both, sweeping off into the kitchen to empty the cardboard cups, and Will retreated to his office to make some calls while Lark went through Howard's post.

An hour later she popped her head around his office door, holding two more cups of coffee, this time from the machine in the kitchen. Will motioned her inside, holding up one finger to indicate that the call he was making was drawing to a close, and Lark put the coffee down, flopping onto the sofa opposite him.

'I just heard from Stan. He'd gone for a cup of tea while Sandra was having her CT scan. There's no news yet, of course, but just knowing she's being well cared for has made all the difference. He told me that Shireen's been really kind to them and he asked me to thank you as well.'

Lark had regained the warmth, the certainty that he'd seen eroded in the last week, and what he'd been wanting to say to her seemed suddenly very relevant.

'I'm glad to hear it. I've been thinking…'

'Yes?'

'We're medics, and Stan and Sandra are the people we're here for. They're at the centre of everything we do.'

'Of course.' Lark's gaze seemed to consume him.

'Howard's our friend and he's going to need some help and support when he's discharged from rehab.'

'Without a doubt. A stroke of that severity means he's facing a long road to recovery.'

'That's what matters. It's what's always mattered. This business with Pete and the trustees, the fooling with our heads, the competition and changing roles… That's all secondary, and we've been spending too much time and energy on it. That has to stop here.'

'Sure, boss. Whatever you say…'

'Lark, I'm serious about this…'

They stared at each other. Lark's response was no different from the jokes that they shot back and forth at each other all the time. But Will's reaction was different. Maybe because everything around them seemed to be shifting, and he could see Lark anew as the one immovable centre of his life. Maybe because he saw her vulnerability too, and felt so darn protective of her.

It didn't really matter *how* it had happened. It just had, and now he was falling a little in love with her. Blossoming love required a lighter touch than friendship, a little more reassur-ance and a little less pretending to ride roughshod over each other, even though they were each in the habit of listening carefully to what the other had to say.

And Lark knew this as well as he did. That a joke had ex-posed the shift in their relationship.

'Sorry, I didn't mean to be autocratic. I'm just a little stressed about all of this.' Particularly since, in Will's mind, the word love always carried the inevitable addendum *and loss*.

Lark nodded. 'You weren't. I always appreciate it when you don't mince your words, and you're right, this does have to stop. If we don't draw a line under it all, this business with Pete and Sir Terence *is* going to compromise everything we do.'

'Solutions?' He grinned at her.

'They want to make this all about personal development, then we'll play it their way. It happens during our personal time, not at work. We take control of it. We've already got a plan for next weekend.'

'And they say that I have all the good ideas.' He grinned at her. However their relationship might be changing, they were still friends. Friends, doctors. Those were the two absolutes that they had to hang on to.

They'd spent the afternoon seeing patients, as usual. Will had made a point of suggesting they stay behind after work to re-view Pete's emailed list of ways they might swap roles, and none of it seemed any fun to him. One of the entries suggested that they swap over who made the tea, and since they usually took turns that seemed a particularly fruitless exercise.

Lark looked up from her laptop, where a copy of the list was displayed, her eyes flashing gold in the evening sunlight that flooded across the room. Her large, impeccably tidy desk dominated the space, the small floral sofa relegated to one corner of the office.

Will leaned back in one of the seats arranged on the other side of the desk, stretching his legs. 'I reckon we can knock half a dozen things off it without even breaking a sweat.'

'Yes. I'm a bit miffed about the tea-making one. I'm going to have to make as much as you do, am I?'

That wasn't Lark's objection to the idea—or his. Will knew that it was the thinking behind it, the assumption that Lark made tea and Will drank it.

'Perhaps we'll have to make a biscuit baking rota.'

The joke had the desired effect and Lark smiled. 'No, I think biscuits are off the table. You know I don't bake.'

'So…since we can tick off half a dozen things from this list pretty much immediately, why don't we concentrate on the weekend? Make it clear to Pete that this is the way we want things to go.'

'Okay. So I'll come to your parents' party with you?'

'I was thinking rather more along the lines of me going with you, actually.'

The idea did seem a little crazy, but every time Will tried to dismiss it, he had a vision of Lark, her hand slipped into the crook of his arm, at the centre of everyone's attention. Shining in public, in the same way he'd seen her shine in private over the last four years. Ever since Friday afternoon, when he'd been so determined to defend her, and Friday evening, when she'd melted into his arms, it had been all he could think about. Will wasn't entirely sure how he could have failed to feel all of this before.

'You're sure about that?' She shot him an unconvinced look.

'Positive. And what did you have in mind—are you going to get on with that painting you've been talking about?'

'I was thinking I might. Trust me, Will, you don't want to spend your weekend painting my walls.'

'Why *are* you painting, anyway. I thought you and Robyn decorated a few years ago, when you first bought the place.'

'Yes, we did. But we couldn't agree on colours, so we compromised and painted everything cream. Now that I have the place to myself, I think it's time for me to try out a few new colours.'

'Perfect. So you're remaking your space, then.'

'You could call it that if you liked. Actually, I'm going to be working pretty hard and getting paint all over me. Have you ever painted anything before?'

'No.' Will decided that body paint didn't count, and that it was probably best not to mention that right now. 'So I'll give you a heads-up on what we're trying to achieve at the party, and you can show me how you want your room painted.'

Lark was shaking her head slowly and the urge to vault across her desk and silence her questions with a kiss tugged at Will. For a start, he wasn't quite sure he could make that kind of leap without disturbing any of the carefully arranged things on the work surface. Secondly, he wasn't in the habit of silencing women, and in particular not Lark.

'If you think it's too much of a challenge...' The suggestion was sure to make Lark's hackles rise.

'No. I'm just worried about my sitting room,' she flashed back at him, and Will felt something stir in the pit of his stomach.

'I'll follow your instructions to the letter. And we have to do something, Lark. Howard's known Sir Terence for a long time and probably has a good idea about how to keep him in check, but I'm not sure that we ever gave him enough credit for the way he protected us and the rest of the staff from ideas like this one. Maybe this *is* the time for us to reassess the way we do things, not because either of us wants to succeed him, but because the balance has changed.'

Lark's face fell. 'I miss Howard. I really do...'

'Yeah, me too. And we're going to have to manage without him for a while.'

'Do you think...? You've seen more outcomes for stroke patients than I have, Will. He *will* be back, won't he?'

'As a doctor...' Will tried to think about what lay ahead dispassionately. 'Howard has everything to fight for right now. His leg's a great deal stronger, and I'm expecting that when he goes into rehab they'll work on that and get him walking again quite quickly. With the right techniques, it'll be possible to release his hand from the clenched position it's in now, although how much fine control he'll have remains to be seen. As he's left-handed, and the stroke affected his right side, he'll be able to manage better with manual tasks.'

'And the aphasia?'

'It'll take a while and a lot of work. But the thing with aphasia is that there's always a potential for further recovery. Howard's determined and he's not going to give up his life's work without putting up a fight, and that's going to stand him in very good stead. You know this, Lark.'

'Yes, I do. I just wanted to hear you say it. It's different that he's our friend, isn't it?'

'Very different. But, as his friends, our job is to believe in him. That means we do whatever it takes to keep this place running, and in good shape for him to come back to. We have to confront this thing with Sir Terence, not just for ourselves but for Howard too.'

When Lark buried her face in her hands, Will recognised the gesture. She was thinking about it, working it through and weighing everything up in her head. The best thing to do was wait, even if he was tempted to add that, in addition to flexing their own authority, it was a scheme that might just allow them to explore each other a little more deeply. That was a temptation that he ought to resist, because all of his common sense was telling him that they already had the best of each other and daring to ask for more was risky.

'You have overalls?' She looked up at him suddenly.

Will grinned. 'Nope. Maybe you could advise on the best ones to get...'

Lark saw where this was going immediately. 'Oh, no. You don't get a say in the dress, Will. I'm drawing that line.'

Shame. From her smile, Lark was probably expecting him to feign a look of disappointment, and Will had no trouble in making it seem real.

'Okay. Fair enough. You've got to give me credit for trying, though.'

Something in her gaze softened. Molten gold showed in her eyes, and the feeling that the only thing he really needed to do was to hold Lark close flooded through him.

'Ten out of ten, Will.' She opened her drawer, taking out a couple of paint charts. 'You want me to show you what you're up against?'

CHAPTER FOUR

WILL HAD GOT in touch with Pete, asking that they move the Friday afternoon session to either the morning or the evening, because the afternoons were ring-fenced for working with patients. Pete had said that the early evening suited him best, and they'd gone to the session with a renewed sense of determination. Will had subtly taken control of the conversation, telling Pete how useful they'd found some of the concepts behind the exercises, and that it had inspired them to take his ideas a little further. Pete had listened, and then Lark had taken over, outlining their plans for the weekend.

And it had worked. Pete was engaged and interested, and Lark felt much happier with the session and less personally confronted. Will had worked his magic.

Only it wasn't really magic at all. She'd known this all along about Will, but before all of this talk of role-playing Lark had never taken the trouble to quantify it. Will's charm seemed effortless because he was actually making no effort to appear charming. Working with him had taught her that he was a nice guy who genuinely liked people, valued them and listened to them. That was all he was doing with Pete—it was all he ever did.

'You know… I think that Pete has a lot to offer. Some of his ideas could be interesting if they were developed the right way,' Will mused as they walked down the concrete steps to the underground car park beneath the building. The weekend officially started now, and he'd said that they had no time to lose taking buses and trains.

Lark turned the idea over in her head. 'Do you feel that your family underestimates you?' Pete had asked the question, but Will had effortlessly deflected it.

This time he answered. 'My parents have always been entirely supportive of my career—of anything I've ever wanted to do, in fact.'

'They value your charm, though.'

Will shrugged. 'Dad's always said I could get away with almost anything. I don't like to think of myself as that manipulative.'

'I've never thought you manipulative. You're not charming either.'

Those baby-blue eyes. The sincerity in them added a whole new layer to their jokes and the smiling compliments they paid each other.

'Thank you. That's a really nice thing to say.'

Lark lived on the outskirts of London, and Will spent the whole of the journey basking in the glow of what she'd said to him. Calling him charming *was* dismissive, because it didn't take account of the work he'd done to succeed. In his father's eyes it had all been easy. Will was the charming one of the family, and everyone else had to work for what they had.

It wasn't meant cruelly. His father didn't even mean to be unsupportive. It was just one of those things. Everyone had a role in their family and Will's place was to be charming. To somehow feel less, as a consequence of that. To interact with people and then move on.

That wasn't easy. But after he'd lost Eloise, it was the only way he could find any peace. Will had been an awkward teenager, in love for the first time, and she'd left him lost for words. He'd been clumsy and blushing when they'd first kissed, but Eloise had forgiven him and taught him how to kiss properly, since she had the advantage of being six months older than Will, and thus more knowledgeable about the ways of the world.

The sweet innocence of it all still made him smile. Eighteen months later, they'd gone to London together, Eloise to study English literature and Will to do his medical degree. They'd traded their virginity with each other, in Eloise's narrow bed in her student lodgings. And Will had known right there and then that she was The One. The Only One. Because what they'd lacked in terms of practical experience they'd made up for with a youthful sense of adventure, which made all of the First Times that they shared so special.

London had been good to them, and Eloise had found work while Will continued his studies. They'd grown from teenage lovers to fledgling professionals who had their lives ahead of them and couldn't imagine spending those lives apart.

And then the unthinkable, a series of chances that had culminated in tragedy. If Eloise hadn't turned to wave him goodbye and wish him a good day, if an impatient driver hadn't been late for work, then maybe she wouldn't have been hit by the car speeding away from the lights. He wouldn't have felt her grip on his arm begin to loosen as he fought to save her, and she wouldn't have died in the road before the ambulance could get to them.

Everyone had been kind. His academic supervisor at the hospital had reviewed Eloise's case with the head of A&E and they'd both assured Will that her injuries were too devastating, and that even the most experienced doctor couldn't have saved her. He'd done the right thing at the end, by simply holding her. He'd been told to take whatever time he needed, and his parents had insisted he stay with them for a while. Will had spent two weeks in a daze, hardly speaking to anyone, and then he'd come back to London.

He'd found that the appearance of happiness was something that could be learned. He'd struggled with sleep, hiding it from everyone, but he'd not been able to hide the migraines that hit him when exhaustion had rendered him unconscious for twelve hours at a time on his days off. On the first anniversary of Eloise's death, Will had promised her that he'd cut back on his gruelling work schedule, and balance his sleep patterns a little better, which had finally lifted the debilitating headaches and sickness.

When he'd started to accept a few more of the invitations that hadn't stopped coming his way, Will had found that concentrating on other people's lives allowed him to forget that he didn't quite believe in the one that he was pretending to live. Piece by piece, year by year, he'd built a new life. One which centred around the present and not the future, and where relationships might come and go as naturally and unremarkably as incoming and outgoing tides, which swept a beach clean and fresh each day.

Lark was the exception to that. She was so different from him that it felt safe to allow her in, past the wall of charm.

Pete had wondered whether Lark was invested in her role as a carer. As she sat quietly in the car next to him, Will wondered whether Pete had attributed the right emotion to the wrong person. Didn't *he* have an investment in Lark's family commitments, because in practical terms they had meant she had little time for a romance…?

And now Will was playing with fire. Spending time with

her out of work, changing places with her. Hugging her. So many things that he'd thought about doing and then dismissed as being way beyond the confines of their relationship. But going back now would be like standing on the beach, expecting the oncoming tide to recede at his command.

It was relatively unusual to find a bungalow in the London suburbs, but Lark had done so, in a street that combined several one-storey properties with larger two-storey houses. He drew into the double parking spot next to Lark's car, feeling a need to stretch his limbs after having been cramped with his thoughts. As usual, Lark was out of her seat before he had time to reach the passenger door and open it for her.

She opened the front door, flipping on the lights and motioning him inside. The right-hand side of the property was taken up by an open-plan seating, dining and kitchen area, and Lark had clearly been busy, moving furniture to the centre of the space and covering it with dust sheets.

'It's an ambitious job. You didn't think of calling in a painter and moving out for a couple of days?'

She grinned up at him. 'Are you saying that it's too much for you?'

'No.' Will knew that in the face of one of Lark's challenges the best way forward was to show no fear. 'You might have waited until I got here, so I could give you a hand with the furniture.'

'I suppose I could have. But I was rather looking forward to the sight of you in painting overalls.'

Will wondered whether she could be looking forward to that quite as much as he was looking forward to the dress for tomorrow evening, and decided that wasn't possible.

'I suppose I'd better go and get them from the car, then.

Those are your colours?' He pointed towards the tester squares painted on the wall.

Lark nodded. 'Yes, the light pinky-beige is for the dining area and the very dusky pink is for the sitting area at the back. The kitchen's going to be much lighter, I'll do that in a warm white.'

'Nice.' Will nodded, feeling on more solid ground with colour choices. Lark had talked about making the bungalow 'hers' when Robyn had left to get married, and he suspected that the hard work involved was partly an antidote to missing her sister.

'I'm not sure how it's going to look.' Lark regarded him thoughtfully. 'But I suppose if I'm redefining my space that allows me to be a bit adventurous. Would you like some dinner before we begin?'

In for a penny, in for a pound. Suddenly Will couldn't wait to get on with the job.

'Or we could make a start, and order in when we get hungry...'

Eight o'clock on a Friday evening. Will probably didn't usually spend Friday evenings at home, but Lark reckoned that he would be attending to his busy social calendar rather than turning his hand to DIY. All the same, he'd changed into an immaculate set of overalls, clearly purchased specially for the occasion, and they'd made a start on the painting.

'It's very blotchy.' Will was frowning furiously at the paint he'd applied to the dining area end of the wall, and Lark walked across from her section of paint in the seating area.

'That's how it's supposed to be—the paint goes a slightly different colour as it dries. And the first coat is always a bit blotchy, when you do a second it'll be fine.'

'I was thinking it would be better to put it on a bit more thickly.'

'No, don't do that, you'll get an uneven finish. Two thin coats is better than one thick one.'

Will was clearly still unhappy with his efforts. 'Where did you learn to do all this?'

'My dad taught me. It's a life skill, isn't it?'

He shot her an unconvinced look. 'My younger brother always used to help my father with any DIY jobs that needed doing. Edward's the practical one.'

'And your brother Joel is the academic. Which doesn't leave you much ground to occupy, does it.' Lark had never questioned the way Will's family did things, but right now it seemed a pertinent observation. One that Will seemed to be struggling to find an answer to.

'He always says that I'm the *"people person".* Will motioned a pair of speech marks in the air.

'So being a doctor doesn't take practicality? Or academic work?'

Will shrugged. 'My thoughts entirely. Families, eh?'

It wasn't much of an answer, but it seemed to be the only one that Will was going to give. And it was accompanied by the look that Will used whenever he was trying to smile his way out of an awkward question.

'So what do you think of DIY then? I find painting quite relaxing.'

He laughed, shaking his head. 'I'm a bit stressed out with it at the moment. Since you've done more than I have.'

Lark glanced at her part of the wall. 'Getting competitive?'

'Isn't that okay, when it's just between us?'

Lark had decided not to admit that she'd been spurred on in her work by comparing the areas they'd both painted. Or that she wasn't unhappy about the fact that her patch of dusky pink was a good deal larger than Will's section of pinky-beige.

'It's not about how much you do, Will. I'll order the pizza and give you a chance to catch up.'

'Ah. If it isn't about how much you do, then why would I need to catch up…?' Will shot her a twinkling smile and started to paint again.

They'd sat in the kitchen, drinking beer and tucking into pizza. Concentrating on painting evenly without leaving too many brushstrokes *had* cleared Will's mind of the worries that the week had brought, and catching up with her—competing—had added a frisson to the task. As he'd leaned back in his chair, taking a sip of beer, he surveyed his work with a satisfaction that he'd thought impossible.

They'd worked on, until it was beyond time for Will to go home.

He returned early the next morning, to find Lark, dressed in the pair of paint-spattered jeans she'd changed into last night, a cup of coffee in her hand. The door to the large front bedroom was wide open, and she'd clearly been surveying the room that had once been Robyn's. An empty space that made Will realise that a hole had been left in Lark's life, which wasn't filled yet.

'Are you going to redecorate this room as well?'

She hesitated. 'I was thinking of it. I might move in there, it's bigger.' When they'd talked about it at work, Robyn's leaving to get married had seemed an abstract idea. Here, seeing the almost tangible space that she'd left, it all felt so much more immediate.

'You miss her, don't you?'

Lark led him into the kitchen and poured him a cup of coffee, then sat down with him at the kitchen table.

'Of course I do.'

'I mean…*really* miss her.' Will ignored Lark's shrugging

smile. It was the one she always gave when she was trying to brush off her own needs, in favour of recognising someone else's.

'I'm really happy for Robyn. She has the life that she wanted, and it's what I always wanted for her too.'

'Of course. No one questions that, but you get to feel something too.' Will wondered why he was suddenly pushing so hard, when he'd already accepted Lark's assertions that she was concentrating on getting on with her life.

She pressed her lips together. 'You know…my parents were always so fearful for Robyn. That was why she came to live with me, she needed to spread her wings and it was virtually impossible to do that at home.'

'And you gave her the opportunity.'

'Yes, but Robyn's always been the adventurous one, and I'm the sensible one. I relied on that to persuade my parents that her coming to live with me was the right thing to do. And Mum used to call me all the time, she was so fearful for Robyn. I felt it was my responsibility to make everything work for her.'

'You never said.' Will was suddenly conscious that they really had moved onto new ground. There were a lot of things he hadn't said either.

'I didn't realise what I was doing. I spent years working out how I could make things go right for her, when Robyn was actually perfectly capable of doing that herself, she just needed a bit of practical help from time to time. The real burden was my own fears, and those of my parents.'

'You've come to see that now?'

'Yes, I have.' Lark smiled suddenly. 'But if you ever tell Robyn that's how I felt, there'll be trouble.'

Will chuckled, liking the idea of sharing a secret with her.

'So you really are reinventing yourself, not just painting a few walls.'

'It's more like finding a part of myself that I lost because I let fear get in my way. But not before breakfast.' She grinned at him. 'Then I reckon I can finish up with a second coat on my side of the wall before it's time to think about getting ready for the party.'

'And it would be a shame if we let a mere party get in the way of painting.' Will was only half joking. Last night, he'd started at the front of the house and Lark at the back, and they'd gradually worked their way towards each other, meeting at the point where the wall had been removed between the two spaces. It would be impossible to allow her to get ahead of him now.

'My thoughts exactly. Maybe the smell of paint will loosen your tongue a bit as well...'

Maybe. But right now Will was in this for the sheer enjoyment of it.

It was just a wall. And paint. If it meant something to Lark, then she really shouldn't have assumed that it would mean the same to Will, and her comment about loosening *his* tongue had been out of order, even if there was a lot more going on behind Will's façade than he ever owned up to. But he hadn't seemed to mind, and apologising might give the slip more importance than it deserved.

And this was a lot more fun than painting on her own. It was clearly the first time Will had done anything like this, but he was a fast learner and his greater height and reach gave him the advantage. It was only the fact that he seemed intent on making his side of the wall perfect that allowed her to keep up with him.

They'd never competed over anything before, and they'd both been adamant that they wouldn't cave in to the trustees and compete with each other now. But laughing together over paint splashes was just one part of the pleasure, and the other part was being the first to reach the square-topped arch between the dining space and the living space.

'If we leave at about five, then we'll get down to my parents' place in time for me to introduce you to the family and show you around a bit.' He'd insisted on keeping working on his side of the wall while Lark went out to the local Chinese restaurant to get a takeaway for lunch.

'I'm relying on you, Will...' Lark's usual strategy at large gatherings of people was to find herself something useful to do and help with that, so that she could avoid the need for small talk. She'd never quite fathomed how Will managed to conjure something interesting to say to complete strangers, seemingly out of thin air.

'You just need to get people talking.' He grinned across the kitchen table at her, reaching for one of the boxes of food. 'Everyone has something to say about themselves.'

She wondered whether this seemed as easy to him as the practical task of painting did to her. Lark dismissed the thought that she'd rather be at home, getting on with the gloss on the skirting boards. Will had risen to his end of the bargain, and she'd rise to hers.

At three o'clock she went to shower and wash her hair, leaving Will to clean the brushes. Clothes and hair were just practical things, arranged to help you fit in with your surroundings, weren't they...?

All the same, her hair and make-up took a little longer than usual, and the red dress she'd bought for the evening reception of Robyn's wedding required a little more scrutiny when she stood in front of the mirror in her bedroom. When she went downstairs her high heels clacked disconcertingly on the tiles of the kitchen floor.

And when Will appeared… She'd seen him in a suit plenty of times before, ready for an evening function. Effortlessly handsome. Charming in a way that didn't seem artificial, but just made it seem as if he was everyone's best friend.

Her heart began to beat faster. Lark couldn't compete with this, and very probably couldn't compete with the other women who would be at the party. And then Will smiled that smile. The one that said that she was the only person in the room—the universe, even—who could draw his attention right now.

'You win.'

She stared at him uncomprehendingly. 'Win?'

Suddenly he was very close. His gaze fixed on her as if even this wasn't close enough. Lark shivered, her hand wandering nervously to her hair, remembering at the last moment not to flatten her curls or push them behind her ears.

'You look stunning. I can't even hope to compete with you tonight, so I'm going to give up gracefully before I make a fool of myself.'

It was a nice thing to say. His words were laced with sincerity, and Lark felt the fluttering of her nerves begin to calm.

'You're making me feel better, aren't you.' Lark still couldn't quite accept the compliment.

Will leaned forward. 'That would be very rash of me. If you were to stop looking so terrified and smile, then I wouldn't be able to take my eyes off you. So while I'm driving, perhaps you could contrive not to feel any better.'

Lark couldn't help laughing. And when Will escorted her out to his car, opening the passenger door to let her get in, and closing it again with a firm sweep of his arm, there was nothing to do but dissolve in the pleasure of his scent, the quiet delight of glancing every now and then at him as he drove. More than an hour later, they drew into the driveway of a large modern house, ablaze with light, in the rolling Hertfordshire countryside.

'Will!' His mother, Priscilla, was looking fabulous as usual, in a blue dress that flattered her curves. As soon as Will stepped inside she enveloped him in a hug. 'And Lark! It's so nice to see you again. I've been hearing a lot about you.'

Will chuckled at the awkwardness of the moment. 'All of it quite unrepeatable.'

'Nonsense, Will.' His mother turned to Lark, holding out her hand. 'He pretends to be such a rogue…'

And, like any mother, Priscilla Bradley saw straight through him. Will's careless charm fooled his mother about as much as it did Lark, and she too ignored it.

The caterers were busy stocking tables at one end of a large high-ceilinged area that was far too grand to be called a sitting room. To one side, a table had been arranged with information about Migraine Community Action's work subtly displayed, so as not to be too intrusive, but there for those who wanted to know more. When Priscilla excused herself, saying that she should go and see what was going on in the kitchen, Will caught Lark's hand, stopping her from following her, and led her through to the back of the house. William Bradley senior was in his study, talking with his son Edward, who motioned to Lark to sit down on the sofa next to him.

It was a nice gesture. Edward shot Lark a quiet smile as his father and older brother went through what was clearly an established routine of challenging each other over who had been the busiest since they'd last seen each other.

Will's father slapped him on the back. 'We have some interesting people here tonight. Your mother added a few to the guest list that you sent, who are all interested in seeing how your charity works.'

'I didn't think she'd be able to resist.'

'Your mother loves a party. She'll be directing the food and drinks operation so that you can get on with talking to people. Ed and I will…' his father waved his hand in the air '…support.'

She heard Edward suppress a snort of laughter. Will and his father were the big personalities in the room, the ones who could hold people's attention, and it seemed that Ed was just as happy to play a supporting role as she was. But Will obviously had other ideas.

'I brought Lark along because it's a great opportunity for her to meet people. You want to join me and Ed in blending into the background, Dad?'

His father's eyebrows shot up in surprise, but then he beamed at Lark. 'Wonderful. Lark, the room's all yours.'

Great. Now she had a whole room full of people to contend with. Will shot her a smile, which was no doubt intended to make her feel she was equal to the task, but for once even Will's smile couldn't penetrate the deep panic that she felt.

CHAPTER FIVE

WILL'S FAMILY WERE welcoming and friendly—but for the first time Lark was noticing how clearly defined their roles were. It sold Will short to imagine him as a charming ambassador when he was so much more than that, and Lark couldn't help wondering if her own attention to detail wasn't inadvertently forcing him into the same role that he had with his family. Maybe she should make an effort to slip into his shoes tonight, and give him some space to show that he was capable of a lot more than just charm.

'What do you think?' Will had extracted her from his father's study, stopping for a moment to exchange hellos with his brother Joel and his wife, who were laughing together in one corner of the empty reception room. Then he'd guided her out onto a covered patio, shimmering with lights and warm enough in the early evening to provide an overflow space from the party.

'I didn't expect your whole family to be here. It's really nice of them all.'

'Yes, it is. They've always been really supportive of whatever I wanted to do.' The corners of Will's mouth turned down for a brief moment and then he smiled, taking her hand and settling it in the crook of his arm in a gesture of intimacy that mirrored the way they worked together. Challenging the hardest issues together, telling each other the truths that would be difficult to hear from anyone else.

'Every family has expectations, Will.' Lark wondered whether the sessions with Pete and the swapping of roles was finally getting to Will.

'Yeah. They all just want the best for me, the way that you want the best for Robyn.'

There was something there. She'd felt it simmering beneath the surface, before it was quickly hidden, so many times and had never had the courage to ask.

'What is it, Will?' She tightened her grip on his arm, as if physical closeness might prompt a greater understanding between them.

'I've told you about Eloise, haven't I?'

'Only that you and she were friends when you were young.' Will had mentioned Eloise once or twice, generally in the context of his schooldays, and Lark had reckoned that they were a little more than just friends from the tenderness on his face. But when she'd asked he'd changed the subject and stubbornly refused to return to it.

'She was my first girlfriend. My first love. We'd been together since we were seventeen. We were going to get married when I finished medical school, but she died in a road accident. I was there, and I couldn't save her...'

His words hit Lark like a blow to the chest. Like every other difficulty in life, Will had skimmed over this tragedy and let everyone think nothing was bothering him. But something like this didn't just go away.

'I'm so sorry, Will.' She felt him shrug and before he could dismiss his own feelings she tugged at his arm to quieten him. 'That's the kind of thing that's never really okay, and you don't get over it. You just learn to live with it.'

'Yeah, you're right. Thanks for saying that.' It was as if a curtain had fallen somewhere behind his eyes, leaving him naked. All Lark could see there was pain and despair, but she couldn't shrink away from that.

'There's more to say, isn't there? Nothing like this simply ends with your parting,' she prompted him.

He nodded. 'Does it sound self-pitying to say that there were times that I wished it had? That I just didn't want to go on without Eloise.'

Will had loved her. *Really* loved her. Lark reproved herself for the jab of envy that she felt. That had never been an issue with any of Will's other relationships—they were all so transient—and she knew that she had the better part of him by being his friend.

'No. It sounds a lot like the reaction of anyone who's lost someone that they really loved. If you have a picture of her that you'd like to show me, I'd love to see it.' If Lark could picture Eloise, then this would all be more real to her and she wouldn't feel so dismayed that Will *had* loved someone. She had no right to feel anything about it at all, other than a sympathetic sorrow over his loss.

He looked around, as if checking that they were alone, and then reached into an inside pocket of his jacket, taking out his wallet and opening a concealed pocket. 'You're not going to tell anyone that I still carry a photo of her, are you?'

'It's not a crime, Will. But no, if you don't want me to mention it to anyone, then of course I won't.'

Will handed her the photograph and Lark caught her breath. 'She's beautiful. You both look really happy together.' The look of open contentment on Will's face made her like Eloise immediately, and Lark could share this reaction honestly with him now.

'Yeah, we were. After she died, Mum and Dad insisted I come back home for a few weeks, and I appreciated that a lot but... I didn't want to talk about it any more. I didn't want people worrying about me either, thinking I was unhappy. So if they asked I'd just say I was fine and change the subject. Get them to talk about themselves.'

Suddenly everything made sense. The way that Will concentrated on whoever he happened to be talking to. The way his relationships never got to the point of being serious, starting and ending without disturbing the pattern of his life.

'So you hid your own pain behind a wall of charm?'

He shrugged. 'I'm not going to deny it, even though it's an uncomfortable thought. I was happier talking about other people and I guess that became a habit.'

'And your family were just happy that you seemed to be getting over Eloise's loss?' It felt a little presumptuous to say her name, but Will smiled suddenly when she did.

'Yeah. This role of mine fitted in with what they wanted for me as well.'

'But you're not comfortable with it now. The way it seems to diminish you.' Lark had been thinking that it ignored Will's very real talents in other directions. But maybe it was his way of rejecting the possibility that he might make a relationship that lasted for more than a few weeks as well.

'I suppose... As you said, all families have expectations. It was a long time ago now, and time heals.' He grinned down at her. 'You paint over the cracks for a while and then suddenly you realise that happiness isn't quite as elusive as you'd thought, and you do actually have a lot to look forward to.'

Maybe that was a veiled hint about Lark's situation. That some day soon she'd step out from behind her own parents' expectations, which she'd so readily shouldered because they fed her own fears.

'So we're going to do this then? I'm going to see whether I can take a leaf out of your book and be the charity's ambassador for the evening?' Lark still felt pretty unequal to the challenge.

He nodded, laughing. 'Trust me. As ambassador in chief, my verdict is that you'll knock them dead.'

Lark had nothing to be nervous about. From the first moment he'd seen her, in a red dress that folded gently around her curves, her beautiful eyes somehow bigger and more lustrous... That wasn't fair. It wasn't the dress or the make-up, and Lark was beautiful any day of the week. The red dress invited Will to look, though, and when he did he felt that he'd discovered something that he'd only half seen before.

All the same, she was nervous. He could almost feel her heart beating faster as her fingers tightened around his arm.

'Over there...' He nodded towards a distinguished-looking man who'd just entered. 'Sir Sidney Chambers. The newspaper guy...'

Lark nodded. 'I've heard of him.'

'And that's Sunil Mehta...'

Lark nodded again. Sunil's generosity, particularly towards medical charities, was well known. Her brow creased and she looked up at Will, clearly wondering what to do with the information.

'We're not here to ask for donations, or newspaper articles, just to introduce you to people so that we're on their radar. Whether they choose to pick up the phone, and when, is up to them.'

'Right. Good.' Lark looked a little relieved. 'Like making friends in the playground.'

Will chuckled. 'Just like that. Remember the newspaper article about different ways to control migraine last year?'

'Oh! I wondered how you'd got involved with that.' Will had been asked to contribute to a double-page spread, and the hits on their website had gone sky-high for a couple of weeks afterwards. Lark aimed a grateful smile at the back of Sir Sidney's head.

'He gave the reporter who was writing the piece my number, and then stepped back and let her do her job.' It had been a great opportunity for the charity to heighten awareness about some of the issues that lay at the heart of their operation.

'Okay.' Lark smiled up at him. 'I'm getting the drift of this...'

She certainly was. Lark was irresistible, honest, natural and beautiful. Will was barely stopping himself from whisking her off to a quiet corner and talking to her for the whole of the evening. Feeling her gaze warm him...

'Who's that?' She nodded towards a woman that his mother was welcoming, deftly catching up a drink for her from a passing waiter. Lark's finely tuned radar had caught the body language between the two of them, the expressions of warmth on his mother's part in response to a slightly forced smile.

'Maya Green. She's a good friend of my mother's and she's here to meet us. Her son's started to have regular migraines recently, and she's dealing with a lot of anxiety over it.'

Lark nodded and then started forward, towards his mother. Will grinned. She'd made her choice between money, influence and vulnerability, and he couldn't disagree with it. He watched as Lark hovered awkwardly, trying to catch his mother's eye, and willed her the confidence to just walk up to Maya and introduce herself.

But his mother saw her and drew Lark in, making the introductions. Whatever. If it worked, it worked. A practised, tactful gesture from his mother brought a waiter over, and Lark jumped, before taking a drink from his tray. She pulled a face and leaned in towards Maya, making her laugh.

By the time he managed to circulate smoothly over to the group, Maya and Lark were talking intently, and his mother was listening and nodding.

'…and what about *you?*' Lark asked the question that she always asked their patients' caregivers, and Maya turned the corners of her mouth down.

'I'm okay. You're only ever as happy as your unhappiest child…' Maya shrugged off the question.

'I hear that. And Leo's always going to be the one to really focus on, isn't he. But you're the one standing here in front of me.' Lark smiled persuasively and Will's mother nodded in agreement.

'It's hard. I can't help wondering why this has happened, and whether there's some trauma he's dealing with that he won't talk about.' Maya grimaced.

'Of course. Stress is a common trigger for migraine, but so are a lot of other things. Each person has different triggers—has your doctor talked to you about this?'

Maya nodded. 'Briefly. He doesn't have a great deal of time, and he gave me some leaflets and prescribed tablets for when Leo has a migraine. But Leo just breaks the rules all the time—he stays out late, or spends hours in his room playing computer games. He says that if he's going to have to put up with the migraines, he may as well have some fun at other times. He's his own worst enemy sometimes.'

'It's hard for teenagers with migraine, and their parents. They feel as if they're missing out on things and that it's you who's preventing them from doing what they want.'

Maya rolled her eyes. 'Sometimes it feels as if he blames me for the whole thing.'

'That must be very distressing for you. We do run groups for teenagers with migraine, and if Leo can chat with people his own age about it, that might help. Or maybe a talk with one of our outreach workers would be beneficial—sometimes when information comes from someone outside the family it strikes home a little better.'

Maya nodded. 'You're right about that. I sometimes feel that I'm the last person he listens to. Can…can I call you?'

'Of course. I really wish you would, so that we can talk some more.'

Now was the time for Lark to produce one of the charity's cards, that Will had insisted she put into her evening bag, but she'd clearly forgotten all about them. She looked around helplessly, and Will reached into his pocket, but his mother beat him to it, producing a pen and a small notebook from her bag.

'Oh. Thank you. May I just tear one of the pages out…?' Lark looked a little flustered, but she was delightful. She scribbled a number down, giving it to Maya. 'Would it be all right if I took your number? I'd love to call you next week some time, if that's okay.'

'Thank you.' Maya took the notebook and pen, writing down her own number, and Lark took it, putting it into her handbag.

'Oh. Look, I have some of our cards.' She flashed Will an

apologetic glance, and he grinned back at her. 'Will made me put them in my bag and I forgot all about them. Take one of these, but don't call the main number—the one I've given you is my mobile.'

Maybe that wasn't quite as smooth as it might have been either, but Lark was incomparable. Charming and effective in a way that Will could only watch and admire, because he never managed to imbue as much of himself in just a smile. Lark caught Maya's hand and squeezed it, before his mother propelled Maya in one direction and he propelled Lark in the other.

'But I want to talk a bit more...' Lark looked behind her, grinning back at Maya.

'That's okay. You've given her your number and you will. If I'm not very much mistaken, my mother's telling Maya right now that she's to be sure to call you.'

'Is she? I suppose that's all right then.' Lark gave him a taste of her scintillating smile. 'Your family... You're like a tag team, it's all quite brilliantly executed.'

Lark would see it like that. Like an intricate plan.

'My parents have been throwing parties like this for ever. It comes naturally.'

'Not to me it doesn't.' Lark was looking around her, her nerves showing again.

'You're doing fine.' Just wonderfully. Beautifully. Lark was actually better at this than he was, because she gave her heart to it. Will wondered how he could ever compete with her and decided that the fun of trying was everything.

'I'll introduce you to Sidney.' He could see that Sir Sidney was temporarily between conversations, and Will ignored Lark's obvious reluctance, guiding her towards him.

* * *

Lark's shyness had made the introductions a little less smooth than they might have been, but once she got talking she betrayed her encyclopaedic knowledge and ferocious passion for the charity's work. And she was open and honest about her own experience of childhood migraine, talking about how it had turned out that chocolate was a principal trigger for her. She'd joked about her chagrin when the various friends and relations who'd looked after her during Robyn's frequent stays in hospital had stopped giving her chocolate treats to cheer her up, but noted that the migraines had become far less frequent.

It wasn't difficult for Will to count how many times he'd made things real and personal by adding his own experience to the mix when talking about migraine. Zero was a number that didn't need a great deal of calculation.

Sir Sidney whisked her away from him, taking her to meet a group of people that Will didn't know. That was one-nil to Lark, although he imagined she didn't think of it that way. He didn't either. Will just was busy envying Sir Sidney her company.

'Going well?' His father joined him, handing him a drink.

'Very well. I'm finding myself slightly redundant.' Maybe he should do the obvious and cover the other side of the room from Lark. Maybe even count the number of cards he managed to give out, but that was actually no contest, because Lark had clearly forgotten about the cards in her bag again and she was currently scribbling her number on a napkin.

'Now you know how I feel when you get into the swing of things.'

'Right. Because overshadowing you is such an easy thing to do.' Will grinned at his father, who chuckled affectionately.

'I've always rather felt you get your charm from your mother. Lark's approach is a little different from yours, though. She leads from the heart.'

Will liked the compliment. 'Yes, you're right. She does.' Maybe he should lead from the heart a little more, although a heart that had been broken was a risky thing to expose.

'You and Lark?' His father's expression made the direction of the innocent-sounding question clear.

'Colleagues, Dad. And she's a friend.'

'I never considered that a problem with your mother.'

'Let it go.' Will felt a shudder of discomfort. He and Lark were something more than the transient lovers who crossed his path from time to time.

'Of course.' His father smiled, giving Will the distinct impression that he knew something Will didn't. 'Don't *you* let it go, though.'

'Oh!' Lark had found her way back to him, and Will could have hugged her. 'I think I'm about to have a panic attack.'

'You're doing fine.' Will grabbed her shaking hand, taking her out onto the patio. The cool air was a welcome contrast with the heat of the room.

'That's better.' Lark leaned towards him and he put a protective arm around her shoulder, hoping that they were out of his father's line of sight. 'This is terrifying.'

'You get used to it.'

'I don't think I ever will. You know I'm a lot happier letting you and Howard do this kind of thing.' She pursed her lips. 'I suppose that's the whole point, though. Stepping out of our roles.'

'Don't look at it like an obstacle course that you have to

complete.' Will reconsidered the advice. 'Although, truthfully, I wasn't sure where to start with the painting.'

'Is that an Achilles heel I can see through the hole in your sock?' She was smiling now, which was all that Will could possibly ask of her.

'My socks don't have holes in them.'

'That's true...' Lark let out a sigh, walking towards the balustrade that edged the patio. He saw her shiver, and Will took off his jacket, draping it around her shoulders.

'Thank you.' She smiled up at him. 'You're such a perfect gentleman.'

'Hey. Enough with the insults.' He and Lark didn't indulge in those games.

'Just kidding.'

Right now—this moment. It was the time he could have moved a little closer, in an indication that he was about to ask whether he might kiss her. Will turned away from it, leaning against the balustrade and looking back at the lights of the party.

'There's a pen in my inside pocket. Why don't you put it in your bag?'

'Thanks. I had to borrow a pencil from one of the waitresses just now.'

'You have cards...'

'I suppose so. They seem a bit formal, don't they.'

Will gave in to the inevitable. 'Okay, next time I'll make sure you have a selection of pencils and torn scraps of paper in your bag. Or maybe I'll just ask Mum where she gets those little notebooks of hers.'

'They are rather cute, aren't they.' Lark grinned up at him. 'But I thought I was only going to have to do this once. I'll need a bit of persuasion to do it again.'

'I can charm the birds out of the trees. Hadn't you heard?' Will laughed as Lark looked around furtively and then poked her tongue out at him.

CHAPTER SIX

THEY WENT BACK into the house through the kitchen, where the caterers were busy setting out drinks and canapés on trays, ready for them to be taken through to the guests. Will's mother had come through to make sure that everything was going smoothly and Lark shot her a smile, making for the sink to pour herself a glass of water.

'I'm sure we have sparkling somewhere, Lark,' his mother called out to her and she shook her head.

'Straight from the tap is fine for me, thanks. I think I've already had too many bubbles tonight.' Lark took a gulp of water from her glass. 'It's a wonderful party, Priscilla.'

'You think things are going well?' His mother hurried towards the kitchen door to open it for one of the waiters.

'It's great, Mum, as always. Thank you, we really appreciate it.'

'It's our pleasure, Will. You know that…'

As his mother turned, her feet went out from under her and she fell backwards onto the tiled floor. Lark was closest and as she hurried over, his mother tried to sit up, pulling at the skirts of her dress, which had ridden up as she fell.

'Okay, Priscilla. Just stay down for a moment…' Lark deftly flipped the material down to cover his mother's legs, kneeling down beside her.

But all that Will could see was Lark's dress, bright red and pluming out onto the floor next to his mother. Like the blood that had begun to leak from Eloise's body as her failing heart had pumped it from her veins and onto the tarmac.

He froze.

'Will... Go and get your father. Tell him that your mum's fine, but that she's taken a bit of a tumble.' Lark's voice penetrated his consciousness and he moved automatically, following her instructions. She had everything under control, and Will had no doubt that she would be doing everything to ensure that his mother was all right.

Movement, finding his father and giving him the exact message that Lark had told him to give, brought Will to his senses. By the time he and his father had got back to the kitchen, his mother was sitting up on the floor, with Lark carefully supporting her.

His father squatted down next to her, a gentle smile on his face. 'What's all this, Priss?'

'Don't make a fuss, Bill. Someone must have spilt something on the floor and I slipped on it. I'm fine.'

His father glanced questioningly over towards Lark and she nodded. 'You came down with a bit of a bump though, Priscilla, and you might well have some aches and pains in the morning. It might be an idea to lie down for a while.'

'Hear that, Priss?' His father picked up the high-heeled silver sandals that his mother had been wearing. 'Your heel's broken. I'll go and get your slippers, shall I?'

His mother nodded, clearly not feeling quite as fine as she'd claimed. Lark beckoned to Will and suddenly he knew what to do. Positioning himself carefully, he and Lark gently lifted his mother to her feet and sat her down at the kitchen table.

His father returned with the slippers, and Will saw his parents safely to the top of the stairs. When he returned to the kitchen, the bustle of the caterers had resumed, and Lark was waiting for him.

'She didn't bump her head, and her reflexes are fine,' she murmured. 'I dare say she'll have some bruises...'

This was no less than he'd expected of Lark. She'd made sure that his mother wasn't badly hurt, and done so kindly and efficiently, even remembering to save his mother's pride by quickly rearranging her dress. He'd worked with her for long enough to be able to trust that she'd done everything that was needed.

'Thanks. I'm—'

She cut his intended apology short, clearly able to second-guess him. 'Seeing her fall like that must have been a shock. You'd only just been talking about Eloise.'

'It's...' Will stopped himself at the last moment from telling her that it was okay.

'It's not okay, Will. You were talking about how unexpected loss had devastated you.'

He looked into her eyes, feeling their golden warmth comfort his fears. Maybe Lark could chase those fears away for long enough to allow him to fall in love. And when that happened, who knew what might be possible?

But for now, he should get on with the task in hand. Tonight—the publicity and the fundraising—was what made the real work they did possible.

'Why don't you go up and sit with your mum?'

'I was going to make her some hot chocolate, and then come back and give you a hand...'

Lark seemed suddenly confident about the roomful of people that her suggestion would force her to face alone. 'I'm on a roll now. I can out party-talk you any day of the week, Will.'

He knew that already. Lost for words, he bent, brushing

his lips against her cheek. It was no more than the brief kisses they'd exchanged at Christmas parties and New Year, surrounded by people who were doing the same, but this was scarily different. He felt her whole body jolt, as if the electricity that was passing through him was running in her veins as well.

'Go on then. Make me proud...' He murmured the words in her ear, and then turned to go upstairs.

The last of the guests had left at two in the morning, just as Lark was beginning to wonder how she might cope if everyone who'd said they'd call her, did. Hopefully, they were just party promises. Will had appeared downstairs to bid everyone goodbye, and to reassure them that his mother was perfectly well and sleeping now.

Will showed her to the door of the bedroom that had been earmarked as hers for the night, swinging it open and glancing inside to make sure that her overnight bag had been carried up from the car and placed on the bed. Clearly, if he set foot over the threshold a silent lever might trigger a series of man traps, and the image of her clinging to him as the walls closed in to squash them, or a horde of scorpions swept across the floor towards them made her catch her breath. Maybe scorpions wouldn't be so bad if Will were there to save her.

'If there's anything you need...' He left the sentence unfinished. Perhaps he knew that Lark would rather face any number of poisoned darts launched from hidden crevices than cross the threshold of *his* room tonight.

'Yes. Thanks.'

'I won't wake you in the morning. I dare say we'll all be sleeping in.'

That was wise as well. Who could foresee the dangers the

morning might bring, if he found her still in the grip of a dream where beckoning him inside was the solution to a thousand problems?

'That sounds like a plan. Sleep well, Will.'

The slight twitch of his eyebrow told her that Will probably wasn't expecting to sleep any better than she was.

'Yes. You too.' He smiled suddenly, turning away, and Lark escaped into her room, closing the door firmly behind her.

The following morning was reassuringly normal. Edward and his wife had stayed overnight too, and the family was gathered around the kitchen table, laughing and talking over a hearty brunch. Priscilla was clearly very stiff after her fall, but the painkillers that Will had given her last night meant that she'd been able to sleep.

Will looked a little tired, but by the time they started out for home, coffee had revived them both. And as soon as they were on the road his mind was onto the next thing on his agenda.

'Skirting boards? I presume that gloss is a whole different ballgame to emulsion.'

'You want to *paint* this afternoon?'

'It would be good to finish off, wouldn't it? If we don't, we'll have to go back to it next weekend.'

That wasn't entirely correct. Lark had been intending to get on with the job on her own this afternoon and during the week.

'You're taking ownership of my walls?'

'Only one of them. At the moment. I may lay claim to the others later.' He shot her a grin. 'Anyway, you may be busy with phone calls today.'

'Today? It's Sunday.'

'Yeah. That's why I put the business cards in your handbag. They have the office number on them.'

'Will! Why didn't you say? Have you let me do the wrong thing?'

'No, it's up to you to give out whatever number you like. Sometimes I give people my mobile number and sometimes our work number, it depends on the circumstances. I reckoned that you were just taking ownership of my party.'

She had a lot to learn, and maybe Will did too. She nodded at the large bag of leftover party food that Priscilla had presented her with before they'd left.

'Okay. I'll need someone to help me with all of this food, or it'll go to waste. You can do some painting as well, if you like.'

Apparently there was a lot more to changing roles than just an evening's playacting. Will was getting on with the painting, and actually making rather a good job of it, while Lark sat at the kitchen table, talking to the CEO of a local charity that she'd met last night, who was excited at the prospect that they might work together in the areas where their interests overlapped.

'How do you *do* this?' She put her phone down on the table, next to the cup of tea that Will had made while she'd talked, her head swimming with vague ideas, none of which seemed to make any sense to her.

He laid the paintbrush down and came over to sit opposite her. 'First of all, it's tempting to give people firm answers straight away, but you don't have to. It's intentions that matter, not specific answers, so stay with the thought that the prospect of working with them is an exciting one, and that we can hammer out the details when everyone's thought about them.'

'Okay. So I've made a few vague promises. What do I do next?'

'Turn your phone off, so you don't get any interruptions.'

Lark hesitated. Turning her phone off, when Robyn might need her at any time…

In the unlikely event that Robyn needed someone, the first person she'd call was her husband. She picked her phone up and switched it off.

'Now write it all down—start with the name and number, then a quick summary of what they wanted, and whatever thoughts you have on that.' He grinned at her.

Lark recognised that format. She picked up her pen and started to write, while Will went back to the painting.

'Okay, I've done that.'

He put the paintbrush back down. 'You can switch your phone back on again now.'

Lark grinned. 'You've missed a step.' She folded the paper in two and held it out towards him. 'Here you are.'

Will frowned. 'I was hoping you might…'

'Oh, no. I've done my part, and now you get to work out how to implement it all.'

To his credit, Will didn't back off from the challenge, taking his seat again at the kitchen table and reading through what Lark had written.

'You're going to want an itemised set of workable suggestions, aren't you.'

Lark nodded, beginning to enjoy herself. 'You can mutter a bit under your breath, and then roll your eyes first. Then you can read it through again and realise that there are a lot of good ideas here, and it probably is something that we'd like to move forward with.'

'I can manage the muttering.' He grinned at her. 'Where will you be while I'm doing that?'

'Probably making you a cup of tea. Giving you the odd winning smile and telling you that you're wonderful.'

'That's entirely true, Lark.' He shot her a wounded look.

'I don't doubt your sincerity.' Maybe she'd taken the game a little too far. 'I'll just make the tea, and then I have a message from someone else who'd like to talk to me whenever I have a moment.'

'You don't need to do that straight away. It's Sunday, and everyone understands that they'll probably have to wait until Monday before they hear from you. Or if they don't, they should do.'

'That's okay. I'm on a roll now. Why don't you try a bit of painting, while you're framing your response to my notes? Doing something practical does wonders for me.'

Will hadn't taken her up on her suggestion of painting, and had taken off his overalls and cleaned his brush before sitting down at the kitchen table to scribble his own thoughts at the bottom of her written notes, while he tucked into some of the party food they'd brought back with them. After fielding half a dozen calls, Lark had decided that enough was enough, and switched off her phone, so that she could read through Will's ideas.

'A couple of these are really good, we can implement them right out of the box.'

'And some of them need a bit of work, still?'

Lark nodded. Will's notes betrayed some of his trademark blue-sky thinking and some of his suggestions needed a bit of work, but others were intensely practical. And, rereading her own notes, they had a smack of Will's recognition of potential, without providing any solid answers.

'This swapping roles is a bit more complicated than we thought, isn't it.'

He grinned at her. 'Yeah. It's making me appreciate what you do even more.'

'I just couldn't do some of the things you do.' Lark gestured towards the plate of food on the table. 'You want any more?'

Will shook his head, picking up their empty plates to put them in the sink. 'I think you've already proved that you can do anything you want to do. It's just a matter of deciding what that is.'

'And that's the hard part. Everything seems to be pulling us both in a hundred different ways at the moment.'

And then, suddenly, there was one piece of solid ground. One person who saw her as she was, and wouldn't let her down. When she followed him over to the sink, brushing her fingers against his cheek, it was as much of a surprise to Lark as it obviously was to Will. But she could see from his smile, the way his eyes darkened, that it wasn't an unwelcome one.

Then he reached out, laying one hand over hers. She could feel his warmth now. Slowly…excruciatingly, wonderfully slowly, they were moving closer. Each small gesture requiring a response, because they were both crossing boundaries.

'Is this okay?' Will murmured the words against her ear, holding her gently in his arms. When she looked up at him, all she could see was his blue-eyed gaze, devoid of its usual relaxed charm and full of a far more potent longing.

'I'm not sure…' As soon as she said the words he drew back, and Lark shivered as the temperature of the air around her seemed to drop by ten degrees. 'I mean… I'm not sure but I'd like to find out.'

'So would I.' His gaze searched her face, still meltingly tender. 'But my track record does very little to recommend me.'

Lark wouldn't have put it quite so harshly. But that was one part of it. 'I don't want to lose our friendship, Will.'

'Neither do I. And I have no right to ask you to believe me when I tell you that this is different. Whatever relationship we choose to have doesn't come with an expiry date, not for me, anyway.'

'I believe in you, Will.' This made it even harder, because Will had just stripped away her best reason for not getting involved with him. 'But over the last few months, since Robyn got married, I've slowly begun to realise that when I promised my mum and dad that no harm would come to her if she came to live with me, I was taking on all of their worries and over-protectiveness. And at the same time I believed in my heart that she could live her own life and be independent of them, and I knew that was what she wanted.'

'And that must have been harder than I ever imagined it was.' He leaned back against the worktop, sliding his hands into the pockets of his jeans, as if to reassure her that he was keeping them out of harm's way. She could still feel his arms around her.

'It was confusing, I felt as if I was torn in two different directions. I need to find my own ground again, and work out what I want from life.'

'Seems that we both have some work to do...' Will was staring at the floor now.

'Will, I'd...' Lark gulped in a breath, which only made her feel even more light-headed '... I'd like to have you on my side while I'm doing that work. And to be on your side.'

He looked up at her suddenly. 'I'm your friend. I'll always be on your side.'

And that was all he'd ever be if she let this go now. The thought opened up a whole world of regret. Taking all of her courage into her hands, she stepped towards Will, standing on her toes to kiss his cheek.

Their bodies never touched, and Will didn't move. But fire ignited in his eyes, the kind that could suck all of the oxygen from a room.

'Are you telling me that you want to take this slow?'

Right now she wanted to take it the kind of slow that would last all night and maybe even into tomorrow morning, before it burned itself out. That wasn't what he meant, and Lark dismissed the thought as a bad idea.

'Yes. Slow gives us both the chance to work out what we really want. We're both so different...'

'We can be different. And I can do slow.'

She really wished he hadn't said that, because now the craving for his touch was becoming unbearable. She leaned forward, kissing him on the lips, and this time he responded, his fingers light on her cheek as he kissed her back.

'Who knew you'd be such a great kisser?'

She felt his smile against her lips, his hand resting on her back. 'It's not me. I'm thinking it must be you.'

'A joint effort then.' Maybe together they made something that was more than the sum of its parts. Something that Lark might never find with anyone else. That was yet another reason to be cautious. She could so easily lose her heart to Will.

But now, in this moment, she just wanted to kiss him again. And Will's gaze was telling her that it was exactly what he wanted too. She reached for him and he took her in his arms. Lark felt herself shiver in his warmth, feeling the press of his body against hers.

'It's okay. I'm going to go home...'

That was the reassurance she needed. They could do as they wanted now, because there would be an ending. Not a final one, but a pause before they moved ahead. Lark kissed him.

Free. At last they were free to be together. Will's reserve, his barrier of charm, had disappeared and she could feel the trembling of his limbs as passion overwhelmed the fear that he had hidden for so long. The thought that this was who she really was, the woman who was bold enough to love Will and demand that he loved her, made her legs buckle suddenly and she felt his arms tight around her, supporting her. And then, when he kissed her again, she found her strength.

'This is…more than I ever knew I wanted.' Will's defences were down, and in this moment he was hers. Lark wanted more than just this one moment.

'You'll be staying with me, Will? For the journey?' Just to give him a taste of what that journey would be like, she dropped a kiss onto his mouth.

'You leave me no choice…'

CHAPTER SEVEN

WILL KNEW HOW to draw the line beneath a kiss, and leave it as an exquisite memory. That was all it had been, a kiss, but still they'd gone further than they'd meant to and promised more than their fears allowed. And yet Will had left her in no doubt that he regretted nothing.

It wasn't over for Lark either. The calls and the ideas could wait until Monday, and furious activity, painting and tidying up, carried her through the hours until she flopped into her bed, unable to do any more. But she could still think about Will, and even the feeling that they'd just stepped over a line and were in dangerous territory seemed to add spice to the sweetness of it all.

And in the morning... Will was just as perfect as he'd been in her dreams. He didn't studiously avoid her gaze, or pretend that nothing had happened between them. But this was no one's business but their own, and he knew that work wasn't the place to talk about it.

'You want to swap offices for the morning?' He finished their Monday morning meeting with a joke.

'Why would we do that?'

'You're going to be on the phone, returning calls for a while. I thought maybe you'd want to pace, or lie on the sofa. Your office, though...' He took in her desk with a sweep of his hand.

'Your office reflects your mindset. It has a pervasive aura of order that might jump-start my responses to your ideas.'

'Don't push it, Will. We're trying out a few alterations to our routine, this isn't a personality swap. I didn't wake up this morning and find my brain in your body.' Too soon, maybe, to be talking about waking up to find herself entangled with anything of his. Lark felt herself redden. Those harmless jokes that they threw at each other all the time probably needed to be toned down a bit.

And then his involuntary reaction made everything okay again. A subtle flush tried his cheeks for size, before it realised that embarrassment wasn't something that Will usually did. He twisted his mouth in one of those gorgeous expressions of regret that said so much more than a smile.

'Good point. Very well made.' His eyes flashed with humour and he rose from his seat, leaving her alone in her office to get on with her calls.

All that Will needed to do was be there. It was an unexpected conclusion to come to, for a man who was used to managing his relationships carefully, being a lover and a companion without ever offering commitment or getting too involved. But that was impossible with Lark. His promise to be there for her was binding. Open-ended, uncertain, and yet still everything that he wanted.

And he could be there. He could wait. The thought of doing both of those things was heady and sweet, and so much more than he'd dared hope for.

Work was promising to be easier this week. Dev would be in the office from Tuesday to Thursday, which took a lot of the pressure off Will and Lark, and meant that they could concentrate more on the clinic and the medical research that lay at the heart of their jobs here.

Maya had called yesterday, clearly distressed, and asked whether she might bring Leo to see them. Lark had offered her an appointment at one o'clock, which was, strictly speaking, her lunch hour, and Will had decided to join them. They walked through to the clinic side of the top floor office space, smiling and joking together.

They'd worked hard to provide an environment here that would be less stressful for people with migraine, carefully lit with warm LED bulbs, well ventilated, and with a water-cooler in the corner of the waiting room. Maya was sitting on the edge of one of the seats, a young man who had to be Leo next to her.

'Maya…' Lark stepped forward. 'It's nice to see you again.'

'It was good of you both to see us so soon.' Leo didn't look too happy, and Maya was clearly under some stress after a long car journey with a reluctant teenager.

'It's our pleasure.' Lark turned to Leo. 'Hi, I'm Lark Foster.'

Maya nudged her son, and he replied with one word. 'Hi.'

Lark ushered Maya and Leo into her consulting room, and Will followed. There was a desk in each of the consulting rooms, but the main space was taken up by a circular table, with comfortable seating, which they both felt emphasised the collaborative nature of the solutions that they usually suggested.

It was difficult to tell whether Leo's silence was because he was sulking or whether he truly wasn't feeling well, and Will decided it was probably a bit of both. Lark caught up one of the clear plastic folders that held all of the leaflets and documentation they needed for new patients, and handed Will the medication sheet.

His questions about the type of migraine that Leo was experiencing, the triggers and the medication that he'd been prescribed, were directed at Leo and largely answered by Maya. Will was forming the impression that he was getting nowhere fast.

'I just need something to make the headaches go away, that's all. The stuff I have from the doctor doesn't work,' Leo interjected suddenly.

'I'm afraid that's not the way it works. The medication your doctor provides doesn't cure the condition, it helps with the symptoms. Do you take your tablets as soon as you feel the first symptoms of a migraine?'

Leo shrugged. 'It depends where I am. Not always.'

'Well, that's very important. And you might also be able to help yourself by making some relatively small amendments to your lifestyle.'

It was already clear that Leo's lifestyle was the root of the problem. Going out late with his friends, and probably having a few drinks, then sleeping late. Missing meals and grabbing something from the fridge when he felt hungry, and leaving his schoolwork until the last minute. It was pretty much designed to provoke a migraine, and Maya seemed frustrated and helpless in the face of it all.

Lark was sitting quietly, listening. A prickling feeling at the back of Will's neck told him that wasn't going to last. But she confined herself to shaking her head slowly at some of Leo's answers to his questions, and watching Maya's reactions to what was going on.

The final straw came when Leo claimed that using the computer for his schoolwork was the root of the problem. Maya begged to differ, saying that he spent far more time playing computer games in darkened rooms than he ever took with his schoolwork. Will saw the twist of Lark's mouth, and leaned back in his seat. Any moment now...

'Sit up straight, Leo.' Her tone was so compelling that Leo actually obeyed her, prompting a half-smile from Maya. Lark was going in a little more strongly than usual, but it was obvious from their conversation on Saturday night that Maya was in agreement with her tactics.

'Now take a few deep breaths. That'll make you feel a little less hazy, and you're going to need to hear what I'm about to say.'

Leo shot her a truculent look, but took the breaths. What Lark was telling him was absolutely correct. Slow, deep breaths would reduce stress and might make someone with a migraine feel better, but Will suspected that there was more to it than that. As an ambulance paramedic, Lark had a lot of experience with reluctant patients, and she was using it.

'Here's the deal, Leo.' Lark had caught his attention now, and wasn't letting go. 'Either you accept that you have migraine, and you spend one day a week in a darkened room with a thumping headache, which is increasingly going to cramp your style, *or* you try to do something about it. It's up to you.'

'The tablets don't work,' Leo insisted, this time a little more forcefully. That was exactly what Lark wanted. She was trying to engage him, and if that meant he argued with her then so be it.

'No, they don't. Dr Bradley's already told you that they can't prevent a migraine, they can only treat it. We're looking for something that *will* work.'

'Nothing works. And I can't live my life cooped up at home, doing as I'm told. I need to see my friends.' From Maya's grimace this was obviously a point of contention between her and her son.

'Yes, you do. Shame about that, because I dare say you'll be missing quite a bit in future because, from what you say, these migraines are becoming more regular.' There was no note of sympathy in Lark's tone. 'I can show you how to deal with them, but you have to give me two weeks of your time.'

Leo was clearly calculating his options. Finally, he gave the right answer. 'Okay.'

'Right then.' Lark wasn't going to let up on him yet. 'I'm going to make an appointment with you in two weeks. Same time, Maya?'

'Yes, that's fine. Thank you.' Maya smiled at her.

'Here are some diet sheets, sleep schedules and general advice on computer use.' Lark extracted the sheets from the folder, sliding them across the table towards Leo. 'There are also some exercises for you to try out, and a diary where you can note everything down. And there's a folder to put it all in and keep it together. You do this, and I'll want to see each page of the diary signed by your mother, so that I know you haven't been cheating.'

'It's…a lot.' Leo was glancing through the printed sheets.

'Too much for you?' Lark threw out the challenge, her mouth twisting in a smile.

'No. It's not going to work, though.'

'You tell me that when you've tried it.'

It *would* work. If Leo did all that was included in the carefully written information pack, he'd at least start to feel a little more relaxed and less tired from the late nights, and there was a very good chance that his migraines would be less devastating as well. Lark had understood that asking him to do all this for the rest of his life was something that Leo couldn't countenance, but he'd give her two weeks, and in that time she'd be calling Maya regularly and suggesting amendments to the plan, in the expectation that Leo would agree to another two weeks the next time she saw him.

'Okay. Deal?' Lark reached across the table, holding out her hand. It was a bit theatrical, but Leo's hesitation before he shook on the deal showed that he knew that this was binding.

Lark got to her feet. 'You're interested in computer games, yes? How about I show you how to set things up to improve that environment?' The light room had been designed to show how lighting could be altered to help with light-sensitive migraines, and patients were encouraged to experiment in there. Lark was giving Leo something practical to do, that he could take charge of, and he'd had to earn that concession.

Leo followed Lark from the room, and Maya hung back, smiling at Will. 'Lark was talking to me on Saturday about putting Leo's wellness into his own hands. She's a wonder...'

Will nodded. 'Yes, she is.' More than Maya could ever know.

The waiting room was still empty and there was time to accompany Maya to the light room, where Lark and Leo were messing around with lamps and the computer that stood in the corner, adjusting the seat so that Leo could sit up straight. Somewhere in the process the two of them started to laugh together, and Maya began to relax a little and smile. When they left, there was a marked difference in Leo's attitude.

Will walked back to Lark's consulting room with her. 'Nice one.'

She grinned at him. 'Talking to Maya on her own helped. Migraine's so difficult for teenagers.'

She'd written about that. The swings and roundabouts that everyone went through in their teenage years didn't help when dealing with migraine. But she'd got Leo on her side now, and that was the first and biggest step.

He'd seen this before, a hundred times. He could be authoritative about the medical steps that needed to be taken, and many people reacted well to that. Lark had a way of getting alongside people, an authentic charm which others reacted to. And somehow Will's own reaction was seeping seamlessly from his head into his heart.

'I love it when you're firm.' The words slipped out before he could stop them.

Lark looked up at him, a surprised grin on her face. 'You do?'

All of the ways that she might be firm with him, and all the ways he might be firm back, were hanging in the air between them. Will froze, afraid that any movement on his part might turn into a kiss. Not here. Not now…

'Wednesday evening? Come to dinner, dress code casual, no implications.' It wasn't unusual for them to meet mid-week, to catch up on anything that needed their immediate attention.

'I'll bring my laptop?'

Will shrugged. 'You could. I'd be crushed if you did.'

'You'll cook? At your place?' Lark raised her eyebrows. They'd eaten together numerous times, but cooking was something that Will had always felt might veer a little too close to seduction. His place had been off-limits as well, for the same unspoken reason.

'Wait and see.' It was a little early in their relationship for cooking, but it was the closest thing to making love that Will could think of right now.

He *was* going to kiss her. He couldn't help it.

Suddenly the buzzer in his pocket started to vibrate and Lark's hand moved to the pocket of her trousers, as hers clearly did the same.

'I'll hold that thought. Patients…' He saw her lips part, as if a full waiting room might be ignored for just a few moments. And then she turned, walking out to greet her next patient.

Wednesday couldn't come around quickly enough. And, by chance, Lark saw Will a great deal earlier than they'd arranged. A patient with a traumatic head injury after a car accident meant that she and her ambulance partner were heading straight for the London hospital where Will worked, which was better equipped to deal with these cases than their local hospital.

She'd worked hard to keep their patient stable during the journey, and it was a relief when the ambulance drew up outside A&E. She and her partner, Alex, carefully transferred their patient out of the ambulance, wheeling him straight through to the rapid assessment centre, where someone from Neurology would be already waiting for them.

'Status?' Will stepped forward, his gaze already assessing the man on the trolley.

'Probable skull fracture, bruising to the right eye and behind his ear—' Lark rapped out her observations a little more concisely than usual, knowing that Will would understand the procedures she'd already undertaken '—he's been slipping in and out of consciousness, and he's becoming increasingly non-responsive.'

'Okay. I don't have anyone to help with him yet...'

'That's okay, I'll stay.' Lark followed him into the cubicle, beckoning to Alex, and they both helped move their patient off the ambulance trolley.

Will's focus was concentrated on examining their patient's head wound, and Lark took off her jacket, pulling on a fresh pair of gloves before she attached the heart and blood pressure monitor to the man's finger. She heard Alex clear his throat behind her, obviously surprised that they weren't already on their way, and she glanced back at him, mouthing that she'd explain later.

'I don't have his name. He was jogging and didn't have anything on him, and no one who saw the accident knew him.' Lark anticipated Will's next question, ducking out of the way as their patient's suddenly flailing arm almost hit her straight in the face. Will caught the man's wrist, gently placing it back by his side.

'He's been doing that a lot?'

'Only once, but he's becoming more restive.'

Will's gaze flipped to the BP monitor and then back again to Lark. A split second of warmth, the sudden recognition that he was glad she was there, and then his concentration was all for their patient again.

'IV fluids and we'll try a mild sedative...' Lark knew exactly what was needed, and focused on finding a vein, while Will rapped out the exact dosage of the sedative.

'Thanks.' Another doctor and a nurse had entered the cubicle now, and it was time for her to step back. Will only had time for that one word, but somehow he made it mean everything—the professional trust and respect between them, and all the other things that she was beginning to feel for Will as well.

'Later...' She whispered the word, wondering whether he'd heard. But now wasn't the time. She pushed Alex out of the cubicle, walking back to the ambulance with him, steeling herself for the inevitable questions.

'You *know* him?' Alex waited for her to stow the ambulance gurney back into the vehicle, and then climb forward into the seat next to him.

'Yes, I work with Will two days a week, at Migraine Community Action.'

'That explains it. Nice to see a consultant who actually realises we're medically trained.'

Lark nodded, and Alex started to manoeuvre the ambulance out of its parking bay. That hadn't been too difficult...

'Gorgeous man.' Alex hadn't finished yet. 'I don't suppose you happen to know...?'

'He's not gay, Alex. Anyway, I thought that you and Jon were back together again.'

'Yes, we are. The rule is that we can look but we don't touch.'

Fair enough. Lark had adopted the same policy with Will, up until very recently.

'What about you?' Alex turned out of the hospital entrance, his mind still on exploring options. 'Is he available?'

'No, I don't think so.' Lark decided not to mention that Will wasn't available because he'd kissed *her* and made a promise to wait. That was all too new to put into words just yet.

'Shame. You could do with a really nice guy, Lark.'

Lark laughed. Will would keep his promises, and she'd be seeing him tonight.

'What, someone that you and Jon can look at but not touch?'

Alex chuckled. 'We won't even look. We'll just make extensive enquiries, to make sure he's good enough for you, and then send you both off to a deserted beach on an expenses-paid holiday. Then we'll enjoy seeing the smile on your face when you get back.'

That would be really nice. Going away with Will somewhere, away from Sir Terence and the constant juggling to keep everything afloat. Away from the nagging thought that losing herself in Will, the man she'd always thought was out of reach, was just another version of losing herself in her parents' unrelenting worries for Robyn. Just Will, and the opportunity to take things slow and work it all out between them.

'That sounds wonderful. I'll let you know when I find the really nice guy.' Lark decided to change the subject. 'What about you and Jon? Any deserted beaches in your future?'

'Yeah, we're thinking about it. We've both got some leave saved, and it would be nice.'

'Do it. You know I've always thought you're made for each other, and you should take your opportunities while you can...'

Will had left work a little later than he'd hoped he would, and rushed home, calling Lark to say that he was delayed, and finding that she too was unexpectedly working late. His cleaner had taken in the food delivery he'd ordered earlier in the day, as promised, and stacked it neatly in the fridge, leaving a note to say that everything was there and thanking him for the chocolate truffles.

He'd been glad to see Lark when she'd turned up in A&E with the patient he'd been waiting for. Even more glad that he didn't feel that he now had to apologise for ignoring her when she and her partner melted away. It was one thing he had in common with Lark that he didn't usually share with his women friends. The demands of his job were usually a stumbling block in their eyes, something that meant that a relationship might be sweet, but it would never work in the long-term.

Will went to shower and get changed, and then got to work in the kitchen. He'd noticed that Lark's fridge was well stocked with good food, but that most of it was easy to prepare, just a matter of finding a suitably sized dish to tip it into then putting it into the oven. He was using ingredients that you had to prepare and mix together before cooking, and he was confident enough in his skill as a cook to know that Lark would be able to tell the difference.

The doorbell rang, and he found Lark outside in the hallway, wearing a pair of cargo pants and sneakers, with a hoodie.

'Sorry… I didn't have time to go home and change.'

The gold in her hair and eyes outshone anything she could possibly wear.

'You look wonderful. I asked *you* for dinner, not your clothes.'

Lark laughed, stepping inside. 'How's our patient?'

'We got a head start on things, thanks to you, and he was operated on this afternoon. He's in Intensive Care at the moment, and we'll need to wait to find out how much he's been compromised by the injury, but I'm optimistic. Oh, and his name was Jack. One of the social workers liaised with the police and they tracked him down and notified his family.'

'Great. Thanks, I'm glad I finally know his name.'

Will ushered her along the hallway and into the sitting room. She looked around and he wondered whether she liked what she saw, in an unusual flash of self-doubt.

'What's cooking? Something smells wonderful.'

'Wait and see.'

'What? You're not going to let me go into the kitchen to take a look?' Lark raised her eyebrows.

'No. If you want to have a look around, the seduction cave is further down the hallway.'

For a moment she took the statement at face value. 'Sorry. You're joking, aren't you.'

'Yeah. It's not down the hallway at all, there's a secret door.'

Will chuckled as Lark rolled her eyes. The slight awkwardness between them, trying to find their feet in a new phase of their relationship, was gone now. This was more like the friendship that they were both so committed to keeping.

'Okay, good to know. I should warn you that it's been a long day and I'm really hungry...'

'Dinner won't be long.' Will took the hint and left her in the sitting room, while he made for the kitchen.

Lark's nervousness about the evening had grown as it became increasingly obvious that she was going to be late. She'd splashed out on a taxi, and by the time it drew up outside the large, solid block of flats in Muswell Hill, she was beginning to feel as if this might just be a mistake.

She'd always wondered what Will's flat was like, and from the outside it seemed nice. The block overlooked the sloping green parklands that led up to Alexandra Palace, and on the other side it was just a stone's throw from a still bustling street of shops.

She'd taken the lift up to the top floor, telling herself that she'd said she was on her way now, and it was too late to back out. When Will had answered the door, the sight of him in jeans and a thin sweater, accessorised with a smile, began to banish all her fears.

And then the jokes and their easy friendship had taken over. When Will disappeared back into the kitchen she was already relaxed enough to take in her surroundings.

The place looked a lot more homely than she'd expected from Will's man-about-town persona. His office had prepared her for the presence of a large, long sofa in front of the open hearth, and Lark wasn't surprised to find that it was very comfortable. But his talent for colour was used to different effect here. Books, plants and the blues and greens of the fabrics gave an atmosphere that was relaxed and soothing.

A heavy oak dining table and chairs stood at the far end of the room, next to the kitchen door. Lark jumped as it swung open.

'Medium well, for your steak?'

Lark nodded. He knew that she liked her steak with just a hint of pink at the centre, and she knew that his would be medium rare. And yet she hadn't even known that Will cooked, although from the aroma that was emanating from the kitchen, he not only cooked but did it well. There was a whole side of him who was a stranger to her.

'You like plants…?' He had none in his office, and Lark nodded towards the three colourful amaryllis blooms that stood on an oak sideboard, in the light of the window. On the other side of the bay was a large ficus, its shiny leaves and exuberant growth evidencing long-term, loving care.

'My cleaner does, she takes care of them.' He grinned.

Maybe this was all a comfortable pretence, created by someone else. Not Will at all. Lark couldn't help feeling disappointed that even his home kept friends and family at arm's length.

'Your cleaner takes care of everything?'

'Everything that you can forget to water. Anything that doesn't need watering is my choice.' He shot her a mystified look. 'Check out the books if you're in any doubt. Josie has no interest at all in medical titles.'

'That's reassuring. And you haven't got a chef in the kitchen, who'll escape through the window when dinner's ready?'

He chuckled. 'Yeah, a chef that enjoys mountaineering, since I'm on the top floor. Whatever made you think that I wouldn't enjoy cooking?'

'I suppose we don't really know each other as well as we think, do we?'

'I guess not. But I'm looking forward to rectifying that.' He looked over his shoulder at the open door to the kitchen. 'Sorry... I've got to attend to the sauce...'

'Make me proud,' Lark called after him.

Will stopped to take a breath and calm his nerves before he carried the plates through to the dining table, which was crazy because this was a simple recipe that he'd cooked a thousand times. But the steak had left the pan perfect, he was pleased with the way that the peppercorn sauce had gone, and the dauphinois potatoes and vegetables... It was tough to mess up a dauphinois or the steaming of vegetables.

But Lark made every second of those nerves worth it. She actually closed her eyes at one point, as if food was all about savouring flavour and not just something that you needed in order to live.

'This is gorgeous, Will. If I'd known you could cook like this, I would have come sooner.'

If he'd known that Lark would come sooner, then maybe he would have *told* her that he could cook like this. He could have made a regular thing of asking her and Robyn round for dinner, maybe broken down the barriers a bit, so that all of this wasn't such a surprise. But that wouldn't have happened, because Will had kept his distance from Lark the way that he kept his distance from everyone.

'I would have gone to your place sooner, if I'd known too.'

Lark's fork hung in the air as she stared at him. The idea that he was a bit more interesting than the steak he'd just cooked was...gratifying. Will wasn't in the habit of reducing himself to a secondary importance to the things that he hid behind, but it occurred to him that the act of hiding might say a bit more about him than he'd thought. It might say everything about him…

'I suppose that we've always made a habit of keeping our work and home lives separate. I've always been rushing off home for Robyn… But the thing is, I never really needed to. Most of the time I'd get home after her, and find her cooking the dinner.' Lark grinned at him. 'Actually cooking, that is. Not just heating things up.'

Will shrugged. 'Everyone's different. Are you giving yourself a hard time over this?' It increasingly seemed that Lark was.

'I suppose… I regret things. Robyn and I used to have such a great time together, and I was so happy for her when she met Matt.'

'And that's something to regret?'

'No. The opposite.' She took another slice of her steak, leaving him mystified, and Will had to wait for a moment while she savoured it.

'I was so weighed down with the promises I'd made to my parents, and the responsibility that I felt. I missed out on what should have been a great time, just me and Robyn making our way in the world and having fun.'

'You *did* have fun together, though.' Will had seen that for himself, when Robyn had been volunteering with the charity. 'There were times when I felt I'd never have fun again, after Eloise died, but I came to terms with it, and I can honestly say that I have a good life. We've both had things to work through, and that's okay, isn't it?'

Lark smiled. 'You make it sound okay. I still feel a bit of a fraud…'

'Don't. The fact is that Robyn *would* have found it difficult to come to a new place, find somewhere to live that was suitable for wheelchair use, and make the most of her years at art school and in a new job. You were there for her, and that's what really matters...' Will felt almost breathless, wanting so badly to lift the burden that Lark seemed to carry with her.

'Thank you.' Her eyes flashed gold suddenly. 'So we're both making a new start, then?'

'Yeah. And I'm just grateful that I have your company in that, because I'm not sure I could do it alone.'

'Me neither.'

She gifted him with a luminous smile before turning her attention back to the plate in front of her. It was always nice when someone enjoyed the food he'd made for them, and Will started to eat again, feeling the quiet enjoyment of having done something to please Lark.

'Do you suppose... Everything seems to be so uncertain at the moment, with so much change. Maybe that's not all bad, and it's a chance to remake things, better than they were before.'

Will hoped so. He wanted so much to find that he and Lark could be together, but if she needed to find her way on her own, then he'd let her go. Finish this before it had even started, which was a record even for him.

'What do you need, Lark?'

'Afters? I can't wait to see what you've whipped up for dessert,' she joked, and Will frowned. He'd perfected the fine art of throwing people off the scent, and Lark really shouldn't try it with him, because he saw right through her.

'Besides that.' He smirked at her, not moving from his seat in an indication that he wasn't whipping anything up until she answered the question properly.

'This. I need this. Someone to question me and force me to

think about the way I do things. Because I don't have the answers to those questions right now, and I want to find them.'

'Pete, you mean?' Disappointment curled around his desire, smothering it.

'No. Not Pete. He doesn't know us at all, and… That may be his aim, but I'm not sure that he's really hitting the mark.' She shrugged awkwardly. 'You asked me what I needed…'

And she'd answered. Lark might not be able to say that she needed him, any more than Will could admit how much he needed her, but there were only three people who were talking about change, everyone else seemed to assume that things were going on just as they always had. When Pete was ruled out, it was the simplest of all equations. One and one made two. And Will knew that Lark would be there for him, just as certainly as he knew that he'd be there for her.

'Asked and answered, then.'

She nodded. 'Does that mean I'm going to get my dessert now?'

Will chuckled, finding that getting to his feet wasn't quite so impossible as it had been moments ago. 'I won't be long. Stay right there…'

'You're not going to let me watch?' She put on an expression of mock pleading.

'Next time. When I've got to know you a bit better…'

CHAPTER EIGHT

CREPES. EASY TO make and they were a neutral canvas that could be tailored to anyone's precise likes and dislikes. Strawberries were always a good option, or something with chocolate sauce, although the latter was out because Lark never ate chocolate. After some thought, Will had decided that two different options would double his chances of success. Cooking was all about knowing who you were cooking for and catering to their tastes, and he reckoned that getting the reaction he wanted from Lark required either crushed raspberries with cream, or sautéed apples with caramel.

He ignored the fact that usually the reaction he wanted was a kiss. A lot more sometimes. Crepes might be an invaluable aid to seduction, but that didn't mean that they couldn't be used to delight a friend as well.

He made up a plate for Lark, topping one crepe with raspberry coulis and the other with caramel sauce, with a dusting of confectioners' sugar for both. Loading a tray with both fillings, and a stack of crepes so that he could make his up at the table and there would be enough for second helpings, he walked through from the kitchen.

'Oh! They're beautiful, Will!' Lark stared at her plate.

'Don't wait for me. They're best eaten straight away.' He tried not to look as she picked up her dessert knife and fork, cutting a neat sliver of the apple crepe. Will had anticipated she might try the raspberry one first and tried not to stare.

'Mmm. This is delicious.' Lark gave her verdict on the apple crepe and turned to the raspberry one. 'More delicious. That one's totally divine.'

Delicious. Divine. They weren't words that Lark used a great deal in the office, but they suited her, slipping from her lips so easily. Will opened his mouth, about to give some clumsy answer, and she shushed him with a wave of her fork.

'I can't talk and eat these at the same time.'

Silence. Let the food do your talking for you. That was the best compliment that any cook could ask for. Will smiled, reaching for the pile of spare crepes.

Lark emptied her plate and leaned back in her chair, smiling.

'Help yourself to more.'

'I don't think I could.' Lark pursed her lips, clearly reconsidering. 'Actually, perhaps I could manage another raspberry one…'

Raspberries and cream. Sweet with a tart aftertaste. Will mentally filed the information away for next time, wondering if they might explore the full gamut of fillings together. It was a new idea, since generally his relationships didn't last long enough to work his way from apples to… Will pondered on what might begin with a 'z' and settled for 'y'. Apples to yellow passion fruit.

Lark helped herself to another raspberry crepe, and then decided on one more apple and caramel, saying that she badly needed to check whether she really did prefer the raspberry or not. Then she leant back in her seat with an air of finality.

'You didn't buy these, did you?' She turned down the corners of her mouth.

'They're really easy to make. You just need to get the right pan and heat it up properly. You want me to show you?'

'Absolutely. I'm not going to miss out on the chance of having a nose around in your kitchen.' She shot him a mischievous look.

'After we've had coffee.'

'I was wondering if you had coffee in your repertoire. Gives people a chance to talk.'

'I talk...' Will got to his feet, stacking the empty plates. This time Lark got the message that she was supposed to stay put, and let him take them through to the kitchen alone. The idea of letting his food do the talking had just taken on a new angle, and he could think about that while he was making the coffee.

He'd got used to approaching any relationship as a matter of delight. Nice places, great food and then really good sex. None of those things gave a lot of time for talking, or even for thinking all that much. Sight, taste and touch were all about the senses, what lay on the surface rather than in his heart. The fact that what he most wanted to do with Lark was to talk with her banished his doubts. This relationship *was* different.

He finished stacking the dishwasher while the coffee brewed, and then took it through. Lark had collected up the place mats and folded the tablecloth, and was sitting on the long sofa. He noticed that she'd taken off her sneakers, so that she could tuck her legs up onto the cushions.

And they *did* talk. Telling each other stories about when they were children, about growing up and going to university. What had happened before the things which had changed them both, into people who had to think long and hard before they took this relationship forward.

Lark had told him how difficult it had been to convince her parents that she could give Robyn the support she needed in

London. How they'd insisted on visiting every weekend at first, inspecting her home and grilling them both on what they'd been doing. And how, even though she was a paramedic, she'd doubted herself sometimes, but that in the end she'd known that she had to support Robyn in reaching out and taking what she wanted from life herself.

How Lark had lost something of herself, that she wanted back now. In the same way that Will had lost something, that he knew he could never get back, when Eloise had died. But Lark had pointed out to him that while he could never get Eloise back, the parts of himself that had loved her were still there, and within reach. No one had ever had the courage to say that to him before, it was too challenging. Far too truthful as well, and much too helpful for a man who needed to move forward.

'It's getting late. We'll have to take a rain check on the cooking lessons and do it another time.' Will was sprawled on the sofa next to her, his feet up on the coffee table.

Lark looked at her watch, turning the corners of her mouth down. 'I lost track of the time. I'd better call a taxi…'

'I'll take you.' Will gave her a stern look when she opened her mouth to protest, pulling his shoes back on and collecting his car keys from the mantelpiece.

'Okay. Thanks.'

She was silent during the fifteen-minute drive. Quiet moments of togetherness, that didn't require the excuse of food or anything else, but just came naturally. When he drew up outside her one-storey house, she collected her bag from the footwell, and then didn't move to get out of the car.

'It's been a lovely evening, Will. Thank you.'

'My pleasure. I enjoyed it too.'

Silence again. Neither of them moved, as if they were both waiting for the one thing that Will wanted to do. That he felt confident in doing now, because here the pleasure of a kiss couldn't escalate into something that they might not be ready for.

Lark began to fidget, laying her hand on the door lever, as if that was what she knew she ought to do. Will took his courage in both hands.

'May I kiss you?'

She smiled suddenly. 'Yes. That would be nice.'

He was hoping that *nice* was a deliberate understatement. Will used all of his self-control, pausing before his lips quite met hers. Hoping that she could see everything that he felt in his gaze, feel it from the brush of his fingers on her cheek.

And then he felt her hand on his shoulder. Not pulling him in, just gently exploring the contours of each muscle, which instinctively tensed at her touch. Will kissed her, letting the molten heat of her golden eyes flow through his veins.

Exquisite. The raging longing seemed even sweeter because he knew that it couldn't be slaked by this one kiss. Not this one or the next. He could stay here for hours, just exploring the softness of her lips.

He was sure that it wasn't hours, but it seemed like an eternity before she drew back from him. Wide-eyed, her cheeks flushed with things that were unsaid, but could never be undone.

'I'd better go.'

'Yeah.' As soon as Will agreed to the proposition, she was out of the car, bending down to graze her knuckles against the window, and Will reached for the control to wind it down.

'Goodnight, Will.'

'Goodnight. Sleep well.'

She gave him a bright smile, as if she would be sleeping with the same sensation that they were still close, that Will reckoned he would. And then she turned, hurrying to her front door. It was acceptable, required even, to watch her safely inside, and she turned to wave to him before closing the door.

He should go now. As Will started the car, he saw the lights flip on in the room to the right of the porch and Lark appeared at the window, drawing the curtains of the empty bedroom at the front of the house. Maybe they were both moving towards filling the empty spaces in their lives. Will drove away into the night, taking with him the feeling of her lips on his.

A kiss. What could just one kiss in the front seat of Will's car hold? Lark was beginning to suspect that the answer to that was *everything*.

Why else could she have gone to work on the following Friday with such a wildly beating heart? Why would she have to reconsider the smile that sprang to her lips when she first saw him, and then relax again when he shot her a look that told her he had the same impulse she felt? Wanting to greet her in a way that would be entirely inappropriate at work.

And why would she jump every time she heard a knock at her office door? But when Will leaned into the room, still holding on to the door handle, he clearly hadn't come just for the pleasure of seeing her.

'Pete's just had a cancellation and wants to come this morning instead of this evening. How are you fixed for that?'

'I can do that. But we were going to carve out some preparatory time at lunch, weren't we?'

Will shrugged. 'We could improvise.'

'I suppose so. Will you take the lead, Will, just so we're not both going in different directions?'

'It's easy enough. Painting and cooking are off-limits, they're our business.' He gave her a delicious smile, and Lark's heart jumped suddenly. They meant as much to him as they did to her. 'The party's okay to talk about, that was a work event.'

'Okay. Call him back and say this morning's fine.'

Twenty minutes later, when Will ushered Pete into his office and flipped the *Do Not Disturb* sign on the door, Lark was feeling confident that this week would be better than last Friday. Pete had listened to Will's description of how they'd mapped out each other's roles at the party, and swapped them, and had seemed impressed that their enthusiasm for the idea of role-swapping had extended so far beyond the items on the list he'd sent.

'I've learned quite a bit about Lark. And myself...' Will finished up with a smile.

'Me too. What Will does at these outreach events isn't just a matter of natural ability, there's quite a bit of work and organisation involved as well.'

Will nodded. 'I think we're finding that we're not quite as different as we thought. Or at least that we're both able to use our own skills to get the same results, even if our methods might be a little different.'

'And this affects your decisions at work?' Pete asked.

Lark could answer this one. 'I think it widens our options. We're both learning that there's no right or wrong way to do something—what works, works and what doesn't, doesn't.'

'Yeah. Well put.'

Pete nodded again. 'You both seem in agreement about all of this.'

'Yes, I think we are. That's the way Will and I work. We don't agree about everything, but we do discuss things and come to a conclusion that we're both comfortable with.'

'So...' Pete paused for a moment, as if he wanted to alert them both to the fact that they should be thinking about that last statement. Lark glanced at Will, and he shook his head imperceptibly. Talking about things was what they did and surely there was nothing wrong in that.

'Who actually makes those decisions? Comes to the conclusions?'

'It's fifty-fifty. Sometimes I do and sometimes it's Will.'

Will nodded. 'I'd agree with that. Fifty-fifty. There are some issues where Lark has a great deal more experience than I do, and I recognise her greater expertise and let her decide—'

'You *let* her decide?' Pete pounced on the word.

'There are other issues where I've got more experience than Lark, and then she lets me decide. The whole point I wanted to make is that working together as we do, and very much at the same level, requires consensus and a willingness on both sides to acknowledge the other's strengths.'

There was a note of irritation in Will's voice, which Lark shared. The idea that Pete expected him to take the lead in any of their decisions was completely misguided, and an insult to both of them.

'You'd agree with that, Lark?' Pete seemed keen on pushing the point.

'Why would you assume that I'd expect anything different from an entirely equal relationship between two people on the same level at work?' She jutted her chin confrontationally. If Pete wanted to insinuate that she did as Will told her because she was the woman of the team, then he was going to have to come out and say it.

'That sounds like the kind of thing you feel you ought to say,' Pete shot back at her.

'So… Let me get this right…' When Will felt strongly about something, his tone became even more measured and affable than usual. Right now his tone oozed good-humoured reason, and Lark waited for the crushingly outspoken punchline that she knew was coming.

'You're taking the step of disbelieving my colleague because of what? Your own belief that when men and women work together, men will inevitably take the lead? And that Lark is so brainwashed by that, that she doesn't even notice anything wrong?' Will smiled. 'I think you underestimate her...'

When Will returned to his office, after walking Pete to the door, Lark was pacing in front of the sofa. It wasn't making her feel any less angry.

'Stop pretending to be so nice to him, Will. Pete's just looking for conflict, when there isn't any. Does he have any actual qualifications in...anything?'

'I looked at his website and I didn't see any. Which doesn't mean that he's not very good at what he does, and I believe that he came highly recommended to Sir Terence.'

'You're giving him the benefit of the doubt when there isn't any.' Lark saw the hurt look in Will's eyes. 'I'm not angry with you...'

Somewhere, deep down, she was. She was angry with the handsome man who'd cooked her a fantastic dinner and who was stealing her heart. The one who'd kissed her goodbye, and made it last right through until the morning, when she'd woken from her dreams still feeling his touch. He should be unequivocally and unreasoningly on her side.

But his job was to do what he thought was right. Which involved putting the other side of the argument to her from time to time.

'I just wish you hadn't threatened to resign.' Lark couldn't help reproving him.

'What else was I going to do? We've already decided that

patients are a no-go area when it comes to role-swapping, and if I can't do what's best for my patients then I shouldn't be here. Pete should never have brought that up again and I'm not going to minimise how important the principle is.'

He was right. Maybe Lark should have threatened to resign as well, but she hadn't wanted to be accused of following Will's lead.

'Why's he doing this, Will? This latest task...'

'Sir Terence has presumably told him that the trustees want to pick just one of us as a temporary CEO, so Pete has to find a way of overriding the way we work together, and making us compete. He couldn't make us question each other by intimating that I've been overruling you, and we won't budge on swapping roles where patients are involved. So he's asked us to work separately on proposals for further development for the charity.'

'And he really thinks we're going to do that. How's he ever going to know?'

Will shook his head. 'I think we'll do it because we said we would. I'm not going to agree to something and then break the rules, and I'm reckoning that you don't have that in mind either.'

'No, I don't. I wish I did—it would be so much easier.' Lark turned the corners of her mouth down.

'Not for me. Trusting you is non-negotiable, Lark.'

This was what it was all about. Two people trusting each other enough to be able to work seamlessly together, for the benefit of their patients. Two people who shouldn't be allowing this to come between them.

'You're right. I'm sorry, Will. I shouldn't be arguing with you because we both think the same way. We'll take the two proposals for further development that we have in hand, and split them up, one each. And we'll work on them alone, as we said we would. It may even get them done a bit faster...'

Will nodded, still looking a little downcast. Lark had forgotten something, and she knew exactly what that was. She walked towards him, laying her hand on the lapel of his jacket. 'And I'm going to break the rules now.'

'Yeah?'

She stood on her toes, kissing him. Suddenly Will's arm was around her waist, and he was kissing her with more passion than ever. Then he drew back.

It was over so quickly, but it meant everything. No stupid disagreement, blown out of all proportion by stress, was going to get in their way.

'Are we good?' Lark smiled up at him.

'I'd put it as *very* good. When we've finished with the afternoon clinic we can go home and beat effigies of Sir Terence and Pete with saucepans?'

Will could always make her laugh. Always propose a solution that worked emotionally, even if there might be a few loose ends on the practical side.

'What kind of effigies?'

'Whatever you like. We can stop off and buy melons, then draw faces on them. That'll make a very satisfying mess of my kitchen.'

'Or you could come back to mine, review my cooking utensils and what's in my fridge, and show me how to make a silk purse out of a sow's ear. Living well is the best revenge, isn't it? I'm assuming that steak and crepes aren't the only thing you can cook.'

Will grinned. 'That's very grown-up of you. Cooking will be no trouble at all, I have a repertoire.'

'I'm already looking forward to trying your repertoire out. Later...'

* * *

Lark's kitchen was the kind of challenge that could break a man. She had lots of fruit, wholemeal bread, brown rice, pasta, four different kinds of cheese and some sliced ham, which he reckoned she must use for sandwiches. Along with jars of apple sauce, burger sauce, salad dressing and a freezer full of made-up meals from the wholefoods freezer shop, that were nice but required nothing any more creative than switching the oven on. He found a can of stout beer in the back of a cupboard and an idea occurred to him.

'Okay, we'll start with the basics. Cheese on toast.'

'Like I've never had it before?'

She was getting the idea. Taking off his jacket and tie, Will rolled up his shirtsleeves. 'Mustard?' She must have mustard. Everyone had mustard.

'Of course! English or French?' Lark gave him an outraged look, and Will laughed.

By the time she returned from her bedroom, in a pair of casual trousers and a crimson sweater, the beer was already reducing in a pan. He gave her the easy job of grating the cheese and when she'd finished she crowded against him, curious to see what he was doing.

'You're in the way!'

'And *you're* meant to be showing me how to do this!' she flashed back at him.

Will gave in to the inevitable and handed over the wooden spoon, which clearly hadn't seen a lot of use. Leaving her to stir the cheese into the sauce he'd made, he cut the bread and put it into the toaster.

'Taste it.'

Lark dipped a spoon into the mixture and wrinkled her nose. 'It tastes like…cheese.'

'That's how it's supposed to taste. Now add a spoonful of mustard and a little of the beer...not too much...' He stopped her from tipping the lot into the mixture. 'Then taste it again.'

She was getting the idea. Lark tasted and then nodded. 'Bit more mustard.'

'Okay, add a little and then taste it again, until you have it right.'

'I'll be full by the time this is done.' Her elbow found his ribs and she nudged him gently.

'You're tasting, not eating.'

Lark wrinkled her nose and tipped half of the spoonful of the mixture back into the pan. Will knew he was hovering a little too close. But she didn't seem to mind, and the pleasure of watching her, feeling her, was too great to miss. A little more mustard, and some more beer, and she was satisfied.

'That's good. Want a taste?'

'I'll trust you. Keep stirring for a moment...' He fetched the toast, laying ham onto each slice, and then poured the viscous cheese mixture onto the top. 'A couple of minutes under the grill and it'll be done. Watch it while I get the plates...'

'Looks nice.' Lark had fetched the cutlery, leaving Will to pronounce the cheese properly toasted, and they sat down at the kitchen table together.

'What does it taste like, though?' Will watched while she sliced into the toast, and was rewarded by the look of sheer pleasure on her face as she took her first bite.

'That's perfect. Really scrummy.'

Scrummy was just what he'd been aiming for. They ate in silence, both clearing their plates.

'So...the trick is to keep tasting it, yes?' Lark asked.

'Yes. You start off with basic ingredients, and you need to

know how much of those to add. But flavourings are a matter of adding a little until it's what you want.'

She nodded. 'You'll write a recipe for me? I'll be doing this again. Are we going to do something for afters?'

Dessert was another challenge, and Will was going to have to think about that for a moment. 'Okay. Have you got an empty notebook?'

She caught on immediately. Scrabbling around in a drawer to find the right scrap of paper when you'd decided to cook something took some of the creative pleasure out of the process for Will. A broad grin spread over her face.

'I've finally found your organised side, haven't I, Will. I definitely deserve something stupendous for afters now...'

He'd finally managed to come up with a spiced fruit dessert that met Lark's expectations of him, and then they'd washed the dishes together, returning Lark's kitchen to perfect order. *That* was part of the pleasure too. Then they'd moved through to the living area for coffee. Lark had finished painting the back wall and put the furniture back in place, and the colour scheme was really coming together.

They chatted over Lark's ideas for finishing off the job, and mulled over paint charts. She'd planned everything, and where the bolder colours threatened to take over, she'd thought of ways to break them up a little.

'It's going to look really great.'

'I hope so. It's something new for me, taking risks and adjusting things as I go.' Lark seemed uncharacteristically nervous about the results, when usually her forward planning didn't leave any room for surprises.

'Have I finally found your experimental side?' He received a tart look in reply and then Lark smiled.

'Maybe. This *is* a bit of a departure for me.'

It seemed so natural to put his arm around her shoulders. Comfort, maybe. Or approbation. Or just the sheer pleasure of having her close, feeling her move towards him to close the gap between them.

'But you're liking it?'

'Yes. As a matter of fact, I am.'

This was nice. Sharing things that they hadn't thought to share before. Carefully treading new ground that seemed full of the promise of delight. But however much Will wanted to take this further, he couldn't. Intimacy with a virtual stranger was so much more straightforward than intimacy with a friend.

'It's getting late. I should go.' He'd done what he'd come to do, and Lark had gone the whole evening without mentioning the challenges they faced at work. Will hadn't thought about them until now either. Maybe in the morning they'd both wake up and see it all in a different, less overwhelming perspective.

She didn't move. In fact, if anything, she seemed to shift a little closer. Will took a moment to appreciate that, and then took his arm from around her shoulders.

'Wait. Will…' He froze, unable to move away from her now. Too entranced with her to go back, and too much at a loss to go forward.

'We know far too much about each other not to talk about this.' Lark's practicality saved him from the agonies of indecision. 'I think we have to say it.'

He was lost now. Lark was braver than he was, and Will felt an exquisite relief wash over him. 'You have this all under control?'

She pulled a face. 'No. I… I know how I feel, though. I think—feel, actually—that I want to know you better. As if I can take a step in the dark with you, because I trust you. And I really want you to stay with me tonight.'

'I feel…a little afraid. Very awkward… I need to hear you say that you're ready to do this.' Will had meant to say that he wanted to be with her more than he'd wanted anything for a long time, but the truth slipped through before he could stop it.

Her eyes, golden in the sudden heat of the evening, gave him a taste of what it might be like to be with Lark all night.

'Probably not. But I want it so much that I don't care, and I trust that we can make things right between us. There's only one thing I have to know. Eloise…?' She pressed her lips together, as if she dared not even frame a question around the name. But this was something that Will *could* answer.

'It took me a long time to come to terms with the fact that I'd lost my future with Eloise. But I have, and I want to make a future with you now. One that's right for us.'

She hugged him wordlessly. Will coiled his arms around her shoulders, holding her tight. Lark seemed as breathless as he felt, caught up in the magnitude of what they'd just done.

'Would you like to see my bedroom? It's painted cream, so I think we're pretty safe in there.'

That was Lark's talent for taking the angst out of any given moment. He'd seen her do it with patients before, breaking what seemed impossible down into small, manageable steps. His familiarity with the technique made it all the sweeter. So much more like an act of love.

'Yes. Cream's good for a bedroom.'

'Sometimes…' She wriggled free of his embrace, giving him a mischievous smile that made Will's heart lurch. Then, taking him by the hand, she led him through to a closed door on the other side of the house.

Her bedroom was *very* cream. Soft, practical and… 'I think it could take a warmer colour.'

She looked round, as if she were seeing the room for the first time. Everything was neat and in order, with pale bedlinen and light oak furniture. 'Yes. You're right, it needs some warmth.'

That was something that Will could give now. He took her into his arms, kissing her, and felt her melt deliciously against him. Then she drew back, staring into his eyes as her fingers skimmed deftly across the all too thin cotton of his shirt. He let her do what she so clearly wanted, feeling the soft touch of her lips on his chest as she undid the buttons.

'Lark…' Her name felt so good, as if it belonged on his tongue. Will craved the sensation of kissing *her* skin.

Her hands moved, plucking at the hem of her top, suddenly awkward.

'Let me…' He whispered the words against her ear, feeling her relax again as she nodded. Will knew exactly what to do, and she gasped as he stripped off her top in one smooth action. Falling together into the unknown, he embraced her tightly, to let her know that he was there with her, all the way.

CHAPTER NINE

WILL WAS THE most exquisite lover. Kind and thoughtful, and yet never letting go of the passion that made everything he did so exciting. He'd undressed her as if it were the most natural thing in the world, and helped her when her fingers fumbled with his buttons.

He seemed to have no insecurities about his body, which was only natural since he looked so much better out of his clothes than in. Will kept himself in shape, often leaving work with his gym bag slung over his shoulder, and it was time well spent. And he lost no opportunity to make her feel beautiful, telling her exactly what he liked about her skin, her eyes…

There was exactly the right amount of time spent in foreplay, long enough to make her forget all of her doubts and fears. The donning of a condom from the drawer beside the bed was so seamless it was practically unnoticeable. He satisfied her completely, and then promptly found his own climax, while Lark was still enveloped in the rosy haze of hers.

And then he curled his arms around her, letting her use his chest as a pillow. Perfect. And…

'You okay?' She felt his lips brush her skin as he murmured the words.

'Yes!' Maybe she replied a little too defensively, because she felt him shift beside her, propping himself up on one elbow.

'But?'

How to break a man's confidence in one loving moment. They'd promised honesty, and she could be honest, without telling him the whole truth.

'It was wonderful, Will. Everything was perfect.'

'Go on.' Something in the clear blue of his eyes told her that he'd hoped for more too.

'I want *you*…' All of the uncertainties, and wrong moves. Everything that lay behind his charming exterior.

He nodded. 'What I really love about cooking is the tasting. Getting it wrong and then getting it right, inch by inch.'

'You won't let me into your kitchen, though. All I get to see is the perfect results.'

Will chuckled. 'Then I've made a mistake. How do you feel about getting this all wrong next time?' His body flexed against hers, as if it heartily approved of the idea.

'It's…a possibility. Is that what you want?'

He drew her closer, kissing the top of her head.

'I want unexpected possibilities, sweetheart.'

Those unexpected possibilities became realities far sooner than Lark had reckoned on. It was one thing for someone with the right knowledge to be able to estimate an average refractory period, and quite another to see Will's blue eyes blazing with desire as they touched and tasted their way to finding something new and different. She was sure that Will would have a bruise after having caught him with one of her flailing elbows, and when they could no longer stand those exquisite moments of play Lark managed to puncture the condom with her fingernail.

But the way his head snapped back and he gasped when she finally managed to roll the second one down over him, the note of desperation as she carefully checked it was in place… The way she lost herself suddenly, when Will moved a little too eagerly. It was real, and imperfect and far more than she'd ever imagined sex could be.

She came too soon, leaving him frustrated, his eyes pleading for something that she guessed Will would never ask her for. Lark made him wait, carefully dropping kisses as she moved down his body. Making him come with her fingers and her mouth was a jagged, uncertain process of trial and error, but when she got it right he lost control, crying out her name.

This time he seemed exhausted, almost unable to move. Lark curled her body close to his and he laid his head on her shoulder.

'Did we do that right?' she murmured as she stroked his forehead.

'No. Let's do it like that again, shall we?' He caught her hand. 'Only next time without the elbows.'

Lark chuckled. 'Definitely. It's just that every part of me is so attracted to you. I dare say that was the problem with your chin and my nose.'

'Sorry about that. Is kissing all right?'

Lark snuggled a little closer. 'Kissing's great. Only don't kiss me as if you're about to make love to me again, because I know you can't.'

He brushed his lips against her cheek. 'That was the best… the *very* best sex…'

'I loved it, Will. Every single moment. Can we sleep now?'

He curled his body around her. There were no barriers left between them now, only new places to explore. 'I was hoping you might say that…'

They both slept soundly. Will woke with her in his arms, happy to watch the hands on the clock crawl from ten o'clock to half past, and then Lark began to stir.

He'd had the best of motives, but had started out doing everything wrong. If Will hadn't known Lark so well, he might have accepted her reassurances that everything was fine and continued to hide behind experience and timing to ensure that everything between them went exactly to plan.

But Lark had overturned all that. She'd torn down his barriers, refusing to accept anything other than the man who hid behind them. Real passion could be awkward, badly timed and frustrating. But it was *real* and that made it the best thing in the world.

Will had learned one important lesson. Getting things right with Lark would take a while, probably longer than the foreseeable future. And he was ready for that now. Ready to spend the time it took to become an honest lover instead of just a good one.

'Will you spend the day with me?' Lark had opened her eyes now, and he couldn't wait to ask the question.

'Good morning to you too,' she chided him gently. 'And I'd love to spend the day with you. What shall we do?'

Will thought for a moment. 'I've got to go home for a change of clothes. Come with me, and we'll play things by ear...'

There was no particular reason to go anywhere else after they'd returned to his flat, so Will showed Lark how easy it was to make maple and pecan bread with a bread maker and she'd sealed her relationship with his kitchen by examining the contents of his cupboards and drawers. They lounged on the sofa together, while the bread maker hummed quietly in the kitchen, and after fresh buttered bread and hot chocolate they'd gravitated towards the bedroom. Talking, negotiating everything about this new phase in their lives.

And then, at four in the afternoon, they found their rhythm.

Lark had undressed slowly for him, and he'd undressed for her. Will had propped himself up against the pillows, and Lark was astride him on his lap. Naked, and joined in the most intimate way. Will stretched one arm around her hips, stopping her from forcing the pace by moving too suddenly, and she squeezed the muscles that cradled him.

'I can't take too much more of that, sweetheart.' Lark had probably already guessed that from the sharp gasp that had escaped his lips.

'Good to know. I want this to last.'

So did Will. He reached for the dish by the side of the bed, that contained halved strawberries. Held one against her lips, then watched her savour it while he licked the taste of strawberries from his fingers.

She gasped as he cupped her breast. 'I'm not sure how much of *that* I can take, Will. Not so fast…'

This was all about voicing every part of their desire. Harnessing it until it could no longer be contained. They were slowly working towards something that was beyond any of the limits that either of them had breached before. That should be terrifying, but right now it was all-consuming.

'How's this?' He moved beneath her, sitting up a little straighter so that he could hold her hips more tightly against his and stop Lark from hastening their pleasure. 'Would my making you beg be of any interest to you?'

Her eyes darkened, the gold gleaming a little more brilliantly in contrast. 'Yes, it would. Does it interest you at all?'

'I was hoping you might ask.' Will brushed his lips against hers. They tasted strawberry sweet. 'Although you've turned me into a complete walkover, so I'll be begging soon, whether you like it or not.'

Lark leaned forward, whispering in his ear. 'Hold out, Will. You want to hold out, don't you?'

His hand found her breast again, and he felt her body. 'I want to. First, you show me how long *you* can hold out...'

Will had made love to her for what seemed like days. Hours, at least. And somewhere, some time between the first awakening of passion and the final quiet after the storm, they'd found each other.

It had been lifechanging. They were moving past the way things had been and into new territory. That had always been too terrifying for Lark to even consider, but a whole weekend where good food, good love and an amazing friendship seemed blended together in one blissful passage of time made taking the risks worth it.

On Monday morning they stood in the queue at the coffee shop together. Not touching, but maybe their body language betrayed that they were lovers. Caught up with Will in a bubble.

'Maybe I'll drink my coffee here.' Lark looked around the busy coffee shop. There were plenty of empty tables—at this time in the morning most people wanted takeaway.

'You're *trying* to be late for work? That's a first.'

She shrugged. 'You know. Arriving together.'

'We arrive together all the time, particularly on a Monday morning.' Will frowned. 'In fact, I think *not* arriving together might be more suspicious. Or more particularly contriving not to arrive together. If someone we know happens to pop in here and sees one of us drinking coffee instead of going straight up to the office, then that's a pretty conclusive indication that something's going on.'

'You've thought about this, haven't you.' Lark bit her

tongue, but not before Will shot her a rueful look. His recent history with women was—history. They'd talked about it and Will had told her that this was different. But she couldn't help feeling a little insecure at times.

'I guess so.' He turned his blue-eyed gaze on her, and suddenly Lark had no doubt at all about Will's commitment to her. 'Would it be too old-fashioned to say that I want to protect you?'

Lark grinned at him. 'I hope that protecting your friends never goes out of fashion.'

'Good point. Did you have anything in mind with regard to protecting me, then?'

He had a way of turning everything on its head and making it feel shining and new. 'Don't you worry, Will. You're quite safe with me.'

No one batted an eye when they walked into the office together, although going to their separate offices and staying there might have raised a few eyebrows. They'd decided that the challenge that Pete had set them—to each work alone on one of the projects that the charity was considering taking forward—would be handled strictly in terms of their agreement. Will would take the proposal for workshops for first responders, aimed at helping them to avoid the very real risks associated with sleep disruption and recurrent migraine, and Lark was going to consider a community outreach scheme for schools, to understand childhood migraine better. Working alone might be a good exercise for both of them.

And so it went. Pete had called, wondering if it might be best to postpone his next session for a week, so that they could concentrate on their proposals, and Will had accepted the idea immediately. Lark had wondered whether Pete sensed that the sessions weren't going too well, but she didn't care because that was one Friday that they didn't have to contend with spending an hour away from the things they really needed to do. There was plenty to keep them busy, follow-ups from helpline calls, liaison with home visitors and, of course, their afternoon clinics. But their evenings and weekends were spent together, even if they were partly taken up with the proposals that they were both writing.

'So...you're nearly finished?' Will looked up from his laptop. Lark was propped up on pillows, her own laptop in front of her, and he'd retreated to the foot of the large bed, facing her. When Will made a promise, he kept it.

'Thirty-four pages.'

He grinned. 'Forty-five.'

Lark frowned at him. 'Forty-five?' Maybe she should change the formatting of her document, so that it at least hit the forty-page mark.

'One and a half spacing. Easier to read. And I've mentioned a few possibilities in the introduction that aren't practical just yet, but might be in the future. I might take them out.'

'There's nothing *wrong* with blue-sky thinking, Will. No one's asking you to stop doing the things you're really good at.'

'You think I'm trying too hard to be you?' He shook his head suddenly. 'On second thoughts, don't answer that. It could be construed as collusion.'

Lark hit *save* and snapped the lid of her laptop shut. 'We work together, Will. Doing one task separately doesn't mean that we can't talk about general principles.'

He nodded thoughtfully. 'Okay. So what do you reckon?'

'I think it's Saturday evening and you could stop working now. Take your clothes off and bring your blue-sky thinking over here...'

Will feigned outrage. 'You reckon that seduction's going to give you an advantage, do you?'

There *was* an element of competition about this. Working together demanded a lot of give and take, and it was usually impossible for either of them to claim full ownership of the planning documents they produced. But working separately invited comparisons, and they'd been joking about those all week.

'I'll give it a go. It might work to my advantage.'

Will closed his laptop and leaned to pick hers up, stowing them both away on the table next to the bed. 'So what are the chances that I'll read what you've done while you're sleeping?'

None, probably. Will could be frighteningly honest at times.

'You think you'll be awake to do that?'

He kissed her. Tenderness spiced with the heat of competition was even more exciting than Lark had expected.

'Let's find out, shall we?'

CHAPTER TEN

SOMEHOW, AFTER A late night working on their proposals, and an even later night spent trying to wear each other out, Will had woken early. He'd taken it for granted that he'd grown out of that sudden burst of energy that accompanied a new relationship, but Lark had shown him differently. Maybe the energy came from the realisation that this time he was prepared to fall in love. Not just fall, Will felt that at any moment he was going to take a running jump.

They emailed both their proposals to Sir Terence three days later, making sure to co-ordinate carefully so that both emails didn't turn up in his inbox at the same time. On Friday evening, when they met with Pete, both Will and Lark expected that should be enough.

'I heard from Sir Terence.' Pete had barely sat down at the small conference table in Lark's office before he dropped his latest bombshell. Will saw Lark straighten a little in her seat.

'He hasn't come back to us yet.' Will decided that a reminder that Pete wasn't actually a part of the decision-making process might be in order.

'He hasn't distributed the material to the other trustees yet.' Pete brushed his comment to one side. 'This is unofficial feedback.'

'Generally speaking, *any* feedback, official or otherwise, is treated as confidential until it's been discussed between How-ard and the board.' Lark voiced his own thoughts.

'Sir Terence has spoken to me because this directly pertains to the work we're doing together.' Pete dismissed Lark's com-ment and Will felt a prickle of outrage run up his spine. 'Your two proposals were both of high quality and strikingly similar.'

'You've read them?' Will tried not to make the comment sound like a challenge, but clearly it did because Pete's usu-ally calm demeanour broke for a moment.

'No, as Lark pointed out, the documents are part of the char-ity's confidential decision-making process. I've just given you the full extent of the feedback I received from Sir Terence. This is a full disclosure environment, and anything that's said here is confidential as well.'

In that case…

'If you want full disclosure, then I think it's fair to say that neither Lark or I are particularly happy with the increasing amount of time we're spending on the tasks you're setting.' Will glanced at Lark and she nodded in agreement. 'We're only here two days a week, and we're trying to run a charity, care for patients who come to us for help, and cover for our CEO. We can do it, but it's not helpful to give us unnecessary work at the moment. And, as we've pointed out before, our patients and the communities we serve must come first.'

'Of course. Noted.' Will saw Lark roll her eyes. This seemed to be Pete's answer to almost anything that challenged him. 'But I think you'll find this next suggestion fun…'

'Fun? Fun!' Lark had been bottling this up all the way back to Will's place. But now he was sprawled on the sofa, watching as she paced back and forth in front of the hearth.

'It's insupportable, Will. What are we a pair of…?'

'Performing seals?'

'Yes, exactly. We're being treated as if we're a pair of performing seals. And what does this Leadership Day involve, anyway?'

'Pete said that we'd be handling unexpected situations. I suppose if they tell you what they are, then it's not unexpected, is it.' Will turned the corners of his mouth down.

'I suppose not. It's too bad—we have things to do on Sunday.' Cook. Eat. Make love. They were things to do, weren't they?

'Do you believe that thing about a cancelled booking?'

'Not for a minute. This is something that Sir Terence has dreamed up with Pete. No doubt we'll be marked on everything we do, and that's going to be part of the decision about who becomes temporary CEO.'

He nodded. 'Yeah, I don't think any of this just happened. Perhaps Sir Terence thinks that having just one of us to deal with will mean he gets his own way a little more often than he does with Howard. And that whoever gets picked will feel they owe him something.'

'I hadn't thought of that. You're right, of course, and that makes it even more annoying.' Lark stopped pacing because it wasn't making her feel any better. Being in Will's arms always made her feel better and she perched on the side of the sofa, next to him. 'Tell me he's not going to get away with this.'

He pulled her down and kissed her. 'He's not going to get away with it. He can't make us compete with each other if we don't want to, and I'm not even sure I want to be a temporary CEO. I'd rather enjoy working under you.'

'Oh, and leave me to deal with Sir Terence. That's not nice.'

'Howard obviously kept him under control. I have every confidence in your ability to be firm.' He kissed her again.

'Stop kissing me, Will!'

'You've heard of angry sex, haven't you?'

'Yes, and angry sex is when we're angry with each other. Not when I'm angry and you're trying to convince everyone, including yourself, that everything's okay.'

He gave her a wry smile. 'Busted. It's not okay, is it. I feel just as wretched about it as you do.'

'Thank you.' His admission took the edge off Lark's anger. 'I know that's hard for you to say.'

'It's time. I don't want to keep living the way I have done, keeping everyone at arm's length. Especially you, Lark.'

She hugged him, feeling his heart beat against hers. 'Let's look at it logically, shall we? It's too late to contact Sir Terence or any of the other trustees this evening, and they won't thank us for stirring things up over the weekend. We'll play along, go on Sunday, and then decide what to do on Monday. Then make a joint approach to the whole Board of Trustees.'

'Are you being deliberately conciliatory? That was what I was going to suggest.' He wound his arms around her shoulders, enveloping her in his warmth.

'I think it's the right thing to do.' Lark kissed him. 'And yes, I'm being deliberately conciliatory. We can save the heavy artillery for when we know exactly what's happening, eh?'

'Good plan. And in the meantime I'll do my best to make it up to you for losing our lazy Sunday together.'

'It's not your fault, Will. You don't have to make anything up to me.'

He chuckled, whispering in her ear, and Lark's eyes widened. 'You can make baked Alaska?'

'Usually. Sometimes it goes wrong and ends up something like a hot Eton Mess.'

'I like Eton Mess as well. And I love a little trial and error with you…'

He dropped a kiss onto her lips. 'You want to make a start, then…?'

At eight o'clock on Sunday morning, after an hour's drive out of London, they drew into a wide, curved access road. The hotel was housed in an older building, which had once been a grand country mansion, and the conference centre in a modern annexe. Will followed the signs, heading for the car park.

'Nice place.' He got out of the car, looking around him. Despite having already made their lunch choices, in response to the emails they'd both received yesterday, they still didn't know what the day ahead held.

In the shining, smartly decorated interior of the conference centre their names were taken and they were asked to check in their phones, before being directed to a large room, with comfortable seats arranged in a circle at the far end, alongside a table that was laid out with drinks and pastries. Two men were already there, talking intently, and a smart middle-aged woman was quietly drinking coffee while she surveyed the room.

Lark gravitated to the coffee, pouring two cups, and Will caught the woman's eye. He smiled and she smiled back.

'Hi, I'm Will.'

'Anna. Do you know what we'll be doing today? All I got was an instruction to be here at eight-thirty, and to dress for physical activity.'

Good to know. At least he and Lark weren't the only people in the dark.

'No idea. I'm here with my colleague, Lark Foster. We work for a medical charity.'

'Really? How fascinating.' Anna smiled at him. 'I'm an accountant. What area of medicine does your charity deal with?'

Will couldn't help a grin. No doubt Lark would tell him that this was a version of how he usually introduced himself, moving quickly past the details about himself and showing interest in the person he was talking with.

'We provide information and support for people who are affected by migraine.'

'Then you must meet a lot of people who are personally interested in your work. I've been suffering with migraines for years…' Anna turned the corners of her mouth down. Will reached into the back pocket of his jeans and proffered his card.

'I dare say you have it pretty much under control by now, then?'

Anna shrugged, 'Ninety-five percent of the time. Whenever we go on holiday my husband plans in a bit of sightseeing on his own for the first couple of days, while I'm lying in a darkened room wishing I was at home.'

'That's not uncommon—you've been working hard and you feel fine, then you get some time off and start to relax and it hits you? I used to get a version of that, when I went through a period of not sleeping during the week and then sleeping more heavily at weekends.'

Anna nodded. 'I always think that's one of the more mean-spirited sides of it. You get some time off and then it hits you.' She tucked the card into the pocket of her immaculate jeans. 'I'll take a look at your website, Will.'

Always use a person's name, at least once. That way, you can remember it, and the conversation becomes more personal. Lark would be suppressing a smile by now, ready to whisper to him later that he'd met his match in Anna.

'Thank you. There's a section on "Holiday Migraine" and we're always interested in hearing from people. It's something we'd like to learn more about…' Will jumped as he felt Lark nudge him. She was balancing two cups and a selection of mini pastries on a plate, and Will took the coffee from her before she spilled it.

'Hi, I'm Lark.' She held out the plate.

'Thanks, these do look nice. I'm Anna.' Anna smiled, choosing a pastry. 'What a pretty name.'

Lark chuckled. 'I'm not sure that my parents thought too much about the expectations it carries. Some people take it for granted that six o'clock in the morning is my best time.'

Anna laughed and the two women started to chat, Anna gesturing towards Lark's serviceable cargo pants, saying that she wished she'd had something in her wardrobe with roomy pockets, since today was about being ready for any eventuality. By the time they got to exchanging information about what they did for a living, Lark's irrepressible warmth was already in evidence between them.

A man had just entered the room, closely followed by a woman, both of them looking around, trying to read the room. It was time for him to circulate and see whether he could find out a bit more about what today might hold…

'Hit me with it, then.' Twenty minutes later he found Lark at his side, and Will automatically stepped back from the five other members of the group.

'Adrian's the headmaster of a private secondary school. Listens to everyone and thinks about what they say, but he doesn't betray too much of what he's thinking. Molly's a lawyer, and she's ambitious, very focused on getting ahead. Graham's in manufacturing, but he's keeping everything else very close to his chest. My guess is that his word is law in his workplace and he's not used to being questioned on any of his decisions.'

Lark nodded. 'And Evan?'

'He's built up his own marketing company and is busy stressing how important he is. I reckon that Anna's the most high-powered…'

'You're good… And you make it seem so effortless.' She'd said that before, but then it had been *very good*. A thrill tingled through Will's veins as she smiled up at him.

'Just *good*?'

'You can't be *very* good at everything, Will.' She shot him a look of reproof and Will decided that on balance it was better to be very good at the things that pleased Lark. Even if the thought threatened to bring him to his knees.

'Anna's a director at…one of the big accounting firms…' Lark frowned, clearly trying to remember which one, and when Will supplied the name of the most influential she nodded. 'And you're a consultant neurologist.'

He could almost see what she was thinking. Lark's habit of assuming that everyone else was more important than she was, wasn't going to help her today.

'And your job is to save lives. If I was going to choose who I wanted to lead me…'

'Okay. Point taken.' Lark frowned. 'Don't you think that sizing everyone up is all a bit…calculating?'

'Of course it is. This is a leadership course, and the first thing you need to do when leading others, or being led by them, is to size them up. Why do you think we've been put into a room alone together for the last half hour?'

'Oh. I was thinking they were just giving us a chance to settle in and eat all the pastries.' Lark's head turned as a young man and woman entered the room, wearing matching sweatshirts with the conference centre logo on the back, and started to beckon to everyone to join them in the circular seating area.

She puffed out a breath. 'I think it's time to get to work now, though…'

Lark was looking a little nervous and Will sat down next to her, trying to radiate some confidence in her direction. Amy and Ben introduced themselves as their course co-ordinators for the day, and told them that they would each be leading the others in completing one task. Each task was expected to take about an hour and there were no rules, apart from keeping everyone safe. Then they were pitched straight in to the first task, which Evan would lead.

Evan rose with an air of showing his fellow course attendees how it was done, and they followed Ben into an adjoining room. There was a small lobby and in front of them a single access revolving door, the glass panels covered with black baize, which concealed whatever was beyond. Ben wordlessly gave Evan a set of key cards and a clipboard.

No instructions. Everyone was looking around at everyone else, obviously wondering what they'd be facing on the other side of the door.

'Okay…' Evan had read through the instruction sheet fixed to the clipboard, and now seemed ready to start. 'We have to go one at a time, and when each person makes their way through the exit door, a buzzer sounds in here and the next person can go inside. Who'd like to try that out and report back?'

Leading from the back was one way of doing it. Evan's gaze moved from one face to the next, clearly waiting for the first person to cave in and volunteer.

'I'll go.' Will stepped forward at the same moment that Lark did, and he nudged her out of the way. She knew as well as he did that Evan's tactic could send the most vulnerable member of the group in first, and that generally speaking it was better to play to people's strengths than their weaknesses. And Will didn't care if he seemed overprotective. Lark wasn't going through that door until he'd seen what was on the other side of it.

'Great, thanks.' Evan gave him the key card and scribbled his name down on the pad. 'I'll time you…'

'Whatever it is, don't rush it.' He heard Lark murmur the words and nodded in acknowledgement, then inserted the key card into the lock, pushing the revolving doors. Suddenly he was plunged into complete darkness.

Okay. That was unexpected. Holding out his hands, he explored the space to his right and felt his fingers brush against something, which on further investigation turned out to be a solid, padded wall. There was another to his left and Will moved forward carefully, one hand in front of his face and the other touching the wall.

As his eyes adjusted to the darkness, he saw a muted light up ahead, and he counted his steps as he moved towards it. Turning a corner, he found himself surrounded by mirrors that reflected multiple shadowy images of himself back at him. Looking around, he could just see a camera trained on him, and he nodded up towards it. Clearly the organisers had taken some trouble to make sure that people going through here were monitored.

Further along, and in darkness again, something brushed against his shoulder and he jumped, raising his hand to find soft door streamers in his way. Then there was a locked door, which he had to find the key for in the darkness. He let it close behind him, then opened it again, checking whether he was able to go back, and storing the information away in case he needed it later. After that, a maze of turns and dead ends, where he completely lost his bearings. More by luck than anything else, he found his way through to another door, which opened when he used the key card in his pocket. Will stepped outside, blinking in the sunlight.

'You made it. Everything okay?' Amy was waiting for him on a wide veranda that stretched the length of the back of the building.

Everything was just fine. Apart from the fact that his three main priorities at the moment were keeping the charity running, seeing patients and spending time alone with Lark, and he wasn't doing any of these things. But that wasn't Amy's fault.

'Yeah, it's all good. You have cameras in there?'

Amy grinned. 'Yep, thermal imaging so that I can watch everyone through.' She turned the screen of the tablet she was holding towards him, and Will saw the blue outline of a figure in the first of a series of small windows, the red heat of its hands reaching out as his had done.

'He's let someone else in, before I had a chance to report back?' Will couldn't keep the tone of disbelief out of his voice.

Amy shrugged, turning the corners of her mouth down in silent agreement. 'Everyone does this differently. You should be back before the next person goes through…' Her head was bent now, watching the image on her tablet, and Will hurried away.

There was no need to worry. The darkness had been challenging but there were safeguards in place. But something about the jerky movements of the small image on the screen had suggested panic rather than disorientation, and that bothered Will.

What bothered him more was that he'd be willing to bet

that Lark had volunteered to go next. She was used to going into potentially hazardous situations so that other people didn't have to, and he'd already had to stop her from going first into the unknown.

Six heads turned towards him as he burst back into the lobby, after having walked the length of the building to get back in through the main entrance.

Evan beamed at him. 'Three minutes and forty seconds. Your friend will have to get a move on to beat that.'

It wasn't all about the competition. Will ignored Evan, making for Ben. 'Where is she?'

Ben's eyes flipped to the screen of his tablet. 'Looks as if she's standing still.'

'Let me see…'

Ben handed him the tablet, clearly a little concerned, and Will saw that Lark was standing in the hall of mirrors. In the low light, she looked as if she were talking to herself.

'I'll go and fetch her.'

Ben nodded, taking a flashlight from his belt and handing it to Will.

'No you don't, we might lose marks for that.' Evan was bristling with indignation. '*I'm* the team leader and that's my decision to make.'

Will ignored him, making for the revolving door. As he swiped his key card he heard Anna speak, cool steel in her tone.

'Be quiet, Evan. Will's more qualified to make this decision than you are…'

In the beam of light, Will could see the corridor in front of him, covered in dark padded material. 'Lark…' he called to her softly.

She didn't answer. Then he heard her whimper quietly.

'Stay right where you are, Lark. Let me find you.' The slight glow up ahead told him that he'd soon be amongst the subtle lighting around the mirrors.

As he turned the corner he saw her. Standing still, her hands up to her face. Something was wrong, and Will shone the flashlight at her feet so that she could see where she was and what surrounded her.

'I'm okay.' As soon as he reached her she flung her arms around him, holding on tight to his sweater. Clearly she didn't realise they were being watched, and at this moment Will didn't care. 'I don't like the dark all that much.'

Yet another thing he'd just learned about her. He'd assumed that her insistence on leaving the hall light on outside the bedroom was because they were still unused to the layout of each other's homes.

'I think there's a mutiny going on outside. Should we go back and save Evan?'

She laughed suddenly. 'As long as they're not going to make him walk the plank in the next five minutes, it's probably best if we turn the light out and I finish the course, eh? Then at least he can say he got everyone through.'

'You're sure? Don't do anything you're uncomfortable with, just for him.'

'I'll be okay if I know you're with me.'

That he couldn't resist. Will still wasn't entirely sure whether a person could overcome their fears for love, but he'd been willing to give it a try, and now it appeared Lark was too.

'Okay. You're ready…?'

'Not quite.' Will felt her body move against his. 'A kiss first?'

'Uh… That's all I can think about right now, but there are cameras in here.'

Lark let go of him, stepping back. 'Oh! Thermal imaging, you mean?'

Will nodded, trying not to grin as he handed her the flashlight. Lark switched it off, looking around in the half-light to find the camera and waving at it, giving a thumbs-up to show that everything was okay. She clipped the flashlight to her belt, and then smiled up at him.

'Stop it, Will. File those notions away for later.'

'You can tell what I'm thinking?' Will couldn't quite shake the idea of being surrounded by mirrors, watching multiple images of themselves making love. Or of being able to see the heat that radiated from them as they kissed.

'When it's about sex, yes.'

Good to know. And it was good to see that Lark was getting over the fright she'd had over being plunged into the darkness without any warning. She took his hand, walking to the edge of the pool of light around the mirrors.

'Don't give me any clues...'

'Why not? If Evan had waited until I got back, you would have heard the exact layout, along with everyone else.'

'If you can puzzle your way through this, then so can I. Give a woman a chance to compete with you, eh?' Lark squeezed his hand, stepping into the darkness.

CHAPTER ELEVEN

THE DARKNESS WASN'T as terrifying as it had been the first time. Feeling Will's hand in hers gave Lark the confidence to find the key to the locked door, instead of sinking to the ground in despair, and the maze was a piece of cake because it was a simple labyrinth based on the age-old principle of turning always to the right. They walked out into the sunshine, then hurried back to the rest of the team, to find that comparative peace had broken out.

Will gave a description of the first part of the course, and when he seemed a little vague about the succession of turns required to get through the maze, Lark was able to close her eyes and visualise them more exactly. That helped everyone through quickly and without incident, and Lark saw Anna roll her eyes when Evan shook Will's hand, congratulating him on his contribution to a great team effort.

Then they all started to have fun. Adrian's task was to assemble a steam-driven vehicle with the help of only a diagram, and somehow he managed to draw everyone together, dividing up the seemingly impossible task into manageable chunks. The engine was ready surprisingly quickly, and when it was taken outside for a test run, everyone cheered when the wheels started to turn and it edged forward.

'Do you think I should apologise to everyone? For messing

up the first challenge.' Lark had retreated to a corner when they broke for coffee, and Will had followed her, his protective bulk suddenly seeming very welcome.

He frowned. 'No, I don't think you have anything to apologise for. We're all afraid of something, and you conquered your particular fear and finished the course. That's walking the extra mile for the team in my book.'

'I just...' Lark shrugged. 'I think if I'd expected to be plunged into complete darkness I might have handled it better though. It came as a surprise, and I don't much like the unexpected.'

Will puffed out a breath. 'You're not going to let this go, are you.'

'Not sure I can.' Lark didn't know why.

'Well... I know you like to plan things out, and you're very good at it. But isn't an aversion to the unexpected something of a disadvantage when you're a first responder?'

Lark shook her head. 'That's not the same at all. We're trained for the situations we encounter, and we can make a difference.'

'May I ask...?' Will was looking at her thoughtfully.

'Anything. You know that, don't you?'

His gaze suddenly captured hers. Lark wondered whether it would actually be possible to live in that gaze, needing nothing else.

'Were you there when Robyn was injured?'

The question took her breath away. Lark remembered that day so clearly, the shock as she'd seen her sister fall from one of the swings at the local playground, lying still on the ground. The awful fear, as she'd realised that there was nothing she could do to make Robyn better, and the way the darkness had lifted when she'd seen the ambulance draw up beside the playground, and two green-clad superheroes hurrying towards them.

'You think…that's why I became a paramedic?' It didn't seem that much of a leap now that Lark thought about it.

He smiled, shaking his head. She'd come to appreciate Will's smile even more now, since it was no longer something that he used to convince everyone around him that everything was perfectly fine, but something that had to be earned.

'Howard once told me that when you were at university, you were the best student he'd ever seen. We're all inspired to do what we do by something, but the commitment required is a life choice.'

'Thank you.' Lark couldn't give Will any answers right now, she had to think about what he'd said, but she knew he'd wait. 'This course…perhaps it's more worthwhile than we thought it was going to be.'

He thought for a moment. 'Yes, I think it is. Although probably not quite in the way that Sir Terence supposed. We're not trying to outdo each other, are we?'

'Aren't we? Who insisted on going first through the revolving door?'

'And who insisted on turning off the flashlight and finishing the course, despite being terrified of the dark?'

Fair enough. Lark's first thought had been that if Will could do it so could she, and competing with him did add a layer of excitement to any task.

'You're right. I think I *am* doing better than you.' Lark knew that Will couldn't resist the challenge.

'Yeah? You'll have to have more up your sleeve than that to beat me.'

'Watch and learn, Will…'

* * *

Molly had micro-managed her way through the first ten minutes of her challenge before Anna tactfully took her to one side for a conversation, and her tension relaxed suddenly. Then it was Will's turn and with the aid of a whiteboard, pens and an irresistible smile, he managed to spur the team on in finding all of the required items of a scavenger hunt.

None of this was supposed to be a competition, but the grin he'd given her when they sat down for lunch, in the pleasant surroundings of the conference centre's restaurant, belied that.

'You've set the bar high.' Lark smiled at him. At first sight, a scavenger hunt didn't have a great deal of application to what Will did in either of his jobs. But actually, enthusing the people around him, encouraging them and playing to their strengths, however trivial a task seemed, was something he did well. He'd make a great CEO for Migraine Community Action.

'Is that an admission of defeat?' His smile told her that he thought it was nothing of the sort.

'Never. I'd rather slay a dragon than a mouse.'

'Nice to know. I'd rather *be* a dragon than a mouse.' He was still chuckling as he turned to chat to Evan, who seemed to have got over his grumpiness at being sidelined in his own challenge, and had made a success of his part in Will's challenge. Will had a way of turning things around and finding common ground in a conflict.

Talk over lunch turned from work to personal, as the team began to bond. Anna observed that the later tasks would be easier than the earlier ones, in a pointed reference which Lark took as a peace offering for Evan, and made sure she voiced her agreement.

Ben smiled. 'Yeah. We know that everyone bonds much better for the later tasks. We take that into account.'

'So they *are* marking us on what we do here...' Will murmured quietly to her.

Before Lark could answer, she heard a shriek from the veranda outside the restaurant. Amy had been sitting drinking coffee with someone, who was now sprawled on the ground.

'Lark! Help...'

One glance told her that the 'man' was actually a full body CPR dummy, dressed up in jeans and a hoodie. But, all the same, the sudden switch from relaxation to purposeful single-mindedness was real.

'This one's mine. Round everyone up, Will...' Lark got to her feet, running through the open doors which led onto the veranda, where Amy was now bending over the dummy.

The dummy wasn't realistic enough to display any symptoms and Lark relied on Amy, who was making a realistic show of panic, to find out what had happened. By the time the others arrived, and Will joined her next to the dummy, she'd unzipped its jacket, gone through the motions of clearing airways and had started CPR.

'I've done this a hundred times...' It didn't seem particularly difficult to just do it again while everyone stood around and watched.

'Make it your own, then.' Will could always be relied on to challenge her and an idea occurred to Lark.

'Take over with the CPR, will you...'

Lark got to her feet, while Will concentrated on the task she'd given him. The dummy was a high-end model which showed a response when CPR was given correctly, and all he had to do was keep the LED in its forehead alight, but the effort involved in that was real.

'This is just an exercise, isn't it? No one's hurt, and no

one's going to die.' He heard Lark's voice. 'As a paramedic, I'm going to tell you that it's not. Because this is my chance to show you all what to do when someone suffers a cardiac arrest for real. The whole purpose of the next hour is that this team saves a life. Maybe not today, but one day.'

Nice one. Will allowed himself a smile at Lark's audacity and glanced at Ben, whose face was impassive. He and Amy didn't give much away during the challenges.

'Has anyone had CPR training before?'

'I have.' Will heard Adrian's voice.

'That's great. Go and help Will, please. Will, make sure that Adrian's doing everything correctly. Keeping CPR up can be exhausting, even if you're a fit man like Will, and if you can find someone to help all the better. But never leave someone who's in cardiac arrest alone…'

'I don't think I'm strong enough…' He heard an unfamiliar note of uncertainty in Anna's voice.

'That's okay, Anna. You do your best. If someone's heart has stopped, then they're dying. Anything you can do to reverse that is better than nothing, and I'll show you how to use your own weight to maximise your compressions. Now—does anyone know if there's an automatic defibrillator here?'

Will sat back on his heels, watching as Adrian took over the chest compressions on the dummy. Lark would have noticed the cabinet on the wall behind the receptionist's desk, it was second nature to her.

'In reception.' Evan spoke up, and Lark nodded.

'Well spotted. Would you fetch it please, Evan. It's good to make a habit of looking out for the green and white sign when you're in an unfamiliar place, just as you might notice fire extinguishers…'

Lark took the team through all the steps, explaining exactly what Will was doing. Everyone was engaged and asking questions and if Will had thought he could compete with this… She was walking all over him. His enjoyment at the thought might be letting Sir Terence down badly, but Will didn't care.

Then Lark gave everyone the chance to practise CPR on the dummy and use the automatic defibrillator themselves. When it was Graham's turn he hesitated, scrunching his fingers up to avoid touching the manikin's chest. Lark grinned at him.

'I can see why you're doing that, Graham, but you're not going to be able to do the compressions properly.' She sat back on her heels, making sure she had everyone's attention. 'Will, would you demonstrate the position of your right hand on your own chest, please.'

He could see where this was going. And it was a very valid point. People who weren't medically trained were sometimes confronted by the idea of touching a stranger in what would usually be considered an inappropriate way. He placed the heel of his hand two inches above his sternum and spread his fingers out.

'You'll see where Will's hand is. Now, if I do the same thing…' Lark's fingers spread across her left breast and Will tried not to grin. The whole purpose of the exercise was to convince everyone *not* to be embarrassed. 'Remember that you're trying to save my life, so I'm not going to mind. And Molly, can you help us with any legal pointers?'

Molly smiled. 'Yes, the law does protect you in this kind of situation…'

It had been a good day. As they walked together across the car park, Lark was still buzzing from the goodbyes.

'I thought for a moment that you were going to ask *me* to

demonstrate where I'm supposed to touch you during CPR...'
Will grinned down at her.

'It crossed my mind. I might have done if your hand hadn't
been right there last night.' Now that they were lovers, Will's
smile would have blown any attempt at professional distance
to pieces.

He chuckled. 'Because I only became aware of the fact that
you're the most gorgeous woman I know two weeks ago?'

'Stop with the charm, Will...'

He spread his hands in a gesture of rebuff. 'It's a matter of
fact. I always thought you were gorgeous. Just unattainable
for someone like me.'

His unspoken question hung in the air between them. There
was no point in denying it...

'I thought you were gorgeous too. But since you were my
friend, I had far too much to lose.'

And now? She'd been Will's friend and colleague for years,
but *lovers* was already becoming more important. Lark had
been telling herself that the three weren't mutually exclusive, but
it was so easy to become lost in her desire for him, and that felt
a little scary. She decided it would be best to change the subject.

'Anna's challenge was fun.' The conference centre had its
own climbing wall, and Anna had been tasked with getting
each member of the team to the top of it.

'You looked as if you could have done with some inappropriate touching when you got stuck on that tricky bit, right at
the top.' Will smiled down at her. 'Although you still made it
before I did.'

'By two seconds.'

'Three. And I'm man enough to acknowledge when I'm
beaten.'

'I notice you stopped to help Molly,' Lark teased him.

He shrugged. 'There's nothing inappropriate about grabbing Molly's trainer to help her with a foothold.'

'And it gives you the moral high ground, even though I got to the top first.' Lark turned the corners of her mouth down. 'Work tomorrow. Is it just me, or is work not quite as much fun as it used to be?'

'These changes. They're unsettling, but I guess we just have to trust that they'll work themselves out. And *home* is a great deal more fun than it used to be.'

She smiled up at him. 'That's true.'

Will's fingers brushed the back of her hand and a wave of longing crashed over Lark. He had that power over her now. Will's smallest gesture could make her forget about everything else.

'Look.' His forehead creased in thought. 'Today's been great, but we're still not happy with the way that we're being asked to change our focus, when we're already having to work hard to cover Howard's absence. I'll be on the phone first thing tomorrow, asking Sir Terence for a meeting. But in the meantime, our time's our own. Would you like to eat on the way home?'

'Not particularly. We had a huge lunch and I've been eating pastries all day...' Lark saw Will's smile broaden and knew he was on the same wavelength as she was. 'I was thinking... maybe see how things go in the dark?'

'I thought you didn't like the dark?'

'I might well change my point of view if you're there with me...'

'And you're telling me this now? With an hour's drive ahead of us.'

'We can think about it on the way home.' Lark liked teasing him. The way his blue eyes ignited with desire left her in no doubt about what Will would be thinking about on the way home.

Wordlessly, he opened the car door for her, waiting for her to get in before he hurried around to the driver's side. A couple of miles and then, as soon as they were on the motorway, the car moved steadily from the slow lane into the fast lane.

CHAPTER TWELVE

SOME MONDAYS, everything just went right. Others took a bit more work. Everyone at Migraine Community Action was beginning to miss Howard now, and Lark and Will were busy talking a variety of issues through with various members of staff. And it took four calls from Will and an email before they found out at the end of the morning that Sir Terence was on holiday for the next three weeks.

'Mexico, apparently.'

'Ah. Nice.' Lark could imagine herself on a plane to Mexico at the moment. 'I assume he's not looking at his emails.'

'Of course not. The email I sent was forwarded on to his secretary, and she called me back to say that he has a free space in his diary in a month's time.'

They were both thinking the same thing. Nothing was likely to change in the next month but Lark would bet that Pete had a few things to surprise them with before they had a chance to speak with Sir Terence. Something had to be done.

'Uma Desai?'

Will nodded. 'Yeah, in the circumstances I think it's justified. She's the Deputy Chair, and Sir Terence never let us know he was going on holiday. We're not going behind his back.'

Lark didn't much care if they were. 'Call her, Will.'

He took his phone from his jacket pocket, flipping through his contacts list until he found the number. Lark tried to return to the paperwork on her desk, but words and numbers were just a jumble of meaningless squiggles.

So much had changed in the last month. Missing Robyn and wanting to take some time out to create her own space. Managing without Howard, and all of the challenges and role-changing that had come at Sir Terence's insistence. Seeing Will at last as a lover, rather than a best friend. It hadn't been all bad—Will had given her more than she'd ever thought possible—but it *had* all been challenging.

In holding on to Will, the only piece of security in a world that was changing, was she losing herself again? Changing roles with him, learning to be like him? Was it his strength she needed or just someone to mould herself around?

'You okay?'

'Oh. Yes, just a bit tired.' Lark hadn't even noticed that Will had finished his call. 'What did Uma say?'

'She has concerns. She didn't say what they were, and I didn't press her, but something's up. She'll be in town on Wednesday, and her diary's full for most of the day, but she can make an evening meeting. So we can both see her then, after work.'

'Yeah. I'll be there.'

He shot her a look of concern. 'Are you okay? This is really good news.'

'Yes, I'm happy we're going to get to see Uma.' This sudden tiredness was a little ominous. Lark hadn't had a migraine in years, but the first signs were always this feeling of exhaustion and confusion. Maybe the last month was finally taking its toll.

'Why don't I cover this afternoon and you can go early? You look as if you need some rest.'

His concern wasn't any different to the attitude that Will had always taken. They'd always supported each other, without questions or keeping score. If one of them needed some time out, then the other covered for them. But this time, Lark couldn't help feeling that Will had been keeping exactly the same hours that she had, and was under the same stress...

Another failure, maybe. Right now, she didn't much care. She wanted to go home so badly that all she could think about was her head hitting the pillow.

'Okay. If you don't mind.' Lark closed her laptop, putting it into her bag, along with the files she was working on.

'No problem. I'll pop in this evening to see how you are.'

Something was bothering Lark. Will knew her well enough to be sure of it, but it seemed not quite well enough for her to share, which was unusual. He told himself that she was just tired, and that the stress of the last few weeks had snapped back at her and hit her in the face.

But when he called in at her house that evening, she answered the door in her dressing gown, looking terrible. He hurried her back to bed, noticing the medication on the dressing table, along with a piece of paper that Lark had used to jot down the times she'd taken her tablets.

'You have a migraine?'

She attempted a smile. 'Yeah. Stupid, eh? I'm busy telling everyone else how *not* to get migraines.'

'You can't avoid every single one of them. I think that's pretty standard advice as well.'

'At least I've stopped throwing up now. Think I'm on the mend.'

Her eyelids were drooping and her speech was slightly slurred. *On the mend* wasn't a description that Will would have applied, but maybe she'd been even worse during the course of the afternoon.

'Why didn't you give me a call?'

'You were taking the clinic for me. Have you only just finished?' Lark pulled at the sleeve of her dressing gown, obviously trying to find her watch, and Will noticed that it was sitting on the bedside table, next to her tablets.

'It's half past seven. And yes, I did stay a bit late, I needed to go through a few things with Dev. He was in the office and helped me with the clinic.'

'Okay. Why don't you go home, Will? I'm no good this evening.'

'That's precisely why I'm staying here. Can you remember when you took your last dose of medication?'

'Uh...' Obviously not. Will checked the paper under the blister pack on the bedside table, and since there was two hours to go before she was due another dose he put it in his pocket.

'I'm going to pop home and get some clothes for the morning. I'll only be half an hour. Would you like anything before I go?'

'Water. Please...'

Will went to the kitchen, fetching a bottle of water from the fridge and a plastic beaker. Lark drank thirstily and then flopped back onto the pillows, closing her eyes. He decided it was best to let her sleep, and picked up her front door keys from the table in the hall, letting himself out.

Lark woke early the next morning, feeling better. She vaguely remembered Will having been there last night, and now he was sleeping soundly on the other side of the bed. She cursed silently, wondering why she hadn't had the sense to send him home.

This was all wrong. Migraine again, after so many years

that it was lucky her medication wasn't out of date. She sat up, finding that her head was still throbbing.

'Hey. How are you feeling?'

'Fine. Didn't I send you home last night?'

He smiled, rubbing his eyes. 'Yes. I didn't listen.'

The obscure feeling of guilt started to grow in Lark's chest. 'That's too good of you, Will. I wasn't sick all over you, was I?'

'No. I managed to avoid that indignity. In fact, you weren't sick at all when I was here, just really sleepy.'

The vomiting must have been earlier, then. Thank goodness for that. Lark sat up in bed, feeling for the piece of paper that told her when she'd last taken her tablets, and Will's neat handwriting showed that she'd not taken any medication since half past nine the previous evening.

'You've got great writing for a doctor, Will.'

He chuckled, getting out of bed. He had great everything. Arms, legs. *Really* great eyes…

Lark leaned back against the pillows. 'I'll be okay when I've had my tablets and a cup of tea.'

'Sure you will. Yesterday you didn't even know how much medication you'd given yourself. Today you're thinking of dispensing medication to other people? You want me to examine your reflexes?'

It was a threat, and he knew it. Lark wasn't going to submit to that. 'You can't examine me, you're wearing boxer shorts. And I won't go to work today.'

'Good decision. You want me to call in for you?'

'No, I'll do it.' Lark closed her eyes. 'In a minute…'

By lunchtime she was feeling much better. And by the time Will got back after work the brain fog had lifted and she'd cooked him a meal.

'This looks great.' He sat down at the kitchen table. 'You cooked it yourself?'

'I went out for a walk and decided to surprise you. So I looked through some recipe cards in the supermarket and found something I liked.' Chicken and leeks in a creamy sauce, with roast potatoes and vegetables hadn't been so difficult, although she'd had to call Robyn at one point and there had been more washing-up than Lark was used to.

'You're hungry?' He nodded towards her full plate.

'I could eat a horse. That's how I know a migraine's well and truly finished, I feel wide awake and hungry.'

She waited while he tried his food. That was what Will always did when he cooked her something, and she hadn't realised what a pleasure it was to see someone take their first bite and then smile.

'That's really good. I would have gone for slightly more mustard, but that's just my preference.'

Lark tried hers. 'Yes, I think you're right...'

Slightly more mustard. Lark had had an early night, and was curled up alone in her bed. She'd told Will that she'd give the meeting with Uma a miss and he'd offered to postpone it, because he wanted her there. And Lark had shaken her head, sending him home to get a good night's sleep, because tomorrow was important to both of them.

And she was *still* thinking about mustard. The woman who never cooked, reading through recipe cards in the supermarket. Going to parties and trying to do his job better than he could. Letting him go to tomorrow's meeting alone, to speak for her, even though she knew he would, and that he'd do it well. Feeling alone now, because he wasn't here to hold her.

Perhaps that was love. And perhaps she'd just found someone else to mould herself around, the way she'd moulded herself around her parents' fears for Robyn. The migraine had been just one of those things, that happened so infrequently now it was barely a problem. But she couldn't help wondering whether the migraines she'd had as a child were because fitting a square peg into a round hole was stressful and required the kind of contortion that was bound to cause pain.

This was the first day off, spent alone and with nothing much to do, that she'd had in over a month. It was bound to let a few crazy thoughts loose in her head, and she should ignore them. She loved Will, and he loved her.

A day at work had dispelled her doubts, or at least not allowed Lark to think about them too deeply. Will had texted at nine o'clock, saying that the meeting with Uma had been really positive and asking if she'd like him to drop round on his way home. Lark had texted back with one word—*YES*—followed by hearts and smiley faces. It was only natural that something so new, so different, would be confusing at times, and yesterday she'd not been well and not really thinking straight.

She was at the front door before Will had a chance to ring the bell. He kissed her and they sat down at the kitchen table, Lark drinking herbal tea, while Will stuck with coffee.

'So tell me everything. How did it all go?'

'Good news. Apparently Sir Terence has been less than forthcoming with the other trustees. He told them that he was managing the situation and, being busy people, they left him to it. But Uma had a feeling that something was up because so little information was getting back to her, which is why she made time to meet me straight away.'

'They didn't know?' Lark stared at him, open-mouthed. The whole point of a board of trustees was that they were a carefully chosen blend of expertise, and their remit was to make decisions collectively, supporting the work of the charity.

'Yeah, I was pretty shocked to hear that. Strictly speaking, Sir Terence has the authority to make decisions on behalf of the rest of the trustees, but only if they're unable to meet. Uma told me that he hadn't attempted to call a meeting, and that any structural changes, like appointing a temporary CEO would definitely warrant one. She didn't say too much because she needs to at least speak to the other trustees before giving us any specific answers, but she's clearly very concerned and on the case. She's going to try to call a meeting over the weekend, and if that's not possible she'll make sure that at least she's spoken to everyone before Monday.'

'Good. That's really good news, Will.' Lark felt a weight lifting from her shoulders. Maybe they could start to get back to something like normal now. 'So hopefully Pete won't be dreaming up any new hoops for us to jump through on Friday.'

'I made sure that it didn't sound as if I was giving Uma a list of demands, but that was the one thing I *did* ask her for. I said that the sessions with Pete, and what he was asking of us, was taking up a lot of our time, and that while personal growth is something we're always up for, we're struggling to keep our heads above water right now. She agreed, got him on the phone straight away and cancelled the sessions until further notice.'

'Oh! That's a relief.' Lark felt tears prick at the sides of her eyes. 'Some of the things he was saying were valid but...'

Will's gaze softened. 'I didn't learn too much from him. I learned a lot from you, and those are the things I'll take with me from the last couple of weeks.'

That was nice. Pete had insisted that they break out of their roles, but all that had happened was she'd felt forced into another role, one that she felt uncomfortable with. Now, perhaps, she could take a breath, and start to reclaim her own space again. Find a place where she and Will could grow together.

'Uma didn't give me any assurances, but she did ask how we would prefer to organise things while Howard's away.' There was a sudden hesitancy in his voice.

'And...?'

'I told her that we both feel that things should stay as they are for the time being. Appointing one of us as a temporary CEO isn't necessary, and it's an unneeded complication. We function best as a team.'

'Uma agreed to that?'

'Until the trustees have had a chance to consult with each other, and us, to make a decision. She said that we do need some kind of plan about what happens next if Howard either can't or doesn't want to return.'

'I don't want to think about that.' The quiver in Lark's stomach wasn't solely out of concern for Howard. There was something Will wasn't telling her.

'Neither do I. But Uma made it clear that if it does become necessary to appoint a new CEO, that she personally would like to see either you or I take the job.'

'No. Will, that's putting us right back into the same position that Sir Terence put us in.'

'We talked about that, and I'm sure that's not Uma's intention, but we do have to be practical.' His chest rose and fell as he took a breath. 'I've told her that if that does become necessary, then I'm not interested in the position.'

'What? Will...' Lark stared at him. 'We haven't talked about that.'

'No, we haven't. But that's my decision, I feel that the best way forward for the charity is with you as CEO.'

'But…'

'You're a versatile and talented medical professional, you inspire people and you make things happen. They'd be crazy not to pick you.'

'And so…you made that decision for me?' Lark felt as if she'd just been submerged in cold water. Suddenly she was fighting for breath, her heart thumping.

'No, I made the decision that I wanted to stand aside. Are you telling me you don't want the job?'

Who wouldn't want it? The chance to steer a place she loved, to make a real difference. Not like this, though. 'Are you telling me that *you* don't?'

He grinned suddenly. That blue-eyed smile that could charm the birds from the trees. 'I did tell you that I thought I'd rather enjoy working under you…'

He had, and when they'd put that into practice it'd had nothing to do with work.

'Don't flirt with me, Will. I seem to remember that I said I didn't much want to have to deal with Sir Terence on my own.'

'From what Uma says, I'd be willing to bet that's not going to happen. She was noting down a list of points, things where you and I felt that our ability to do our jobs well had been compromised, and where Sir Terence had ignored proper procedures. I didn't ask, because she obviously didn't want to say, but I'm sure she'll be taking those to the other trustees. You're the best person for the job, Lark, and I don't think that Sir Terence is going to be getting in your way.'

'So you're just going to back off, are you? You're not thinking straight, Will, the charity needs someone like you at the helm. But this isn't about that. It's about you making a decision about my life without asking me first.'

He couldn't see it. A look of annoyance showed in his face,

before it was quickly hidden. 'If you didn't want me to make decisions, why did you ask me to go alone? But that's okay, I'll call Uma in the morning and tell her that I want to compete with you for the CEO's post. Because that's worked so well for us so far.'

'What exactly *has* worked for us, Will?'

He shrugged in frustration. 'You don't know?'

Lark knew. For the last few weeks, she'd had a lover who was a friend. Someone who she could show her own life to, and who had shown his in return. It had been wonderful, but even that wasn't enough, if she couldn't find herself.

'I wanted to create my own space, where I could find out who I am. Everything seemed so uncertain and I clung on to you...' The enormity of what she'd done hit Lark. Will didn't deserve this. 'I was your friend, and I tried to mould myself into something else. Someone who could change roles with you at work and who could be a part of your life.'

'Is there anything wrong with that? I did the same, and... I know you better now. I think I know myself better.' Will seemed at a loss, suddenly. Beneath all of his charm, he was a kind, careful man, and Lark wondered whether he could even begin to appreciate what she was talking about.

'You have a place in the world, Will. You know who you are. I'm not sure that I have any idea who I am, I just feel pulled backwards and forwards, as if I have no real anchor.'

'By me, you mean?' His face darkened. 'Pulled back and forth by me?'

She couldn't deny it. But that wasn't Will's fault, he'd never asked her to do anything, let alone pulled her. 'It's me, Will. Not you.'

Chagrin showed in his face. *It isn't you, it's me.* Maybe he'd said that a few times, to nameless women, who Lark had never paid too much attention to because she'd known that Will's relationships never lasted. This must be new to him, someone who couldn't hold down a relationship as long as he could.

'I'm in this for keeps, Lark. I always have been, ever since we first became friends, and I couldn't imagine a time when we wouldn't be there for each other. And when we became lovers...' He shook his head. 'I can't even say how much you mean to me. I don't have the words.'

She loved him too. And that was the problem, because there was no going back from it now, no return to that easy friendship that they'd both valued so much. She'd given herself to Will before she'd really worked out who she was and what she wanted in life, and that had made the gift worth nothing.

She realised that she'd been staring at him silently, and that Will had been waiting for her to say something. When she didn't, because she honestly didn't know what to say, he said it for her.

'We've got a decision to make, haven't we.'

He was braver than she was. He always had been.

'Yes, we do.'

'You have to tell me what you want, Lark. Whatever that is, we can work out a way to keep the charity running. The one thing I won't have is for you to be unhappy and feel you don't have a way out.'

'You're an honourable man, Will.'

'And that's not an answer.'

He was hurting, that was obvious. And Lark owed him an answer, even if it hurt her to give it. 'We have to stop. *I* have to stop, before I tear us both into little pieces.'

It was all breaking apart. Four years of relying on each other and a few short weeks that had been sweeter than anything that Lark could imagine, even if they'd ultimately proved to be the catalyst that separated them. Lark swallowed down her tears, knowing that she needed to go through with this, if only to save a great deal more hurt later on.

And there were no words. The ones that they always used— *See you later...tomorrow...on Monday. Have a good weekend...a good evening...a great holiday*—suddenly they had no future.

'I'll...' The words died in her throat, because Lark had no idea what she was going to do next.

'Yeah. I'll miss you too.' Will had the courage to make that sound like the ending that Lark couldn't quite get her head around yet. Or maybe he just had more experience with endings...

Not fair. She was the one who was saying goodbye, not him. And Lark didn't even know how to say it. But Will knew how to leave. He got to his feet, picking up his coat and briefcase, and walked away.

CHAPTER THIRTEEN

LIFE. IN ALL its rich variety, its careless cruelty, and all of the moments that couldn't be taken back. Will had flagged down a taxi, and in fifteen minutes he was back home, slumped on the sofa, staring at the wall. Then he tried out a little pacing, while he formed the words that he hadn't been able to say to Lark.

We can work this out.

They couldn't. Lark needed some space to work out what she really wanted in life, after having put her parents' fears before her own needs for so long. He needed to be able to untangle the complex web that had been spun around them, the roles that had been questioned and changed in both their work lives and their personal lives, and to find something solid to hold on to. But the more he thought about it, the more he felt that there *was* nothing to hold on to, and he was just groping in the darkness.

I love you.

Of course he did. Not loving Lark was beyond his capabilities, but it didn't make any difference. He should have taken what he had, and when the temptation to want more had seized him he should have resisted it. Hadn't he already resolved that he'd never again put himself into the position of having to lose someone who was everything to him?

Don't do this, Lark...

That was the most outrageous proposition of all. Letting go

was all he knew how to do now, and Lark needed someone who would fight for her. He hadn't fought tonight, and he wasn't going to go back and do it tomorrow or the next day. Losing her had flipped a switch somewhere deep inside him, and he couldn't go back and risk doing it all over again.

Pacing really wasn't doing any good. He could keep it up all night, and still not find the answers he was looking for. There were a few invitations propped up on the mantelpiece, all of which he'd politely declined in favour of spending time with Lark, painting different coloured squares on her kitchen wall. Maybe a little bland conversation, saying everything and meaning nothing, was what he'd be needing in the days and weeks ahead.

Howard's sister, Petra, was a nice woman, clearly worried for him and trying hard to restore as much normality to the situation as she could. Alyssa had phoned Will, going round the houses until she got to the point of her call. If it wasn't too inconvenient, and he didn't mind…

Yes, he'd be there, and Alyssa should take Sunday afternoon for herself, as usual. Not being able to get a word in edgeways didn't normally bother Howard too much, but it had gained a new meaning recently, and Will would try to steer things in the direction of the new normal.

Petra looked around at the plants and the tall windows, which made the visitors' room light and airy. 'It's very nice here, isn't it? Now that you can walk it must be so much easier to make friends.'

Howard nodded.

'I suppose I'd better go now, though. I wish I could spend some more time with you, but just seeing you looking so well is an enormous relief.'

Howard *did* look well. That wasn't his problem. The twist of his lips was masked by the slight droop on one side of his face.

'It's such a long drive...' Petra looked at her watch. 'Next time, maybe I'll stay overnight with Alyssa, and we can have a really good talk.'

Howard opened his mouth to speak, but only managed a few jumbled, incoherent sounds. Clearly the idea was engendering a strong emotion, which made it more difficult for him to concentrate and form the words he needed. Will saw a slight movement of Howard's left hand, the familiar over-to-you gesture that he used in business meetings.

'Everyone appreciates your having come so far. I know that Alyssa's been struggling to find some time to herself and she's been able to relax this afternoon, knowing you're here to visit.' Will tried to tactfully steer Petra away from the idea.

'Of course. We all need a little me time.' Petra nodded sympathetically. 'Maybe I shouldn't bother her. I could send her a box of fruit or some flowers, perhaps. Or something for the bath...'

'Good idea!' Automatic speech—the everyday phrases that were said without thinking—was often unimpaired by aphasia and it was sometimes startling to hear Howard speak so fluently. Even Will jumped a little, and Petra's face was a picture of astonished delight.

'That's what I'll do then, Howard. A bath before bedtime with a few favourite luxuries always helps me sleep...' She was chattering nineteen to the dozen again, and Howard seemed to relax a little. Goodbyes were said, kisses were blown in Howard's direction and then suddenly the room fell silent.

Will waited. Howard was making the difficult connections between thought and the physical process of speech, and no doubt he'd be saying what was on his mind when he was ready.

'She…means…well.' The three words were carefully modulated. Howard's therapist had been teaching him to slow down and space his words out, beating time with his hand. The technique was clearly working.

'She seems very concerned for you.' Will supplied the words that he guessed Howard might be looking for. 'Maybe a little too much of the talking *at* you and not *with* you?'

Howard rolled his eyes and nodded. Sometimes actions did speak louder than words.

'Anything you want me to do?' Will waved his hand, dismissing his last question as far too broad. 'Sorry. Would you like me to get someone to mention that she needs to give you a bit more time to put what you want to say together? Kindly, of course, so as not to hurt her feelings.'

Howard nodded. He didn't get away with that with the staff here, they'd wait until he answered, even if it was just a *yes*. 'You…'

'You'd like *me* to call her? Maybe give her an update on your therapy and the techniques they're using to help you speak again?'

'Yes!'

Automatic speech again. Will had heard it before, many times, but he was still getting used to hearing it from a friend. Those sudden glimpses of how Howard had spoken before the stroke, when now he had to struggle to frame his words.

'Okay. I'll speak to Alyssa and get her number. Now that she's seen you I'm sure she has a lot of questions, and I'll do what I can to answer them.' Howard had no doubt thought all of this through already. It was a fine line between putting words into his mouth and checking that Will understood his intentions properly, but this time the process worked and Howard nodded.

'And I'll be tactful.'

Howard gave a short laugh, his raised eyebrow saying that he'd expect nothing less from Will. Tact. Kindness. Making out that everything was okay, even though his own life felt as if it were falling apart. He and Lark made copious use of email, but he hadn't actually laid eyes on her for the last two weeks. The gnawing pain seemed worse every day, and Will knew from experience that it wasn't going to get better any time soon.

A smiling nurse wheeled a tea trolley towards them. 'Would you like a drink, Howard?'

The nurses here knew exactly how to approach each patient. Every stroke was different, and each person had different physical or cognitive damage to contend with. Howard could deal with one question at a time much better than a whole string of choices.

'Yes. Thank you.' Howard got the words out and smiled up at the nurse.

'Tea or coffee, then?'

'Tea…' Howard clearly wasn't finished yet and the nurse waited quietly. 'Thank you, Marie.'

He got a luminous grin in return. 'Nice one, Howard, you're welcome. One cup of tea coming up. You want something, Will?'

'Tea would be great, thank you.'

Biscuits were offered and accepted, and Marie gave a cheery wave as she wheeled the trolley out of the room. No doubt the next person would be expected to practise whatever skills their stroke had robbed them of, as well.

'How is…work?' Clearly, the matter was of some importance to Howard and he'd been practising the phrase.

'I thought we'd decided that you could do with a break from

that, Howard.' Will shot him a reproachful look, and got one back in return. 'Okay. You're not going to stop wondering, just because I don't talk to you about it, are you?'

Howard shook his head pointedly.

'In that case…' Will wondered whether *Everything's fine* might wash, and decided it wouldn't. 'Lark and I are taking one day at a time. We've been through everything that was on your desk and it's just whatever comes in, now. I'm not sure either of us realised just how much you deal with in the course of a working day, but we're managing.'

'Any…questions?'

'Not at the moment. But we'll ask if we do have any. Is that okay?'

Howard nodded emphatically. Maybe the strategy of not bothering him with anything that was going on at work was beginning to outlive its usefulness. He was kept pretty busy with his therapy, and fatigue was a normal after-effect of a stroke, but Will imagined that he would have concerns about his work too, if he were in Howard's shoes.

'All right. I'll email Lark and we'll get together a list of questions…' Will amended the thought. 'One of her famous yes/no decision sheets, maybe.'

'Yes. Good.' That seemed to satisfy Howard, but when Will opened his mouth to reply he waved his hand impatiently. There was more, obviously.

'You…' Howard grimaced, struggling for words that wouldn't come. 'Email?'

Right. There was clearly nothing wrong with Howard's perceptive abilities, and Will found himself wishing that they didn't have to go in this direction.

'Yeah. We've both been pretty busy, naturally, and we're finding that being in the office on different days has helped. I haven't seen much of her in the last couple of weeks.' For that, read *nothing*. Now Will was groping in the dark for the right words, because the idea of living without Lark left him wondering how he could make any sense of his future.

Howard nodded, taking a sip of his tea. 'Trustees…?'

Yeah. Good question. Happily, things seemed to have settled a bit on that front. 'They've been great. Sir Terence is looking to explore other avenues at the moment, and Uma's taken over as Chair of the Board. She's been great, really supportive of both of us.'

The mention of Uma Desai's name mollified Howard a little. Clearly he'd been wondering exactly what was going on, and the suspicion that he'd done more to protect him and Lark than they ever knew solidified into certainty.

'Don't…' Howard frowned, lost for words again, and then shook his head.

'We can come back to that.' Will leaned back in his chair, picking up his tea. Relaxing and then coming back to what he wanted to say often seemed to help.

But Howard didn't want to let go of the thought just yet. He picked up the pencil and pad that lay on the table next to him and started to write, then scribbled the words out angrily when he saw that they weren't making any sense. Yet another of the effects of the stroke—Howard could read with understanding and, being left-handed, he could manipulate a pencil, but the aphasia prevented him from writing coherently.

'Do…not…allow…any…' Howard paused and Will waited. 'Nothing…to…get…in…the…way.'

The careful separation of each word seemed to give particular emphasis to them, and they hit Will with such force that he almost dropped his teacup. As usual, Howard had thought about the situation and got right to the heart of it.

'You mean between Lark and me?' That was Howard's obvious meaning, but this time Will needed to confirm it for himself.

'Yes.'

'We shouldn't allow anything else to get in the way of our friendship, you mean?' It was good advice, but sadly a little late.

Howard nodded, reaching for his tea, but Will couldn't let this go.

'You're talking about the trustees?'

Howard shrugged. 'Any... Nothing.'

Clearly he was having difficulties with the word *anything*. But Will had the message, loud and clear. Howard knew them both well, and his insights had helped them to use their different approaches to good effect when they'd first begun to work together.

And it was a good thought. Will's past, Lark's past. The different roles that everyone had expected them to take, and which they'd obligingly clung to. All of the things that he needed now, and the things he'd tried to give Lark but hadn't been able to. If you took them out of the equation was there somewhere, a quiet place at the centre of it all, where they could meet?

It was too big a thought to be able to put anything into words. And Howard had said what he'd made his mind up to say, and seemed content now.

'Thanks for the advice. I'll make sure to act on it...'

CHAPTER FOURTEEN

LARK HAD BEEN FUNCTIONING. For the last two weeks she'd kept on top of her work commitments, and that was really all she needed to do. Going out wasn't something she'd done all that much in the past. In fact, it had usually been Robyn who had dragged her out for the evening.

Functioning was a good word for it. Numb, unthinking, like a cog in a massive machine. Trying not to think about Will, or how much it hurt to be apart from him, because she was sure that was the right thing to do. She'd written him a carefully worded email and he'd returned an equally carefully worded one. The roles that they'd both taken on had been smashed, and they couldn't be together while they were both beginning to explore what that meant. They should remain friends.

The last part of that was a piece of blue-sky optimism on both their parts. Friends would be an agonising reminder of all they'd lost. At the moment, even seeing Will's name on her email list made her heart jump, and seeing him would be far too much to bear. Their fragile working relationship needed to continue, for the time being, anyway. But Lark had already explored the possibility of increasing her hours working as an ambulance paramedic, and as soon as Migraine Community Action didn't need her any more she'd be gone. There would be no working over Will, or under him, or next to him.

Robyn and Matt drove down for one of their semi-regular

Sunday meet-ups, and her sister looked around the sitting room, grinning.

'Love the new colours. Very you. Warm and soothing...'

'And bold.' Matt added his opinion.

'Yeah, definitely bold,' Robyn agreed.

'You think so?' The warm and soothing part fitted in with Lark's picture of herself, but she'd never reckoned on bold. Of the two of them, bold more nearly described Robyn.

'Absolutely. I wouldn't think of painting a sitting room this colour, but now that I can see it it's stupendous. When did you have the time to do all this? I know you've been pretty busy at work.'

'Will helped me.' The words slipped out before Lark could stop them. That was the trouble with actually talking to people face to face, her ever-present thoughts about Will were a lot more difficult to disguise.

'No!' Robyn yelped in amusement. 'You mean you had that gorgeous hunk of manhood in your sitting room in a pair of overalls?'

'Hey! Do I have to worry?' Matt grinned.

'Of course not. He's not my type.' Robyn shot her new husband a dazzling smile. 'You're my type. And you're great with a paintbrush as well.'

'Thank you.' Matt looked around the room again. 'Does this mean we'll be getting the paint charts out again when we get home?'

'No, because our colours say it all about us. That gorgeous green that you didn't think was going to work in the sitting room but we had it because I wanted it. And the blue that you chose for the hall, which I didn't think I'd be able to bear, but I've discovered I rather like it after all. They're proof positive that we're madly in love, because we'd never have said yes to them for any other reason.'

Matt thought for a moment. 'True. Good point.'

'And Lark's colours are bold and brave. With a lot of warmth.'

'Bold's not me, Robyn.' Lark tried to laugh the idea off. It hurt, because if she'd been bolder then maybe she could have cut through her uncertainties and fears, and found a way to stay with Will.

'But it is. Really. You're a paramedic and you help run a charity. You've written academic papers and...' Robyn reached for Lark's hand. 'I couldn't have achieved half of what I've been able to do without you.'

'That's not true. Your achievements belong to you, not me.'

'You didn't see what it was like at home, Lark. Mum and Dad were so fearful, and there was so much conflict, so many arguments. And then, remember that weekend when you turned up, sat everyone down at the kitchen table and gave us a plan that we could all live with? That was a way forward for me, and one for Mum and Dad as well, only it took them longer to really come to terms with it. I reckoned that if you could be that bold, then I could stop listening to all of Mum and Dad's fears, and be bold too.'

'I... I don't know what to say...' Lark reached over to hug her sister.

'Have I said the wrong thing?'

'No. It was the right thing, and I'm happy that you feel that way.' It was too late though. The time for being bold, for believing in herself and hanging on to the love she'd lost, was gone now.

'Um...' She heard Matt clear his throat. 'Sorry to interrupt... But is the oven meant to be smoking like that?'

'No!' Robyn yelped, and Matt sprang to his feet and hurried into the kitchen. Smoke plumed upwards as he opened the oven door, and he drew out the casserole dish that contained their lunch, carefully peeling back the foil lid.

'I think that's... I can't actually tell what it is, but it's beyond saving. Perhaps I should open a window.' Matt turned the corners of his mouth down.

'Never mind. We'll go out for lunch, shall we? My treat.' Robyn grinned.

The heavy despair that had been weighing Lark down seemed to lift suddenly. 'Yes, let's do that. There's a new place next door to the coffee shop we used to go to that I've been meaning to try...'

Bold. It was the kind of word that could change a life, and when Robyn and Matt had left Lark was still turning it over in her head. She sat down at the kitchen table and opened her laptop, the impulse to reach out impossible to ignore.

Then she saw it. Before she'd had a chance to think, she'd clicked on Will's name in the list of unread emails. The message wasn't a long one, just two paragraphs inviting her to meet with him next weekend. He thought that lunch, somewhere out of town, might be easier for both of them.

It was the first time that either of them had alluded to anything being easier, because that implied that it might be hard. And for Will, the man who always tried to make out that everything was okay, it was practically outrageous. She snapped her laptop shut, as if that might create some distance between her and the email and allow her to breathe again.

Bold. She opened the laptop again, staring at Will's email. Then typed a few lines, saying that she thought a meeting would be a good idea, and did he have any thoughts about where they might do it. Then she read it over twice and pressed *send* before she had a chance to read it again for a third time.

Will wouldn't be sitting watching his email on a Sunday evening, and there was no point in staring at the screen waiting. Lark walked over to the coffee machine and then decided that she wanted tea and flipped the kettle on. Over the bubble of boiling water she heard the distinctive ping that announced she had new mail.

She wouldn't even look. It was just another spam email. But when Lark returned to the screen to shut her laptop down, there was Will's name again, right at the top of the list.

Tunbridge Wells station at noon on Saturday. It was a bit of a trek, but getting right out of London seemed sensible. Whatever happened in Tunbridge Wells probably stayed there, and if something *did* go wrong then they could leave that behind them.

Her fingers shaking, she typed a line to say that the time and place sounded good, and that she'd be there. Then Lark closed her laptop and put it away in a drawer in the sitting room where she couldn't see it. Even so, visions of Tunbridge Wells were circling her thoughts like a pack of lions...

The week had been ordinary. Will's emails had been just the same, pleasant and businesslike, and Lark's replies had been the same. She'd spent an inordinate amount of time thinking about what to wear on Saturday, and then he'd emailed and said that he had somewhere in mind that involved a short walk, and that a pair of sturdy shoes might be in order. Lark decided not to ask, and that jeans and a nice top would probably be more appropriate than the dress she'd had in mind.

She'd missed breakfast and spent the whole of the train journey to Tunbridge Wells staring at the pastry she'd bought at the station, and telling herself that it was okay to feel nervous, but she mustn't show it when she met Will.

He was leaning against his car in the station car park. Jeans that fitted like a glove and a dark blue sweater, which would no doubt complement the colour of his eyes perfectly when she got close enough to see them. But she had to forget all of that, because suddenly Lark knew exactly why she was here. Loving Will meant that she wanted him to be happy, and she had to be bold enough to fight for his future, whatever it might cost her.

Will smiled, looking uncharacteristically nervous, and she smiled back. He opened the car door, and Lark got in. They drove in silence, taking the main road out of the town and then upwards towards the top of one of the surrounding hills.

'Such a lovely view.' Perhaps he was heading for a restaurant on the look-out point that was signposted up ahead.

'Yeah. It's nice to get out of town sometimes.' Will smiled suddenly, as if he'd been wondering whether that was permissible. On the whole, Lark would rather he didn't as it made her stomach do a sudden loop-the-loop.

'Yes, it is. And it's a beautiful clear day.'

The reference to the weather silenced both of them. The road dwindled into a one-lane track and Will pulled to one side, onto a small hard-standing area at the top. Lark got out, looking around. There was a large cairn of stones, which marked the look-out, and a few benches. Apart from a couple of dog-walkers, trudging to the top of the hill and then turning to go back down again, it was deserted.

'We have to walk?'

Will had ducked back into the car, grabbing a zipped backpack. 'No, we're here.'

Okay. Lark followed him over to the bench that was furthest from the footpath that led up to the beacon and when he sat down she did so too, leaving as much space as she could between them.

The strong breeze seemed to pull at her, taking the city air from her lungs and replacing it with something fresher. Tugging at her hair, making Lark feel that she wanted to shake her head and knock out all the cobwebs that had formed. It was nice, but she was sure that wasn't what they were here for.

'I thought of making a booking at a quiet restaurant…' Will was looking at her intently, displaying none of the easy charm that had become his hallmark. 'But I wanted to bring you somewhere like this. I hope you don't mind.'

'It's nice. Refreshing.'

'And it's just the two of us.'

Alone with Will. Those moments in the night when he'd seemed like the only person in the world. Lark ruthlessly drove the thought from her mind.

'That's good. We can talk here.'

'I was hoping so.' Will took a deep breath. 'Just you and me, Lark. Nothing from the past, nothing from our families or our work. Maybe here we can find out what's really keeping us apart…'

She was staring at him, wide-eyed. The sun chose that moment to come out from behind a cloud, and Will was suddenly bathed in the golden gaze that he loved so very dearly. It gave him the courage to press on.

'I walked away from you without putting up a fight, and that was wrong of me. Because all we are, all we've ever done, is meet problems head-on and solve them together.'

'Because we're different, Will. Two points of view is better than just one in a work situation.'

'I don't accept that. How could I love you the way I do if we didn't have the same goals, the same way of looking at things?'

Too much. He'd said the word, and meant it, and he couldn't take it back now. A tear rolled down Lark's cheek.

'Don't say that, Will. Please.' There was pain in her voice, but that gave Will hope. If she couldn't love him then there would be no pain, and she probably wouldn't be sitting here next to him.

'Okay, I won't say it again. And if you want to go home I'll take you back to the station, whenever you say the word. But if you'll stay and fight for what we have, then here's the place to do it. Just you and me, with nothing and no one else.'

She was staring out across the magnificent view of the countryside that the hilltop afforded, although Will doubted that she could see much of it because Lark's eyes were full of tears.

'Robyn told me that I was bold, the other day.'

'That's the way I've always thought of you. You have a bold heart, Lark.'

She turned towards him, and Will saw something ignite in her eyes. 'We were wrong, Will. We let go of what we had without a fight. You've got coffee in that bag?' She nodded at the backpack that he'd put between them on the bench.

'Yes.' He fumbled with the zip, trying not to hope too much. 'And sandwiches.'

'Okay. I'll take the coffee. And then we'll do battle, shall we?'

They'd talked for hours. Broken it all down. They'd both struggled against the confines of the roles they'd found themselves in, but it had been difficult to let them go. Admitting that he was human wasn't quite so hard, because Lark had admitted she was human too. They'd made mistakes, and they'd been hurt.

But they could both move on from that. They could leave the hurt and the mistakes behind, and make new lives. Fresh and clean as a hilltop on a summer's day, always remembering the past but never being bound by it.

Will was falling in love all over again. With a bold, complex woman, who was fighting every step of the way. Finally, they were alone. Sitting on a bench together, with nothing to come between them.

Lark was silent for what seemed an age. And then she turned to him. 'I love you, Will.'

He'd promised he wouldn't say it again, but it was the only thing he wanted to tell Lark. Will hesitated and she grinned suddenly. 'You can say it if you want to now.'

'I love you, Lark. I want to love you every day...' Maybe it was a little too soon to mention the rest of his life.

'We'll keep each other honest, eh?' She leaned forward and kissed his cheek. It took Will's breath away.

'That was...'

'Different. Special...'

'Nothing between us...'

She smiled, laying her hand on his shoulder. 'You can kiss me back. If you want to.'

It was all that Will wanted. More than he'd even known he might want. 'I love you, Lark. I'll love you always.'

She gave him that brilliant, golden smile of hers. 'That's good, because I'm going to love you always too. Starting now.'

All he wanted was to feel her close. Suddenly bringing her here, to the top of a hill that was miles from home, didn't seem such a great idea. But for now, being here with Lark, feeling his heart open and fill the space that had previously contained only doubts...

'How long does it take to get back home by car?' Lark grinned up at him.

'A while. But I have an admission to make. I wasn't sure how this afternoon was going to go, and if it went badly... I didn't want you to have to choose between going home late on the train or having to take a lift from me.'

'So—let me get this right. You considered the possibility that we'd be arguing until we didn't have any breath left, and then I'd be stranded here and have to accept a lift from you. Which I might not want to do.' She kissed him again. 'And you planned for it. Will, that's so sweet of you. What did you do?'

'I booked a room in your name at a hotel, close to the station. It's all paid up for the night.'

'I've got a hotel room?' She flung her arms around his neck, kissing him again. 'Will, I just happen to have a hotel room. Would you consider coming back there with me?'

EPILOGUE

Six months later

TUNBRIDGE WELLS. Everyone had to have a special place, and Tunbridge Wells was theirs. It was two days before Christmas, and everything was beginning to shut down. Lark had booked a room in a small hotel she knew, close to Tunbridge Wells station.

'This is nice.' Will lay on the bed, his hands behind his head. 'A day to ourselves before we plunge into sharing our Christmas with two different families.'

'Your mum and dad aren't going to mind us turning up on Boxing Day and missing Christmas with them?' Lark was sitting in front of the mirror, applying her make-up, ready for a special dinner that Will had booked.

'No. Wait until you see the party they have planned for New Year. They're pretty happy that we'll be making that.'

'Good. It was nice of Howard and the trustees to insist that we take time off together over Christmas.' Lark turned, resting her arm on the back of her chair. She could spend any amount of time just looking at Will. 'Nothing's going to go wrong, is it?'

'Nothing. You've planned everything with your customary skill, and everyone knows exactly what they're supposed to be doing. Uma's approved the plan and she's even put herself on the list of people who'll accept a call. That's a first for the Chair of the Board of Trustees.'

'She's such a breath of fresh air. I have a good feeling about the charity's future.'

Sir Terence had resigned, after the other trustees had confronted him about a number of things he'd been keeping from them, and his general high-handedness. Howard was back at work part-time, and was improving every day. Recovery was a long road, but it was good to see how he thrived in the atmosphere of the charity's offices, where everyone gave him time to say what was on his mind. He'd proposed that he, Will and Lark would steer the charity into the future together, and that when he finally did retire they'd take over. But no one expected that he'd be stepping back just yet, there was still more for him to do.

'That's enough about work.' Will seemed to know what she was thinking. 'We're officially on our first holiday for six months. No one wants to hear from us until the New Year.'

'Best Christmas present ever.' Lark watched as he got up from the bed, buttoning his shirt and putting on his tie and jacket. 'Just you and me.'

'I have an idea.' He grinned at her. 'I'll need you to stand up, though.'

'So that when I fall into a swoon at the audacity of it, you can catch me?' Lark teased him, putting on her shoes and getting to her feet.

'You look so beautiful.' His hand skimmed the dark blue material of her dress.

'Is that the idea?' Lark stood on her toes to kiss him. 'I'd like to modify it a bit and include you in the definition.'

His blue eyes darkened suddenly and Will fell to one knee in front of her. 'That's not the idea, sweetheart.'

Lark's hand flew to her mouth. 'Is this… Will, is this what I think it is?' They'd talked about the future, made plans even, but this was different. Suddenly that future was here and now…

He reached into his pocket, taking out a ring that flashed in the light. 'Lark, will you marry me?'

'Yes…'

'That's not the whole plan. I want to love you for the rest of my life.'

'I'll love you too, Will. And we'll have children?'

'Absolutely. They were the next item on the list. They'll have your brains and…your looks as well.'

'They'll have our love, Will. That's what they'll really need.'

His eyes took on an imploring look. They were both shaking, and Lark hung onto his hand, knowing that Will would always be there for her.

'I only need one word. Say yes.'

'Yes, Will. Yes to everything that we can do together, for the rest of our lives.'

'Do you like the ring?' A note of uncertainty sounded in his voice.

She'd barely noticed it, because his eyes were so much more lustrous. But Lark held out her hand, and when he slipped it onto her finger the three diamonds sparkled.

'It's beautiful, Will.' She pulled him to his feet so that she could kiss him.

They'd made a promise and everything had changed. All of the things they'd talked about were no longer just hopes and dreams but had become real and tangible. Will's kisses were even more precious now.

'You're ready to go and celebrate?'

'Yes. And it'll be a definite yes for champagne, just in case you're wondering.'

Will kissed her. 'So it's *yes* to everything tonight, is it? Should I take advantage?'

'No.'

He chuckled. 'At last. I was beginning to worry that you were going to give me carte blanche on every idea I come up with.'

'Just keep coming up with ideas like this one, Will. Then I'll keep on saying *yes*.' This was rapidly shaping up to be the best night of Lark's life. And unless she was very much mistaken, there would be many more to come...

* * * * *

SNOWED IN WITH THE CHILDREN'S DOCTOR

LOUISA HEATON

MILLS & BOON

For Soraya, my editor, who helped me tremendously
to whip this story into shape!

CHAPTER ONE

'YES, THANK YOU very much, Joe. Well, for anyone who's got a window, it is snowing heavily here in the Midlands. A large area of low pressure has been moving up the country, bringing with it *unprecedented* amounts of snow, and it looks like we'll have this for at least the next twenty-four hours. Experts are predicting *over ten inches* of snow to fall over the next few hours, causing drifts, whiteouts and generally hazardous conditions. People are being advised *not* to travel, unless *absolutely* essential, and if you do, please take precautions. Visibility is down to just a few metres in some more rural areas, so do take care. Here at Clifton FM, we'll be bringing you all the latest weather reports on the hour, every hour...'

There was a burst of Christmas pop music, with jingle bells.

Nell reached forward to turn down the car radio. It was just what she'd expected to hear from the traffic report. The weathermen on television, before she'd set out, had advised against travel, too. But nothing—no snow, no blizzard, no unprecedented area of low pressure—was *ever* going to stop her from visiting Lucas's grave on the anniversary of his death.

It was just snow, after all. There'd never been this amount of panic over a bit of snow when she'd been a child. Not like today. It was health and safety gone mad.

So it was dark. Evening. Yes, the snow was heavy, and the wiper blades on her car were having trouble clearing the thick white flakes that blew against her windscreen. And, yes, she was creeping along in low gear, because drifts were already forming, sweeping up to meet hedgerows and tree trunks. And, yes, visibility was bad, and this part of the road didn't have streetlamps, but it was perfectly doable. All she had to do was stay on the road.

Which, she had to admit, was difficult, because she was on a remote country lane, near Elmbridge Manor and this was a notorious spot even on clear days. She'd lost count of how many times she'd read about an accident here when visibility was bad. Deep ditches on either side of the road, lots of bends and curves, like a sinuous snake… Normally the lane was edged with dark, spiny hedgerows, but tonight even those were covered in snow. Everything looked white.

It was difficult to judge, but she figured if she just stayed in the centre then everything would be—

A deer suddenly leapt over her car, hooves clipping the bonnet, and Nell screamed and yanked the wheel in panic, sending the car spinning on the ice beneath the snow and plummeting into the left-hand ditch with a sudden, sickening thud.

She found herself gasping, heart pounding, her entire world tilted by forty-five degrees, the back end of her car sticking up, her mad wipers going as fast as her heart.

'Oh, my God! Oh, my God…' Her whole body trembling, she burst into tears.

This was not how today was meant to end! She'd wanted to do what she always did. Lay flowers on Lucas's grave, then drive home and watch his favourite Christmas movie whilst wrapped up in a blanket, sobbing quietly to herself whilst she ate giant amounts of Lucas's favourite ice cream. Mint choc chip.

It was something she'd done the first year after losing him, on the anniversary of his death. Without thinking. Doing the things that he'd enjoyed in a bid to feel closer to him. To pretend that he was near. And now it had just become a thing. She'd done it last year, too, and today she'd known for sure what she was going to do because she recognised it as a routine. A self-soothing ritual that marked the day of his passing.

She'd made it to the cemetery. Laid a wreath at his grave, staring at his name etched into the stone as the thick flakes had swarmed around her in the strong winds. How long she'd stood there she didn't know. Only when the cold had begun to penetrate her bones, and her toes and fingers had gone completely numb, had she walked back to her car and begun the drive home.

And now she and the car were stuck in a muddy, icy ditch in the middle of nowhere, miles away from home and with no idea how she'd get there.

Nell searched blindly for her phone, but it had fallen from its place in the middle of the console and into the passenger footwell. She unclipped her seatbelt and leant forward to reach for it, cursing and swearing quietly until her fingers grasped its leather cover and she pulled it to her, looking for the small card that held the details of her breakdown cover.

She'd never called them before, but she'd seen an advert on the television for them recently, telling their customers that they'd be treated like family and that if you were a woman, stranded alone, then you'd be made a priority customer. She hoped that would be true as she dialled the number, listening to the robotic voice telling her all the options before she finally got through to a human being.

'Oh, thank God! Yes, I've had an accident and my car's in a ditch. A deer leapt across the road.'

Had it been a deer? She could have sworn it was a reindeer,

complete with jingle bells, now that she thought about it, but that couldn't be right. She'd not been drinking, so why would she think it had jingle bells?

'I'm by myself...can you get someone out to me?'

She'd already tapped in her membership number, but the young man called Evan, on the other end, apologised. He told her that because of the extreme weather they didn't have anyone free to help her right now, but someone should be with her within a few hours.

'A few hours? What am I supposed to do whilst I wait? Freeze to death?'

'I'm so sorry, Miss Bryant, but we simply don't have enough technicians free. As I'm sure you can appreciate, with this freak weather we're having, the demands on our services are unprecedented.'

Unprecedented. There was that damn word again. She'd got sick of hearing it during the Covid pandemic and now it seemed people used it all the time.

'Do you have anything in the vehicle to keep you warm?'

She had a blanket. But with the engine off and all that snow outside how warm would she be?

'Maybe...'

'Are there any properties nearby that you could go to? Knock at the door and see if they could help?'

She shook her head. 'No. This area's remote.'

She knew she was on a lane at the rear of the Elmbridge Manor estate, but there were a few acres between her and the house and she couldn't imagine tramping through all that snow just to speak to some snobby butler, or something. And there were obviously wild deer around here! Also, if she remembered correctly, a lake in the grounds somewhere.

What if she were to fall in? Because the snow would have

covered that, too, over the ice that must have frozen it over in the preceding weeks.

'Well, then we advise you stay with your vehicle, Miss Bryant, until help arrives.'

Nell ended the call, feeling so angry she wanted to throw the phone back into the passenger footwell. But she didn't want to break it. She might need it again.

The breakdown service had been useless! But, to be fair, it was probably to be expected. She had been warned against coming out in this blizzard and yet she had stubbornly refused to let a bit of bad weather stop her. It was hugely important to her that she visited Lucas on important days. His birthday. Easter—which he'd loved. Halloween. Christmas. The anniversary of the day that he'd passed.

She couldn't look after him any more, but she could look after his gravesite. Keep it neat. Tidy. Weed-free. With fresh flowers whenever she could. He wasn't here any more, but she felt close to him there. Felt that she could talk to him still. It gave her comfort. She was still of a mind that her journey had been essential. A mother needing to be with her son. What could be more important than that?

But now...? She sat in the dark car as it filled with shadow, the snow blocking out the available moonlight. How long she sat there she didn't know. Thirty minutes? Forty?

She glanced at her phone.

Just over an hour!

The chill had penetrated the car and outside looked just as bad as ever. Should she get out and walk? Try and stick to the road? If she walked in the direction she'd been headed, she'd come to a house in about two miles...

She vaguely became aware that the inside of her car had brightened slightly, as if another car was approaching from behind. Nell turned to peer through the rear windshield, but the snow was thick upon the glass, allowing only glimmers of light through the flakes and frozen crystals. Could she hear an engine?

The light stilled and she heard the noise of a car door slamming and then the heavy thud of footsteps. It looked as if whoever it was had a torch. Light flashed this way, then that. She heard a curse. Maybe someone stumbling.

Should she lock her doors? It could be anyone. Her fear manifested itself first. This was such a remote road and she hadn't seen any other cars for ages. It would be the perfect spot to take advantage of a woman on her own. But her fear was balanced equally with the desire to get home as quickly as possible. And if she was inclined to believe that someone was coming to attack her, surely she ought also to believe that this could be her knight in shining armour.

Or dame in shining armour...

Her heart hammered in her chest as the person outside got closer and a darker shadow passed over her car door. Whoever it was looked tall. Powerful.

A sudden rap on the window made her jump.

Of all the stupid things in all the world to be doing in weather like this, Dr Seth James, Lord Elmbridge, had not expected to be out rounding up escaped reindeer. On nights like these, when the windchill factor had dropped the temperature considerably, and every gust felt as if the world was trying to take a bite out of his face, he'd have much preferred to be indoors, before a roaring fire in the drawing room of his private quarters, enjoying a nice glass of his finest whisky.

But, no. The heavy snowfall had spelled the death of the fencing at the reindeer enclosure. Its posts had given up the ghost and begun to lean heavily, and before he'd known it, he'd had a call from Ned Hoskins, who lived at Hilltop Farm, to say that he'd got reindeer wandering about his cowsheds and did he want to fetch them before they made it to the village?

The reindeer had been Granny's idea. She'd thought it would be a fine final touch to the Christmas Experience they offered at Elmbridge Manor. They had Santa, and a grotto, and even some well-paid elves to help corral the children who would wait in line with their parents to meet St Nicholas and his endless sack of free gifts, and she'd suggested that this year they have reindeer too. Decked out with jingle bells. The whole shebang.

And he'd agreed. Stupidly. Not realising how much extra work the reindeer would be. But then again, why would he? He was a paediatrician, not a reindeer farmer, and when he'd hired the reindeer for the festive season he'd thought he'd also hired an experienced reindeer wrangler. Only Sven had finished early for the day, when the snow had begun to fall thick and heavy, citing that he wanted to be back home with his heavily pregnant girlfriend, just in case she went into labour.

Fair enough. Seth remembered the anxiety he'd felt himself as Dana's due date had got closer and closer, and they'd not even had to worry about snow. Dana had been pregnant through summer, complaining only about the heat.

And so, instead of warming himself before that roaring fireplace, he'd instead donned his thickest coat, scarf, gloves and boots and headed out into the cold to hitch the trailer to the back of his car.

He had not been happy about it. Every newsreader, every weatherman, had warned people about going out in these conditions, but what else was he to do? Let the reindeer terrorise the local village? If they'd already made it to Hilltop, then they were only a mile or so away from people's homes, and he didn't want to imagine the calls the local police would get when the villagers started to notice giant deer in their back gardens.

And he didn't want the animals being darted by animal control and taken away—not when he'd paid for them and they were in his care.

It had been a difficult hour or two at Hilltop. Up there, exposed to the most biting winds of this blizzard, he and Ned, with the help of his sheepdogs, Buzz and Rex, had managed to round up eight of the nine reindeer into the back of his trailer, which he'd filled with warming hay and straw. One was still missing, and hadn't been found anywhere.

Ned had invited him in for a warming hot cocoa, but Seth had declined. He'd wanted to get back. Put the reindeer in the stables opposite the horses, so that tomorrow he could work on the fencing and get that sorted. He'd just have to hope the ninth reindeer showed up somewhere.

It had been a long day. He hadn't been able to feel his fingers. His toes. His nose had to be as red as Rudolph's…

And then, to top off the perfect evening, he'd been driving back to Elmbridge and had got to that sharp turning at the rear of the estate, the part of the road that had taken Dana's life, when he'd seen the fading taillights of a car in the left-hand ditch.

A sick feeling had made his stomach feel like lead. He'd stopped and sat there for a moment. Staring at the car that was already half covered by snow and in a drift, frozen in place. It had been as if he couldn't move. As if he'd been thrown back in time, pinned in place by fear and dread.

But then his medical instincts had kicked in.

Someone might need help.

They were most likely okay…had just driven off the road, that was all.

Switching on his own hazard lights, he'd grabbed a torch from the glove box and got out into the blizzard, wincing at the icy touch of every snowflake blasting into his face. He'd felt the snow gathering on his face. On his beard. His eyebrows. His shoulders. Felt the cold sinking in through the thick woollen coat that was now splashed with mud.

He'd tramped through the snow, wondering who on earth had been stupid enough to come out in this weather when the whole world and his wife had been telling everyone to stay indoors except for emergencies.

When his boot had slipped on some hidden ice and he'd fallen to one knee, he'd cursed and sworn like a sailor, before getting to his feet once again and tramping angrily over to the car.

Now he rapped the torch against the driver's window.

At first he thought that the driver must have walked off to look for help, but then the car door cracked open an inch.

'Hello…?'

The thickness of the blizzard stopped him from seeing who was inside, but the voice sounded like a woman's.

'Are you all right? Can I help?'

Okay, so maybe he didn't sound as friendly as he'd wanted to. But he was exhausted, cold, muddy, and now his knee hurt from the slip on the ice. He just wanted to be at home with Granny and Olly. He didn't get to see much of his son, what with work, and now that he'd started his first year at school he'd been hoping to spend some quality time with him. Not be out at all hours rounding up reindeer and helping a woman out of a ditch.

The door closed slightly. 'Who are you?'

He still couldn't see her face in the darkness and through the blizzard, but he really wanted this to be over sooner rather than later.

He shone the torch on his own face. 'I'm a doctor. I work at the local hospital.'

'I don't recognise you.'

Seth frowned. What the hell was that supposed to mean? 'It was my first day today and it's a big hospital. Who are you?'

Two could play at this game.

'I'm a phlebotomist.'

A vampire. One of those people you could call on to come and take blood and place IVs because doctors were too busy to do everything.

'What are you doing out in this storm? Don't you know it's dangerous?' he asked, just as the wind howled in response, whipping around him in a gust designed to lift him off his feet.

But Seth was tall and broad and, he thought, strong. It would take more than a blizzard to move him.

'You think I'm stupid? Of course I know.'

'Then why are you out?'

There was a brief pause, then the door was pushed open and a woman in a long puffer coat, beanie and thick scarf attempted to climb out of the car.

But her car was at an odd angle and it was not an elegant disembarkation.

Seth stifled a wry smile as he watched her awkwardly clamber out, cursing and muttering to herself as she tried to do so with dignity. He'd seen more graceful newborn giraffes. He proffered a hand, but she glaringly refused to take it.

'Do you not have roadside assistance?' he asked.

She turned to glare at him. 'They can't make it—they have no one free.'

'How long have you been here?'

'Long enough to think I'd be found years into the future trapped in the permafrost.'

'And you didn't go for help?'

She stared at him as if he was an idiot. 'From where, exactly? Are you familiar with this area?'

'A little.'

'Then you'd know there isn't anywhere to ask for help from around here—unless you fancy tramping a mile or so across unknown ground to beg for help from some crusty landowner.'

Crusty landowner? Hmm...

'So you thought you'd take a drive in the worst weather this area has experienced in a decade. Pray tell me what was so important you had to come out in this?'

'*You're* out. Why are *you* out?'

She peered past him to his four-by-four and trailer. But he could hardly tell her he was out rounding up lost reindeer. It sounded crazy even to him.

'Rescue mission. You?'

She didn't meet his gaze. She looked uncomfortable. 'Well, as much as I'm enjoying this inquisition at the roadside, I'm wondering if you can you help me or not?'

He could. 'I've got ropes.'

She nodded. 'Wonderful.'

'We can attach them to the rear of your vehicle and pull you out.'

'If it's not too much trouble.'

It was. He'd wanted to be warm and back home with his son by now. He gave a mock bow. 'You're welcome.'

She didn't seem thankful. Not really. She seemed pissed off—which was fine, because so was he. He still had no idea what she was doing out on a night like this. Clearly it wasn't a good reason or she would have told him. Instead, she'd evaded the question, which made him think that she'd thought that her errand—most likely something trivial or stupid—was too important to put off. She'd probably popped out to get a pint of milk.

Muttering under his breath, he fetched the ropes and began to attach them to both vehicles. He was aware of her standing back and watching him, hands crossed over her chest, rubbing at each arm as she jiggled to keep warm in one spot. It was hard to tie the knots with no feeling in his fingers, but somehow he managed it, and then he told her to stand back whilst he got back into his own vehicle and began to reverse, hoping to pull her car from the ditch.

It was a struggle. The snow had grown thick and deep around her car, and because of the width of the lane and the fact that he had the trailer behind his own vehicle, he couldn't get the angle he needed to pull the car out. It just kept sliding back through the ditch.

It was pointless.

After much toing and froing, he let out a heavy sigh and got out of his vehicle. 'It's no use. I can't get it free.'

She looked at him, frowning above her thick knitted scarf, already rimmed with snow. 'What am I going to do?'

'Anyone you can call to pick you up?'

'No.'

Damn. He couldn't leave her out here, stranded. 'I can drive you back to my home. You can stay warm, let people know you're all right. Sort something out...' He shrugged.

She peered at him. 'You could be anyone. An axe murderer.'

He showed her his empty hands. 'No axe.'

'A normal murderer, then.'

Really? He didn't have to put up with this crap. He was

cold! He wanted a warm bath. Not to be dealing with this prickly phlebotomist.

'Fine. I'll see you around.' He began to tramp back towards his car.

'Wait! Are you just going to leave me here?'

He turned. 'I offered you a lift. Shelter. If I recall, you're the one who'd rather stay here. And, as warm as your manner is, it's not enough to make me want to stay with you.' He got into his vehicle, slammed the door.

She came over to his window and knocked on it.

He pressed the button to lower it. 'Yes?'

She looked torn. 'Well…where do you live? Close by?'

He nodded. 'Pretty close.'

'Where?'

'Elmbridge Manor.'

A frown and then a raising of her eyebrows. 'The Manor?'

He nodded again. Smiled. 'Crusty landowner—at your service.'

CHAPTER TWO

HE WAS NOT a crusty landowner. He looked like anything but. Tall. Dark. Bearded. His black coat billowing around his legs as he'd stood there in the road as if he was about to pull a broadsword, or click his fingers and conjure up a ball of flame.

But he wasn't a fantasy swordsman or a mage—he was a doctor, he'd said. Looking like that! He wore black leather gloves. The kind you'd see on a bad guy in a movie, instantly marking him out as a hitman or someone who didn't want to leave any trace.

But he certainly left an impression—that was for sure.

As she stood there, in a blustery whirl of snow, cold to her bones, with numb ears, fingers and toes and God only knew what else that would need to be thawed, she tried to decide if she should get in the vehicle with him. And as her teeth began to chatter she figured that if he was going to kill her, then he would have done so by now, and he most certainly would not have spent a considerable amount of time trying to pull her car out of the ditch.

But she had insulted him. 'Crusty landowner', she'd said. She was sure, if it had been daylight and not so cold, he would have seen that was making her blush with embarrassment.

'I'm sorry.'

He flashed a momentary polite smile. 'In or out, blood-sucker. I want to get home.'

Bloodsucker, huh?

'Fine.' She stalked around the bonnet of his vehicle, stumbling in a particularly deep spot of snow, and yanked open the passenger door.

She met his gaze. Inside the car, his face had begun to thaw in the warmth from his car heater. The snow was gone from his facial hair and she could see his beard was as black as his hair. His eyes as dark as his soul. Or so it would seem. Her imagination was running rampant.

She got in, closing the door behind her, putting on the seat-belt and then leaning forward to rub her frozen fingers and hands together in front of the heating vent. It was almost pain-ful, having the feeling return, and as the vehicle began to move away from her accident site she risked another glance at her dark-eyed saviour.

'Who were you rescuing?'

He frowned. 'What?'

'You said you were out on a rescue mission. Who were you rescuing? Or do you just drive around in snowstorms, looking for damsels in distress?'

'It's not a who—they're a what,' he answered grimly.

Nell frowned. 'What?'

'Reindeer. I was rescuing some reindeer that had escaped their enclosure.'

Reindeer? So maybe I wasn't hallucinating!

'Were they by any chance wearing jingle bells?'

He risked a glance at her. 'Why do you ask?'

'Because one of them leapt over my bloody car and caused the damned accident in the first place! I should sue you!'

'Sue *me*? What were you doing out and about in this weather? Did your nails need doing?'

His sarcastic tone did nothing to appease her. 'Don't be ridiculous!'

'Then why were you out?'

She clammed up. She did not have to explain herself to this man. Even if he was helping her.

They drove in silence for a while. The snow was blowing onto the windscreen. And then he was indicating a right turn and pulling past two enormous gatehouses before heading up a long, partially cleared driveway to a house that she had only ever seen from the road.

Elmbridge Manor. A vast mansion of a house. Beautifully lit up with white fairy lights and multitudes of lit Christmas trees.

She wanted to gaze upon it and soak it all in, or even ask some questions, but she wouldn't give him the satisfaction. All she wanted was to get warm, call her breakdown service and let them know where she was, and how they could contact her when they finally arrived at the scene of her accident. Then she could go home and never see this man ever again! Because, like he said, it was a big hospital with hundreds of staff. They might never cross paths again.

He pulled up in front of the main doors. 'Ring the bell.'

'Don't you have a key?'

He smirked. 'I need to get the reindeer into their stables, which are at the rear of the property, so would you please ring the bell? Jeffreys will let you in.'

'Jeffreys?'

'The butler.'

'You have *a butler*?'

'Who else would open the door?'

A wry smile crept across her face. 'Right. Well, thank you,

Mr Lord of the Manor, for your assistance. I will get out of your way as fast as I possibly can.'

'I will enjoy that very much, Miss I Should Never Have Been Out In This Weather.'

She got out and smirked at him before slamming the car door, hoping the vehemence of her slam would tell him just what she thought of him. As he drove away, she was very tempted to follow up with a hand gesture, but the wind was howling and she was getting cold again, so she did as he'd asked her and hurried to the doorway and rang the bell.

She thought for a moment that no one would answer, and that perhaps this was all an elaborate joke and maybe there were hidden cameras somewhere, when the door swung open and she saw a butler dressed in smart black and white peering at her in enquiry.

Jeffreys led her into a vast hall with a chequerboard floor and the tallest Christmas tree she had ever seen. Adorned with lights and baubles in tasteful rose golds and soft pinks, it looked like something she'd see in a huge American department store.

Beyond that were vast hanging tapestries and two suits of armour guarding a sweeping staircase that wouldn't have looked out of place on the *Titanic*. Her gaze was drawn up along the fir-and-pinecone-laden balustrades, past a multitude of oil paintings of lords and ladies of old, to the vast arched dome of the ceiling, adorned with carvings and grotesques, a fresco of a hunting scene, and the biggest crystal chandelier she had ever seen in her entire life.

It was so big it would probably take up her entire bedroom, and it put the cheap, fringed flowery lampshade that she'd bought for her living room in a sale to shame.

'Wow.'

Briefly, she forgot how cold she was. How damp her clothes felt. Awe and wonder were the order of the day.

The grumpy doctor lived *here?*

She'd always been curious about this place, driving past it each day on her way to work. Elmbridge Manor was open to the public on most days of the year, and although she'd always told herself that one day she'd join a tour and take a look around, see how the other half lived, she had never quite organised the time. She'd been so busy with Lucas, and then he'd got sick, and then her marriage had broken down after he had died.

After that there just hadn't seemed any point. She'd thrown herself into her work, taken on extra shifts so she didn't have to stay at home alone, in her poky little flat. Listening to the silence. Living in that Lucas-free space. She already had so much missing from her life—she didn't want to see how rich other people's lives were compared to her own.

'May I take your coat, madam?' asked Jeffreys.

'Oh… Sure.'

Unused to such attention, Nell hadn't noticed the butler patiently waiting and watching her. She was going to just shrug it off, but then she paused as she saw Jeffreys was standing behind her to help her off with it. She blushed, embarrassed, and really not used to people serving her.

'Thank you. You're very kind.'

Jeffreys neatly folded her cheap puffer coat over his arm. 'Lord Elmbridge is unavailable at the moment, madam, but might I be allowed to show you into the drawing room?'

'Oh. Yes. Of course.'

Nell followed the silver-haired butler across the hall and through two large double doors into a room that was bigger than her entire flat. It was filled with baroque-inspired furniture, with walls lined in what appeared to be pale green silk, and her gaze was instantly drawn to the large fire crackling away beneath a huge stone mantelpiece.

'Would you like some refreshments, madam?'

'I wouldn't want to be any bother...'

'It's no bother, madam. Something warming, perhaps? Tea? Cocoa? Hot chocolate?'

Hot chocolate sounded amazing. She'd not had one since Lucas had been alive. 'Hot chocolate, please.'

Jeffreys gave a polite bow and disappeared from the room.

As she stood in front of the fire, hands out, enjoying the warm embrace of the flames, she let her gaze drift upwards to the portrait above the fireplace.

It was of an elderly gentleman, with white hair and thick white mutton chops either side of his frowning face. He wore wire-rimmed spectacles and at his feet lay two hunting dogs.

Peregrine Edward James, Fifth Lord Elmbridge, she mouthed, reading the inscription beneath.

'My husband,' said a woman's voice behind her.

Nell turned and smiled, blushing slightly. This woman probably had no idea who she was, or why she was standing in her drawing room. 'He looks a very fine gentleman.'

'He was a bloody awful man and I'm glad he's gone.'

Nell's mouth dropped open in amused shock.

'But portraits always make people look finer than they actually are.' The old woman smiled and hobbled towards her, using a cane. 'I'm Emily James. Dowager of this fine house. And you are...?' She peered up at her, with rheumy, kind eyes.

'Nell Bryant. I live in Clifton, but my car went into a ditch and a young man helped me out and brought me here.'

'Which young man?'

'Er...tall, dark hair. Bearded. Lives here?' she said, as if this might still be some joke and her rescuer was actually the groundskeeper, or something.

A warm smile crossed the Dowager's face. 'My grandson. Lovely boy. Heart of gold. Nothing like that one.' The Dowager indicated the painting again and then ambled over to one of the dark red sofas and slowly lowered herself onto it.

Nell stared at her in surprise, deciding she liked this older woman immensely.

'Do sit down, dear. You'll give me a crick in my neck.' The older woman pointed at the other sofa opposite her.

'I'm waiting for my breakdown people to arrive.'

'In this weather? You'll be lucky if you see them before morning.'

Nell's heart sank. Morning? The clock on the mantelpiece told her it was nearly eight o clock at night. She couldn't impose on these people for that long—it wouldn't be right.

'Maybe if I give them another ring...'

'Nonsense! Stay here tonight. There's no going anywhere—not in this storm.'

'I wouldn't want to impose.'

'You wouldn't be.'

'Well, only if you have the room. I'll sleep anywhere.'

'My dear, there are sixteen bedrooms in this place. We have more than enough room.'

She reached out and pulled a bellpull beside her chair. It must be connected to something in the staff quarters, because before she knew it, a maid had appeared in the doorway.

'Ava, my dear, would you prepare a guest room for Miss Bryant? She's going to be with us overnight.'

'Yes, my lady.'

Ava disappeared, just as Jeffreys entered with a silver tray upon which sat a large cup of hot chocolate. Beside it, in two small bowls, were some whipped cream and some tiny marshmallows.

'Thank you.'

'May I get you anything, my lady?' Jeffrey asked the Dowager.

'A whisky, please.'

'Of course, my lady.'

He went over to a drinks cabinet hidden within a large globe and quickly prepared a glass of whisky for the older woman. Then he disappeared again.

It was quite a marvel to experience such service! The closest experience Nell had had to someone serving her was if she sat in a café that had a waitress. To experience proper maid and butler service... It was amazing! But obviously not something that she ought to get used to. Lucas would have loved it... No doubt he would have been pulling on that bellpull to see how quickly someone would arrive.

A cloud must have crossed her face, because suddenly the Dowager was peering at her with interest. 'What's that you're just thinking about?'

'Oh, nothing...'

'Didn't look like nothing.'

The Dowager was astute. Her eyes might be rheumy, but they didn't miss a trick.

'Your grandson mentioned he's a doctor?' said Nell.

'Changing the subject? Okay, then. Yes. He's a children's doctor. A paediatrician.'

Nell had just been taking a sip of her hot chocolate and she felt the hot liquid burn her throat as she swallowed too fast in dismay. A paediatrician! Nell worked on the children's wards. She was specially trained to take blood from children and babies, having trained as a play specialist, too. He was going to be working on *her* wards?

She coughed, trying to clear her throat, her eyes streaming, as she struggled to breathe. They'd been after a new paediatrician for ages, and she'd known he'd be starting today, on her day off.

'And what is it *you* do?' asked the Dowager curiously.

'She's a leech,' said a now familiar voice from across the room.

Nell turned and stared as the man who'd rescued her from the roadside—grandson to the Dowager—entered the room, heading towards his grandmother. The billowing black coat was gone and now she saw a solidly built man, holding a steaming mug, wearing dark jeans and a black fisherman's jumper, stalking across the room. He bent low to drop a kiss upon the older woman's downy, wrinkled cheek, then stood in front of the fire, all tall and brooding, as he warmed his hands.

'A leech?' asked his grandmother.

'He means I'm a phlebotomist. I take people's blood,' she clarified.

'And she also goes out and drives in dangerous weather for no reason,' he mumbled as he sipped at his drink.

She glared at him. 'I was not out for no reason!'

'*Seth!* Is that any way to talk to our guest?'

Seth. So that was his name. Yes. He looked like a Seth. Like an Egyptian god. She could imagine him perfectly, striding about, bare-chested and bare-legged, with gold circlets on his upper arms, emphasising his muscles...

Or was that Set?

She didn't know. Couldn't remember exactly. She was getting confused. And something about him—maybe it was his arrogance—had her feeling...exasperated.

'My apologies,' he said low-voiced, without looking at her.

It didn't sound like an apology at all, and she bristled with a controlled anger that she refused to release out of respect for the fact that she was in someone else's house. A stranger's house. Elmbridge Manor! Certainly not somewhere she belonged.

She stood up, smiled at the Dowager. 'If you'll excuse me? I'll just make another call to my breakdown service.'

'Of course, dear.'

She shot a look at Seth, then left the room to stand in the massive entrance hall with its chequerboard floor.

The breakdown service call-handler—this time a young woman called Lisa—thanked her for her call updating them on her situation, and said that now she was safe and warm they would get someone to her car first thing in the morning, when the storm was expected to have passed.

It wasn't ideal. She had no idea how she would get home. Or even if her car would be rescued by the time she needed it to get to work. But she figured she would just go to her room here and hide away until it was time to leave.

Ending the call, she sucked in a deep breath, relaxed her shoulders and went back into the drawing room.

The Dowager and Seth stopped talking the second she entered.

'So, you're staying the night?' he asked, one black eyebrow raised.

'Yes. Your grandmother was kind enough to offer me a room. But don't worry. I'll be out of your hair by the morning.' Nell settled back into her chair and took a sip of her hot chocolate. It was warm and rich. The perfect sweet antidote to feeling cold.

'Ignore my grandson, dear. He can get grumpy when he hasn't eaten.'

'That's all right. I've dealt with worse,' replied Nell.

She noticed Seth frown.

'Maybe once he's had something to eat Seth could give you a tour? What do you say, Nell?'

'*Nell?*'

She looked at him. 'Yes. That's my name. It's short for Eleanor.'

He smirked. 'I prefer Leech.'

'I think Eleanor is a delightful name—and, again, don't be rude to our guest,' said his grandmother.

Nell smiled her thanks at the Dowager. 'I wouldn't want to bother Seth any more than I already have this evening.'

'Oh, pish! It's no problem at all. Is it, Seth?' the Dowager gave her grandson a look that brooked no argument.

Nell could have sworn she heard him growl.

He'd returned to Elmbridge Manor to look after his granny on two conditions. One, that he still be allowed to work part-time at the local hospital and two, that she stay out of his life and stop trying to fix him up with ladies she considered to be a good match.

Granny was sweet. Lovely and charming. But after Dana had died she had allowed him a mourning period of one year and then had begun to oh-so-sneakily start arranging things so that he ran into certain available, single, suitable women.

The first had been Lady Sarah Darling. The granddaughter of one of her bridge partners. He'd turned up for his granny's birthday dinner at Elmbridge Manor to find Lady Sarah awaiting him. All glossy-eyed and glossy-lipped. Though he'd tried to be polite, he'd found her dinner conversation about the politics of fashion to be completely uninteresting.

Last year when he'd visited, because his granny had had a fall and broken her hip, he'd found himself being pushed towards the private nurse she'd hired—Laura Jennings—who'd just happened to be the daughter of some business mogul. Granny had hoped that he and Laura would bond over the fact that they were both medics, but thankfully that was not to be. Laura had set him free of any obligation almost immediately by informing him that she knew her granny was trying to set them up together, but was asking him not to bother because she was into girls, not boys.

Happily, they'd enjoyed chatting and being friends, and he'd been let off the hook most gratefully.

He didn't want to be forced into a relationship. He had a lot of baggage. An estate to manage. His inheritance. And a son to look after. A son who'd lost his mother and was still getting used to that. There was absolutely no way in hell he was going to get involved with this Nell woman, no matter how pretty and doe-eyed she was.

The woman was infuriating, for a start. And a risk-taker. Going out in this storm! There was no way he was letting a woman like that anywhere near him or his son. The sooner she left Elmbridge Manor, the better.

Granny had disappeared up to bed, citing tiredness, but he knew her motivations. He'd seen the smile on her face as she'd retired and knew exactly what she was up to. What she was hoping would happen if she left the two of them alone.

Now she'd gone, Nell stood up, facing him. 'You don't have to give me a tour. I don't need it and I'm rather tired, too.'

'Fine. Goodnight.'

He stared back at her. Glad not to be spending any more

time with her than was necessary. If she thought he was going to insist on the tour, then she was wrong. Something about her irked him. Whether it was the stupidity of going out in this weather, her argumentative nature, or the rich darkness of her brown eyes, he wasn't sure. Maybe it was all three? He just wanted her gone so he could breathe again.

'You know, you're very rude. I just hope that your bedside manner makes you a much better doctor than you are a human being.'

He took another sip from his coffee, contemplating a sharp retort, but thought better of it. Because each time that she argued with him he felt a stirring within his blood that he didn't want to think too hard about.

He placed his now empty mug on the mantel and looked at her. 'It's late. I'm going to bed.'

Why was he suddenly furnished with images of her laying naked beside him, dark hair splayed over his pillow?

'I trust you'll be gone in the morning.' And he stalked past her, towards the door, thinking he'd reach it and be able to leave without hearing her retort.

Only he wasn't so lucky, and he paused, one hand on the door, as her words reached him.

'Too right. I don't want to stay here a moment longer than I have to.'

CHAPTER THREE

THE SEEMINGLY EVER-PRESENT Jeffreys escorted her to her guest room. Following him up the staircase that had caught her eye earlier, she passed portrait after portrait of the Lords Elmbridge and their ladies dressed in sumptuous rich clothes of velvet, silk and lace. The James family. Abraham James... Lady Emilia James... Thomas James...

They all seemed to have the same dark eyes that Seth had, so it felt as if every painting of his ancestors was staring at her and judging her in her torn jeans and the jumper she'd found in a bargain bin at the local charity shop as she passed.

The guest room had a plaque on the door. It was called The Blue Room, apparently, and when Jeffreys opened the door she saw why. The room had dark wood panelling all around, except for the wall that held a small fireplace with a crackling fire going. The carpet was a soft blue, as were the ceiling-to-floor drapes and the counterpane on the bed. The *four-poster* bed. She'd only ever seen those in movies.

Nell remembered to close her mouth quickly enough to turn and thank Jeffreys and wish him a good night.

When he'd closed the door, she'd stared at the bed—and then jumped on it, landing flat on her back, legs and arms splayed as she laughed and chuckled at finding herself in such a marvellous place! She was having a sleepover at Elmbridge Manor!

She stared up at the ceiling, then got up to explore, finding a small en-suite bathroom behind a door that looked like part of the wall. The bathroom had a shower stall, a toilet, and a large, sunken bath in the floor! Maybe she could have a quick wallow in that in the morning before she left?

It would be a shame not to take full advantage of the facilities.

She washed her face and brushed her teeth, with the brand-new toothbrush that she found on the side of the sink in a small marble jar, and then got into bed.

It was extremely comfortable and warm, and as she lay there in the dark, listening to the fire and to the wind still howling outside, she just knew she would have a good night's sleep.

'Goodnight, Lucas,' she said out loud, thinking of her son.

She might not have watched the movie he loved. She might not have eaten the mint choc chip ice cream. But she had managed to visit him. And, believing that he was always with her anyway, she just knew that he would have loved this room and this bed.

'I love you, sweet boy. I miss you. Sweet dreams.'

And she fell fast asleep.

She couldn't remember dreaming, but something woke her early in the morning. A sound?

Her eyes blinked open, adjusting slowly in the dark of the unfamiliar room, until she suddenly sat up with a start at the sight of a ghostly boy standing at the side of her bed, staring down at her, holding a teddy bear against his chest.

'What...? Who are you?'

She reached for the bedside lamp, struggling for the switch, nearly knocking it over in her fright, certain that once the light was on the ghost would go. Or maybe it was part of a dream? Lucas had used to wake her in the middle of the night all the time, and she had been thinking of him before she went to sleep.

But when she turned back the boy still stood there. Golden-haired, but with those same dark eyes she'd seen in Seth and all the James ancestors. Her heart pounded.

'Hello?'

The boy smiled at her. 'Hello. Who are you?'

He was so like Lucas! The colour of his hair... The way it was all mussed up, as if he'd just got out of bed and hadn't combed it yet... It was most unsettling.

'I'm Nell. Who are you?'

And then she heard a voice. Seth's voice. Calling in the corridors outside of her room.

'Olly? Olly?'

She looked at the boy, noticed his brief smile, then he chuckled and ran from the room.

Nell stared after him, her heart thudding strongly in her chest.

'There you are! What were you doing in that room?' she heard Seth say.

She pulled the covers up over her chest and stared at the semi-open door, hoping Seth and the boy would just go away and leave her alone. She didn't need this.

But there was a slight knock on her door and it swung open further. And Seth was suddenly standing there.

He looked just as dark and dangerous as he had last night. Devilishly so. Did he only have black clothing?

'Did Olly wake you?' he asked.

'Oh... I was awake anyway,' she lied.

He nodded. 'He knows not to wander the corridors and go into people's rooms. I'll have a word with him.'

She stared at him, wondering what his face would look like if he smiled. 'Like I said, I was getting up anyway.'

He didn't look at her. Didn't meet her gaze. Was he just being polite? Not looking at a strange woman whilst she was in bed? Or did he hate her so much that he just couldn't look at her?

'Breakfast is in the morning room. Ring that bell when you're ready and someone will take you.'

And then he was gone again.

Nell let out a breath she hadn't known she'd been holding. Did she really want to go downstairs and share breakfast with that man? Or with that little boy? Olly? Who was he? Seth's son? Some kind of ward? Neither Seth nor his grandmother had mentioned the little boy last night. The topic of conversation had seemed to be her, more than them. Which was fair enough if they were going to let a stranger stay overnight in their home.

She could have been anyone. She could have been a thief and they'd trusted her. Perhaps she ought to be more grateful to Seth, after all? He need not have stopped in that snowy blizzard. He might have driven by and *not* helped. And yet he had, and all they'd given each other since was grief.

Nell got out of bed, performed her morning ablutions, and looked longingly at the sunken bath. But her stomach was rumbling and she knew she needed to go downstairs to thank her hosts for their kindness. And then maybe call the breakdown service again.

Once dressed and presentable, she pulled on the bell and after a minute or two there was a knock at the door.

'Come in!'

Ava stood there. 'You rang, madam?'

'Could you show me to the breakfast room, please? Er... the morning room?'

Ava smiled and nodded. 'Of course, madam. Come with me.'

As they walked along the corridor and down the curving staircase, Nell couldn't help but be intrigued. 'Do you like working here?' she asked the maid.

'I do.'

'And the Dowager and her grandson? They're good employers?'

'The best, madam. Very kind and considerate. They look after all their staff very well.'

Nell raised an eyebrow. She could imagine the Dowager being kind and considerate, but Seth? 'And... Lord Elmbridge?'

She still couldn't get used to the idea that that man was a *lord*. A peer of the realm!

Ava nodded. 'The best. Kind... Considerate... Lord Elmbridge and his grandmother get us birthday gifts each year, and in a few weeks there will be the servants' ball. He and his friends look after us and serve us.' She smiled.

Nell was surprised. She couldn't imagine him being thoughtful and kind at all.

Opening another set of double doors, Ava led Nell into a large room filled with light from all the windows. The walls were a bright daffodil-yellow colour and a long table sat in the middle, set with a fine china and laden with food choices. Cereals. Hot food, like bacon and eggs. Toast. A butter dish and a variety of jams, honeys and marmalades. Croissants. Pastries. Fruit already chopped up and mixed into a fruit salad. Yoghurts. Fruit juices.

'Lord Elmbridge didn't know what you'd like, so he asked us to prepare everything.'

'Oh, right… Well, yes…that is kind.'

'Take a seat, madam.'

'Am I to eat alone?'

'The Dowager will join you in just a few moments.'

'And Lord Elmbridge? And… Olly?'

'They've already eaten. Early risers. Poor little Olly doesn't sleep well since…'

Ava's eyes clouded as she clearly thought better of what she'd been going to say.

'If you need anything, just ring the bell.' She gave a nod of her head, another quick smile, and then she disappeared.

Nell turned back to look at the table groaning under the weight of food. She normally just had toast in the mornings. She couldn't afford much else. But now that all of this was arrayed in front of her… She decided to eat her fill, and began loading a plate with bacon and eggs.

She was halfway through her breakfast when the door opened and the Dowager arrived, smiling and holding onto her cane. 'Good morning, Nell! Did you sleep well, my dear?'

Yes. Until that little boy had startled her. It had been most unsettling to find him in her room. Waking her like Lucas used to. Thank goodness she would never have to endure that ever again!

'I did, thank you. And thanks again for your hospitality. You didn't need to go to so much trouble just for me.'

'Nonsense. We love having guests here. Have you heard any more about your car?'

'I called the breakdown company just a moment ago. My car has been pulled from the ditch and everything still works. Just a new dent in the bonnet and a bit of mud. They're delivering it here. I hope you don't mind?'

'Not at all. We'll be sad to see you go.'

Maybe the Dowager would be—but Seth? She knew he would be glad to see the back of her.

Pixie Ward was the paediatric pre-surgical ward and Nell's favourite. She would often be called there, either to take some bloods or place an IV, or just to help calm a frightened child by distracting them with play activities so that the doctor could examine them.

Some children arrived in quite an unwell state. But Nell knew that on Pixie they would start their journey to being fixed, and that was the very best part for her. Seeing them get better. Seeing them begin to thrive. Smile. Laugh. Seeing the strain leave their parents' faces and waving them goodbye when they all went home.

It was therapy for her. *Good* therapy. Occasionally one of the children would get really sick and they'd have to go off to the PICU—the paediatric intensive care unit—but mostly her patients' stories had happy endings and that was what she tried to focus on.

Today, she'd been called to attend to a four-year-old girl who was scared of needles. As were her parents, apparently. Nell had been told by the ward sister in charge that though they'd tried, they'd failed after the child got hysterical.

Arriving at the nurses' desk, she smiled at Amy, one of the paediatric nurses, and asked for more on the patient's background.

'Oh, I'm not sure… I've just come on shift and she's a new patient.' Amy looked around. 'No one else is free… Oh! That's her doctor, over there. The new paediatrician guy—Dr James? Maybe ask him?'

Dr James. Lord Elmbridge.

Dread filled her as she turned around to see her grumpy,

brooding rescuer heading towards them in dark trousers and a black shirt, with a stethoscope draped around his neck and his hospital ID clipped to his belt.

'Dr James.'

'Leech.' He gave her a smile.

She decided to let that go. 'I'm here to draw blood on Kalisha Smalls. What can you tell me about her?'

He settled into a chair at the desk and began tapping away at the keyboard. 'Four years of age…brought in due to complications of sickle cell anaemia.'

Sickle cell was a disease that caused blood cells to be of an unusual shape. Because of their sickle shape, they often didn't live as long as normal blood cells, and could also block blood vessels, causing extreme pain and infection.

'She's to undergo a hip arthroplasty after suffering necrosis to her femoral head. We had IVs in situ, as well as a catheter and cannula, but she's pulled them all out. We need them replaced, but she won't let anyone near her, and someone said that you're very good.'

Was that a compliment?

'Oh. Well, that was very kind of "someone" to say. And the parents? What are they like?'

'Extremely needle phobic.'

'Which Kalisha has probably picked up on?'

'I need you to get the IV and cannula back in.' He looked up at her then. Met her gaze. 'Can you do that?'

His eyes were so dark! So mysterious. And yet so cold. Closed off.

'I'll give it my best.'

'That's all I ask.'

She was about to walk away, to go and see the patient, but

she felt she had to say something first. 'I didn't get to see you at breakfast.'

Seth looked up, seemingly annoyed. He was checking around to see who might be listening. Amy was on the phone, talking to a parent and giving an update on their child.

'I was busy.'

Maybe. But she really needed to establish the parameters of their working relationship after the difficulties of how they'd met. Work was her haven and she didn't need to be avoiding anyone.

'I just wanted to say thank you. For helping me out and giving me a place to stay for the evening.'

He was silent for a moment. Then he let out a breath and his face softened. Just a little. 'You're welcome.'

'The young boy... Olly? Is he your son?'

She saw the walls go back up instantly.

'Yes.'

Nell waited for more. But Seth just stared at her. Challenging her, almost.

Wow... This guy was a paediatrician? Most paediatric doctors she met were warm and kind. Sometimes a little silly, so they could engage with their patients. This man was... Well. There wasn't a word for what this man was. Except maybe *Lord*. Someone who looked down on everyone else.

'And?' he asked.

She smiled. Why did she bother? Why bother trying to get to know him? He wouldn't be staying.

'And nothing. I'll go and see Kalisha.'

He hadn't meant to be so prickly, but there was something about Nell that made him feel on edge, and when she'd started asking him about Olly...the boy he felt he'd failed...he'd instantly felt under attack. Maybe he didn't need to be so defensive, but he wanted to protect Olly as much as he could, and he wasn't going to have her criticising him. He did enough of that himself.

So when had Nell looked at him as if she wanted to kill him, just before she'd stalked away, he'd let out a breath and run his hands through his hair in exasperation. He'd been rude. He could admit that. And if he and Nell were going to have to work with one another then maybe he ought to offer some sort of olive branch?

He loved his job. Loved interacting with his patients. He felt at home on the wards. This was a place where he felt in control and that he knew what he was doing. He didn't need it to become a battlefield.

Seth finished typing his notes, updating a patient's drug chart, and then decided to go and see Nell at work with Kalisha. See what made her so special and the phlebotomist of choice for Pixie Ward, whose praises everyone sang in perfect harmony.

Kalisha was in a six-bed ward. The walls were decorated with a mural that made it look as if the children were in a land full of pixies. There were flowers and mushrooms, all of which were homes for pixies that seemed to have been caught in a snapshot of their lives. One purple pixie was holding a small basket filled with flowers and fruits, another pixie, this time in pink, was listening to music and pirouetting in a dance beneath a large daisy, and by Kalisha's bed a pixie lay on her tummy, by a pond, watching all the fish swimming below.

Nell was by the bed, smiling and laughing with the parents.

Seth decided to watch.

Nell began talking to Kalisha. 'So, I hear you're a very brave girl and going to have an operation?'

Kalisha nodded shyly, clutching onto her teddy bear.

'Does anything hurt, my lovely?'

The little girl nodded.

'Can you point to where it hurts?'

Kalisha pointed to her left hip.

'I bet it does! You poor thing… I'd really like to help take your pain away. Would you like that?'

Another nod.

'Well, we can give you some magic medicine that will do that.'

'She doesn't like needles,' said Kalisha's mother.

Nell smiled. 'I know.'

Seth watched with interest.

'See this little cup of juice here, that the nurse brought earlier? That will help take away some of your pain. All you have to do is drink it.'

'I don't want to,' said Kalisha in a small voice.

'Oh, honey, why not? Do you think it'll taste bad? It doesn't. It tastes of strawberries—do you like strawberries?'

'I do…'

'She's worried that it will put her to sleep and she'll wake up with needles in her again,' said the mother.

'Well, I can see why you'd be upset about that, Kalisha. I wouldn't want that, either. Not without my permission.'

Seth frowned. They had already told Kalisha that when she came round from her surgery there would be tubes and wires in her arms, and how important it was that they stay there.

'But what you had in your arms weren't actually needles. They were just very small tubes, helping keep you well before your surgery. You've been through a lot, huh?'

The little girl nodded.

'And those little tubes? Well, we need to put them back if

we're to make you better. They help us give you medicine to take away that pain. And you want to feel better, don't you? So you can go home?'

'Yes...'

'How about I promise to do that for you and you won't feel a thing?'

'But needles hurt.'

'Not with my magic cream, they don't. Here, let me show you. No needles, just cream—okay?'

Kalisha let her put some cream on the back of one of her hands.

'We'll let that sit there for a moment and do its magic. Hey, do you like bubbles?'

Kalisha smiled and nodded.

Seth watched as Nell got out a bubble wand from her bag and began blowing bubbles for Kalisha to reach out and touch. Then she passed the wand and the mixture to the little girl, to play with herself.

A smile crept onto his face as he watched Nell with the little girl. She was good. He had to give her that. She used words that were easy for a four-year-old to understand, and hadn't been patronising nor talked down to her at all. Nell had talked to her as if her very real concerns were extremely valid and he liked that.

After a short period of time during which bubbles filled the ward, Nell suggested that she wipe away the magic cream.

'And now I'm going to touch your skin where the cream was. Can you feel me touching you?'

Kalisha looked at her in amazement. 'I can't feel it! Mummy, I can't feel it!' She laughed.

'That's good. You see! So if you'll let me put the tubes back in, we can use this cream and you won't feel a thing. And if you like, whilst I do it, you can blow bubbles and look at Mummy and Daddy and have fun, and you won't have to worry about anything at all. And afterwards, you'll feel so much better. How does that sound?'

'You promise?'

'Cross my heart.' Nell made a crossing motion over her chest.

Kalisha looked at her mum and then her dad.

'Want me to do Teddy first?' Nell asked.

After a quick nod from Kalisha, Nell put a dot of magic cream on the teddy, then gathered her things, wiped off the cream and inserted an IV into the toy.

'See? Your turn now. Are you ready to be a twin with Teddy?'

'His name's Toby.'

Nell smiled. 'I love that name. So…are you ready? Here's the bubbles. You look at Mummy and Daddy and I'll be done faster than you can say lickety-split.'

Kalisha began blowing bubbles, looking away from her.

Seth could see Nell would need to work fast. But she had gained Kalisha's trust and that was the most important thing. He was impressed. Nell's reputation was true. And when she got the IV in first time, all hooked up without Kalisha even flinching, he knew he was in the presence of a master.

'There you go. All done.'

Nell watched as Kalisha looked at her arm.

'I didn't even feel it go in.'

'Magic cream!' Nell laughed. 'Now, remember, it's not a needle in your arm—just a small bendy tube. So you can use your arm as normal, okay?'

'Okay.'

'Will you and Toby be all right?'

'We will. Now we're twins.'

'Good.'

Nell got up and turned around, and saw him standing there in the doorway, watching.

Was that a blush he saw? he wondered.

Interesting.

As she moved towards him, carrying her kit, he stood up straight.

'That was good...what you just did.'

She shrugged. 'It's just my job—nothing more.'

He smiled. 'I'm giving you a compliment.'

'Oh. Well, I didn't recognise it because I didn't know you could say nice things.'

'I say nice things. On occasion. When they're merited.'

'Noted. Do you need me for anything?'

No. He didn't. But he wasn't ready for her to go yet, strangely. What was it about Nell Bryant that intrigued him so? Her spiky nature? The way she couldn't give two hoots about who he was or where he lived? Most people upon finding out who he was would suddenly change and become obsequious, which he hated. So the fact that she didn't... He kind of liked it. Kind of liked their argumentative banter. It was fun.

'How's your car?' he asked.

'Dented. Muddy. But working.'

'Good.'

'How are your reindeer?' She laughed. 'That's not a sentence I ever thought I'd say.'

'Safely contained. We found the last one.'

Maybe it was her eyes? She had nice eyes. Dark. Chocolatey...

She stared at him, as if trying to figure him out. Then she frowned. 'Okay, then.'

And she walked past him to the nurses' desk to add her procedure to Kalisha's chart.

He watched her go, realised he was admiring her pert behind, and then instantly turned away. He had a post-surgical check to do—best to get on with that and stop thinking about Nell Bryant.

Not her eyes, nor her behind.

CHAPTER FOUR

'So, THE NEW DOCTOR—Dr James. What do we think?' asked Beth, one of the nurses, as they sat together in their lunch hour.

There were four of them. Beth, Nell, a healthcare assistant called Lou and another nurse, Angel.

Nell had plenty to say on the subject of Dr Seth James, but she was intrigued to hear what the others thought.

'I think he's hot,' said Angel. 'He's got that dangerous, devil-may-care look about him. All rough and ready. He looks like he'd be good in bed, right?'

The others made appreciative noises.

'He looks like a real man. Solid. Strong. You can tell he's fit,' said Lou.

'I think he looks like a pirate,' said Beth. 'That dark hair and that dark beard... You'd expect him to wear a gold hoop earring and have a parrot on his shoulder... I mean, swoon alert—am I right?'

Nell felt as if they were waiting for her to agree. 'You don't think he's a little...standoffish?' she asked.

They all turned to look at her as if she were crazy.

'No! Not at all. What makes you say that?'

'He just... I mean, he...' She could feel herself getting flustered.

All the things the other girls had said were true. Dr James

was very attractive, in that rough and ready kind of way, but she felt she'd seen a side of him that they hadn't.

'You know he's a lord, right?'

'A lord? Of what?'

'Like a real lord...a peer and a landowner.'

'You mean he sent off for one of those certificates where you own a tiny scrap of land in Scotland and you become a laird, or something?'

'No.' She shook her head. 'He's Lord Elmbridge. Of Elmbridge Manor.'

They all looked at one another in surprise.

'Well, knock me down with a feather... Should we curtsey?' asked Beth, laughing. 'How do you know this?'

Nell didn't want to tell them what had happened. Not at all. 'I just heard, that's all.' She must have blushed, because suddenly they were all pointing at her.

'Come on! Spill! You know more than you're letting on!'

'I swear, that's it. That's all I know.'

At that very moment, the Lord in question walked into the hospital cafeteria, grabbed a tray and began to line up for some food.

Beth pointed. 'He's here! Do you think he knows how to serve himself?'

'Who cares?' Angel laughed. 'Let's just take a few moments to enjoy his rear view.'

The girls sighed and chuckled, but Nell didn't know where to look. She regretted telling them he was a lord, but she'd been stuck for something to say, and to take the pressure off herself—not wanting to admit that she did indeed find him very attractive—she'd presented the group with a tasty morsel of information.

Now, unable to resist as everyone gawped at Seth, she looked up and risked a glance.

He was very fine indeed. All that they had said and more. And maybe that was the problem? Or an added problem, seeing as he didn't seem to like her very much. Not that that mattered. Nell wasn't looking for a relationship. With anyone.

Why would she risk getting involved in something like that again? She'd only end up getting hurt and left behind, her heart in tatters and shreds, held together by scars and pain. And Dr Seth James, or Lord Elmbridge, or whatever it was he wanted to be called, would never, ever—not in a million years—be the man for her.

Never.

So why was she still looking at him? Why was she still engaged in noting those wide, broad shoulders in a tight-fitting, surely bespoke black shirt? Looking at the way his dark, almost black hair curled around the collar? And why did she note, with appreciation, the neatness and flatness of his waist? And why on earth was she admiring the curve of his backside in those dark jeans?

Flustered, she took a bite of her sandwich and deliberately looked away. She would not be caught gazing at him when he turned around. She would not give him the satisfaction, even if everyone else was clucking like a gaggle of hens around a new... *Ahem.* Male chicken.

'So, what's everyone doing for Christmas?' she asked.

'Well, not *him*, sadly.' Lou chuckled. 'I'm off to the outlaws. What about you?'

And just like that her friends were distracted into talking about Christmas plans.

Nell had none. As usual. Christmas was something that she never really wanted to bother with any more, but she still decorated, still bought a turkey with all the trimmings and made dinner on Christmas Day, because it was what Lucas would have wanted. It was what Lucas had loved. By doing so it brought him closer, and she would take that over anything.

'Me, too,' said Beth.

'Me three,' said Angel.

'Dinner for one,' Nell said, smiling a smile that said, *Don't feel sorry for me.* 'As usual.'

'Maybe you should have Christmas with the Lord?' suggested Beth. 'There's no ring on his finger. Maybe he's single?'

'Looking like that?' said Lou. 'There's no way that man is on his own.'

Seth sat in the hospital cafeteria, trying to eat the chilli con carne and jacket potato that he'd selected from the hot food section. He noticed Nell Bryant the phlebotomist on the other side of the room, sitting with a group of friends.

Her hair was down, and as the winter sun shone in through the window behind her it gleamed and shimmered, revealing hidden streaks of red and copper amongst the dark brown as it fell in waves down her back.

He looked away and pulled out his phone, determined not to spend more time than was necessary thinking about or noticing Nell. Nothing could ever come of it. He had bigger priorities right now. Looking after Granny and Olly. Getting into running the manor as a business. And he wanted to make Christmas really special this year for his son.

The last couple of Christmases had been hard, down in Devon, but he'd told himself it was easier to be away from where the accident had happened. Olly had missed his mother intensely—still did, no doubt—only as more and more time passed his pain didn't show as much, and he'd felt that it was the right time to return to Elmbridge.

It was his childhood home, and it always felt good to return there. Even if it did bring back memories of Dana's accident and alongside that all his regrets. His guilt. His shame.

If only he hadn't wanted to enjoy a drink at that Christmas party…

If only he hadn't let Dana offer to collect him and bring him home…

If only…

If only…

Without realising what he was doing, he let his gaze drift back over to Nell. She was laughing now, enjoying a joke or something, and he was amazed at how her face lit up with her smile. He'd not seen that yet. Not a true smile. He'd seen her sarcastic one, but it was nothing compared to this. Genuine. Warm. Her doe eyes gleaming with mirth and enjoyment. He wondered if he'd ever get to make her smile like that. What would it feel like to make her smile and know he was the reason for it?

His phone beeped, dragging him from his reverie. It was a text from Sven, to let him know that the delivery of hay for the reindeer had arrived, as expected. He texted back. And then a text arrived from his grandmother, reminding him that tonight Santa's Grotto would officially open and he was to be there at six sharp to cut the candy-cane-striped ribbon.

Part of him rued the day he'd taught his grandmother how to text. The other part actually liked it. Granny, apart from Olly, was all he had left of his family, and she was like a cat with nine lives. Every time she got sick, or hurt, she'd end up in hospital and he'd worry he was going to lose her—only for her to bounce back.

One day, he knew she wouldn't. And then he'd miss her

texts and her love. So he smiled, and messaged back that he would be there on time, and that, no, he hadn't forgotten.

He suddenly became aware of a presence beside his table. He looked up. 'Leech...' He smiled.

Her head tilted to one side as she rolled her eyes. 'You could just call me Nell, like everyone else, you know.'

'But where would the fun be in that?'

'Perhaps I should come up with a name for you?'

'Like what?'

She shrugged. 'I don't know... My Lord? Lord Grumpy?'

'They're not very inventive, are they? Aren't you embarrassed?'

'Well, I'm trying to be polite. They're not the first names I came up with for you.'

'Which were...?'

'Well, let's just say they were a whole slew of swear words.'

'That's rather mean...and not really in the spirit of Christmas. Don't you think?'

'Since when have *you* been in the spirit of Christmas?'

He smiled and got to his feet, towering over her. 'As always, it's a pleasure talking with you, Leech, but I have things to be getting on with. I'm a very busy person.'

'As am I.'

'I'm sure you are. Enjoy your day.'

He grabbed his tray and returned it, and then headed out of the cafeteria back towards the ward. He felt confused. He enjoyed their banter. Enjoyed baiting her. And at the same time he found himself drawn to her. His eyes sought her out in places, almost as if they were out of his control—which was ridiculous, because his body was his own and he felt sure his brain was in charge, and not something lower.

So why did he keep running into her?

As he'd said to her before, it was a large hospital. They might never run into one another.

And yet they did.

Over and over again.

Nell was feeling mightily annoyed with Lord Grumpy after their encounter in the hospital cafeteria. She'd only gone over to tell him that she'd accidentally let it slip that he was a lord to her friends, but the conversation had not been what she'd expected. He was still calling her Leech, which was funny in one way and annoying in another. She kind of liked it that he had a nickname for her, and that they could argue without it actually being mean, but she didn't like the feeling that he had somehow bested her.

So when she got back to Pixie Ward and overheard Paula, the ward sister, on the phone, talking about how their usual Santa couldn't visit the wards to give gifts to the children who'd be stuck there over Christmas, she had a wonderful idea.

She waited for the ward sister's conversation to be over, then knocked with her knuckles on the door. 'Hi. Couldn't help but overhear about Gordon. What's happened to him?'

'Broke his hip after falling over in that snow we had at the weekend. So we need to find another Santa fast.'

Nell smiled. 'I have one in mind… I'm sure he'd love to do it.'

The ward sister perked up. 'Oh? Who?'

'Dr James! He loves Christmas! He was just telling me. And he's only part-time, so he could do it. I'm sure he wouldn't want to let the children down.'

'Do you think he would?'

'I'm sure he would if you asked him. I believe he's even got his own reindeer.'

She didn't explain when Paula raised an eyebrow at that. Maybe she'd think Nell meant he had a collection of reindeer. As in ornaments.

The more she thought about it, the more it seemed to her that Dr James was perfect! He had reindeer. His own Santa's Grotto, which the Dowager had told her about. And it would be hilarious, seeing him all dressed up in a Santa outfit and a white beard, ho-ho-ho-ing with the children and having to be happy and cheery. She'd get a real kick out of it…maybe even make him pose for a photo or two.

'Okay. I'll ask him. Know where he is?'

'He should be on the ward somewhere.'

Paula stood up and smiled. 'Perfect! I'll go and find him. Thanks, Nell.'

'You're very welcome.'

Nell went to see her next patient feeling rather pleased with herself, imagining the look on Lord Grumpy's face when Paula tracked him down. She couldn't imagine that he'd be able to get out of it. How did you say no to a determined ward sister who needed a Santa for her ward?

Daniel Cohen was a ten-year-old boy who was in for a liver surgery and needed a liver function test, group and save, as well as a full blood count before his operation. He was a charming young man. Very polite even though jaundiced-looking. Hopefully once he'd had his surgery he'd be back to his normal self again.

'Hey, Daniel. I'm here to take some of your blood. How are you with needles?'

'Do they hurt?'

'No. I have magic cream. Want to see?'

Daniel nodded.

Nell placed a splodge of cream on the back of his hand, covered it with a dressing, and drew a happy smiling face on top.

'In a minute or two you won't be able to feel anything there. So, tell me, Daniel, when you're not in hospital, what do you like doing?'

'Playing football. But my parents have stopped me since I got sick. They say it's too dangerous for me.'

'You must miss it?'

'Yeah.'

'Who do you support?'

As Daniel went into a long answer about his favourite club and his favourite players, Nell removed the dressing and the cream and showed him that the crook of his elbow was now numb. She inserted the needle without any trouble at all, and got the blood draw.

'See? All done. Want a sticker?'

She opened her packet of stickers and he picked one with a green dragon on it that said he'd been brave today.

'Thanks. Are you in trouble?' he asked.

Nell frowned and looked at him with a smile. 'Trouble? No. Why do you say that?'

'Because that man behind you is looking at you funny.'

Nell turned to see Dr James standing at the foot of Daniel's bed, arms crossed.

She blushed. 'Dr James.'

He forced a smile for Daniel. 'Might I have a word with you, Miss Bryant?'

She stood up, knowing what this was about and rather looking forward to hearing him bluff and curse and bluster about how she'd set him up to be the ward Santa.

'Of course,' she answered, all sweet and innocent, as they

headed away from the ward and into the corridor. She looked up at him, all smiles. 'What can I do for you?'

But instead of the anger and irritation she'd expected, he disarmed her and smiled. 'You may have heard... I'm going to be the ward Santa this year.'

'I might have heard something.'

Another smile—but this one was dangerous. 'I was honoured to be asked, being so new to the ward, and I told Paula I'd be pleased to do it. But I might need an assistant to help me. An elf assistant.'

The pleasure in his eyes told her exactly where this was heading.

'I can't be an—'

'Oh, but you can! There's even an elf costume for you. Paula's dug it out and I think you'll like it. It's very...fetching. We're going to be the perfect partnership.'

Nell stared at him in horror. Be his elf? His assistant? Spend hours with him trailing around the wards, being the butt of his jokes? It was going to be impossible!

'I can't.'

'You would let down the *children*?' he asked in a soft voice of mock horror, his arms crossed over his chest as he leaned casually against the wall.

No. She would not let down the children. She would be his elf just to spite him.

'Fine. I'll be your elf.'

'I knew you would.'

'I should have known you wouldn't be able to do it without a servant!'

He chuckled in amusement. 'And I should have known that *you* would do the unexpected. But I think I'm getting to know you now, Little Elf. And you and I are going to be very close from now on, because it's the only way I'm going to be able to keep an eye on you.'

He gave her a wink and walked away.

What have I done?

She thought she'd played a prank on him. Thought she'd got one up on him after the rude way he'd spoken to her in the cafeteria, calling her Leech. Now it seemed she had a new name. Little Elf was nicer than Leech, but he seemed to have the upper hand here. But he would, wouldn't he? He'd been born into it. And no matter what she tried, she'd never pull him down a peg or two.

Dr Seth James was the most infuriating man she had ever had the misfortune to meet!

CHAPTER FIVE

THE OPENING OF the grotto went really well. Seth cut the ribbon, posed next to Santa and his elves for a photograph for the local newspaper, then stood by and talked to the journalists who wanted quotes for their articles as parents lined up with their children to see Santa.

But he wasn't used to being in the limelight like this. It wasn't something he sought out. It was why he stayed away from Elmbridge, usually. His other home was in Devon, on the south coast. A nice little cottage, tucked away against a rock face, where he and Olly could live their lives and just be like everyone else.

He'd returned to Elmbridge because of his grandmother. Because she'd asked. Because she'd told him the time was coming closer when he would have to be the Lord Elmbridge he'd always been meant to be and that Olly needed to know about his history and his heritage.

She was right. Elmbridge would be Olly's one day. And so he'd come back as soon as he'd secured the hospital position. He was lucky in that money was no object. But he couldn't *not* work. He loved being a paediatrician.

Children were so honest. So open. That was why he'd agreed to open a grotto in the grounds of the Manor this year with no charge, so any child could see Santa. And it was why

he'd agreed to be the ward Santa when the sister had told him
that Nell had volunteered his name.

Nell Bryant.

She was a funny one, that was for sure. Okay, so they hadn't
got off to the best start with one another, but now he felt as if
it had become a series of small battles between them, and he
had to admit he was beginning to enjoy it. But there was no
way he was going to let her get the better of him. She'd thought
she'd wind him up by volunteering his name and that he'd say
no. So of course he'd had to sidestep that and do the complete
opposite! Plus he'd have fun doing it. His Little Elf was going
to rue the day she'd ever messed with him.

Amadi Babangida was a seven-year-old boy who had been
admitted for surgery on his twisted foot. He had been born in
Nigeria with the deformity, and a charity had arranged for him
to be brought over to the UK to have the surgery that would
straighten it and allow him to walk without crutches. His meta-
tarsals and ankle joint would need pinning, with plates and
screws to straighten the foot and allow him to bear weight on
it, as so far he could not.

Amadi was a cheerful young boy, who had travelled over
with an aunt. His mother had stayed at home with her other
four children.

'How are you doing, Amadi?' asked Seth, standing by his
bed.

'Okay.'

'Nervous? It's a big day today.'

'But I will be better after.'

'That's right. Not only better, but awesome! We'll have you
up and walking in no time!'

'And playing football? And cricket?' Amadi asked with a light in his eyes.

'Absolutely!' Seth looked him over. 'Let me guess…fast bowler?'

Amadi nodded, his teeth gleaming in his bright smile. 'Do you play?'

'I haven't played cricket since I was your age. Rugby was always my game. So, Mrs Chiagozie, do you have any questions?'

Amadi's aunt smiled and shook her head.

'Okay. Well, we've got an hour or two before Amadi goes to Theatre, so if you do think of anything you want to ask, then grab a nurse and someone can come and find me. I'm not a surgeon, so I'm always here—okay?'

A nod.

Seth held out his hand and shook Amadi's. 'See you soon.'

'See you.'

He gave the boy one last winning smile, winked at him, and then headed to a side room to check on a patient who had spiked a fever before her planned surgery and then developed a cough. Concerned about Covid, the nursing staff had isolated her, and he was going in to tell the parents the bad news.

Once he was gowned, gloved and masked, he entered the room and looked at the parents, before settling his gaze on Holly, his patient.

'You've tested positive for Covid, I'm afraid, Holls, so we're going to have to postpone the tonsillectomy until you're better. But because your fever is quite high we're going to keep you in and transfer you to another ward to keep an eye on you. How do you feel about that?'

Holly coughed hard. 'I don't know…'

'Is she going to be all right?' asked her dad.

'Kids are resilient. We'll keep a close watch on her…try and keep that fever down.'

'Will it affect her tonsils? She already suffers so much.'

'It could aggravate them. But, like I say, we'll keep a look-out for any complications.'

'Whatever's best. But it is disappointing. We were hoping to finally be rid of the damn things. They've been trouble for her ever since she was born.'

'I get that, and I know it's hard to wait, but it's safer to do the operation when she doesn't have Covid.'

Both parents nodded and the mother reached out to squeeze her daughter's hand. 'Where will she be moved to?'

'We have a paediatric Covid ward. It's best for us to put her there…just because her oxygen saturations have been up and down.'

'Is that bad?'

'It's not ideal. We like them to be over ninety-four, and Holly's have been dropping into the eighties. We'll give her some oxygen therapy too—get her feeling better.'

He understood the parents' frustrations. No one wanted an operation to be cancelled. You'd build yourself up for it, get mentally prepared, and then for it to not happen… But there was nothing they could do. It would be safer to operate when Holly was Covid-free and maintaining better oxygen levels.

'When will she be moved?' asked the father.

'Soon. We have to take some precautions when moving a positive Covid case through the hospital.'

The parents and Holly nodded, before Hollt coughed once again. Seth told them he'd come and see them later, when Holly was settled on her new ward, and then left, removing his PPE and depositing it in a special collection bin. Then he washed his hands and checked his watch.

It was time for him to go and see if this Santa costume would fit him. The usual Santa was considerably shorter than Seth, so he needed to know if there were any problems. If there were, he'd simply buy a new Santa outfit. It might even be fun. He could wear it for Olly, too.

But as he headed down the corridor towards the bank of lifts he saw Nell coming his way. She was on her mobile. Smiling. Laughing. Catching her like that, in a spontaneous moment before she noticed him was nice. She looked good…he couldn't deny that. Those dark waves were tied up and out of the way now, but she had allowed some longer tresses to come loose and frame her heart-shaped face.

And then she noticed him, and he watched as her face and posture changed. It was as if she'd gone on the alert as she ended her call, snapped her phone shut and placed it in her pocket.

'Dr James.'

'Little Elf.'

She rolled her eyes. 'I told you before… It wouldn't hurt you to call me Nell.'

He smiled. 'I know. But it annoys you when I don't, so why don't we stick with that?'

'Okay. Fine!' she said, as if it didn't really matter. 'Are you done for the day? On your way back to your palatial mansion?'

'Santa costume fitting.'

'Ah, yes. You're going to look marvellous with a big, fat belly and a bushy white beard.'

'You like beards?' he asked, stroking his own dark one.

'I read something quite interesting about them the other day, actually.'

'Oh? Pray tell.'

'That a beard is not linked to testosterone levels at all.

Women like men who are clean-shaven as well as bearded, so men don't grow one to attract a mate.'

'So, what's the reason?'

She smiled. 'They do it because men with beards are perceived as older, wiser and more aggressive than other males. It's science. A beard is meant to be intimidating, to frighten weaker males away from the available females. Interesting, don't you think? That in an evolutionary way you're nothing more than a peacock, trying to look more impressive than other men.'

He laughed, amused by her suggestion. 'I'm not competing with anybody. I happen to like how it looks. That's all.'

Nell smiled. 'You keep telling yourself that.'

And she passed him by, heading towards Pixie Ward.

He narrowed his eyes as he watched her walk away. Her hips drew his gaze and he shook his head as he thought about what she'd just said. He was no peacock! He felt no need to display his feathers and have others admire him. He needed no one's admiration, and nor did he look for it. All he wanted was to be a good dad for Olly. It was just, what with the manor, and working at the hospital, he'd forgotten to shave. Sometimes he was so tired he didn't have the energy for it, and had figured the beard would have to do. And now he liked how it looked, that was all.

At least it had grown through the same dark colour as the hair on his head. He remembered his father having dark, almost black hair, but his beard, when he had grown one, had come through auburn. With his greying eyebrows, he'd looked mismatched, as if put together by a child, so after that he'd kept himself clean-shaven every day, no matter what.

Seth's father had died young. A sudden heart attack that no one had seen coming. He'd grown up without a father and then, a couple of years later, without a mother. He remembered his childhood as being empty and strange, being raised by a granny who did her best, but…

Now Olly had no mother. And Seth was determined to be the best father he could for his son. And if that meant lying on the floor, playing with cars or blocks or doing jigsaws, rather than shaving his beard, then that was what he was going to do! Little Elf could come up with as many crazy theories as she liked, but he knew none of them were true.

He was trying to be a good dad and that was all that mattered.

The dreaded day had arrived.

Elf Day.

It wasn't Christmas yet. There were still a few more days. But on Pixie Ward Santa made visits early—and if Santa was doing his rounds, then he would need his elf, too.

Nell stood in the staff room, staring at the outfit with which she'd been provided. She had to wear that? In front of *him*? This was just going to give him a whole other level of ammunition to torment her with.

When she was finished dressing, she stared at herself in the mirror.

Soft red velvet shoes with jingle bells on curled over her toes. Green-and-white-striped tights. A red tunic and breeches. A green hat with more jingle bells.

Behind her, the door opened and in walked Beth. 'Oh, wow! You look…'

'Stupid?'

'*Festive* was the word I was going for.' Beth stood behind her, peering into the mirror, too. 'Mind you, I feel like there's something missing…'

'Missing? Are we looking at the same reflection?'

'I know!' Beth rummaged in her own locker and pulled out her make-up bag. She turned Nell to face her. Then she drew a large red spot on both her cheeks and, using an eyeliner pencil, added freckles over them. 'There. Perfect!'

Nell felt ridiculous, but had to admit the kids would probably love it—despite her own misgivings.

Beth snapped a couple of pictures on her phone and passed it to her. 'So you remember?'

'Remember what?'

'That Lucas would have loved this. Seeing his mum being silly.'

It was true, and it made her smile. She could do that now. Once upon a time she hadn't been able to hear his name or be reminded of him without breaking down into a weeping mess. But now…? Now she could think of him happily.

She'd not had him in her life long. Only four years. But she'd known him inside out. What he loved. What made him laugh. What made him seek her out in the middle of the night.

Lucas had often had wild and crazy dreams, and when they'd woken him he'd ambled into her room, holding on to his teddy bear, so he could tell her about them. And then she'd invited him into her bed, and they'd snuggled together for a while before they both fell asleep.

Her husband hadn't liked it. He was a man who believed that children should stay in their own beds, in their own rooms. But perhaps if he'd known how short a time they'd actually have Lucas he might have allowed it, instead of arguing with her about it all the time? Did Blake regret it? All his rules? His regulations? His firm belief that babies ought to be left to cry themselves to sleep? That they shouldn't be in their parents' bed? That breastfeeding should end at six months?

She and Blake had had so many arguments about so many silly things, when what they ought to have been doing was soaking up every millisecond they had with their son. But Blake had always been standoffish. Nell had put it down to the way he'd been raised as a child himself. His parents had been cold. Only showing love through buying their son gifts, rather than giving him hugs and kisses.

When Blake had walked away after Lucas died it had seemed easier for him to get over the loss. She'd never seen him cry. Not even at the funeral. His face stoic. Stone-like. That was what they'd argued about. How unfeeling he'd seemed when all Nell had wanted was for him to hold her and tell her they'd get through this.

And they had.

Just not together.

'You know, I put pictures like this in a giant folder on the computer...as if I'm still saving memories for him.'

Beth looked at her with a soft smile. 'That's nice. You should.'

'He'll never get to see them, though, will he?'

'No. But the children you see today will see you. And they'll remember Santa and his elf visiting them that time they were in hospital. You'll be in those children's memory their entire life.'

'You're right. And I want to make this special for them. Jingle bells and all.'

She lifted a foot and jiggled it. The bells sounded and they both smiled.

'Where's your Santa?'

'Getting changed in the men's changing rooms.'

Beth laughed. 'Now, *there's* a man who could rummage in my stocking.'

Nell raised an eyebrow. 'I don't know… I can't imagine him being…*romantic*, can you?'

'I don't need romance with a man who looks like him. Just getting down and dirty would do it!'

At that moment the door to the men's changing area opened. The first thing that emerged was Santa's giant belly, clad in his familiar red suit, and then the rest of him.

'Ho-ho-ho! Merry Christmas!' Seth said in a deep voice, eyes twinkling as he carried his large sack of presents behind him.

The gifts had all been donated. Collected throughout the year, wrapped by hospital volunteers and kept ready for the festive season.

He stopped to admire Nell. 'My, don't you look jolly?'

'So do you! And here was me thinking that the only character you could play convincingly would be Ebenezer Scrooge. Are you ready to put some smiles on children's faces, or would you prefer to stay here and count all your money?'

He sidled up to her and pulled down the long, white curly beard that covered his own. 'Oh, I don't know… Just putting on the red suit makes me want to make people happy. Even you, Little Elf. What do you say?'

The fact that he'd chosen not to wind her up surprised her. 'All right. Maybe you ought to always wear it, if it makes you nicer.'

'Well, only good boys and girls get what they want for Christmas. Tell me, Little Elf, have you been a good girl?'

She coloured under the intensity of his gaze. The Santa hat, padded belly and fake beard ought to have made him look a figure of ridicule, but he managed to pull it off and be ridiculously sexy. It was annoying!

'I'm always a good girl. How about you?'

He smiled and raised the beard back up. 'Now, that would be telling. Come on!'

And he began to walk out of the staff room.

Nell looked at Beth with a look that said *Can you believe this guy?* Only to see her friend and colleague staring at her in surprise.

'What?' she asked.

'Are you and he...?' Beth trailed off.

'Are he and I what?'

Beth grinned. 'Flirting?'

'Absolutely not!'

'Are you sure?'

'Most definitely!'

'Well, honey, maybe you ought to tell the rest of you. And him. Because that...? What I just saw...? That was the very definition of two people flirting with one another.'

'You're crazy. He's the most annoying man I've ever had the misfortune to meet.'

'Little Elf!'

They heard his voice calling from the corridor.

'Oh, sweetie... You're in trouble with a capital T.'

Nell frowned at her friend, wanting to retort, to dismiss what Beth had suggested, but there were no words in her brain.

Exasperated, she simply said, 'Bah, humbug!' and stalked from the room.

Seth was having enormous fun as Santa. Normally at the hospital he had to keep a professional distance with his young patients. It protected him for when things went badly—as they sometimes did. But as Santa he wasn't at their bedside as a doctor, advising them on pain management or talking through surgery with a parent. He could be as jolly as he wanted! As friendly as he wanted! And it was so wonderful to see the smiles he put on the young kids' faces.

The next kid he was visiting was Peyton Swan. A young girl on the post-surgical ward who had been in to have a meningioma removed from her brain.

Her first visit to the hospital had been when she was three years old, to have the tumour removed then, but due to its positioning they hadn't been able to get it all. So she came in every couple of years to have more taken out. She was now seven, and this was her third surgery. She lay in bed, her head wrapped in thick bandages, looking pale and tired.

'Peyton Swan! Ho-ho-ho! It is so good to see you again! How are you doing?' Seth asked in his jolly Santa voice.

'I'm okay...' she answered in a quiet voice.

'I've brought someone special with me this year. One of my elves from the North Pole. Little Elf, say hello to Peyton!'

Nell stepped forward with a jingle and took hold of Peyton's limp hand. 'Nice to meet you, Peyton!'

Seth grinned behind his fake beard. 'Have you been a good girl this year?'

Peyton nodded shyly.

'Good! I'm glad to hear it! Good boys and girls get presents for Christmas! What have you wished for this year?' Seth was now kneeling beside the bed.

Peyton was thoughtful for a moment. 'To not have to come into hospital any more.'

He got that. She'd already been through so much. Her childhood so far had been spent in and out of hospitals and recovering from brain surgeries. Had this young girl ever had the chance to go skating? Or to ride a pony? Or go to gymnastics class?

He knew she would not get her wish. Peyton faced a lifetime of maintenance surgeries. She would be constantly coming in to hospital to have the growing tumour cut away in order to maintain her quality of life.

'I hear you, Peyton. I really do.' Seth reached for her hand and squeezed it. 'But that's up to the doctors. I may be Santa, but I don't have a magic wand to take your tumour away from you. The only thing I can do is to try and make you smile and be happy...if only for a little while.'

He hated feeling helpless. Hated it that he couldn't make her feel better. But he was not a surgeon. He didn't know the true extent of her case.

'So tell me...what can I do right now to make you smile?'

The little girl thought for a moment more. 'Sing for me?'

He smiled. 'You like singing and music?'

'I do.'

'What song would you like us to sing?'

'The one about Rudolph the reindeer.'

Seth nodded. 'Ah, Rudolph...my favourite reindeer of them all!' He leaned in and whispered. 'Shh, though. Don't tell the others. Dasher and Dancer and Donner and Blitzen will not be happy!'

He got to his feet and stood, straightening out his belly and turning to Nell, motioning that she was to join in.

He noticed the fear in her eyes. Did she not like to sing? Or was she just embarrassed?

'A one, two, three...'

They began to sing, and instantly he flinched and turned, shocked at the sounds coming out of Nell's mouth.

She couldn't sing!

He wanted to laugh so hard, but he didn't want to ruin the song for Peyton. So he turned away from his Little Elf and tried to ignore the caterwauling behind him as she bravely tried to hit the notes with him and continued on with the song.

He made eye contact with Peyton, who was chuckling, and made a *Have you heard this?* motion with his thumb at Nell behind him.

He boomed out the lyrics and noticed the smiles on all the other children's faces as they listened and laughed at Nell, whose face was going redder and redder. But he had to give her points. No matter how awful she sounded, she bravely ploughed on, singing the song for Peyton. As they reached the final line Nell's voice cracked and she made a weird choking sound. He couldn't help it. He laughed. Laughed so hard his belly began to jiggle. And then all the children joined in.

Yet when he looked at Nell, expecting her to be embarrassed or to run away, cheeks burning, he found that she was laughing too, barely able to breathe, clearly enjoying her own inability to sing and how awful she sounded, but not caring because it had made Peyton and all the other kids on the post-surgical ward laugh.

They'd brought joy and song and laughter to a ward that didn't often have any.

The kids all began to clap, and one, the little boy in the far bed, cheered and whooped.

Seth reached into his sack and pulled out a wrapped gift for Peyton. 'Merry Christmas,' he said, leaning in so she'd hear him. 'I shall hope and pray that one day your wishes come true.'

'Thank you, Santa.'

He gave her a wave and then, with his Little Elf, went to the next ward.

* * *

Afterwards, Nell and Seth made it back to the staff room at the end of a long afternoon. She'd not realised how exhausting it would be, and she had new-found respect for Santa's grotto staff all over the globe.

She pulled off her red velvet hat and her jingling boots and flopped down on the sofa. Behind her, Seth peeled off the Santa jacket and his fake belly and beard and sat opposite her in just Santa's trousers and a fitted white tee. He had muscular arms that spoke of time spent in the gym. She wanted to look away, but to be honest she was kind of surprised.

Seth as Santa had shown her an entirely different side to the man she'd thought she knew, and now she wondered if there was more to him than she'd initially suspected. For her, the battle lines had come down, at least for a short while, and she wanted to know more about this man before the cease-fire ended.

'We did a good thing today,' she said.

He nodded and ran his hands through his thick dark hair. 'I hope so. Not sure my ears will recover from that voice of yours...but we're in a hospital. I can get ENT to take a look before I go home. Make sure no real damage has been done.'

He grabbed a biscuit off a plate and bit into it.

Nell smiled. 'Yeah. I should have told you before that I can't sing.'

'Can't sing? It sounded like there was something mortally wrong with your vocal cords. Cats for miles around were wondering why their queen was calling them. I wouldn't be surprised if when we leave the hospital it's surrounded by moggies.'

She laughed. 'I know! But I wasn't going to stop. Peyton wanted us to create magic today, and we couldn't, so instead she asked for a song. I would have given that girl whatever was in my power to make her happy.'

He nodded sagely. 'Some of those kids have it tough. That old saying, *Well, at least you have your health*... They don't even have that.'

No. Nell knew all about kids who didn't have their health.

Lucas's face flashed into her mind. How he'd looked lying there in that hospital bed, all pale. It had been better when he was sleeping, because then he hadn't felt unwell. He'd been in a land of dreams.

That was how she'd dealt with his coma. She'd told herself he was just sleeping. She would carry the pain, the hurt and the grief, whilst Blake sat beside her in a chair, sighing and playing some stupid game on his phone to pass the time.

Thankfully he'd only come on occasion. He'd told her that there was no point in them both sitting there, day after day, as Lucas had no idea they were there. But the nurses had told her that maybe he could hear their voices, and so she would sit and read Lucas stories, hoping that her voice would somehow bring him back to them after his aneurysm.

Before he'd got sick, Lucas would often wake in the middle of the night, come and tell her his dreams. She would have given anything for him to do that back then.

Only he'd never woken up. He'd just faded away. Slowly. Day by day. And there'd been nothing she could do to prevent it.

So Nell knew how those parents felt as they sat beside their children's beds, hoping and praying that they'd get better and come home. And she knew how scared those kids were, too. Not truly understanding what was going on, but trusting the adults and the doctors and nurses to make them better.

Seth sat forward suddenly, arms resting on his knees, looking intrigued. 'Where did you go just then?' he asked in a soft voice.

Nell met his gaze. Should she tell him? Did he need to know? Did she need to share Lucas with him? Maybe. Perhaps he might look at her in a kinder, more compassionate light.

'I was thinking about my son.'

A pause. A raised eyebrow as he looked at her differently.

'You never mentioned you had a son.'

She smiled grimly. 'I don't have him. Not any more.'

Seth's eyes darkened as he frowned. 'I'm sorry.' He sounded it too. 'You don't have to tell me anything if you don't want to.'

Nell appreciated that respect. This was her choice. He wasn't demanding information from her, and yet somehow that made her want to give it.

'His name was Lucas. He died three years ago. The night you and I met, when my car was in the ditch, was the third anniversary of his death. I was returning home from visiting his grave. I couldn't miss it. Not even for bad weather.'

Seth managed to look completely and utterly ashamed. He looked down at the floor. 'And I was awful to you... About being out in that weather. I'm sorry. I should have realised you'd have a good reason.'

'You weren't to know.'

'No. But I could have been kinder. You were having a difficult day already. Then your car ended up in a ditch. I ought to have been more...considerate.'

He had the decency to look shamefaced.

She smiled. 'Yes. You should have been.'

'I'm sorry. I mean it.'

Nell was kind of enjoying this version of Dr Seth James. She'd seen a completely different side to him when they were with the children. He'd been kind and funny and generous.

Warm! And, although she'd been dreading having to be his elf for the day, it had actually been fun. And now, seeing this tender side of him… She was beginning to realise that she had misjudged him completely. That the Seth she'd met on that winter's night in a blizzard was not the real Seth.

'It's okay,' she said.

'No. It's not. And I guess if we're being honest with one another perhaps I ought to tell you why I wasn't in the best of moods when we met, either.'

'Go on.' She was intrigued. Anything to explain that night…

'That bend where your car went into the ditch…'

She nodded.

'It was the exact spot in which my girlfriend was killed, when she skidded on black ice and careered into a tree at speed. I survived. As did our son, Olly. But Dana succumbed to her injuries.'

'Dana!'

Of course! Nell remembered hearing about her accident! Dana had once been a friend. They'd met at secondary school, never in any of the same classes, but often in the school plays. They'd both liked to act, and one year had both auditioned for the role of fairy godmother in the pantomime. They'd had a bit of a rivalry. Friendly and fun. Joking and winding each other up. They had known one another. A little anyway.

Nell had been away in Austria with Blake when the accident had happened. She'd found out about Dana's death when she'd returned and her obituary had been in the local newspaper.

'You knew her?'

Nell nodded. 'Once upon a time. Many years ago. At school. I remembered reading that she'd died… I didn't know she was your girlfriend.'

Seth looked down. 'So, finding you in that spot, in a car,

in a ditch, in the middle of a blizzard that everyone had been advised not to drive in… It shook me. I'm not ashamed to admit it.'

'I get that. And I'm sorry. How is Olly coping?' The boy… The boy who had been standing in her bedroom that morning when she'd woken at Elmbridge Manor. Standing there holding that teddy…

'He's doing okay. As well as can be expected. He asks questions about his mum sometimes, and I guess he'll find out the truth one day.'

'The truth? Of the accident?'

'The fact that if it wasn't for me wanting to have a drink at a Christmas party she'd still be here today.'

To give her credit, Nell tried to say it wasn't his fault.

'You can't blame yourself.'

'Can't I?' He sat back on the couch and let out a long, low breath. 'I wanted a drink. A *drink*, for crying out loud! And because of that she offered to fetch me and bring me home afterwards. With Olly in the car! If I hadn't had a drink… if I'd driven myself…then she'd still be here and Olly would have his mother.'

'Maybe, but no one could blame you for wanting a drink at Christmas. At a party. She did a nice thing, offering to pick you up. And who's to say that *you* wouldn't have skidded on that same patch of ice as *you* drove home? Then Olly wouldn't have his dad.'

'Better that than not having his mum…'

'You can't think that. What happened, happened. No amount of guilt or regret will change the past. But you can be the one to give him all his future happiness. The love of a father who will no doubt be his bedrock and his go-to guy.'

'You're sweet to be so kind. Especially after how I've spoken to you.'

She laughed gently. 'We have had our moments.'

He sat forward again and held out his hand. 'Ceasefire?'

He didn't want to be on her case any more. Didn't want to tease her or rile her or any of those things. They'd both been through loss. They'd both lost someone special. Her, a son. Him, the mother of his child. There was no need for them to be at war any more. They ought to be united in their shared pain.

'Ceasefire.' She leaned forward and shook his hand. 'The official peace treaty begins now.'

He let her hand go, trying not to think too hard about what it had felt like to touch her. Had it been something magical? Something warmly intriguing? Or was it just relief that they had made a pact to be nicer to one another?

Dismissing it as nothing more than that, he smiled and stood up. 'Well, time to get changed. I don't want to drive home like this.'

She looked down at her own outfit. 'No.'

'And don't forget to take off all of that.'

He pointed at his own face, indicating the make-up on her cheeks. The big circles. The freckles. They were cute, though. Made her look impish. Like a pixie. A beautiful pixie.

'I won't.' She stood and met his gaze for a moment. 'It's nice to finally meet you, at last, Dr Seth James.'

He nodded and smiled. 'Likewise, Nell Bryant. Likewise.'

CHAPTER SIX

IT BECAME HARD not to notice Seth after that. Now, when they had to pass each other on the wards or see each other across the room, instead of feeling a rising irritation and waiting to defend herself from his smarmy comments, Nell found herself smiling at him, or nodding, or saying hello and asking how he was doing.

And it was having a strange effect.

It was odd how sharing the story of losing Lucas had opened up a whole other avenue of friendship between them. She liked this new intimacy they shared. Liked it that they now understood one another and where they were coming from.

One lunchtime, just as she was heading off the ward to get something to eat, Seth bumped into her and asked if he could join her for lunch.

'I'm starving. Haven't eaten all morning.'

'Sure,' she answered.

The hospital cafeteria was busy and there weren't many hot food options left, but Nell settled on a chicken pie with some mashed potatoes and veggies, and Seth had fish and chips with mushy peas. There was a table by the window, overlooking the memorial park, so they sat there.

'How's Olly?' she asked.

'Good. He's been given a role in his school's Christmas play and the first show is tonight. He's nervous, even though he's only got a small bit to do.'

'What's the play?'

'Something called *The King's Christmas Cherries*.' He laughed at her expression. 'No, I've never heard of it, either.'

'What part has he got?'

'He plays a knight. Only one line. He has to bow before the King and say, *"Your Majesty! I bring you Sir Cleges!"*'

'Has he been practising?'

'Are you kidding? I've heard every iteration of that sentence for the last week or two. It's driving me mad.'

'But you won't feel mad when you hear him say it in the play. You'll be proud.' She pointed her fork at him and smiled. She would have loved to see Lucas in a school play, but he'd been sick. But she would never get that chance now. 'A proud papa.'

He nodded, obviously thinking hard. 'Yeah. Would you want to come with me? Go and watch it together?'

What?

Her heart suddenly pounded in her chest at his suggestion. *Isn't that... I don't know...a little odd?*

'I barely know him.'

Seth looked embarrassed. 'Of course! Sorry. I don't know what made me ask. It's just... These things, you know? Things that both parents usually go to. I hate going on my own. It just makes me think that Dana should be there, too. Reminds me that she's not there.'

Without thinking, Nell reached across the table and squeezed his hand. Just briefly. 'She would have loved it. Seeing her son in a school play like she used to be...'

He frowned, looking up at her. 'How do you know she liked to act?'

'I told you—I knew her at school. We usually went after the same parts in the school plays and pantomimes. She loved acting. I think she'd love the fact that her son is doing the same thing even more.'

Seth smiled sadly and she made a sudden decision.

'You know what? For Dana's sake I will go. I'd love to go and see *The King's Christmas Cherries* with you.'

'What made me say I'd go?'

The question kept going around and around in her brain that afternoon at work. Seth had left for home. He'd worked the early morning shift and stayed until two in the afternoon, and now he had left after giving her a time to meet.

Suddenly their ceasefire, their friendship, seemed to be heading in another direction, and she was worrying that she was getting too close.

As she helped place an IV in a young patient who was going to be having surgery that evening for the removal of a foreign object—she had a coin stuck in the distal end of her oesophagus—she saw her friend Beth looking at her.

'What's up? I've never seen you frown so much.'

'Oh, nothing.' She didn't want to talk about it in front of their patient.

'No, come on. Something's bothering you!'

'Mummy always says a problem shared is a problem halved,' said the patient.

'Mummy's right,' insisted Beth. She slipped her arm into Nell's and pulled her away from the bedside. 'Come on—spill.'

Nell sighed. 'I've agreed to go somewhere with someone and I'm not sure I should have.'

'Well, that's a little vague... Is the someone a guy?'

She nodded, biting her lip.

'Whoa! Okay. You've not been on a date since Blake.'

'It's not a date! I've just agreed to accompany him to something, that's all.'

'Honey, that's a date.'

'What am I going to do?'

'You could cancel if you're uncomfortable. Say something's come up. Do you like him?'

A few days ago she would have said no. But since he'd been Santa and she his elf, and since that moment of sharing their painful pasts in the staff room, things had changed. She'd seen another side to him, and if she were truly being honest then, yes, she liked him.

It must have shown on her face, because Beth's eyebrows rose in surprise. 'Okay. Well, I guess the question is...do you feel ready to date again?'

'I'm not sure he sees it as a date. He didn't ask me out, exactly. Well, he did, and I said no, and then I changed my mind and offered to go with him.'

'Wow. The romance!'

Nell smiled ruefully. 'It's just as friends, I think.'

'You need to be sure.'

'I only ask because if things don't work out and get awkward, you're going to have to continue to work in the same place, and that can get uncomfortable.'

Nell nodded. But she'd already dealt with the uncomfortable with Seth, and if they ended up back there again she'd deal with it. Somehow. But he wouldn't be interested in her in *that* way. Would he? He had a son to think about, and she... Well, she didn't. And she wasn't looking to be anyone's stepmother, or anything. She wouldn't be able to handle that.

'I'm just going to support him on what could be a difficult thing. That's all.'

'He needs a bit of hand-holding? I see… Okay. Well, then you need to make it clear what you're offering here. Friendship. Nothing more.'

But again something must have shown on her face, because Beth tilted her head, smiled and leaned in closer.

'Unless…you *do* want something more with him?'

Nell blushed. She'd be lying if she said she hadn't thought briefly about what it might be like to be kissed by Seth. He was dark and brooding. The lord of the manor, with a tragic back story of heartbreak and looks to kill for. He was strong and broad-shouldered. He looked the kind of guy who would be able to protect you for life.

And she knew he loved deeply. He had been devoted to his girlfriend, Dana. Had given her the kind of love that Nell could only dream of.

Blake had never been demonstrative. Never been one for public displays of affection. She had yearned sometimes for him to hold her hand or tell her he loved her in public. But their relationship had never been overly physical. It was something that had plagued her for years, but she'd accepted it because back then she had loved Blake and wanted to accept him for the way he was. The way he showed love. It would be enough, she'd kept telling herself.

But then Lucas had died and the wedge, the gap between her and her husband, had widened. His inability to show emotion, or anything of what he was feeling, had been the final nail in the coffin of their marriage, and she couldn't remember the last time she'd been held. The last time she'd been kissed.

She yearned for human touch.

To be cherished and loved for who she was.

Made to feel important to someone. As if she was the only one who mattered. The only girl in the world.

So, yes, she did want something more.

The question was…did she want all that from Seth?

And, more importantly, was he even capable of giving it?

It had felt strange, asking Nell to join him at his son's school to watch him in a play. It wasn't even as if Olly had a big part! It was just one line…it would be over in a jiffy.

But the idea of sitting in the audience alone, with all the other proud parents…

Dana would have loved it! She'd have been excited, telling Olly how proud they were, and that he was going to be amazing and not to be nervous. She would have tried to get a front row seat and recorded it on her phone, or taken pictures, and she would have cheered the loudest at the end, standing to clap and maybe even give a wolf whistle or two when the cast came on stage to take a bow.

He knew this because that was what she had done when Olly had been an angel in his first ever Christmas play at nursery.

Since Dana's death, Seth had endured these torturous events for Olly's sake only. Sitting at the back of the auditorium, trying not to notice all the couples, all the proud mums and dads sitting together, and trying in vain not to hate them because they had what he and Olly didn't. And when the play was over, he'd collect Olly and whisk him home again. Telling him that he was proud. That Olly had done well.

Why had he invited Nell? Just so that he wouldn't be there alone again? So that Olly had two people applauding him? Who would Olly think she was? He'd not thought that through, and that bothered him—that he'd asked her so impulsively. She didn't really want to go. She'd said no, originally. Well, kind of…

'I barely know him.'

She was right. They'd met once. When she'd been sleeping over at the Manor. And if he were to turn up at his son's school with her in tow what would Olly think? She was just a friend. A work colleague he'd helped out once. But would his son understand that?

He'd dropped his son off and left him with the teachers, so that he could get dressed in his knight's outfit, and now Seth was standing outside the school, waiting for Nell to arrive. He'd told her a time to meet him.

He glanced at his watch. She should have been here ten minutes ago.

Had she changed her mind? Did she think the invitation was weird and regret accepting it? She'd taken pity on him, that was all. It had been an impulse offer to come.

Seth managed a polite smile at the one or two parents he knew, whom he saw on drop-offs and pick-ups. He watched the couples, walking in excitedly. One or two were arm in arm.

The Painters, as always, held hands. They had twins. They said the months of sleepless nights had helped bring them closer together. That as the twins babbled in their own secret language that they didn't understand it made them talk to one another more. Brought them closer.

Seth envied them that. He'd always thought he'd grow old with Dana. Marry her.

He'd never understood her reasons for not wanting to marry. She'd said her parents should never have married. That they spent all their time arguing. Told him how she constantly had to hear how her mother could not afford to move out so had to stay with a man she hated.

It had had an effect on Dana. She'd remained steadfastly independent in their relationship. Kept her own bank account. Worked at her own career and always been wary of the title that would come if she married the Lord of Elmbridge Manor. She'd said that anyone who married into that kind of rich history would be taking a lot onto their shoulders, and he'd agreed, but he'd thought they could do it.

They'd been happy, hadn't they? But though he'd asked Dana to marry him more than once, she'd kept saying no.

It had hurt. But he had loved her and respected her wishes. Even if he'd felt that she was never truly his. That somehow she always had one foot out through the door, ready to bolt.

He checked his watch again. Five more minutes and then he'd go in. He was probably being a fool to expect her to turn up. Olly was nothing to do with her. She wouldn't feel any pride in watching him perform. She'd be polite, smile and clap, maybe, but that was it.

No. He'd asked her here for himself. And if she didn't show up wouldn't work be awkward? Especially since they'd called a ceasefire after their initial meeting?

And then suddenly he saw her. Or rather, heard her first. There was the sound of running footsteps, heavy breathing, and then there she was, dark hair streaming behind her as she ran up to him, smiling, laughing, panting.

'Oh, thank God! I thought I'd be too late!'

'It's fine. Why are you running?'

'My car. I swear it's more trouble than it's worth.'

'What happened?'

'It conked out on me halfway here. Steam rising from under the bonnet... I'm wondering if the accident cracked something and it's finally given up the ghost? Anyway, I've had to abandon it a few streets away.'

He smiled. 'You're going to get your money's worth out of your breakdown membership.'

'Well, they've had enough money out of me over the years.'
She looked past him. 'Where's Olly?'

'Getting into his costume. Ready to go in?'

She nodded.

'Thanks for this. I do appreciate it.'

Her eyes met his and he saw them soften. 'You're welcome.'

If she had been Dana he would have taken her hand, kissed
her cheek, and they'd have walked in together. But he couldn't
kiss Nell or take her hand, so he awkwardly put his hands
into his jeans pockets and said, 'This way, I think. Follow
the crowd.'

He showed his parent pass to the teaching assistant who
was manning the door and then they walked down a school
corridor that smelt of paint and clay and books. They were
herded, like sheep, into the school hall.

Up at the front was a raised stage, with red curtains covering its entirety, and the rest of the room was filled with mill-
ing parents, looking for the last good seats.

Seth scanned the rows, looking for two seats together. He
and Nell were the last two people in, it seemed, and he wasn't
sure where they would sit—until he saw the headmistress, Mrs
Janlin, trying to get his attention and pointing to a couple of
seats two rows back from the front, hidden by a sea of heads.

'Thanks,' he said, as they passed the headmistress, and then
he stood back to let Nell go first.

Sitting down, he saw they had a good view of the stage.

Nell leaned in. 'I did some research and I think this play is
based on a story involving King Arthur.'

'Really?'

He was impressed that she'd done any research at all. Olly
wasn't her kid, so for her to show that kind of interest… He
was kind of pleased.

As the lights were lowered and some medieval-sounding music began to play, the hubbub of the crowd decreased, spotlights rose on the stage and the curtains pulled back to reveal a king sitting on his throne, examining a bowl of grapes and frowning.

'These grapes taste of nothing!' said the boy dressed as the King, loudly. 'I wish I had some fruit that tasted delicious!'

The play was more interesting and a lot funnier than Seth had thought it might be. At times, the audience roared with laughter. And they clapped and cheered when a nervous young girl performed a solo vocal, tremoring with fear to begin with, but eventually gaining confidence and letting her voice soar like an angel.

They smiled quietly when some of the children stumbled or fumbled through their lines. And then suddenly Olly was there, striding on stage in his knight's uniform and standing before the King.

He gave an exaggerated bow and announced in a loud voice, 'Your Majesty! I bring you Sir Cleges!'

Seth couldn't help it. He beamed with pride. It was only one line. Olly didn't have a major part. But his son had acted the part of a noble knight perfectly. And as the tattily dressed Sir Cleges entered, stage right, Olly stood behind the King's throne, relieved that his part had gone without a hitch. He sought out his dad's face in the crowd and gave him a little wave.

Seth waved back.

'He did brilliantly!' whispered Nell.

'He did.'

Was that a tear he could feel in his eye? A tear of pride? Because he'd never felt so proud as he did in that moment, and he hoped that if Dana was somehow able to see her son, she would feel proud, too.

Seth stared at his son until he left the stage, and then he watched the rest of the play, laughing with the audience when Sir Cleges chased the knights with his stick and all devolved into chaos on stage as the kids went crazy.

The King's Christmas Cherries turned out to be an amazing play, and when it was over the entire audience stood and gave the kids a standing ovation.

Seth whistled loudly, and beside him Nell clapped heartily.

'That was so good!' she yelled, so that he could hear.

She was right. It had been more than good. It had been amazing. And he couldn't have been more proud of his son than he was in that moment.

Afterwards, Mrs Janlin gave a few announcements and handed out some award certificates. Olly was called up to receive a certificate for 'Asking the Most Awkward Questions in Assembly'.

Seth felt there must be a story or two behind that certificate, and he couldn't wait to hear what it was.

As they stood outside, waiting for Olly to appear, he took the moment to thank Nell again for coming. 'I really appreciate it,' he told her.

'Hey, I had a great time! Back when I was Olly's age school plays were awkward, embarrassing affairs, with difficult silences when everyone forgot their lines. Kids today seem much better at it than we were.'

He laughed. 'I think you're right. Olly did so well… I feel I ought to treat him. Fancy a bite to eat? Or do you have to go? I don't want to take up all your free time if you have somewhere else to be.'

He watched her think about it for a moment. 'No, I don't have anywhere to be. If that's okay with you and Olly?'

'I'm sure he won't mind.'

At that moment, Olly came barrelling out of school, grinning, his face lit up, holding on to his certificate.

'Look, Dad, look!'

'I saw! Congratulations!' Seth read the certificate that had been waved in his face, then passed it to Nell to look at. 'You remember Nell? You met her at home the other day?'

Olly peered up at her. 'You had a sleepover at our house.'

'Er…that's right,' said Nell, awkwardly.

'I thought we could grab a bite to eat, Olls. Is it okay if Nell comes, too?'

'Sure.'

Seth smiled at Nell, and they began to head out of the car park.

Olly was a bundle of energy, clearly high on his stage debut and being awarded a certificate. He held on to his dad's hand, but he was so bouncy and so full of adrenaline Nell felt exhausted just watching him.

She'd forgotten how vital and high-octane some little boys could be. Lucas had been the same when he'd got excited. She was dismayed at how difficult she was finding it, being in his company. Olly was so full of energy, so full of life. It simply reminded her of what she'd lost.

Seth took them to a pizza restaurant, where Olly ordered cheese and tomato. Seth ordered a meat feast, and Nell asked for a small vegetarian pizza with extra mushrooms and jalapenos.

She was relieved when Olly disappeared to play in the soft play area whilst they waited for their food to arrive.

'You okay?' Seth asked.

She nodded, forcing a smile. 'Yes. You?'

'I am. I spent a long time dreading tonight and you made it easier.'

'Oh, I'm sure it was nothing to do with me. Olly is the star of the night.'

'Well, that too. And now I'll never have to hear about Sir Cleges again!'

'Bonus.' She laughed, twirling the straw in her glass of water.

'I know this must be hard for you... Christmas is a time for families. Especially those with young children. You should be the one watching your son in a play, and yet there you were with me, watching mine. That was more than generous. That was brave and kind and I won't ever forget it.'

Nell wasn't used to a man saying nice things about her in public. She wasn't used to sitting in a restaurant across from a man and having him stare into her eyes and tell her how much he appreciated her.

It was weird.

It was strange.

But most of all it was wonderful, and delicious, and she craved more. But they were just friends, right? She'd done this as a favour to him. It hadn't been a date. This wasn't a romance. And yet it didn't stop her from blushing and thinking what it might be like if it were...

What kind of romantic partner was Dr Seth James, Lord Elmbridge? She'd seen and experienced his sarcastic side. The smart-aleck side. She'd seen the sort of doctor he was—kind and warm. She'd seen him as Santa Claus and knew he could be funny and generous and thoughtful. Clearly, he was a complex man.

But could he love?

He'd been through loss, just as she had. She'd lost a son and a marriage and it had left her wary of ever being with someone again. Her marriage had taught her a lot about what she didn't want from a relationship. And what she did want. If she were ever brave enough to dip her toe in the dating waters ever again she'd want to be loved openly. By someone who was physical in their love. Who believed in the power of hugs and cuddles and kisses. Who was openly demonstrative. Someone she could hold at night and fall asleep in his arms feeling that she was adored and valued and cherished.

What did Seth want? After Dana, did he ever feel he could date again?

'What are you thinking?' he asked.

Blushing, she laughed. 'Oh...deep thoughts.'

'Want to share?'

'Here? In a pizza restaurant?'

'Why not?'

She stared at him, wondering if she was brave enough to ask. Feeling her cheeks burn. 'Okay... I was wondering if you ever saw yourself dating someone again.'

Seth let out a short laugh of surprise and leaned away from her in his chair. 'Not what I was expecting!'

She saw him check to see where Olly was.

'Maybe. One day. But at this point I'd be pretty surprised if I did. That person would have to be amazing enough to thaw my ice-hardened heart and warm it up enough to make me go through all that palaver again.' He stared hard at her. 'What about you?'

'Me? Oh, I don't know... I think Blake might have ruined me for a while.'

'Your husband?'

She nodded. 'It was just so awful and so difficult at the end... The person who is meant to love you shouldn't treat you like that, you know? And if someone who is meant to love you can treat you so badly...? Well, I've heard enough shocking dating stories from my friends at work that I'm not sure I want to enter that world again. Maybe one day I'll be brave enough, but not right now.'

'What made you think of that now?'

She sipped her water. 'Tonight. Seeing all those happy families at the school. Realising I'm not one of them any more. I felt lonely. I may not have Lucas, but I'm still a mother. A mother without a child. And it's Christmas. A time for families. I really feel it at this time of year.'

'I get that. I don't feel like I'm one of them, either.'

'You don't?'

'Absolutely not. Olly should have his mum here with us. Getting excited. Watching his shows. Going to parents' evenings. Every time I go to one of those things on my own I'm harshly reminded that I shouldn't be. On my own, that is.'

'Don't we make a pitiful pair?' she said ruefully.

At that moment a server arrived, carrying their pizzas.

Seth called out to Olly, and when the young boy came to the table made his son clean his hands, using an antibacterial wipe from a small sachet. 'Okay, now you can eat.'

Nell watched as Olly smeared his pizza with extra ketchup and smiled. Lucas had liked ketchup, too.

It felt odd to be sitting there with Seth and his son. She was a part of this small group, yes, but she didn't belong. Not really. She was an outsider, allowed in by Seth's grace. Nothing more.

Her pizza was perfect. Oozing with melted cheese and soft mushrooms, with a kick from the jalapenos and peppers. It hit the spot. And although she felt on edge, she had to admit it was much better than being at home in her flat alone, searching the channels on the TV to find something that took her fancy.

Christmas was always difficult without Lucas. Far too quiet. Far too tidy. She'd put up some decorations and a tree, but it was something that she did out of duty now. Before, she would get Lucas to help her decorate. Lifting him up to place the star or the angel on the top of the tree. Getting him to put his stocking over the end of his bedpost. Her stocking hung alone now on the mantel. A glaring reminder of her solitude.

Her mum and dad always suggested that she go to them at Christmas. But with her work commitments she'd have to take too much time off from work. And besides, she'd spent enough Christmases with them and really didn't want any more.

Not with Mum getting angry with Dad for having one too many extra drinks as he cooked dinner, or Dad getting leery and making one too many jokes at Mum's expense, so that by the time Christmas Day turned into Christmas Night there'd be an atmosphere that could be cut with a knife, punctuated only by her father's deep, resonant snores from the couch. Her mum only ever wanted her there as a buffer. So she'd have someone to moan to.

Nell didn't want that any more. She wanted to sit and remember the good times. Reflect and quietly toast her son as she sat down to Christmas dinner.

'Are you my dad's girlfriend?' Olly suddenly asked out of nowhere, with smudges of ketchup around his mouth.

Nell flushed and glanced with embarrassment at Seth.

'No, she is not,' said Seth, firmly and sternly to his son. 'I told you. She's a girl who happens to be a friend.'

'I know. But Jacob said that when *his* daddy has a lady sleeping over at their house, it's because she's his girlfriend.'

Nell's cheeks felt as hot as the surface of the sun. 'That's different,' she managed. 'The reason I was at your house was because my car had broken down in the snow storm and your dad offered me a place to stay. Otherwise I would have frozen in my car.'

Olly shrugged. 'Okay.'

Nell glanced again at Seth, glad she'd cleared that up. It had been awkward… Olly suggesting she was his dad's girlfriend.

'But Daddy will have a girlfriend one day, won't he?' Olly went on. 'Like Jacob's daddy?'

Nell swallowed hard and tried to redirect the conversation. 'Who's Jacob?' she asked.

'A boy in his class,' said Seth darkly.

'He has a mummy…but sometimes his daddy has a girlfriend, too.'

Nell looked to Seth for clarification.

'Jacob's parents are divorced.'

'Oh. I see.'

'Jacob says one day he will have *two* mummies.'

'And how does he feel about that?'

'I think he's happy. He smiled when he said it,' said Olly. 'But I don't think it's fair that he should have two when I don't even have one.'

Nell stared at the little boy, feeling his pain. She waited for Seth to say something, but he seemed tongue-tied, so she spoke instead. 'You do have a mummy, though, Olly. She will always be your mummy. She may not be here, in person, but you are never without a mummy.'

'You think so?'

She nodded. 'Absolutely. She loved you. I know it. With all her heart.'

The way she still loved Lucas. He wasn't here, but that didn't mean the love was gone. Not one iota.

'Love carries on,' she told Olly. 'Even when that person we love is no longer with us in person. It's still here,' she placed a hand over her own heart, 'and will stay with you for ever.'

Olly smiled and then took another bite of pizza.

Nell met Seth's gaze and he smiled and nodded at her, mouthing a silent *Thank you*.

The rest of the meal went on without any more difficult conversation. Seth asked his son what the 'awkward questions' were that he'd asked in assembly, and before they all knew it they were laughing and enjoying each other's company.

For a very brief moment—a millisecond of time—Nell forgot that she was alone. Forgot that she wasn't a part of this small family group. But when it was time to go home, and she realised that she would have to walk away from them and leave them, she remembered, and the harsh reality of life almost took her breath away.

'Well, thank you for tonight. I had a great time,' she said to Seth. 'It was nice to meet you properly, Olly.' She shook the little boy's hand. 'And you made an excellent knight.'

'Let us drive you home,' said Seth. 'Your car's broken down, remember?'

'You don't need to rescue me twice. I'll be all right.'

'On the contrary. At least let us drive you to your car and wait with you until the breakdown service arrives.'

She shook her head. 'No. You go home. Olly's tired. Look at him yawning. I'll see you at work.'

Seth glanced at his son, who looked almost asleep on his feet. He'd had a long day. 'If you're sure?'

'Absolutely. Go.'

'All right. Thanks for coming with me tonight. I appreciate it.'

Nell smiled at him. 'You're welcome.'

And then he surprised her by leaning in and dropping a kiss on her cheek.

Nell held her breath and closed her eyes, slowing down time, feeling the moment as if wanting to treasure it. To remember it. His lips against her cheek…the soft bristles of his dark beard tickling her skin. The scent of him… Aftershave. Soap and sandalwood. Something deeper. Earthier.

She wasn't used to public displays of affection. Blake had only ever kissed her once in public, and that had been on their wedding day, when the vicar had said, 'You may now kiss your bride.' And he'd even looked awkward doing that!

And then Seth was pulling away, with something like regret in his eyes, taking his son's hand and helping him get into the car and do his seatbelt.

She stood there, watching them, knowing she ought to walk away. But she couldn't.

There'd been something in Seth's gaze when he'd kissed her goodbye…

He closed his son's car door and walked around to the driver's side. 'One last chance?'

He meant for a lift, but she found herself wishing he meant so much more.

'I'm good. It's not far. You get Olly home to bed.'

'Okay. See you at work tomorrow.'

She smiled. 'Yes. Yes, you will. Bye.'

She raised her hand as he got into the vehicle and continued to stand there as he drove away, her eyes tracking every last moment that his vehicle was in sight. When he disappeared around the bend she felt all the tension in her body flow out, and she practically sagged as she headed in the direction of her own car.

Alone once again.

CHAPTER SEVEN

SETH HAD BEEN called to the paediatric assessment unit. A young boy had been sent up from A&E with a week-long history of sickness and diarrhoea. And now he was reporting bad stomach pains.

When he got to the boy's bedside, he saw Jaxon Hunter's vitals were all alarmingly low. He saw a pale boy, clearly underweight, who was also looking a little jaundiced, lying listlessly in bed, his anxious parents at his bedside. He was hooked up to an IV of fluids to help rehydrate him, and had been given anti-nausea and painkilling medication.

In A&E they'd taken blood, performed scans and an X-ray, and now it was Seth's job to report on the results.

'Mr and Mrs Hunter? I'm Dr James and I'll be looking after Jaxon. Do you want to tell me about how his symptoms began?'

Jaxon's mother spoke. 'He came home from school a week ago, complaining of a tummy ache. They'd had the school Christmas dinner that day, and the teacher said the kids had all had pudding and sweets, so we just thought he'd indulged too much.'

Seth nodded.

'He seemed to be a little better the next day, but by the time he came home after school he said his tummy ache was back and he felt sick. That night he spiked a fever and had diarrhoea, so we thought maybe a tummy bug. Norovirus is around at this time of year, isn't it? Is that what this is?'

'We don't think so. Was he urinating frequently?'

'I don't know. Normally, I guess…'

'We'll need to get a sample from him. They weren't able to get one in A&E, so when he wants to go, if you could get it in a bottle so we can test it?'

'What do you think it is?'

Seth sighed. 'Well, normally these kinds of symptoms *would* be associated with a tummy bug or winter virus, but the yellowing of his eyes and skin indicate an issue with the liver. There have been some cases of healthy children this year suddenly developing acute hepatitis-like symptoms, due to an adenovirus, and at this moment in time I'm veering towards that.'

'*Hepatitis?* Isn't that serious?' the mother asked in shock.

'It can be, but if I'm right this isn't hepatitis as we normally imagine it. The adenovirus creates hepatitis-*like* symptoms—liver inflammation—so right now we need to treat Jaxon's symptoms and perform a PCR test to confirm.'

The polymerase chain reaction test would detect genetic material from a certain virus.

'And then he'll be okay?' asked Jaxon's father.

'We need to confirm our suspicions first, and then work from there.'

He didn't want to tell the Hunters that on occasion some children required liver transplants because of this virus. Why worry them until they knew for sure? They had enough to worry about with their son being in hospital as it was. He would tell them when they needed to know. When the evidence pointed in that direction.

'We'll need some more blood from Jaxon. I've already put the request in, so someone will be along soon to do it.'

'I'm here.'

Seth turned at Nell's soft voice and smiled on seeing her at the end of the bed. He'd not heard her approach. He turned back to Jaxon.

'This is Nell and she's going to take another small sample of blood from you—is that okay?'

Jaxon nodded.

Nell approached and sat on a chair beside the bed. 'Hi, Jaxon. I know you're feeling poorly, but I need to take some more blood from you.'

'They took blood in A&E. Can't you use that?' asked Jaxon's mother.

'That was used to test for other markers. I need a fresh sample for the PCR test. How are you with needles, Jaxon?'

'Okay... They pinch.'

'They do. But only for a little while.'

'The nurse in A&E struggled to find a vein,' said Jaxon's father. 'We don't want him poked all over again.'

Nell turned to face them. 'I get that. Totally. They might have struggled due to Jaxon's dehydration, but he's been on fluids for a while now, so hopefully I'll have better luck.'

Seth admired the way she was handling the parents' concern. She really was good at her job.

Nell palpated both of Jaxon's arms, focusing mainly on his left antecubital fossa—the crook of the elbow. Then she tied the tourniquet around his upper arm, swabbed with an alcohol wipe, gave it a brief second to dry, then inserted the needle and got a sample right away.

Seth had been holding his breath, but now he let it go. 'This is why we call Nell to do this,' he said, and smiled. 'We'll have the sample checked ASAP, so we can get the results to you.

In the meantime, if you have any questions, don't hesitate to get a nurse to find me.'

'Thank you, Doctor.'

Seth escorted Nell back to the nurses' station, where she stood labelling Jaxon's sample, ready to bag it up and send it off to Pathology.

'How's your car?' he asked.

'Poorly. At the garage having its head gasket fixed, or replaced, or whatever it is they're doing.'

He grimaced. 'Sounds expensive.'

'It's fine. Christmas is meant to be expensive, right?'

'Not in that way. How did you get to work?'

'Bus.'

'Ah…'

'I bet you've never had to catch a bus in your entire life, huh?'

He smiled. Caught out. 'No, I haven't.'

'How the other half live…' She smiled as she sealed the bag with the blood sample. 'I'll get this off to Path.'

'Thanks. Hey, what time do you finish today?'

'Five.'

'Perfect. Me too. Let me give you a lift home.'

'You don't have to do that.'

'You helped me last night, so now it's my turn. Honestly, I don't mind.'

'Don't you have to get back for Olly?'

'He's at a friend's house. Sleepover.'

'Oh. Well, if you're sure…?'

He nodded. He absolutely was.

It was snowing again. But not as hard as the blizzard that had originally caused them to meet. This snow was gentle. Fat flakes drifting down and disappearing into the already wet ground. It wouldn't settle. Not this time. The ground was already sodden from the melt of the last snowfall.

It was nice being in Seth's car. It was a different one from the one that had been pulling the trailer that night they'd first met. This was a saloon car, with cream leather seats, and it was warm and comfortable. Gentle Christmas music played from the speakers.

'Left or right?'

She pointed ahead at the traffic lights. 'Right where that car's turning—see?'

'Yep.'

She wasn't sure how to feel about Seth seeing where she lived. He lived out in the sticks—in a manor, for crying out loud! She wasn't sure he was used to suburban life and all that it entailed. Her flat in a tower block was all she'd been able to afford after the divorce, when they'd sold their marital home. She didn't plan on staying there for ever. She was saving hard, and she kept her expenses to a minimum, as much as she could—which was why the car breaking down was a big deal.

She needed the car for work, but repairing it really was money down the drain. She had considered telling the garage to scrap the car and be done with it, but in the end she'd not been able to. The car was her lifeline. It got her away from the town when she needed to breathe clean, country air. It got her to Lucas's grave at Wilford Hill. It got her away from the stresses and strains of living near a city as big as Nottingham.

'Take this left…then there's an immediate turning into the car park for my place.'

She saw him glance out at the huge tower block as he pulled into a parking spot.

'This is it,' she said. She didn't feel embarrassed about

where she lived. She'd made it a home and she had good neighbours who helped each other out. But she just knew he'd be comparing it with where he lived and the vast differences between them.

'Which floor are you on?'

'Twenty-first. Top floor. I get a great view of Clifton and the city. Especially on fireworks night.'

'Must be amazing.'

'On occasion. Want to come up and see?'

The invitation was out of her mouth before she could even think to censor her words, and then she felt her cheeks burn as she blushed. Of course he'd say no. He wouldn't want to come in. Wouldn't want to risk leaving his car here.

'Sure!'

Nell blinked, surprised, but then she smiled and alighted from the car, waiting for him to lock it, then headed towards the entry doors. She swiped her security key on the front door pad. It buzzed and let her in.

On the ground floor was a security office, where Paul was on duty as usual.

'Hey, Paul, how you doing?'

'Hey, Nell! I'm doing fine. Readying myself for the night.'

'Can you do me a favour? Keep an eye on the silver saloon in the car park? The one under the lamp.'

'Can do.' He saluted her as they walked past and she punched the button for the lift.

She'd never have thought that she'd be bringing Seth back here! As she waited for the lift she tried not to let nervousness bubble up inside her, but she couldn't help it! What would she do once they reached her flat? Talk to him? Make him a cuppa? Give him a tour? It wouldn't be much of one. It'd be over in less than a minute. A tour of Elmbridge Manor would take a good hour in comparison!

The lift doors pinged open and they stepped inside. She was suddenly acutely aware of the graffiti within it. Perhaps it would have been okay if it was artistic, but it was just people's names. Tags. Nothing more.

They rode the lift in silence, with Nell struggling for something to say. Just when she'd decided on a topic that might be safe, the lift doors pinged open and they were at the top. Her flat was directly opposite the lifts.

'This is it. Home,' she said, unnecessarily.

But she was still nervous. Because the last time she'd been with Seth on a social level he'd kissed her goodbye, and when she'd finally got home to her flat and sat down she'd replayed that kiss over and over again.

It had just been a kiss. Friendly. It had said *Thank you for joining me tonight*. Nothing more. That was what she kept telling herself. But she was struggling to admit to all that she had felt as Seth had leaned in to kiss her. The heart in her mouth moment, watching him come closer, as if in slow motion, the anticipation of the kiss…

She'd been hesitant.

Afraid.

Excited.

She'd wondered what it might be like to have a real kiss from Seth. To have a man like him be interested in her. To have him be attracted to her.

No doubt it would be a wild ride!

But was she only wondering about it because it felt like far too long that she'd been starved of affection? Lucas had given great cuddles, but he'd been her little boy, and although she cherished the memories of what his hugs had felt like, after his death she had yearned to be held by her husband.

Blake had let her down in more ways than one, though, and the slow decay of their marriage had been extremely lonely as they'd drifted further and further apart.

Nell still wanted that physical contact. To be held. To feel safe. To feel cherished and important. Could she get that from a man like Seth? Was he even interested in her in that way?

'Living room. Kitchen through there.' She walked a little further down the hallway. 'Bathroom.' There was a long pause before she decided to push open the other door. 'My room.'

She gave him a polite, embarrassed smile. The decor of her flat was nothing to write home about. It did not have the sumptuousness or decadence that Elmbridge Manor had. There were no chequerboard floors here. There was carpet and linoleum. No tapestries or wall-hangings. Just a couple of pictures that she'd found in a local charity shop and liked. No sweeping staircases. Just a short, dark corridor, with a sad-looking Monstera plant in the corner.

'Looks great.'

She laughed. 'Now I *know* you're just being polite. This isn't what you're used to.'

'Sit down for a moment,' he said. 'I've something to show you.'

Intrigued, she led them back to the living room and sat down on the sofa. Alarmingly, Seth sat right next to her, his mobile phone in his hand as he began to thumb through his photo album. He got to the spot he wanted and passed her his phone.

'Keep swiping left.'

Nell frowned and looked at the first picture. It was of a

small living space. Yes, it had French doors that led out to a small balcony overlooking the sea, but the living space itself was minimal. A wooden floor with a rug. A simple sofa and a chair. A bookcase. A television.

'What am I looking at?'

'My home in Devon. Where Olly and I were living before we came back to Elmbridge.'

She swiped left. There was a small galley kitchen. Only a tiny bit larger than her own. More modern than hers, but the space was practically the same. *Swipe*. A bedroom. A double bed, one small side table piled with books. A lamp. Some reading glasses. *Swipe*. A young boy's room. Single bed with a football team duvet. *Swipe*. A bathroom, with both a bath and a separate shower cabinet. Simple. White tiles. Potted plants hanging from a shelf.

'We live quite modestly. Elmbridge belongs to the public. We've always had an open house. The place is all about allowing the public access to a historic building. It's not just mine, though we do live there now. But that...' he nodded at his phone '...was where we used to call home.'

She passed the phone back. 'It is rather modest. Lovely, but modest.'

He smiled. 'It's hard to be comfortable amongst so much history.'

'How long are you planning to stay at Elmbridge?'

'We're back for good. Granny isn't getting any younger, and it's time that Olly began to learn about where he came from and what his responsibilities will be when he gets older.'

'And your Devon home?'

'It will always be there if we need to go back, or just want to spend some time by the sea.'

She heard something in his voice. 'You're missing it?'

He nodded. 'I was free there. Not bound by dark memories. Here… I've got obligations.'

'Being Lord Elmbridge instead of Dr James?'

'You've got it in one.'

'But there must be a part of you glad to be back in your ancestral home?'

'Of course! Granny makes it easier, and it's good for Olly to know his great-grandmother.'

'What about your parents?'

His eyes darkened. 'They died when I was very young.'

'I'm sorry.'

'It was quick. Or so the doctors tell me. My father had a massive heart attack one day and my mother died a few years later. After that, Granny raised me.'

She reached for his hand tentatively. Squeezed it in a show of support. Trying to say, *I'm here for you.*

Seth looked down at their hands, then away and over at the mantelpiece. At the pictures there.

'Is that your son?' He pulled his hand free and got up and walked away from her.

Nell felt her overture of affection had not been well received. Was Seth like Blake? Was she going to follow a pattern of falling for men who were uncomfortable with displays of concern or care?

'Yes. That's Lucas.'

The picture was her favourite one of him. He'd been outside in their back garden, building a snowman as the snow continued to fall. Lucas's nose and cheeks were bright red. He had snow crystals in his hair and it looked damp. He was in his coat and wellies and gloves and he looked so happy. She'd snapped his picture as he'd stood there, holding glovefuls of snow to add to their snowman. He'd turned. Looked at her. Grinned. *Snap.*

Afterwards, when it had been time to eat, time to go in and get warm, she'd made hot chocolate and they'd watched a Christmas movie. When they'd got up the next morning all that had been left of the snowman was a small mound of frozen snow, two broken twigs and a stubby carrot lying alongside them.

'He looks like you. He has your eyes,' Seth said.

That pleased her. That her son had taken after her, more than he had his father. Lucas had had blond hair, unlike her. But brown eyes like hers. He might have had his dad's mouth, and most definitely his dad's ears, but everything else was all her.

'Thanks.'

'You must miss him.'

She took a shuddering breath, determined not to cry. 'I do.'

Seth turned to look at her, obviously hearing the catch in her voice. 'I'm sorry. I didn't mean to make you feel sad.'

'You don't make me feel sad. Not having him here does that. All the time. I can mask it in most places, but here... I'm afraid you've caught me without my usual armour.'

He was looking at her strangely. Intensely. His gaze drifted over her features, his eyes searing into her soul.

'Tell me about him.'

'Lucas? He was the kindest boy. Generous in every way. He'd offer to give you his last sweet. He'd let you lick his ice cream. His laughter was the best sound ever...'

If she closed her eyes she could almost still hear it.

'And when he hugged you he would squeeze you so tightly...'

She could feel tears approaching. Normally she would fight to keep them back, but here, at home, sharing this moment with Seth, she wasn't sure if she should or not?

She sniffed and gave a nervous laugh, wiped her eyes. But Seth reached up to still her hand.

She stopped breathing. What was he going to do?

He looked into her eyes. Saw her soul. Her tears. Her pain. But it also seemed as if he could see something else worth pursuing. Because suddenly he was wiping underneath her eyes with his thumb. Catching her tears.

Her heart began to thud. She'd thought that maybe he was like Blake when he'd pulled his hand away from contact with her earlier, but maybe she'd been wrong? Maybe he'd felt something between them too? Maybe he'd been afraid?

But now his touch was gentle. Caring. Warm and soft.

Looking up into his dark gaze, she could feel herself getting lost. But she didn't want to assume anything was going to happen, so she kept her hands still, by her sides, desperately afraid to reach up and embrace him. What if she was reading the moment wrongly? If she was wrong, that would be embarrassing.

But she didn't think she was. Not with that look in his eyes. Not with the way he'd wiped away her tears. Not with the way he was now holding her face. Tenderly. Cradling her as if he couldn't quite believe he was standing this close and gazing into her eyes.

'There's something about you, Nell...' he said softly.

'Oh?' Her heart was hammering in her chest.

'I can't get you out of my mind.'

'Sorry about that,' she whispered, knowing she wasn't sorry at all.

'I wondered if…if it would be all right if…'

'If…?'

'If I could kiss you right now…'

She felt her eyes widen. Felt all the remaining breath leave her lungs. Her blood pressure was soaring, her pulse thundering, every nerve-ending and every cell in her body lighting up, as if on fire.

But she couldn't speak. Couldn't answer him. Fearing if she did try to speak her voice would squeak so high that maybe only dogs would hear it.

Instead, she gave the slightest of nods.

Yes. You can. Yes, you must. I want you to.

His gaze dropped to her mouth and then moved back up to her eyes, as if taking in every detail of her before he finally allowed himself to succumb to his desire to kiss her. He came closer. Closer still. Until they were millimetres apart.

She gazed deeply into his dark blue eyes, finally allowing her hands to rise up and rest upon his chest. He felt solid. All muscle. Just as she'd hoped he would be. And her touch seemed to make his breathing unsteady.

It was a heady moment.

His mouth was tantalisingly close to hers. 'You're sure? Because if I do this, I don't know if I'll be able to stop,' he whispered, arousing her instantly.

She nodded. 'Then please don't stop. I beg of you,' she whispered.

And that was enough to make his mouth claim hers.

Atoms split. Fireworks exploded. His brain went into absolute meltdown as his lips met hers. It had been a long time since he'd kissed a woman in this way. There'd been no one since

Dana. Years of keeping himself walled off from everyone and not letting anyone get close. But the one thing he'd learned about putting up walls was that, yes, they kept everyone out, but they also kept you prisoner. He'd been in solitary confinement for too long and Nell was setting him free.

At last.

There was a moment of guilt. A moment in which he almost stopped. Stepped away. Told her that this was wrong. That he was sorry. Asked her if she could forgive him.

But that moment passed the second their lips met. Because kissing Nell felt so right and so good he couldn't imagine himself ever wanting to end this. His hunger for her simply grew. He knew he wanted more, but he couldn't presume she felt the same way—even if she had sunk against him and was now kissing him back with just as much fervour as he.

He paused briefly, to take a breath. Pulled back to stare into her eyes. Eyes that were dazed with lust and yearning. A look that almost felled him.

'Nell…'

'What?'

'You're sure?'

She nodded. 'Are you?'

It was as if she was searching his soul now. Looking for signs of regret. He knew she didn't want to do this unless he felt absolutely ready too, and he appreciated that so much. She must know there might be doubts because of Dana.

'Most definitely.'

He trailed his lips along her jaw, giving her featherlight kisses as he exposed her neck and ran his lips down it, feeling the heat of her, the rapid pulse in her carotid, the warmth of her skin. And her scent! Like flowers in a meadow. Her hair soft and silken in his fingers.

Somehow they moved to her bedroom, stumbling past furniture, against walls, not willing for a moment to let each other go. Against her bedroom door, he felt her reach for his belt, pulling it free and loose before she attacked his buttons. He kicked off his shoes. Felt her go for his zip.

It was a disrobing frenzy, with clothes strewn only God knew where, but they finally made it to the bed and he laid her down upon it, gently lowered himself onto her. Their tongues entwined. They both knew that this moment would happen, that...

We don't have protection.

The thought unloaded itself and he felt himself curse inwardly.

'What is it?' she breathed.

'I don't have a condom.'

He looked into her eyes with regret, saw it mirrored there. 'Me neither.'

His arousal was straining at the leash. He wanted her. Badly. But he could not allow anything to happen in case it put either of them at risk. She must have seen the look of apology in his eyes, because she reached for his face and turned him towards her.

'Hey...' She smiled. 'There are other things we can do until we get one.'

Mmm... I like the way you're thinking!

'Say more,' he whispered.

She stroked his face, ran her fingers over his mouth. 'We have lips. And tongues. Hands. And fingers...' She bit her lip as she looked up at him with daring. 'What do you think we could achieve with any of those?'

'Let's find out,' he responded, smiling, and began to kiss her again.

CHAPTER EIGHT

SHE WOKE, NAKED, in Seth's arms. Totally satiated. Warm and cosy. She'd not slept so well for years, or felt so safe as if she did there and then.

She didn't want to move and spoil the moment. If she could have stayed there for ever, she would have. But she knew she had to go to work, and Seth probably did, too.

Turning her head ever so slightly, she tried to peer at the clock.

Eight-fifteen. She needed to be at work by nine o'clock and she hadn't showered yet. But to deliberately pull free from his embrace when she was the little spoon and Seth lay wrapped around her...

She was starving, too.

Last night had been...bliss. Heaven. Perfection. Okay, maybe not exactly perfection, but close to it. She would have loved to have felt the length of him inside her, but all the other things they'd got up to instead had been pretty terrific!

If this was Seth's foreplay what would the main event be like? She'd never known intimacy like it. Blake had been good at sex—when they'd actually engaged in it—but it had never felt like this!

With Blake, sex had been hurried, almost. As if he was embarrassed to be engaging in it and only scratching an itch he felt from time to time. She'd tried initiating it with him on occasion, only to be shot down and made to feel like a sex-crazed fool who could only think of one thing, when she wasn't like that at all.

All she'd ever wanted was the intimacy. The becoming one. The feeling that she mattered and that her desires would be sated when she felt them.

Last night Seth had been intent on making sure she was satisfied. He'd taken his time. Enjoying her pleasure as much as he'd enjoyed his own when she'd returned the favour. They'd discovered each other's bodies like explorers. Teasing. Tempting. Bringing each other to the heights until they'd finally fallen asleep with exhaustion.

It was no wonder she was hungry and didn't want to move.

Because she'd never felt like this before.

Ever.

Who'd have thought she'd be experiencing it with a man she'd really not been sure she even liked when she'd first met him?

He must have felt her shift, because he groaned slightly as he emerged from sleep and squeezed her against his body. 'Where are you going?' he asked, his voice husky with sleep.

Nell smiled happily. 'Believe you me, I don't want to be going anywhere—but it's a quarter past eight, and I don't know about you, but I need to be at work for nine.'

She felt him nuzzle into her hair. 'Urgh… Me too. Fancy playing hooky? We could call in sick.'

And now she felt other parts of his body waking up in response to being right next to her… But although his suggestion was deliciously tempting, she could not allow herself to let down her colleagues. They depended on her, and if she didn't show up it might mean a patient receiving a delay in treatment or surgery.

'That is *so* tempting…but we can't.' She allowed her hand to reach back and caress his hip and thigh.

'Careful…' he growled.

She grinned. 'Why? What are you going to do?'

'Hmm…'

Suddenly he had rolled her onto her back and was above her, smiling.

'So many things.' He kissed her, then pulled back again. 'But you're right. We have patients. Enjoying you will have to wait until later.'

He rolled over and let her go. Nell grabbed a robe and slipped into it.

'I'm going to grab a quick shower.'

Seth growled and pulled a pillow over his face. 'Aargh! Please don't make me think of you all soaped up in the shower.'

She chuckled. 'Okay… Unless you want to join me?'

He pulled the pillow off his face and stared at her. 'We'd never get to work on time.'

She shrugged. 'Five minutes late is better than not turning up at all.'

He threw off the covers and stalked towards her, totally naked.

'Let's make it ten.'

He took her hand and pulled her, laughing, into the bathroom.

Ward rounds were always Seth's favourite part of the day. He got to check in with all the patients and see how they were doing. Find out how they'd progressed overnight and oftentimes send them home, where they belonged. This was even more important as Christmas crept ever closer.

His last patient of the day to check on was Amadi, the young boy who'd been brought over to England to have his twisted foot operated on. The surgery had been a huge success, and Amadi was on day three of recovery.

Seth examined his wounds and checked for sensation and capillary refill on Amadi's toes. It all looked great. 'We'll need to get you set up for some physio and some exercises you can do in the meantime. But if you keep going like this, Amadi, then I don't see why you can't go home next week.'

'Home' wasn't really home for Amadi. It was a room in a hotel being paid for by the charity that had brought him over from Africa. He would stay there with his aunt until he began weight-bearing and learning to walk properly.

'Thank you,' Amadi said.

'Hey, it was absolutely our pleasure to have you here and to help you. When you're up on your feet and able to do more stuff, we'll have to have a game of football. What do you say?'

'Cricket?'

Seth laughed. 'Okay. Sure! I'm not very good, but I'll give it a go. It's a deal.' He held out his hand and Amadi shook it.

Once ward rounds were over, Seth was headed back to the desk to make a phone call when he saw Nell pass by on her way to Pixie Ward.

He paused in what he was doing, just to watch her. She moved with such grace. He felt a smile creep across his face as he watched her—until he noticed one of the nurses watching him. He stopped smiling and put his head down, as if reading some paperwork, and then he picked up the phone.

Last night with Nell had been…out of this world!

They'd laughed, talked.

Played.

And, dear God, that woman could do things to him…

He'd thought it might feel odd. His first woman to be intimate with since Dana. And, yes, it had. It had felt strange, especially as he'd not been sure he could ever be with some-one again. But Nell had got through all his defences so eas-ily. She'd got under his skin from day one, to be fair, although he'd never thought it would end up like this.

But why shouldn't he try to find some fun? Some happi-ness? It wasn't as if they were getting into a serious relation-ship here. It was lust. He'd had a lot to deal with these last couple of years, so why not let the lid off the pressure cooker once in a while?

His gaze returned to her briefly as she disappeared through the doors to Pixie Ward, and all he could think of was the way she'd looked in the shower that morning. Dark hair streaming down her back, hands placed on the shower tiles as he'd helped make sure that every inch of her was soaped…

Seth tried to think pure thoughts. Work thoughts. To get himself back under control again. But it was proving difficult.

He and Nell had been able to spend last night together be-cause Olly had had a sleepover at a friend's house. He'd have to be back at the Manor tonight for his son, but he didn't want to take Nell there to stay, because what if Olly crept into his room in the middle of the night?

He'd told Olly that he and Nell were friends. Nothing more. He didn't want to confuse or lie to his son. And he couldn't say, *I don't know what she is* and then have her in his bed every night. He needed to be his son's role model, and that meant teaching him how to treat people.

No. They'd have to find another way to be together.

Nell was sad. She'd been tasked with getting an IV into a newly admitted patient, but there'd been absolutely no veins to access—even with the vein finder—so the medical team had had to take the time to drill through the leg, just beneath the knee, and create an intraosseous infusion, giving them access to deliver medications, fluids or blood products directly into the marrow of a bone.

The team had given their tiny patient a local anaesthetic and Nell had tried to distract him with bubbles and teddy bears and puzzles, but it had been a difficult case, and seeing the child in such distress had really upset her.

On occasion, her job made her feel helpless. Impotent. As if she had no power to help. Most days her work went by without a blip, and she would go home feeling she had accomplished something. But the days when it all went wrong and she felt she'd done nothing left her feeling wasted. It was a sting that never went away. She would always remember those days, and she hated that it was easier for her to remember the failures than all of her successes.

A psychotherapist she'd sat with at lunch one day had told her that it was a natural thing. That if Nell were to be given ten sets of feedback and nine were good but one was bad, she would focus on the bad one the most. It was part of being human. Wanting to be liked and accepted. Because hundreds and thousands of years ago it had meant safety to be part of a group. Feeling disliked, feeling ostracised, played on your nerves because it made you feel alone.

She pondered that for a while and wondered if it was true. If it was still the most primitive part of the brain that controlled how people felt today? Or maybe it was nothing to do with evolution. Maybe it was what had happened to Lucas?

She'd felt helpless watching her son lie in his hospital bed. Her role had switched from being staff to being a patient's mother. Having to just stand by and wait whilst doctors made decisions on her son's behalf had been frustrating. Of course they'd tried to include her and Blake in their thinking, but really there'd been nothing they could do to help Lucas except make him comfortable before they turned off the machines that were keeping him breathing.

All her medical knowledge, all her years spent looking after other people's children, and she hadn't been able to help her own. That inability to take away his pain, his suffering… She felt the same way when she couldn't get IV access. When she couldn't draw blood from a patient. When she couldn't site a cannula.

It was a reminder that she wasn't perfect. That she couldn't solve all the ills facing children when they came into hospital. She wasn't a superhero. She was just a phlebotomist. She was human and fallible and sometimes she'd fail.

As she headed back to the desk to find out what her next job was, a linen cupboard door opened, and an arm reached out and pulled her inside.

Seth.

She smiled. Laughed a little.

'What are you doing?' she asked as he pushed her up against a rack of blankets and pillows.

'I have something for you.'

'You do? What is it?'

'This.' He bent forward to kiss her on the neck. 'And this.' His next kiss was by her ear. 'And this.' The final kiss was on her lips.

Then he gently tipped her chin upwards, so that her lips could meet his, and she allowed all the stresses of the past hour to fizzle away into nothing.

Kissing Seth was perfection. Kissing Seth took away all the

worries and the concerns of the world and all she could think of was what he was doing to her in that moment.

Their morning shower had been an enlightening moment. She'd never shared a shower with another human being. She was used to standing under the hot spray alone and having a perfunctory wash. This morning she'd discovered how sexy shower gel could be. How it felt to have a man's hands soap her and wash her all over. She trembled at the memory.

'And this.' Seth lifted a condom into view.

She laughed quietly. 'Where did you get that?'

'Oh, you know…store cupboards in hospitals are amazing things.'

'You stole it? You naughty man.'

'"Stole" is a strong word. *Purchased* is a better one. I dropped a few coins in the donations tin at the genito-urinary clinic.'

Nell laughed. 'So it's ours? And we're free to do with it what we wish?'

'Absolutely.'

His dark eyes had a devilish glint in them that aroused her in an instant, and she couldn't believe she'd have to wait until much later before she could take advantage of that.

'Where should we meet? My place?' she asked.

'I'm not sure I can wait that long. The door behind us has a lock, you know…' He winked.

'You want us to have sex in a linen cupboard? On a children's ward?'

He groaned. 'Maybe not. I guess you're right. That would be bad. Okay… Let's meet at yours after work. I'll call Olly's school and ask if he can stay in the after-school club. They'll feed him and I'll collect him later at six-thirty.'

'Are you sure?'

'Most definitely. Let me show you how sure I am...'

Nell emerged from the linen cupboard with hair that was more messy than when she'd gone in. She tried to straighten it and look normal and presentable, and hoped that her cheeks weren't too flushed by all the naughty things Seth had whispered into her ear.

This thing with Seth was incredible. She'd never felt so desired! Never felt she had such power over a man. It was heady. Powerful. She wanted to enjoy it for what it was. Fun. Exciting. Exhilarating.

But a small voice at the back of her head kept screaming at her. *What are you doing?*

As she settled in at the desk to write out her worksheet, Beth appeared.

'Hey, stranger.'

'Hey.'

'Everything all right? You look a little flushed.'

Nell felt her cheeks flame even more. 'Oh, you know... I got a little upset after not being able to help that little boy in Bed Four. They ended up doing an intraosseous access. I'm okay now.'

Beth sat down next to her. 'Yeah, it's hard watching them do that. But sometimes the patients just don't have the veins for us to work with. You need to let it go. Think of how many kids you get first time, without even an iota of pain.'

'You're right...'

'Listen, me, Lou and the others are meeting for a drink tonight after work. The White Rabbit? You know it? Why don't you join us there? There's a quiz on. We could make a decent team and it would take your mind off today. Grand prize is a meat hamper!'

Nell laughed. 'What am I going to do with a meat hamper?'

'Share it? Come on—what do you say?'

It sounded fun, but she had other plans with Seth…tempting plans…and she didn't want to cancel them. Not one bit.

'Thanks, but I can't tonight.'

'Why not?' Beth said in a whiny voice. 'You never go out! Come on! It'll be good for you!'

'I can't because I'm meeting someone.'

Beth raised an eyebrow. 'The guy?'

She must have blushed, because suddenly Beth was all excited.

'You're meeting a guy! Oh, come on—spill! Who is he? It's someone here, isn't it?'

'Why would it be someone from here?'

'Because this is our only dating pool! So who is he? Do I know him?'

'You don't know him,' she lied, hating herself for lying, but not wanting to have gossip spread about her on the ultra-fast hospital grapevine just yet.

She wanted to keep all the pleasure to herself and not have it sullied by whispers and gossip. Was that wrong? She didn't think so. Because right now what she had with Seth was fun and exciting and it was early days. Keeping it just between them would help the magic last longer. And it was Christmas. Traditionally the hardest time of the year for her. And now suddenly, because of Seth, it was a little bit brighter. A little bit better. Was it wrong to want to hold on to that happiness?

'Damn! Well, he'd better be amazing, because you're missing out on what will be an amazing night.'

Nell smiled. 'Oh, don't worry. I won't be missing out at all.'

* * *

'Don't go?' she said, when Seth looked at his watch and said he needed to leave.

He squeezed her against his bare chest as they lay in her bed. 'I don't want to, but I have to go and fetch Olly.'

'I know. I just... I don't want this to end. I like the cuddling.'

'Just the cuddling?'

She laughed and looked up at him. 'All of it.'

He kissed the tip of her nose. 'Good.'

He rolled out from under her, stood and began to dress. She couldn't help but lie there and admire him. His taut muscles. His flat stomach. His arms. How good his backside looked as he slid on jersey boxers.

'I have a whole afternoon free tomorrow and so do you. I checked. Why don't we spend it together? We could go into town, do some Christmas shopping, then spend an hour or two here before I have to pick up Olly from school. It's his last day tomorrow before they break up for the school holidays.'

'Will I get to see you when Olly's on holiday?'

'Absolutely.' He began to button his shirt. 'Granny is always happy to keep an eye on him. She couldn't do it today, because she was off playing bridge with some friends, but she generally looks after him when I work. The staff help, too.'

'Okay. Christmas shopping in town sounds fun.'

'Great.' He scooted over to give her one last kiss. 'Have I told you today how amazing you are?'

Nell smiled happily. 'No, you haven't.'

'Well, you are. Amazing. Beautiful. Talented. *Bendy.*' This last was said with a grin and a kiss.

She laughed. 'Go. You'll be late.'

He checked his watch one last time. 'I'll see you tomorrow.'

'You will. Now, go!'

Seth blew her a kiss and disappeared, grabbing his jacket from the back of her bedroom chair before doing so.

As the front door to her flat slammed shut she felt herself sag in disappointment. He had gone. The flat suddenly seemed so empty without him there. How quickly she had become used to his presence.

Stretching her hand out across the sheets, where he had lain, she could already feel them becoming cooler. She rolled over, grabbed his pillow and inhaled his scent and groaned.

Seth had been amazing. Worth waiting for. He had taken her to heights that she had never believed possible. The first time they'd both been so excited that it had been over in a matter of minutes. But the *second* time... The *third* time... Those had been masterclasses in sex and foreplay.

Seth had known how to bring her to the edge of the precipice and then, just as she'd thought she might explode, just as she'd thought she might fall, tease her in another way. Another place. Until her entire body was screaming with need. Only then would he give her what she desired. It had seemed only fair to do the same to him in return.

God only knows what my neighbour thinks all that noise was.

Would she be able to look Mrs Goodleigh in the eye ever again?

For now, she was quite content to lie naked in bed, staring at the ceiling and thinking of all the things that Seth had done to her body. It would keep her going until she saw him again. She wanted him back here with her. So she was no longer alone.

Is that why I'm enjoying him being here? So I'm not alone?

Christmas was such a difficult time of year for her. What if she was just using Seth to blot out the pain she felt? Because when she was with him she stopped thinking about the world.

Stopped thinking about her pain over Lucas and how alone in the world she felt. How isolated.

Seth changed all that.

Or…was it something more?

His last job for the day was to check on a post-operative young lady called Laura Kemp, who had spiked a fever. Her temperature had been steadily rising over the last two hours, after a long and complicated arm surgery to remove a benign growth just twenty-four hours ago.

As he stood by her bed, the nurse, Lou, took Laura's temperature again. 'One zero two point four,' she said, looking at him grimly.

'Okay, let's get her on some antibiotics. I also want full bloods done and a urine sample—just to make sure we're not missing something. And could we get a swab from her surgical site?'

'Of course.'

'I'm going to be away this afternoon, but Dr Peters will be on duty from lunch, so I'll fill him in on Laura's situation when we do the handover. Hourly obs, please, Nurse.'

'Of course,' she said again.

He typed his directions onto the portable tablet that he carried with him, so that Laura's notes would be instantly updated. 'Okay… I've got ten more minutes and then I'm gone. Anyone else you need me to check before I hand over my patients?'

'Amadi is about to leave. Do you want to say goodbye?'

'Of course! I've got him something. It's in my locker. Hang on, I'll go and fetch it.'

He went to his locker and pulled out the gift he'd wrapped earlier, then headed to Amadi's ward, where he was sitting dressed in the chair beside his bed as his aunt gathered all his belongings and his TTOs—drugs and forms *to take out.*

'Amadi! My friend! How are you feeling? Big day!' Seth shook the young boy's hand.

'I am happy.'

'Good. Good! I've got you a little something for later... when you're better.' He passed over the gift.

'What is it?' asked Amadi in his beautiful accent.

'You'll have to open it to find out.'

Amadi ripped open the packaging and then beamed a huge grin. 'A cricket bat! And a ball!'

Seth grinned at the delight on the young boy's face. 'So you can practise when you're better.'

'Thank you so much!'

'Hey, it was my pleasure. We're going to miss you around here.'

'Thank you.'

He chatted with Amadi and his aunt for a little while, and then it was time for them to go. He waved them off, noting that Nell stood in the doorway too, giving the young boy a little wave.

Seth went to stand by her as Amadi left. 'It's always good to see them leave looking so happy.'

'It is. That was a nice thing you did. The bat and ball.'

'Oh, anyone would have done the same.'

She looked at him. 'Not everyone. Are you ready to go? I'm done for the day.'

'I'll just grab my things.'

Nottingham City Centre was bedecked with Christmas lights and festive music blared from every shop they passed. One minute they'd be singing along to a song about someone driving home for Christmas, the next a merry jingle about a reindeer with a red nose.

They entered a shop selling soaps and bath bombs. It had an overwhelming sweet scent. Nell bought a gift box of bath bombs that looked like Christmas puddings and tree baubles for her mother. Seth bought his grandmother a similar gift box, but this one was filled with whipped soaps that were meant to be moisturising for dry skin.

Next they entered a bookshop, because Seth wanted to get Olly some books. Apparently the little guy liked to read. Nell felt weird, going with him into the children's fiction section. She'd not been in one since losing Lucas, and it felt strange to be there. On a display table was one of the last books she'd ever bought for him. The story of a lonely astronaut who met an alien and became friends with it. Seeing it struck her quite hard, and she thought she must have gasped, because suddenly Seth was asking her if she was all right?

'That book... The one with the spaceman on the front... I bought it for Lucas just before he...'

He reached out for her hand and brought it to his mouth, kissing it. 'Shall we go?'

'No! You must get something for Olly. It's why we're here.'

'But if this hurts you...'

'I'm okay. Just shocked, that's all.'

She was glad of his hand in hers and though he picked a few books off the shelves to look at, he didn't let go.

It felt good to be holding his hand. In public! Something that had never happened with Blake... It was as if Seth wanted the world to know that he was with her. That she was his. She kind of liked that. Even if it was all new and fresh and fun, and she had no idea where it might lead. She never let herself think of the future, because then she'd feel afraid of what she might lose next. It was best to just stay in the present and just enjoy it.

Seth picked up a book about a knight. 'Think he'd like this?'

'I don't know.' How could she know? She didn't know Olly. Not really. They'd had a pizza together. That had been it. But he had played a knight in his school play. 'Maybe. What's he into?'

'Knights. Dragons. Quests.'

Lucas had liked the same things. 'Well, probably he would, then.'

'I'll get it. And once we're done here, let's grab a drink.'

'Okay.'

Seth paid for the book and then they went upstairs to the part of the bookshop that had a café where they could sit. They both ordered hot chocolate, with whipped cream and marshmallows. Nell opted for a spiced ginger one that was on special offer.

'This is delicious!' she said, as they sat down at the one remaining table, which had just been cleared and wiped down by a member of staff.

'It's good to sit down. My feet are killing me today,' said Seth.

'Mmm… Want to try mine?' She proffered her drink and he took a sip.

'Nice. Not too spicy, but a nice after-kick with the ginger. Warming…'

'Have you thought about what else you might get your gran and Olly for Christmas?'

'Olly wants a new bike. We left his old one behind in Devon, because it was getting too small for him, so I've ordered a new one. I'm hoping it will arrive in time. Granny's always difficult to buy for. She's got everything.'

'That's how I feel when I buy stuff for my mum and dad.'

'You don't talk too much about them.'

'They live so far away, so it's mainly phone calls or video calls. Mum was hit hard by losing Lucas. He was her first and only grandson. She struggles sometimes…feels like she's lost her role as grandma.'

'I can't even begin to imagine what it must be like to lose a child. You see it happen to parents at the hospital on occasion, and though you try to be there for them to lean on there's that professional distance that keeps you safe, you know? Even though it's upsetting, and you might shed a tear or two with them… I can't imagine what it would be like to lose Olly.'

'It's not something you can imagine, is it? You know growing up that you will one day lose your grandparents, and then your parents, but you never imagine you'll ever have to face losing a child. Especially one so young. When it does happen…' She was lost for a moment, thrown back to those dark days of grief and pain. 'It's difficult to accept. Like it can't be happening. Not for real.'

He reached across the table and took her hand in his. 'You are so strong.'

She looked down at their hands, felt a warmth inside that did not come from the spiced ginger hot chocolate. This was what she'd always wanted! A man not afraid to show affection in public. A man who admired her and cherished her. A man who could rock her world in bed and be just as hungry for her body as she was for his. A man who made her smile. A man who listened to her cares and her woes without one eye on the clock.

Dr Seth James was simply amazing, and she was so lucky to have him in her life.

I'll have to get him an amazing Christmas present.

'Thank you,' she said. 'So are you. I think we've both been tested where loss is concerned.'

'Ain't that the truth?'

They drank their hot chocolate, and Nell reached across the table with a napkin to wipe the cream moustache from Seth's upper lip, laughing. It felt good. Free. Fun. It was a feeling she could get used to. She enjoyed his company. It made her feel good just being around him.

'Where to next?' she asked.

'Jewellery shop. I think I might get Granny a new necklace or some earrings.'

'Perfect. I'll get the same for Mum,' agreed Nell.

The jewellery shop was sparkling with silver and gold decorations when they got there. Oversized baubles bigger than beach balls hung in the window, and up above, from the ceiling, hung silver and ice-white snowflakes. The necklaces, earrings, rings and bracelets glittered beneath the shop lights in their pristine glass cases, so that it was hard to know where to look first. It was a veritable feast for the eyes.

'Oh, look at that!' said Nell, admiring a rose gold bracelet with charms on it like a cluster of flowers.

'Gorgeous. Think you'll get that for your mum?'

Nell looked at the price tag and winced. It was almost a month's salary. 'I couldn't afford that. No, she'll have to make do with something considerably cheaper. Ooh, those are nice!' She pointed at the next case where a pair of gold earrings lay. Studs, with small dangling cascades attached, and on the end of each one a small round ball, like the stud above. They were simple, without being too busy, and just the kind of thing her mum might wear. They were an affordable price, too.

It was a while before a shop assistant became free and she could ask to look at them more closely, and Seth wandered off to look at the other display cases. Up close, she could see that the gold studs had a pattern printed on them, which made them even prettier.

'I'll take those, please,' she said.

As she waited for the assistant to wrap her purchase, she turned around to see where Seth was. He was on the opposite side of the store, admiring the necklace he held in his hands, before nodding at the assistant who was serving him. The assistant, a young woman with slicked-back dark hair and a tight black turtleneck jumper that emphasised her perfect figure, smiled and fluttered her eyelashes at Seth.

He didn't appear to notice, and Nell smiled to herself before turning back to pay for her mum's earrings.

She felt so incredibly lucky right now.

This Christmas was shaping up to be one that she might even enjoy. Since losing Lucas, she did her Christmas shopping from home, buying online. This was the first time she'd ventured out into the world to do it for herself. It felt good, to be doing this with Seth. He was like a safety blanket. A constant reassuring presence at her side. She was *with* someone.

But how long would it last?

She didn't want to think about that at all.

After Christmas shopping they went back to Nell's place and fell straight into bed and each other's arms.

Seth felt great, just lying there, holding Nell in his arms, entwined around each other. It brought him a peace that he'd not felt for a very long time.

'What are you thinking about?' she asked him.

'About this. You.' He felt himself stir and knew that she could feel it too.

Nell laughed. 'I can tell! You want to go again?'

'Always, with you.'

She played with his chest hair with her fingers. 'Me too.'

'I wish I'd met you earlier.'

'You do?'

'Yeah... I guess you could say I was lost in the wilderness for a while, after losing Dana. I was beginning to accept that I'd always be alone. And I thought I was okay with that. But since knowing you I've come to realise that I was never okay with that. Being alone means never truly being happy.'

He felt her smile upon his chest. 'I make you happy?'

'You know you do.'

She looked up at him. 'You make me happy, too.'

'Good.' He kissed the top of her head and gave her a little squeeze.

'Do you ever worry about what the future holds?' she asked.

'I don't know. Maybe. Sometimes. What about you?'

'I try not to think about it. It scares me. All the stuff that hasn't happened yet. Losing Lucas was the worst thing ever, and now I know what real pain is I'm scared of losing anyone else. Losing Lucas broke me, and I can't be broken again. I'm not sure you can fit that many broken pieces back together.'

'I get that.'

They were quiet for a moment or two. Thinking.

'Losing Dana... It made me realise that happiness is fleeting. So when it does come you should grab hold of it, because you never know how long you've got it for.'

'You mean like this?'

He felt her hand drift lower and take hold of him, begin to stroke.

'Hmm... Maybe,' he said, feeling his body awaken once again.

Her touch had the power to revive more often than he'd ever believed possible. It was as if he simply couldn't get enough of her. As if his body wanted to be fed the drug that was Nell Bryant over and over again. Like an addict.

He rolled her onto her back and lay atop her, staring down into her eyes. 'Let's just enjoy the happiness we have in the present and not worry about what's ahead for us, okay?'

'Why would we worry? It's good.'

'I know. But if it keeps being good, then it's going to lead to it being a proper relationship, and then we'll have to start asking ourselves some pretty deep questions about what we want from this.'

Had he felt her stiffen beneath him? Just slightly? But he'd had to mention it, because she'd lost her son. Her precious son. And he came with one. If they got serious, she'd have to consider the possibility that she'd have a greater role in Olly's life than she'd thought about. And that scared him, too.

What would Olly think about him bringing Nell into their lives? He'd hate to think that Olly might believe he was trying to replace his mother. He might not be ready.

Seeing the look of uncertainty and, yes, even fear, in Nell's eyes panicked him, so he kissed her. Once. Twice. Three times. He didn't want to think of scaring her away. He didn't want to imagine it. He wanted what they had now. The fun. The joy. The happiness.

'But we don't need to worry about that now,' he whispered into her ear, before he began to trail his lips down her body.

He wanted to take them both to another place. A place where they didn't need to think. A place where she *couldn't* think and nor could he.

He didn't want to fill their minds with what-ifs, because he didn't want to spoil this.

He just wanted to escape into ecstasy.

It was simpler there.

* * *

When Seth left for the evening she stood in the doorway to her flat, dressed only in her bathrobe, her body aching deliciously as she kissed him goodbye. She was smiling and waving as he stepped into the lift, but the second the lift doors closed, taking him from view and whisking him down to the ground floor, her smile faltered.

She closed the door and leaned back against it, her mind filled with what he'd said.

'But if it keeps being good, then it's going to lead to it being a proper relationship, and then we'll have to start asking ourselves some pretty deep questions about what we want from this.'

He'd thought about that. Did it worry him? It must do. And, worst of all, he was right. They *would* have to start asking themselves some pretty deep questions about this. For example, could she accept the fact that he came with a little boy of his own? Olly would be a daily reminder of all that she had lost in Lucas. He also came with a manor house, a rich history and a title—a type of living that she just wasn't used to.

Were they fooling themselves right now? The sex was great, it was true, but a relationship couldn't be built on just sex. There had to be more to it than that. And, yes, she enjoyed his company—they could talk and laugh about anything—but had they ever talked about anything serious? Like people in a real relationship would?

Nell headed into the kitchen and opened the fridge, hoping for some inspiration as to what to cook for dinner. No doubt Seth would go back to the Manor and have a meal cooked for him. They lived such different lives. Came from two different worlds. Were their differences insurmountable? Were they fooling themselves that everything would be fine whilst they hid their relationship from reality?

Neither of them had told anyone that they were sleeping together. Olly didn't know. The Dowager, Seth's grandmother, didn't know. Their friends didn't know. What would happen when everyone found out and the real world entered to complicate everything? There were so many unanswered questions that were beginning to trouble her.

And this is why I don't allow myself to think of the future. Because it just upsets me.

There was a lonely chicken breast in the fridge, and half a jar of sweet and sour sauce. She knew she had rice in the cupboard...

That would have to do.

The next couple of days were strange ones for Nell. She saw Seth at work and they stole kisses in linen cupboards...secret smiles during handovers. Occasionally their hands would brush one another's as they passed by a patient's bed. Each touch, each kiss, was a reminder of the happiness he brought to her, but also a stark reminder that they would soon have to face reality.

They were good together. That much was clear. He made her smile. He made her sigh. The way she felt when she was with him was something that she couldn't clearly articulate because there were not enough superlatives in the world for that. But she couldn't help thinking that she'd gone from a relationship with a man who couldn't show love in public to a relationship with a man who was afraid to show love in public. Because if he did, everything would change.

Keeping their relationship secret was the only thing that kept it alive in its current state, and she wanted to remain in that blissful state for as long as she could. Because losing Seth... Just the mere idea of that was enough to make her want to hide from the world and its cruelty. That it should give her a taste of such fine happiness only to take it away again.

So as Christmas Eve arrived Nell went about her work as normal, determined to stay busy, determined to keep her head down, knowing she wouldn't be spending Christmas with Seth. He would be at the Manor, with his grandmother and his son, whereas she would be home alone.

She popped in to see Ruth, her supervisor, in her office, midway through the shift. 'Hey, Ruth. I was wondering...do you need me to come in tomorrow? I'm free... I could do it.'

'Christmas Day? No, no. I told you. You've worked the last two Christmases. You deserve to take this year for yourself. Besides, Marie and Owen are in.'

'Oh... Well, what if I swapped a shift with them?'

'Take the day off, Nell! Enjoy Christmas,' Ruth said in a stern voice, yet she was also somehow smiling.

'Okay...'

Maybe she could go to Lucas's grave? Take him some flowers. Take a present for him and leave it there. Just something small. Unobtrusive. Something that wouldn't get stolen.

The ward had a different atmosphere today. Christmas was nearly here and the doctors were trying to safely discharge as many patients as they could. So there were a few empty beds and her beeper didn't go off nearly as much as it usually did, and she actually found herself at a loose end. Determined to do something useful, she headed to Pixie Ward and the small play area and began to tidy up.

There were books all over the floor, rather than in the bookcase, and the dressing up clothes were half off their hangers.

One princess outfit was on the floor. The building blocks and the cars were all in disarray.

She spent a good fifteen minutes tidying up, and was busy keeping her mind off all her feelings and the idea of spending Christmas alone in her flat with nothing more than a pathetic attempt to make a turkey dinner for one, when suddenly Beth came looking for her.

'Nell? I need you.'

She stood up. 'What's going on?'

'We've got a patient being sent up from the ER. A young boy who keeps having grand mal seizures. I know you don't normally help with new admissions, but I've just sent Lou and Angel off for a break as it was quiet. Can you help me get him settled?'

'Of course.'

She didn't mind at all. In fact it would be nice to help. She hated having nothing to do.

'Where's Dr James?'

'He had to go and see Dr Soong in Theatre, and the on-call doc is with another patient right now.'

'Okay. Just tell me what you need me to do.'

'I can do the kid, but could you assist the parents? You never know what state they'll be in when they come up here. No one wants their child to be admitted to hospital—and especially not right before Christmas.'

No. They didn't. Nell remembered her own bewilderment at having to rush to a hospital a few weeks before Christmas. Seeing her pale, lifeless son in a hospital bed. He'd looked so small! So helpless! And there'd been nothing she could do to fix it. And no one to hold her hand.

Blake had been there, eventually. But he'd stood opposite

her, looking down at Lucas, his jaw rigid and firm. More than anything she'd wanted him to come and stand beside her, clasp her hand. When he hadn't she'd gone to him and taken his hand, but he'd pulled it free, almost as if he was angry at her. As if it was all her fault that their son was in this place.

Parents could turn on one another. She'd seen it many times. Fear would push most people together, but for others it tore them apart. As it had to her own marriage.

There was a beep at the double doors to the ward and Beth responded to it, buzzing through the nurses and the techs from downstairs as they wheeled a boy on a trolley into the ward. Behind them were two parents. A mum and a dad. The mum with a tear-stained face, the father pale and shocked as their son was manoeuvred into a side ward and transferred from the trolley onto the bed.

Nell, feeling their pain and fear, went to stand by them. 'Hi. I'm Nell. A phlebotomist and play specialist here on the paediatric floor. Don't worry, we're going to get him settled and monitored first, and then the doctors will run any further tests they might need. Has your son had seizures before?'

She got her first glimpse of the boy in the bed and felt rocked to her core. This little boy looked so like Lucas! The same shock of blond hair. The same pale skin and freckles over his nose. He was even wearing a pair of pyjamas the same as one Lucas had once owned.

The mum began a fresh burst of crying. 'No! Never!'

The dad put his arm around his partner. 'He's been complaining of headaches for a few days now. We thought it was just so he could get out of the last few days of term. We should have known something was wrong.'

Nell tried not to stare at Lucas's double. Tried to pull herself out of the shock she was feeling and be helpful to these two worried parents. *Lucas had suffered with headaches.*

'You couldn't possibly have known. Did they do any scans downstairs?'

'Yes, but the results haven't come back yet. Do you have them here? What do they say?'

'A doctor would have to take a look,' Nell said, looking away from their son and guiding Mum and Dad towards two plastic seats against the wall. 'What's your son's name?'

'Luke.'

Nell felt her stomach drop to the floor. *Luke?*

'Can I get you guys anything? Tea? Coffee? Some water?'

'Tea would be great, thank you. We've not had time to get anything for hours.'

'Okay, I'll be back in a minute.'

It was such a relief for her to be free of the fear in that room. Free of the trepidation. The hope for good news. The hope to hear that this was all just something and nothing. That it would pass. Or it would be something easily controlled by medication.

But hope could be a terrible thing. Sometimes it blinded you. Sometimes it lured you. And when all hope was gone...

That was the most difficult thing of all.

That little boy, Luke...

She shook her head to clear the image of him in that hospital bed. It was like looking at her own son all over again. Would she have to watch him deteriorate, like she had Lucas?

She'd rushed to the small kitchenette, wiping tears from her eyes with her sleeve, when behind her the door opened.

'Hey, what's the rush?'

Seth.

He would know. He would understand. She turned to him

and buried her face in his chest as she cried tears that she'd kept behind barriers for way too long.

'Hey...what's going on?'

She felt his arms surround her, felt his protection and his concern as he began to rub her back and stroke her hair, waiting for her to cry it out. It meant so much, in that moment, that he was there for her, and that he allowed her to experience her emotions without trying to ignore them.

When the torrent finally ended she was able to just stand there, her head against his chest, sniffing gently. 'A boy has just been brought onto the ward. He looks so like Lucas...and his parents...they're so scared... I just felt... And then the mum said his name is Luke. I don't know... You probably think this is silly, but it was like looking at my own son all over again.'

There was a pause whilst he took in all her words. 'I don't think it's silly at all.'

She was so grateful to him right there and then! To not have her feelings dismissed. To not be told she was being silly. Or hysterical. Or over-emotional. Blake had used to accuse her of that kind of thing all the time whenever she got upset. Because he himself was uncomfortable with such a show of emotion. He couldn't handle it, and had often berated her for behaving in such a way.

'Thank you,' she said. 'I've said I'd make the parents a cup of tea. I don't think they've had anything for hours. They're waiting for scan results, too.'

'Want me to go check on them?'

'Please.'

'Okay.' He kissed the top of her head. 'Meet me at the desk when you've made their drinks. We'll go in together.'

She gave him a thankful smile and set about making the tea, feeling slightly better having let out all the emotion that had been stirring in her ever since she'd laid eyes on Luke and his parents. She still felt apprehensive about going back into that boy's room, but with Seth at her side maybe she could achieve anything?

With the drinks on a tray, she headed out to the nurses' desk, where Seth sat. He was on the phone, his face grim.

She put down the tray and waited for him to get off the phone. 'What is it?'

'Luke's CT scans. Come and take a look.'

Frowning, she headed round to his side of the desk.

She didn't need to be a radiographer or a doctor to understand what was wrong and why Luke was having grand mal seizures. There was a growth in his brain. A large one. Easily the size of an egg.

'A tumour…? That poor boy.'

'I've just spoken to the neurosurgeons. They've taken a look, and want a further MRI to be sure, but they're hoping they can operate to remove it. They're going to come down and talk to the parents with me.'

The parents… Her heart broke for them. It was Christmas! To receive news such as this on Christmas Eve! Any time would be horrible, of course, but at this time of year… She couldn't imagine how they were going to react to this. But at least they would have hope. At least the surgeons thought they could operate.

He had more options than Lucas had had.

'What will you say to them?' she asked.

'I'll just have to be honest. Come on. Let's go get this over with.'

Luke's parents took the news exactly as he'd expected they would. In abject shock and horror, looking at their son as if they couldn't quite believe what was happening to them as a family.

Seth was thankful that Nell was there. She was being a superstar, despite her own upset. Sitting with them...comforting them. Trying as best she could to make them look at the positive side of things.

But she would know, wouldn't she? Exactly how these parents were feeling and what they needed?

Luke had been given anti-seizure medication and had returned from his MRI when the neurosurgical team arrived. He and Nell left the Sanderton family in their capable hands and vacated the room for a breather after what had been an intense couple of hours.

'I feel so sorry for them. They've got a long road ahead,' Nell said.

'Yeah, but at least they have a road. Not everyone gets that chance.'

She looked down at the desk, lost in her own thoughts. 'Yeah...'

He didn't like seeing her so down. Didn't like the idea that he wouldn't get to spend Christmas with her and she'd be home alone in her flat either. She'd had a difficult day. Old memories must have risen from the darkness to torment her.

On impulse, he said, 'Look, I know this is going to sound crazy, and if you want to say no, then please do so, but...why don't you join us for Christmas? We could go to your place and pick up whatever you need. Come and stay at the Manor with Olly and me and Granny. We often have guests. Olly needn't know what you mean to me just yet. We'll simply say you were going to be alone and it was a nice thing to do for us to invite you.'

She looked at him, smiled. 'Are you saying I mean something to you?'

He leaned forward. Looked right into her chocolate eyes. Whispered, 'You know you do.'

He could see her mulling it over in her mind. Considering her reservations. The down side of such a deal. Surely there weren't that many?

Then she nodded. He saw the resolution in her eyes that she would look for happiness this festive season.

'All right. You've got yourself a deal. Christmas at Elmbridge Manor it is.'

CHAPTER NINE

As SETH DROVE up the long drive towards Elmbridge Manor, this time in fading sunlight, as the afternoon, turned to dusk and more snow began to fall, Nell felt considerably more relaxed than the last time she'd been driven to his home.

This time she could appreciate all that she was seeing.

Elmbridge was a vast expanse of a building, built out of what looked like sandstone. A myriad windows reflected the dying sun, and the fir trees outside it had all been decorated with white fairy lights and golden baubles. Yellow light shone out from the ground floor and a couple of the first-floor rooms, and she saw some of the staff drawing curtains and preparing for the evening chill.

'I still can't believe you live in a place like this.'

He laughed. 'Only a small part of it. A lot is open to the public, remember?'

'You still can't get away from the fact that our childhoods were vastly different. I played in the street. You had *grounds*.'

Seth shrugged. 'I didn't know any different.'

'Nor me.'

'We're both still good people, though. Does background matter all that much?'

'Maybe… My background holds no expectations of me. While yours…' She paused as she gazed at his impressive home, filled as it was with portraits of past generations. 'Yours has a history and a future to uphold.'

He was quiet for a moment as he pulled the car up in front of the house. Then, 'Does that bother you?'

Of course it did. If she was going to stay involved with him then she needed to think about that. Dana hadn't married him. She'd wanted to keep her independence. Seth had said he'd always felt she had one foot out through the door, ready to bolt, which had bothered him. He would want someone as fully committed to this place as he was, and she didn't know if she was strong enough to carry the burden of Elmbridge past, present and future.

She smiled, hiding her thoughts. 'Of course not.'

'I'm glad.' He turned off the engine and got out of the car.

Nell blew out a breath. This place was imposing. How could it not be? And maybe it wasn't just this place? Maybe it was Seth who was imposing and, like Dana, she was ready to bolt in case things got scary.

Seth came round to open her door for her. She took his hand as she alighted from the vehicle. 'Am I going to get the tour this time?' she asked.

'If you want one. Let's get inside first, and tell Granny and Olly that you're going to be staying with us.'

'Okay...'

She was nervous about spending Christmas with them. She'd not had a family Christmas for a long time, and although she was excited about how they might go about it at Elmbridge, she was worried too. But to not be alone... To not have to sit and watch the King's speech on Christmas afternoon with her meal for one, in an empty flat, listening to her neighbours' merriment all around her...

Everyone was so excited to have snow for Christmas. It

wasn't ever a given in the United Kingdom, despite its penchant for bad weather. Usually Christmas only merited cold or rain. But this year they were going to get that white Christmas that so many singers sang about on the radio.

It was going to be a fine time. A time for hope. A time for joy. She needed to try and remember that.

Before they'd left the hospital Nell had called in to say goodbye to Luke's family. Luke's mum had told her that their son was going to go down for surgery immediately, and that the surgeons had high hopes of removing the tumour. And Seth had told her that the neurosurgical team had promised to call him when the surgery was over to let him know how it had gone.

Neither of them had work now until the day after Boxing Day. Hopefully by then Luke would be recovering. Children usually bounced back from surgeries so well—she could only keep her fingers crossed that he would do the same and that after Christmas she would be able to go into his room and see his smile. No more headaches. No more seizures. No worried parents gazing anxiously at their sick son. Maybe they'd even still have time to enjoy Christmas?

Jeffreys appeared at the front door.

'Can you take Miss Bryant's bags up to my room, please?' Seth asked.

Nell turned to look at him, surprised that he'd said that. They'd be sleeping together? She'd just assumed she'd be put in a guest room, like last time. But she didn't mind. There was no need to hide it. The staff would notice more if she didn't sleep in her own room, or caught her creeping back to there before morning. If this was how he wanted to play it, fine— but would he be open with his family? It was one thing to tell them that she'd be staying with them for Christmas, but sleeping in his room…?

As they stepped into the hall with its chequerboard flooring she smiled. It seemed almost familiar! She looked up the sweeping staircase at the portraits and the tapestries and wondered if she'd ever be able to get used to such a place. Would the grandeur ever become normal?

Another staff member arrived to take her coat and she slipped from it with ease, marvelling at how smoothly and efficiently the staff worked at taking care of their guests.

'The Dowager and your son are in the playroom, my lord,' said Jeffreys. 'Shall I let them know you've arrived?'

'Please. And if you could inform them that Miss Bryant—Nell—will be our guest for Christmas? We'll see them later in the dining room, but for now I want to give Nell a tour of the house.'

'Very good, sir.' Jeffreys moved away with her bags, disappearing through a door behind a suit of armour.

Nell turned to look at Seth and grinned. 'This is crazy!'

He smiled and came closer, wrapping his arms around her and pulling her close. 'What is?'

'All of it! This house…the staff…you. Why did you tell Jeffreys to put my stuff in your room?'

He frowned. 'You want your own room?'

'Well, no. But your gran… Olly… They don't know that we're together, do they?'

'Not yet, no.'

'Won't you have to tell them? Properly? Face to face? Olly will need it explained to him and…'

Seth kissed her, stopping the flow of words, the flow of worry and concern. The press of his lips against hers very quickly absolved her of all worry as she sank into the wonder of his kiss, and when it was over she was almost breathless.

'Everything will be fine,' he whispered.

'Will it? Sometimes I wonder.'

'This scares you? This place?'

She nodded.

'Why?'

'It's just so much. It's like I can't take it all in. And there's also what you said before about us needing to ask ourselves some questions if this gets serious…'

'And is it? Serious?'

She nodded. 'Don't you think so? I need to know what you want from me. What you expect if this goes any further. It's not just you and me, Seth. There's a little boy involved here too, and we have to think of him.'

'I do think of him. Always.'

'I know you do. As I think of Lucas—even though he's not here any more. If you tell your family I'm your girlfriend, or whatever you want to call me, then Olly will… Olly will think I'm trying to take the place of his mum, and I'm not sure if I'm ready for that.'

Seth nodded and let out a sigh. 'I know. It worries me too. He's been through so much… I don't want him being hurt again.'

'And I don't want to be the one to hurt him.'

He smiled. 'You could never do that. But let's not worry about all this yet. It's Christmas. Let's just enjoy being together for now. I'll let Olly and Granny know it's something new, nothing established just yet. Then there'll be no expectations.'

'There's always expectations, Seth.'

He took her hand. 'I know. But for now let's push them to one side and just enjoy being here together. I want you to have a good Christmas. I don't want you to be alone with your thoughts. And if you want to cry then that's fine too. Just cry on me, okay? Let me be here for you—that's all I ask.'

That meant something. That meant a lot.

And maybe he was right. Maybe she was worrying excessively when she didn't need to be doing that yet.

Not here. Not at this time of year.

'Okay.'

Seth reached for her hand and led her down a corridor and through a set of double doors. They passed through a small interconnecting corridor that was plainly decorated, then turned a corner and came to another door.

'This is the side of the house that's open to the public,' he said, before opening it and leading her out into another vast reception hall, with the same kind of chequerboard floor. But this time all its adornments—the pictures and the tapestries—had little white cards beneath, filled with information about what the object was. Where it came from, who commissioned it, and its place in Elmbridge's heritage.

There was a pair of ornate vases at the base of a sweeping staircase. Mainly white, but patterned with large flowers of pink and cream and adorned with gold leaf. The card beneath said that the vases had been a gift from a grateful Albert, Prince Consort, who had stayed at the house in 1846.

'Prince Albert? Queen Victoria's husband?'

'Yes. I believe he stopped here once for a hunting weekend, to break up his journey to Scotland. He was very good friends with one of my great-grandfathers.'

'Wow…'

She knew she shouldn't be surprised. Elmbridge was a great house, and in the past would have been a perfect place for people of importance to stay. To think that royalty had stayed here...in the very same building where she would lay her head tonight.

'Are you still friends with royalty?'

He laughed. 'Not as much as you might hope. I know people who are third and fourth cousins of the King, and we see each other on occasion, but it's just like when you and your friends get together. We're all just people at the end of the day. We're nothing special.'

Of course he'd think that. Those were the circles he moved in. Nell could claim no knowledge of any cousins! Her friends were Beth, Angel and Lou. Nurses. Doctors. X-ray technicians. Physiotherapists. If her friends visited her place the only things they left behind were take-out containers and empty wine bottles.

As he led her around the parts of Elmbridge open to the public, it really began to hit home how different they were and how they came from entirely different worlds.

But she admired Seth. He had not sat back on his laurels, believing that his title meant that all he had to do was manage his tenant farmers and lord it over the local village. He'd got himself an education. Had gone to university. Studied medicine. Become a doctor—a paediatrician. And he worked for the NHS—he wasn't a private doctor. He was devoted to his son and was raising him without nannies. He was kind and considerate and hot and—

Oh, boy, am I in trouble!

She held his hand as they wandered through the corridors and rooms. She particularly liked the library, with its green leather sofas, the morning room, with its bright daffodil-yellow walls, and upstairs the Pink Bedroom, where the card on the door informed her that this had once been the bedroom of the notoriously bad-tempered Lady Ethel.

'Why was she so bad-tempered?'

'She wasn't a well woman, by all accounts. Suffered terribly from migraines and couldn't abide loud noise. She used to demand that all the servants in her room wore slippers on their feet, as their shoes clunked too loudly on the wooden floors. There's a portrait of her on the stairs. I'll show you when we go back down.'

They climbed to the next floor. Here were all the guest rooms. Smaller than the family bedrooms, but only just. There was the Hedley Room, the Polly Suite, the Rose Room... Each one decorated tastefully and kept in pristine condition. Some were roped off by thick red rope hung between brass posts. As was a small staircase. Another door.

'Why can't we go past those?'

'Repairs and maintenance. An old house like this one occasionally springs a leak. To get ahead of any real damage we close off certain areas on a regimented cycle each month, to maintain what's there and preserve its history. Do you want to see the old staff quarters at the top of the house? Jeffreys and the others live in the village now.'

'Oh, yes, please!'

Seth led her up a narrow staircase and opened the door at the top into a narrow corridor. This one wasn't decorated as beautifully as the rest of the house. It was simply painted white. There were no paintings, no tapestries. Just the occasional narrow window with a candle on the ledge, or an old oil lamp or two. The doors to the servants' rooms had no cards. Each room was plain and simple. A bed. A wardrobe. A table and chair. In one there might be a pile of books next to the bed. In another a piece of embroidery, as if the owner had just set it down to go and get a cup of tea, or something.

'It's a different world. They'd work so hard downstairs and then come up to this.'

'I know. But that was the way back then.'

'You still have staff today.'

'Only because it would be nigh on impossible to maintain this house on our own. And the public have expectations, too. They expect a house like this to have staff. I like to think I look after them as much as they look after me. The pay is good. The hours reasonable. I like to think of them as old friends, really.'

'But doesn't all this get a bit too much? You work so hard at the hospital and yet you still have to deal with all this. Your home being open to the public, employing staff, maintaining the grounds and the house, budgeting, overseeing tenants, business meetings…'

'I have managers and I delegate. A lot,' he added with a rueful smile.

'And are you a good employer, Seth? I mean, are you a kind boss?'

'I'd like to think so. You are, of course, at liberty to ask any of my staff if they're happy. I can assure you that I don't crack a whip.'

She smiled at his joke and remembered Ava, the maid, telling her how Lord Elmbridge was a brilliant boss. 'I should hope not. And Olly…he'll have to take all this on when it's his turn?'

'I won't ever force him to do anything he doesn't want to. If he decides to become an actor or an astronaut or a busker in the street, I will support him and simply arrange for staff to take care of the estate in his stead. And when he becomes the next Lord Elmbridge, then I'll make sure he'll be ready for that, too.'

She nodded. 'You're a good dad.'

'Thanks. I'm trying to be.' He paused for a moment, then glanced at his watch. 'It's nearly dinnertime. We ought to go down and get changed for dinner, and then say hello to Olly and Granny.'

'And you're sure they won't mind me being here?'

She was very aware that Christmas was a time for families to be together. The James family had such a long and distinguished line, and she was intruding on their private time. They already shared so much with the public...shouldn't Christmas be just for them?

'How could they?' He lifted her hand to his lips and kissed it. 'Come on, let's go down.'

'You remember Nell?' Seth stepped back so Nell could step forward to say hello to his grandmother once again.

The two women shook hands.

'Of course! Seth very rudely called you a leech the last time you were here. I do hope he's stopped doing that?' His grandmother turned to look at him with one eyebrow raised.

'He most certainly has.' Nell laughed, glancing at him.

'Olly? You remember Nell, don't you? She came to see you at your show and we went for pizza.'

His son nodded. 'You said you weren't Daddy's girlfriend,' the little boy said, much to her embarrassment.

His great-grandmother chuckled. 'Oh, yes, I remember Oliver mentioning that you'd gone out with a lady,' she said with a twinkle in her eye. 'You didn't say it was Nell.'

'Didn't I?' Seth grinned and winked at her.

The wink told his grandmother that she knew full well why

he hadn't mentioned it—in case she started to play match-maker. Well, he didn't need that. He'd been able to start a re-lationship with Nell without his grandmother's interference, thank you very much, and now it was teetering on the edge. Neither of them knew where it was going. He knew where he wanted it to go, but he still wasn't sure whether he was ready for it.

'You must sit beside me at dinner, Nell. Tell me all that you've been up to,' his grandmother said, as Seth helped pull out chairs for the ladies to sit.

Nell settled obligingly next to her, as requested, opposite Seth and Olly.

They were in the grand dining room, at the big dinner table. This one was capable of seating up to thirty dinner guests, and though it always seemed silly to sit and gather at just one end of it, it was the nicest room to have dinner in. There was a crackling fire behind them and there was something about the room that felt intimate, despite its size.

'Not much, I'm afraid,' said Nell. 'Mainly working.'

'The bane of many a life.'

'Yes, but if you love what you do, then it's not really a problem.'

'And do you? Love what you do?' asked his grandmother.

'I do. I work with a great team, which makes it easier.'

'But it must be hard, working with all those sick children. It must break your heart sometimes. Seth doesn't say much about it, but sometimes he comes home with a dark, sad look in his eyes and I know it must have been a difficult shift.'

He caught Nell's eye. She'd had a difficult day today, with that young boy Luke. He would still be in surgery... He hoped it was going well.

'It can do, yes.'

'But your friends and family get you through it?' his grandmother persisted.

Nell nodded.

'Tell me about your family, Nell. Could you not make it to them for Christmas?'

'Granny...!' he warned.

'I'm just asking, Seth!'

'Well, maybe Nell doesn't want to talk about her family.'

'Nonsense. Everyone loves to talk about the members of their family. The weird one. The drunk one. The embarrassing one. Come on, Nell—I bet you've got some tales to tell. Everyone has!'

He could see the discomfort in Nell's eyes. The first course hadn't even been served yet and his grandmother had grasped Nell with her talons and would not let go. Not now that she suspected there was more to his and Nell's relationship than she'd first believed.

'It's okay, Seth. I don't mind. My parents live quite far away from here. They did invite me for Christmas, but I would have needed to take too much time off work, which I can't afford to do.'

'Any siblings?'

'No.'

'And you and my Seth have been getting along?' his grandmother asked with a cheeky smile.

'Yes, we have.'

Some of the staff arrived then, walking into the room with an air of grandeur as they prepared to serve the first course. He saw that Cook had made her special chicken liver pâté, and was serving it with strips of sourdough toast. Another secret recipe that she guarded carefully.

'This is lovely,' Nell said.

'It's one of Cook's favourites,' said his grandmother. 'She always makes it on Christmas Eve. I'm afraid we're a family rather steeped in tradition.'

'And history. Seth gave me a tour of the half of the house open to the public. It's an amazing place you have here.'

'Where do *you* live, if you don't my asking?' his grandmother asked, probing for information again.

'Nowhere as palatial as this! I live in a flat. It's quite small. Barely enough room to swing your arms.'

'Hmm...'

Thankfully, his grandmother went quiet as she delved into her pâté and toast.

Seth sent Nell a look that tried to apologise for his nosy grandmother. But he should have expected it, really. This was the first woman he had brought home since Dana, and although his grandmother had loved Dana, she'd always disliked the fact that Dana never wanted to marry. It had gone against all her own beliefs. That Elmbridge needed its Lord to walk its Lady up the aisle and place a ring on her finger.

As if on cue, his grandmother spoke again. 'What are your thoughts on marriage, Nell?'

Seth winced as Nell choked on a piece of sourdough and set down his own toast. Dabbing at his mouth with a napkin, he looked at his grandmother.

'That's enough, now. Nell didn't come here to be quizzed.'

And he didn't need his grandmother scaring her off when she was nervous enough as it was. All those questions she'd asked on the tour... He wished he had answers for her, but the truth of the matter was that he just didn't know. This was scary for him, too. Bringing her here. Admit to his grandmother that they might have something between them. That he might be taking a step away from his past and further into the future.

Nell was right. This wasn't just about them, but Olly, too, and he had to get this right. He didn't want Olly to be upset in any way shape or form.

'Seth, she came here to be part of our family Christmas. All I'm doing is finding out a little more about her. It's hardly the Spanish Inquisition, dear boy.'

'Marriage is a fine concept,' answered Nell. 'If two people truly love each another and have the respect for one another that they deserve. They shouldn't be married if they don't intend to make the other person happy for the rest of their life.'

'A good answer!' His grandmother smiled. 'And an answer that sounds as if it has a story behind it.'

Nell smiled back at her. 'I was married once. Divorced now. My husband was not the man he first appeared to be, and he married me not because he wanted to make me happy for the rest of my life, but because I was pregnant with his child and he thought it the dutiful thing to do. So did I, in a way. I thought we could make it work because of the baby. That we owed it to our child to try and make it work.'

Seth looked at his grandmother and then at Nell. He'd not known that about Nell and her husband. But he could imagine it. Her trying to do the right thing by her son by giving him a dad. By being a traditional family unit. Trying daily to make it work between them but struggling. Because marriage was hard enough when you loved someone deeply. When that love was conditional it was more difficult still. He admired her even more than before. Putting her child first, before it was even born, and trying to give her son the family she'd believed he needed.

'You have a child?' his grandmother asked.

Nell's eyes darkened.

'*Gran*. No!' he warned.

But his grandmother was like a dog with a bone, and she was not willing to give up on her juicy titbit. 'You have a child?' she asked again, but this time more gently, as if sensing something awful was about to be shared.

'I had a son. His name was Lucas. He died three years ago.'

His grandmother reached out to take Nell's hand, enveloping it with her own fragile, liver-spotted ones. 'My dear, I'm so sorry. He must have been very young when he died?'

Nell nodded, unable to speak.

Beside him, Olly crunched loudly into his toast, oblivious to the tension in the room.

'You must miss him every day. Tell me about him. What was he like?'

Nell glanced at his grandmother in surprise. She'd told him once that she didn't like to mention that she had a dead son to people because normally they'd act as if they were extremely uncomfortable and would change the conversation, or simply walk away as quickly as they could without seeming rude. She'd said hardly anyone asked her to tell them about him.

'He was beautiful. Funny, in a dry way. I often used to say that he was an old soul in a young body. He had this adult way of speaking that just used to make me laugh.'

Nell's eyes glistened as he watched her from across the table.

'We had this calendar on the kitchen wall that had a "Word of the Day" on it and a description of what it meant. Every day Lucas would try to find a way to shoehorn that word into a conversation.'

She smiled and Seth thought she'd never looked more beautiful.

'He was stoic. Wouldn't complain if he fell over and grazed his knee...or bumped his leg and gave himself a bruise. He liked cartoons and cuddly toys. He liked to help me bake cakes. He liked chasing butterflies in the back garden, when we had one, and he wanted a dog so badly. We never got one, because my husband said he was allergic.'

There was silence around the table then. Except for Olly's chewing.

'He sounds like the most wonderful little boy. Do you have a picture?'

Nell nodded and reached for her phone from her back pocket.

His grandmother and Nell spent a few moments scrolling through her pictures. Laughing and smiling. At one point, his grandmother laid her head against Nell's, as if in solidarity. It was a familiarity that he'd not expected.

Maybe he'd been wrong. Maybe his grandmother had not been questioning Nell to try and decide if she was good enough for him, but was instead questioning her to find a way she could connect with her? He knew that his grandmother had lost a baby once…a miscarriage. But back then those sorts of things had never been spoken about. You were expected to just get on with life and leave it in the past.

But you never forgot. How could you?

'From now on, every time we meet, tell me something new about Lucas,' his grandmother was saying now. 'I want to remember him with you.'

Nell nodded and threw her arms around his grandmother. 'Thank you,' she whispered, her eyes wet with tears.

His grandmother was an amazing woman. One of a kind. He must never forget that.

And Nell? With every moment he found himself admiring her more and more. For her quiet strength. Her fortitude. Her kindness and her huge heart.

Was he falling in love with her?

He thought that maybe he might be. He could imagine her at this table. In his bed. Walking the halls. Being the new Lady Elmbridge.

But could she see herself as a new mother to Olly? A stepmother?

If she did, or if she didn't…either way scared the hell out of him.

CHAPTER TEN

APPARENTLY THE JAMES FAMILY tradition was that on Christmas Eve, before they went to bed, everyone would open their Christmas stockings. So they sat in the parlour in chairs, around a gently crackling fire, and watched each other open their gifts.

Olly went first, zooming his way through all his little gifts. A remote-controlled car no bigger than his thumb. A small bag of chocolate coins. A torch in the shape of his favourite cartoon character. A computer game. A yo-yo that apparently he'd been begging his dad for, for ages, and a chocolate Santa.

The Dowager had soap and perfume, a pair of soft woolly socks, a box of candied jellies, which were her favourites, and an ornamental brooch.

Seth received socks, gloves, a beard-trimming kit and a large bar of white chocolate.

'I've got you a little something, but you're going to have to wait until tomorrow,' she said to him.

'And I got you a little something,' Seth said, reaching into his pocket and pulling out a small box that was beautifully wrapped.

'Oh! You didn't have to!'

'Of course I did. Now, open it.'

Feeling all eyes on her, Nell pulled apart the ribbon, gently prised open the taped-down silver paper and pulled out what looked like a jewellery box. Her heart beating fast in her chest, she opened it—and gasped.

It was the rose gold bracelet with flowers that she'd admired in the jeweller's that day they'd gone shopping!

'Oh, Seth! It's beautiful!'

He helped her put it on. Fastening it around her wrist and then giving her a kiss on the cheek.

'Ooh!' said Olly in a sing-song voice, making everyone laugh.

She couldn't believe it. If someone had told her that she'd be enjoying Christmas as part of a family, with a little boy in tow, sitting around a crackling fire in an amazing manor house, she'd have stared hard at them and told them not to be so incredibly ridiculous!

It was wrong, wasn't it? To be sitting here like this? Shouldn't she be at home, in the quietness, mourning the loss of her son? What did this even mean? Was she moving on? She would never forget Lucas—of course not—but should she be smiling? Should she be enjoying herself?

And yet here she was. Feeling a part of things. A part of *them*. Not just as a guest, but as someone who belonged. Someone who'd been welcomed.

And Seth kissing her like that in front of his son... Well, it had only been a peck on the cheek, but it was a sign, wasn't it? Not just to Olly, but also to the Dowager, and maybe even to himself, of just what Nell meant to him. And the fact that he'd bought her this bracelet...

She was falling for him. There was no denying it. Perhaps she was already in love with him? How could she not be? A little part of her most certainly was. She just needed to be brave enough to accept that maybe she was wholeheartedly.

But every time that thought entered her brain she heard Seth's voice that time.

'But if it keeps being good then it's going to lead to this being a proper relationship, and then we'll have to start asking ourselves some pretty deep questions about what we want from this.'

She'd posed some of those questions earlier today and he'd listened. Really listened. He hadn't dismissed her concerns, because no doubt he had them himself, but it had all seemed so overwhelming right then, and so they'd agreed just to enjoy the present for a little while and worry about all that other stuff later.

But what if she couldn't?

Because whether she liked it or not—whether she liked Olly or not—Seth came with a little boy in tow. And because of him, they couldn't mess around. Olly had already lost one mum…he didn't need to lose a second mum if she ever decided to become that.

Could she?

Be a mum to someone else's son?

She looked at him now, as he sat playing with his remote-controlled toy car. He was wearing penguin pyjamas and fluffy slippers, cross-legged on the floor. Such an innocent. Such a young boy. And yet he unnerved her. He was Seth's son, and she knew how much Seth loved and adored him. How much Seth had tried to protect him since his mother's untimely death.

Up until now, he'd pretty much kept them apart, except for that one time she'd gone with Seth to see Olly's show. Now he'd taken the step of inviting her for a family Christmas. He'd had her things sent to his bedroom. He'd kissed her in front of him. Seth was making a declaration, wasn't he? Showing the people he loved how much she meant to him. And now this bracelet. This beautiful bracelet that he'd remembered her admiring.

Was this all moving a little too fast?

It had taken her this long even to decide to enjoy the relationship, but now it was starting to become public and she didn't know if she was ready. It was one thing to sleep with Seth, but if this went any further could she step into the role of mother once again? Because mothers loved their children. And if she grew to love Olly—who really was a sweet little boy—then there'd be no turning back. No escape route. If she got scared and left it would upset not only Seth, but Olly, too.

Was she making a mistake in being here?

Had her need not to be alone at Christmas propelled her into this dilemma? Forcing an issue she wasn't ready to confront?

'I have a gift for you,' she repeated. 'But it's upstairs in one of my bags.'

She went to stand, needing a moment or two alone to think, but Seth grabbed her hand and shook his head.

'That's okay. I don't mind waiting until tomorrow,' he said, smiling at her, winking again.

She smiled back.

He had no idea of the turmoil in her brain.

And as she sank back down into her seat she hoped he never would.

'It's late. I'm off to bed. Come on, Oliver! You've stayed up way past your bedtime. Come with me, and we'll go up together,' said his grandmother.

'Goodnight kiss first,' said Seth, kissing a sleepy Olly on his cheek as his grandmother took hold of her great-grandson's hand and led him away.

'Goodnight, all.'

'Night!' said Olly, grabbing his teddy and giving them both a wave.

When they were gone, he heard Nell let out a long sigh.

'Tired?' he asked.

'A bit. It has been a long day. Full of emotional ups and downs.'

'They never tell you that in the recruiting posters, do they? There's always some fresh-faced nurse or doctor standing there, arms folded, in a pristine uniform. Do you think more people would sign up if they showed someone with messy hair, bags under their eyes and a uniform covered in mysterious stains?' He smiled at the thought.

'Probably not…' She rolled her shoulders, tilting her head from one side to the other.

'Here, let me help.'

He went to stand behind her and began to massage the knots from her shoulders. She was incredibly tense. But her little moans and groans as his fingers soothed her sore muscles fed his desire for her.

It *had* been a long day. A whole day in her company when he hadn't been able to touch her the way he'd wanted to. Even at dinner they'd had to sit opposite one another, and then afterwards, opening their gifts before the fire, she'd sat on a chair far away from him, closest to the flames.

He'd found himself staring at her many times, wondering where their relationship was going. He'd thought Nell seemed to be a little on edge, but maybe that was just nerves at being someone's house guest? Or maybe it was something more?

He knew he would be asking a lot of Nell if he decided they were properly a couple. He came with a son, and she'd lost hers. If Nell took him on, then she also took on his little boy. Was she strong enough to do that? Was she ready? It was hard for him, too. He'd never imagined finding someone else he wanted to share his life with, and yet here he was, moving on, losing his heart, imagining what it might be like to go down on one knee to this woman.

Dana had always refused to marry him and he'd told himself he would never propose again—not to anyone. But dammit if Nell didn't make him dream of what might be... And he could imagine himself down on one knee, opening a small box and looking up into her face, asking her to marry him.

He'd thought his love for Dana was something he would never find again, but somehow this love, for Nell was different. Stronger... He didn't want to scare her away. Didn't want to lose her. But at the same time he was terrified of getting close again because he really couldn't bear the idea of having his heart broken all over again.

To love like that...and to lose that love. Was that why he was holding back? Why he kept telling Nell they didn't have to answer those serious questions yet? The ones that kept cropping up time and time again...

'You seem tired. Want to go up too?' he asked as he continued to massage her shoulders, her soft brown hair falling over his hands.

'Yes. I do. Could I grab a shower first? Or do you only have baths here?'

'We have all the modern conveniences a woman could desire.' He laughed and held out his hand. 'Come on. We'll go up. Maybe I could join you in the shower?'

She smiled. 'Maybe you could. But I'm just going to be quick. Why don't you wait for me in bed? The best things come to those who wait, they say.'

'Okay. I'll wait.'

He didn't want to wait. He wanted to consume her. But he knew he would honour her request.

'What about the fire? Shouldn't we put it out before we go up?'

'Jeffreys will take care of that.'

'No, we should do it. Help out a bit more.'

Afterwards they headed upstairs. He would have loved to have joined her in the shower again, but he figured he'd have plenty of time in the future to do that. Hopefully. She was tired. She probably just wanted to freshen up before getting into bed and then they could enjoy themselves.

He was looking forward to exploring her body again. He was hungry for her. Tonight had gone well. She'd fitted in with his little family unit perfectly. His grandmother loved her, he could tell, and Olly had just accepted that she was there without question. Maybe this was something adults worried about more than kids? Olly was young. Kids adapted better than adults. Grown-ups were the ones who made life complicated.

In his private bathroom, he showed Nell how to operate the shower and change the temperature, and then he closed the door behind her and began to get undressed, ready for bed. He already felt aroused at the thought of what was to come when she came out of the bathroom. He couldn't wait to be with her again. Hold her. Taste her. Feel the tremors in her body as she came, over and over. Her gasps, her sighs…

Each little moment with her like that was a gift in itself. Something he could treasure. Moments he could lose himself in. And he was going to spend Christmas Day with her. And Boxing Day, too, before they had to return to work.

Maybe it would be time, then, to start telling everyone that they were a thing. It was going to be difficult to hide it. Already he believed one or two people might be beginning to suspect. Dr Claridge had made a comment to him. Professor Meyer had raised an eyebrow or two.

Part of him wanted the world to know that he was with Nell. Another part wanted to keep her all to himself and not let anyone else in. But he knew that was impossible.

He heard the shower being turned off and the sound of the shower door opening and closing. He could imagine Nell, wrapped in a towel, and indeed, moments later, she came into his bedroom wearing just that. He wanted to unwrap her and lick off any remaining water droplets. He would be diligent and make sure he didn't miss any, and that would mean a careful exploration of her body...

'What are you thinking about? You've got a strange smile on your face,' she said.

'Thinking about you and all the things I could do to you.'

'Oh, really?' She smiled, releasing her hair from the topknot she'd tied it in and letting it fall over her bare shoulders. It looked slightly damp, but glossy and wild.

'Really...' He took hold of the covers on his bed and drew them back, inviting her in. 'Let me demonstrate.'

She stood there, smiling at him, and then, without breaking eye contact, she reached for her towel and undid the knot, allowing it to drop to the floor. She stood before him completely naked in the soft darkness of the room. A vision. A goddess. And he couldn't bear to be apart from her a moment longer.

He reached for her hand and pulled her, giggling, towards him.

As she'd stood under the hot spray she'd toyed with the idea of going back into his room and telling him that maybe this was a mistake. Maybe this was going too fast. Maybe she ought to sleep in her own room, whilst she clarified her thoughts?

But the idea of not getting to spend at least one more night with him was too much.

He was just in the next room! And she wasn't ready yet to see the smile on his face falter. Not at Christmas. He'd generously invited her into his family home for Christmas Day, and Christmas Day they would have! In front of Oliver and his grandmother they would be able to control themselves and keep their relationship less obvious, and then... Then she would say she needed to go home. She'd be able to get some space to think about what they were doing and whether she could handle where it was going—because she'd accepted his invitation here without thinking.

She'd just not wanted to be alone, that was all. She had not accepted because she wanted him to think that this relationship might be more than it was. But the truth was, it had already become more than she'd expected. Unexpectedly, he had found his way into her heart.

It would break her to walk away. She knew that. Just thinking about doing it had caused tears to fall in the shower. She loved Seth. She knew she did. But Seth was part of a package. She couldn't have him without Olly, and she didn't know if she was strong enough to be what Olly needed her to be.

She'd always imagined that if she did meet someone in the future they would take their time. Learn about one another, get used to one another, fall in love with one another. And then, and only then, if their love was true they'd get married? That would be the time to get used to the idea of having another child.

Olly was great. He was sweet and lovely and she'd enjoyed watching him in his school play, and tonight, playing with his little remote control car. He'd even let her have a go with it, and she'd crashed it into the fireplace. But there was a big difference between enjoying moments like that and becoming a potential stepmother.

What am I doing? she had asked herself. *Am I just assuming, here? Seth hasn't even asked me to be Olly's stepmother!*

So she'd shaken off her doubts and her fears and gone into his bedroom, determined to enjoy her Christmas with Seth. And all her worries—along with that insidious voice that kept whispering to her that she ought to run—were pushed to the back of her mind.

It would be fine.

It would all be fine.

She'd been dreaming of walking the halls of Elmbridge with Seth. Holding his hand. Smiling. Laughing. The world had been in slow motion. Seth had wanted to show her something, and had taken her to the head of the staircase to see a new painting he'd had commissioned. There'd been a velvet cloth over it, and when he'd pulled it off, he revealed an oil painting of her. Eleanor James. The new Lady Elmbridge. And when she'd turned there'd been paparazzi, shouting her name, cameras flashing, screaming questions at her.

'How does it feel to become a mother again?'

'Do you feel like you're replacing your son?'

'Do you think you belong here?'

She'd woken with a start, sweating, gasping, only to find herself in the dark, with Seth sleeping soundly beside her.

No. I'm not in the dark.

The bedroom door was open. Odd... She felt sure it had been closed after they'd made love. But a shaft of light from the hall fell through the gap. She looked around the room, into the shadows, and realised that Olly was standing beside her. Staring at her. Clutching his teddy.

The way Lucas had used to.

'O-Olly...what are you doing in here?' she whispered, her heart hammering in her throat.

'I think I heard Santa Claus,' he said in soft tones, clearly not wanting to wake his father.

She stared at him. Lucas had been a light sleeper, too. The slightest sound—a dog barking, a car alarm, a storm—would wake him and he'd come to their room and want to climb into bed with them.

'You need to go back to your room,' she said, more firmly than she wanted to.

But this was freaking her out. He'd found her in his dad's bed!

'Can't I sleep with you?'

No, no, no! She couldn't deal with this. It was all too much! This was exactly what she'd feared!

'Your dad's asleep.'

'He normally lets me, if I can't sleep.'

'Santa won't come if you sleep here.'

'He's already been. The presents are under the tree. I've checked. So, can I get into bed with you?'

There'd been nothing she loved more than those occasions when Blake had been away from home and Lucas had climbed into bed with her, snuggling against her, and she'd wake in the morning to find him starfished across the bed, his hair all mussed and smelling of sleep.

But if she stayed in this bed with both Olly and Seth in it...? That would say something about their relationship that she wasn't ready to face yet!

'Okay. You get in. I'll just go and...erm...get myself a drink.'

She clambered from the bed gently, helped Olly get in and

pulled the covers over him, tucking him in without thinking about it.

Seth murmured and rolled over, and she froze, but his breathing remained deep and steady.

'Be quiet and go back to sleep, all right?' she told Olly.

Olly nodded happily from the bed and closed his eyes.

Nell stared down at the two boys. One she most definitely loved and the other… She didn't know. She *liked* Olly. But could she allow herself to love him? And if she did love him, did that mean she'd love Lucas less? No, of course not. Lucas would always be her little boy.

A lump of grief tore through her at the thought that Seth still got to enjoy night-time cuddles with his son when she couldn't, and she quickly gathered the clothes she'd been wearing earlier and rushed from the room, closing the door behind her quietly.

She couldn't bear to stay there a moment longer.

CHAPTER ELEVEN

CHRISTMAS MORNING. His favourite morning. Seth had enjoyed an amazing sleep, and moreover he'd got to share the night with Nell. He rolled over to snuggle with her, to spoon her—only to discover that the body in the bed next to him was considerably smaller than he'd been expecting.

He opened his eyes.

Olly?

Damn. He must have crept into the bed in the middle of the night. Where's Nell?

She must have got up and switched rooms. He could understand why she might not feel comfortable about sharing a bed with his son just yet.

I'll go and find her in a minute.

'Hey, sleepyhead.'

Olly slowly blinked open his eyes and smiled. 'Hey, Daddy.'

'Merry Christmas.'

'Merry Christmas.' Olly yawned and stretched, pulling his teddy in tight for a cuddle.

'Did you wake in the night?'

'I heard Santa downstairs.'

'You did?'

'I told Nell.'

'Did you? Where is she? Did she go downstairs?'

'I don't know. She took her clothes.'

Seth sat up and peered at the chair upon which Nell's clothes had rested. They were gone, and the first stirrings of alarm began to spread throughout his body. He told himself to calm down. She was probably downstairs already, having breakfast with Granny.

He looked at his watch. Just gone eight. 'We should get ready for breakfast.'

'And then can we open presents?'

He smiled. 'Of course. Come on.'

He chivvied Olly into getting ready, fetched his robe from his bedroom. There was no sign of Nell. She had to be downstairs, surely? Already eating breakfast. She was an early riser, like him. She was probably already on the black peppercorn and smoked salmon bagels and the Buck's Fizz?

He was keen to see her. To reassure himself that he was actually getting to spend Christmas with her, as he'd planned.

Olly seemed to take an age to brush his teeth and comb his hair and wash his face. Seth was getting quite twitchy! He kept telling himself not to be silly, that she'd be there, in the breakfast room, all smiles, ready to wish him a Merry Christmas. But as they headed downstairs the sense of dread he was feeling began to grow stronger and stronger. And then, just as they were about to enter the breakfast room, Jeffreys came to him with a note on a silver tray.

'Merry Christmas, my lord. This is from Miss Bryant.'

A cold lump settled in his belly. He took the slip of paper and turned to Olly. 'You go and get your breakfast with Granny. I'll be in in a moment.'

Olly nodded.

Seth dismissed Jeffreys and stood alone in the hall, afraid to open the note.

And then he did.

Seth,

I'm sorry. A million times I'm sorry. But I'm just not sure I can do this with you. I wanted to enjoy Christmas with you. You know I didn't want to be alone on Christmas Day, and I do think your family are lovely. You have all made me feel so welcome. You. Your gran. Olly.

I can deal with us. But it's not just us, is it? You come as a package deal, and Olly is the sweetest. It's not his fault. This is mine. My fault. I'm scared of what this all means and I need time to think about if it's what I want.

Please enjoy Christmas. And please don't hate me. I can't help but be afraid.

Love Nell x

His first impulse was to go rushing after her and bring her back. But then he read the letter a second time. A third time. A fourth.

Had Olly climbing into his bed been the straw to break the camel's back? She wasn't blaming Olly, but he couldn't help but think that this was what she meant. Lucas had used to wake her in the night. She'd told him that once. Had Olly doing the same thing upset her? But he was just a little boy. That was what little boys did.

She was right, though. He came as a package. Him and Olly. Him and Elmbridge, even. It was a lot for anyone to take on if they weren't used to it. Nell had been ready to bolt. One foot out through the door. Like Dana had always been. Maybe that was why he felt like he couldn't fully commit to her.

He took a moment to steady his breathing. It had become juddery and uneven. Shallow and weird.

He wouldn't get to spend Christmas with her.

His heart broke at the thought. He'd really wanted to show

her Christmas, Elmbridge-style. He'd wanted to make today the best Christmas she'd ever experienced! He'd wanted to watch her open his presents. Pull crackers with her at the table. Clink champagne glasses. Go for a walk with her around the estate after dinner. Build a snowman. Sit with his arms around her in front of a crackling fire. Share a bath with her. A bed with her.

A lifetime with her.

The thought stopped him in his tracks.

A lifetime. With Nell.

He'd been afraid to want it. Afraid to tell her he did. Maybe that was why she'd run? Because she didn't know how committed he was to her. What he really felt. He'd kept telling her they would discuss it another time, but maybe that had been wrong? Maybe they should have discussed it as soon as she'd spoken about it?

Was he being crazy? Would she even want what he could offer her? Her letter said she needed time to think about what she wanted. Well, if that was the case, then surely she needed to know what her options were and what exactly he was offering?

There was still time to rescue the day.

He entered the breakfast room and pulled on the bell that would summon Jeffreys from the bowels of the house.

'Morning, Seth. Where's Nell? Still getting ready?' asked his grandmother.

'Kind of… We've just got to pop out briefly. We won't be long.'

'The hospital, is it? Try to make it back for dinner, Seth. It's *Christmas*.'

He smiled. 'I promise we won't be long.'

Jeffreys appeared. 'Yes, my lord?'

'Have my car brought round immediately, please.'

Jeffreys bowed. 'Of course, my lord.'

The flat seemed empty and cold.

Nell stood in the doorway that led into the lounge, noting the Christmas tree with no presents underneath. The Christmas cards that adorned her windowsill and mantelpiece, from friends and work colleagues. The big one in the centre from her mum and dad.

Had she made a terrible mistake? Should she have arranged to go and spend the festive season with her parents? If she had she might have avoided last night. She might have avoided running out on Seth and Olly and the lovely Dowager.

Were they awake yet?

Did they know she had gone?

She would never be able to face them again.

But the feelings that had rushed up out of nowhere when Olly had arrived in the night had been too strong and everything— *everything*—had come crashing down on her. Reality and realisation.

If she stayed with Seth, she would have to become a mother to Olly. If she stayed with Seth, she would have to become steeped in the history and tradition and responsibilities of Elmbridge. And he might realise that she wasn't up to the task of any of those.

How could she be?

She wasn't used to his world. She didn't move in his circles. She'd lost a son, and a husband who'd seemed incapable of loving her. Maybe she just wasn't deserving of all-consuming love? And Seth would realise that eventually. It was best that they just remained friends. If he still wanted her as a friend.

What she'd done was awful! Running out on him on Christmas morning? How would she ever face him again?

Entering the kitchen, she wiped away her tears and switched on the kettle. She needed a cup of tea. And then, maybe, just so she wasn't cooped up inside all day, feeling morose and miserable and alone, she'd go out for a walk. It was pretty out. It had snowed again overnight, casting everything in a fresh sprinkling of white. Painting the world afresh.

Maybe she should think about getting a cat. So she had something to come home to of an evening. A rescue cat. The mangiest, oldest cat they had. One that had been overlooked and unloved. She would give it happiness in its final years. Love it. Give it a home despite its sad history. That would be a good thing to do, right?

The kettle had long since finished boiling, but she was still standing in the kitchen, poised by the open cupboard where she kept the mugs, when there was a knock at her door.

Nell jumped in surprise, heart thundering, pulse racing.

There was only one person it could be.

Should she just pretend she wasn't at home? She could ignore the knocking and when she saw him at work in a couple of days say that she'd gone to stay with her parents after she'd left him.

But guilt, or something else, drew her to the door. She peered through the small spyhole and saw Seth standing on the other side.

He was so close! She laid her hands against the door and then gently put her head against it, desperate to be back in his arms, but afraid to be.

Another knock. 'Nell? Are you in there?'

Yes. Yes, I'm here! And I love you so much! But I'm afraid to love you. I'm so scared.

'Nell?'

She sucked in a breath and stepped back. If he kept yelling he'd wake her neighbours, and she didn't want a scene. Maybe it was best to open the door. Explain quietly. Apologise.

The need to look into his eyes just one last time was overpowering.

Her hands reached for the lock. Turned the key.

No going back now.

She pulled open the door.

Seth looked at her.

He didn't look angry. He looked bewildered, if anything.

'Hey...'

'Hey. Can I come in?'

She dithered. Maybe it would be easier to turn his love away on the doorstep? Maybe it would be easier to be a disappointment to him while she was standing right here? But no.

She stepped back. 'Come in.'

He moved past her. That familiar scent of him filled her nose and overrode her senses, making her want to reach out and touch him.

He waited for her in the lounge. Stood staring at her as she entered.

'Talk to me,' he said.

She didn't know what to say. Or how to start. How could she explain her scary, illogical reaction of fear?

'I don't know what to say.'

'Well, let me talk, then.'

'Okay...'

She settled down on the couch next to him, ready for his onslaught of anger and disappointment.

'I'm a lot. I get that. I have a history. A title. A manor house. A grandmother. A dead girlfriend and a motherless son who is the sweetest boy I know, despite all that he has gone through. And I also have a deep and abiding love for a woman. For *you*. You're right. I come as a package deal. And that's not easy. Accepting me means accepting everything about me—and that's a lot. I know it's a huge ask, after all that you've been through. But I love you, and I believe you to be the strongest woman I know. And if anyone can handle me—us—it's you. What we have has happened fast, but the rest of it doesn't have to. We can go at your pace, move on when you're ready.'

He paused to reach out and take her hand in his.

'I'm in no rush to get you down the aisle, although one day that would be nice.' He smiled. 'And Olly's in no rush to have a new mother. You need to get to know one another. Get used to one another. I get that. And if you feel you can't do it right now, then I'll give you time. I'll give you space until you do feel ready. But please don't walk away from us because you're scared.'

He lifted her hand to his lips and kissed her fingers.

'Let me hold your hand and be by your side. Let me help you face these challenges. I believe we can have a future together. A wonderful future. A wonderful *life*.'

She looked at him, stunned that he could be so willing to wait for her!

'Oh, Seth...'

'I love you, Nell Bryant, and I would do anything to make you happy. If you need me to walk away right now, then I will. But know this. I will keep coming back for you. I will never leave you. I will be here whenever you are ready. Because you are special, and you mean so much to me. I can't adequately explain it. There aren't enough words for how you make me feel.'

He was saying all the right things! Could she do this? Would she be able to? If they went at a pace that suited her?

'But I ran out on you. What's your gran going to say?'

'She thinks you've had to go to the hospital with me for an emergency.'

Nell blinked. Okay… So Seth's gran didn't know. Nor did Olly. She didn't want the little boy to think that she had walked out on them. She knew Seth would have protected him from that, but this…this was a second chance.

Was she brave enough to take it?

'I don't know what to say…'

'Do you love me?'

She looked deeply into his eyes. Met them with an intensity of love that was impossible for her not to feel right at that moment.

'I do. With all my heart.'

'Then let's step off into the scary unknown together. Let's take a chance on this love we've found. This love that neither of us expected. Even if it is terrifying. Let's take a chance, Nell. Take it one day at a time.'

She wanted to. So much!

Tears of happiness pricked her eyes. Because he loved her, and he was willing to help her get through her days of adjusting to a new life. A life with him. She knew he would be patient and kind. She'd seen it. Experienced it. And a life without love would be empty and unfulfilling.

This was her chance.

'All right. Let's do this!' She laughed.

He beamed a smile and let out a huge breath. He must have been holding it. Then he pulled her to her feet and kissed her. Kissed her so softly and so delicately, awakening her body to want and need.

It had only been a few hours since she'd lain in his arms, but she had missed him so much!

'I love you, Seth James,' she whispered, looking directly into his eyes.

'And I love you. Are you ready to come home?'

She nodded.

She was.

Ready to go home with him.

EPILOGUE

Two years later

CHRISTMAS MORNING AND Nell awoke in her husband's arms, feeling tired and happy. Seth was draped over her, cradling her large belly, which was filled with their overdue daughter.

She could feel the baby kick and then stretch, and she had to rub at her side with her hand, to move a foot that seemed to be stuck under her ribs. It was still dark outside. Just gone five a.m. And yet she felt wide awake—as if she was waiting for something important to happen. She could sense it. An impending sense of change and expectation.

Feeling a little bit of heartburn, she managed to pull herself into a sitting position on the edge of the bed. On the bedside table was a large glass of water, so she drank a little bit—and then realised she needed the loo.

Behind her, Seth slept on, and on the far side of the bed was Olly, slumbering also.

She smiled at them both. They looked so cute lying there like that. Innocent and dreaming.

Let them sleep. We've got a long day ahead.

They had guests to take care of this year.

The first Christmas they'd spent together almost hadn't happened, because of her freaking out. The second year they'd spent it in the Alps, at a skiing resort. This year they'd decided on a proper family Christmas at home. She'd even got her mum and dad to come and stay at the manor. Mum had said she'd made her dad promise to behave.

And even though the majority of the work would be done by Jeffreys and his team, and the cook, Mrs Brough, there were still things that Nell wanted to do to make this Christmas special.

She grabbed her robe from the end of the bed and put it on, tying the belt over her large belly and waddling to the en-suite bathroom, switching on the light and closing the door gently so as not to wake her two darling boys.

Peering at herself in the mirror, she wrinkled her nose and ran a hand through her messy hair. She was just about to go to the toilet when she felt something strange.

Nell paused, glanced at her reflection again. It had been an odd sensation. As if something had…

Drip…drip…drip…

Wetness splashed onto her feet and she looked down at her toes almost in disbelief. Had her waters broken?

As if in response to her question, she felt her first contraction. Mild, low…but enough to be noticeable and to say *I'm here. Let's do this.*

Nell almost laughed in surprise and shock. Then she turned away from the loo and headed back into the darkness of the bedroom, waddling her way across the expanse of the floor to the bed. She leaned over Seth and laid a hand on his shoulder, gave him a gentle shake.

'Hey…'

Seth groaned, then blinked open his eyes suddenly. 'What's up? Is everything okay?'

'My waters have broken.'

His eyes widened and he shuffled into a sitting position. 'You're sure?'

'I've had a contraction.'

'It's baby time?'

She smiled and rubbed at her belly. 'I think so. Elise is on her way.'

He reached for her hand, squeezed it. 'You sure know how to make Christmas mornings exciting.'

She smiled. 'I know. Do you think we're ready for this?'

He cradled her face. 'I am. Are you?'

'With you by my side? I'm ready for anything.'

Seth kissed her. Then opened her robe and cradled her belly, kissing it.

What a perfect day to have another baby.

The best Christmas gift of all.

* * * * *

COMING SOON!

We really hope you enjoyed reading this book. If you're looking for more romance be sure to head to the shops when new books are available on

Thursday 26th October

To see which titles are coming soon, please visit

millsandboon.co.uk/nextmonth

MILLS & BOON

MILLS & BOON ®

Coming next month

THE NURSE'S HOLIDAY SWAP
Ann McIntosh

Those penetrating hazel eyes locked on hers, searching and sending heat cascading through her veins.

"If you're in pain, you could go home. No one would blame you."

"Don't be silly," she replied. Her breath wanted to catch in her chest. He was so close his warmth and delicious scent touched her, making her heart beat erratically. "I...I'm fine. Besides, we're short staffed."

She didn't think he moved, but suddenly the moment seemed incredibly intimate.

"Well, if you have to leave, just let them know I said you could."

It suddenly occurred to her that with the way they were positioned, if she lifted her chin just a little, she'd be perfectly positioned for his kiss, and her heart went from thumping to racing.

What are you thinking?

Totally flustered, she forced her gaze down to her lap and away from the temptation he offered. Had she really been about to make a fool of herself with her boss? Imagining the warmth in his gaze was more than friendly concern?

Gathering her composure and giving her head a mental shake, she straightened, making her face impassive.

"Don't fuss." She made her voice as firm as she could, adding a bit of a shooing gesture with her right hand in emphasis. "Go back to work and I'll be out in a minute."

Javi's gaze dropped to where her bare legs poked out from beneath the drape, and she immediately felt naked.

Exposed.

Funny how when he was bandaging her up that hadn't even crossed her mind!

"Right," he said, abruptly turning for the door. "See you on the ward."

And it was only when the door closed behind him that she could breathe again.

Continue reading
THE NURSE'S HOLIDAY SWAP
Ann McIntosh

Available next month
www.millsandboon.co.uk

LET'S TALK
Romance

For exclusive extracts, competitions and special offers, find us online:

- **f** MillsandBoon
- **𝕏** @MillsandBoon
- **⧉** @MillsandBoonUK
- **♪** @MillsandBoonUK

Get in touch on 01413 063 232

GET YOUR ROMANCE FIX!

Get the latest romance news, exclusive author interviews, story extracts and much more!